Moontachi Gaiden:

VIPER'S
LABYRINTH

Max Mathesius

Also by Max Mathesius

From the Moontachi Gaiden series

The Rise of Baronia: Book 2

Maiden of the Silver Light: Book 3

Crystal Symphony: Book 4

The Neon Prism: Book 5

Moontachi Gaiden:
Book 1

VIPER'S
LABYRINTH

MAX MATHESIUS

Max Mathesius

Copyright © 2015 by Max Mathesius.

Illustrations by Max Mathesius. Editor: Steff Chen & Seneca

ISBN-13: 978-0692473368 (Moontachi)
ISBN-10: 069247336X

This book was printed in the United States of America.

To order additional copies of this book, visit online at

www.amazon.com

<u>Synopsis</u>

When the Sun leaves, the Moon shall rise.

Legends tell of the Great Moon—the savior for all humanity during the reign of the Hundred Hands Emperor.

Wanting to be like the Great Moon, Alistor yearns for an adventurousness his everyday life. Until one fateful day, Mr. Rare crosses into his path and grants his wish. Now he must survive the countless demons attacking his world as the Aggerona Empire arrives in full force.

Yet, despite the dangers he faced, Alistor wasn't ready to give up after his school permanently closed. With the odds against him, he'll need more than power and lady luck to survive the onslaught of the Aggerona army.

So, with the help of a money-obsessed chef named Bamboo, Alistor embarks on a hilarious adventure to change his fate, forever changing the life he once knew.

Max Mathesius

Chapter 1

Lost Legacy:

A star-crossed beginning

It's been long....way too long.

A mysterious dark warrior confronts a great goddess before him. He removes a thickly layered cloak concealing his body. Flocks of green and purple hair flowed by his face. His red glowing eyes glared back as she began to pass judgment.

"Are you ready to accept your fate? All you have done will be lost through history and time. Your struggles, feats, and memories are all erased. You'll cease to exist."

"Then so be it. Eternal sleep, I accept. As long as I sleep, you can never see the light again."

He points his blade toward her. A seven-branched sword emits a negative aura.

"Our holy blade Shichishito. It's tainted! But how can it be? How are you worthy to wield it? It makes no sense." She muttered.

"There's no need for gods. In fact, gods do not exist. It's just a mere class to express one's measure of power. It only shows how weak you are."

"You went this far, allowing the Hundred Hands Emperor to surface. You killed our members and guardians and even desecrated our symbol. You have betrayed us."

"The Hundred Hands Emperor is the least you should worry about. It's the human race you should be fearing."

"Why do you care for them so much? They're a pathetic race. Answer me!"

Max Mathesius

"The human race is pathetic, but I have already foreseen a future. When the Sun leaves, the Moon shall rise. The great Moon will be the one who'll make this change. For the greater good."

She gives back a dirty look to him.

"You were always a fool and forever will be."

"Heroism was always overrated anyway." He merely shrugged. "Let's finish this; I'm tired of the long wait."

He slams the Shichishito deep into the ground. A shroud of darkness begins entrapping everything around them. Massive earth-shattering quake commences as huge walls begin to form all around. Vines and serpents wrap across the entire scene.

"A labyrinth? You intend to spend eternity here?" She hesitantly asked.

The dark warrior begins to fade away. His eyes closed as he muttered his last words.

"And so my final mission comes to an end. Moon…the rest is up to you. The future is yours to shape. We shall be eternal out of the light and into the night."

"Then so be it; may none ever speak of your name. Forever taboo HAVOK."

Decades later…

The great Moon is in the middle of his final battle against the One Hundred Demon tribe. A relentless demon tribe freed from the Devil's Gate to take revenge on humanity.

"I have no need for such fickle weapons of legend. My power alone is enough."

He tossed the Moon Sword aside.

"You fool! If that's how you feel, you can perish with her. The Moon blade is the only thing capable of hurting me." The Emperor explained.

Moon faced head to head against the Hundred Hands Emperor.

"Enough messing around; I want to face you at full strength. No holding back." Moon pointed out.

"So cocky, yet if you wish to invite death early, so be it."

The Emperor begins transforming. A hundred times as many hands burst into the scene.

"So…this is your true form. Nice makeover!"

Viper's Labyrinth

"Now feel the wrath of my ten thousand hands."

The Emperor dives in for his final attack as Moon calmly stands by with his eyes closed into a deep trance, focusing his thoughts together.

"The Moon is high, and the sky is blue. This night is ours, so let our oceans cross as one. Be eternal, and allow me to end this now."

The Emperor impacts Moon with his entire body. He had a smirk on his face as he saw blood rushing down from him. Suddenly an excellent crack split on his face. Parts of the Emperor's body begin breaking apart.

"What? Impossible, you've bested me? How!"

Moon casually walks away, picking up the sword he tossed aside.

"True, this blade was only capable of hurting you. But there was never a rule stating you couldn't hurt yourself. A simple afterimage, in fact. You ran right into your own attack."

Both of them were down for the count. He then shatters the Moon Sword in half, confusing the Emperor.

"You break your own people's regalia? I don't understand? Whose side are you really on? Tell me! Who do you think you are?" The Emperor demanded.

Moon dramatically turns around one last time.

"I'm the Great Moon."

The scene ends from there to the present time in the year 79. A young boy is interrupted in the middle of his reading.

"Still daydreaming again? Come on, you've been obsessing over these old stories for the last couple of weeks. It's time to get out more."

"Katty! Give those back."

Alistor, age 14, A student currently attending Emerald Jr. High. Past history, birth record, and parents are now unknown. However, he was taken under the care of Sairori at a very young age. Raised by an infamous swordsman, he recently left to explore what academic life had to offer.

"So, how has this school life been treating ya?" He asked.

His long-time best friend Katty, age 15, is his current roommate across his door. Has trouble getting dates and is often left behind.

Max Mathesius

"I don't think it will work out for me." Alistor nodded.

He so far attempts to go to school, like an average person fitting in society. He favored this over being with the old man.

"How come? Why is this not working?"

"Dunno, what I'm looking for was more for an adventure. I never knew where I came from, and my parents are believed to be long gone."

"Well, you can always return back to Sairori."

"What are you kidding me? No! He's completely crazy, and no one likes him. He's always bragging about being ready for a monster attack. So everyone thinks he's nuts. That's the first reason why I had to leave."

The two took a moment to look at the clouds as a slight breeze passed.

"What I think you need is a break. Come on, let's get some lunch or something."

A moment later, at the cafeteria…

"Yeah, I'll have the usual," Katty replied.

The two are served their meals. Then, from a ladle pouring some food into their bowl, they make their way to a table.

"Thanks, Bamboo."

The cafeteria chef is named Bamboo. His age is currently unknown. However, he has a deep passion for cooking and dreams of someday opening his own restaurant.

"So why have you been attached to these old folk tales? I know it's entertaining, but it can't be true. They are long gone."

"Well, that's what I'm looking for," Alistor admits. "Just to imagine what it was like during their time. The experience from their tales."

"Are you serious?" Katty laughed. "Well, I'm sure anyone would love an adventure, but nothing ever happens in Mathias."

The two continue to talk. Bamboo had the urge to listen in on their conversation.

"To just one time know what it was like before. If I could stand by their side for just one day."

They continue looking over the illustrations from the old stories.

"I'm still wondering about the other half of Moon's tale. I can only wonder how it really ended."

Katty merely shrugged.

"All we know is the remainder of Moon's tale was lost through time. Whether it was ever finished or not, no one knows."

Bamboo creeps up on them, interrupting their conversation.

"I've heard a rumor it was something bad. The way it ends is not what you think." He briefly mentioned. "If the school life is not working, you can always help in the kitchen."

"I think we'll pass." Alistor nodded.

The two head back outside as Katty immediately parts ways with him.

"I have something I need to do. Catch you later."

With one wave, he was gone. Alone, Alistor walks through the barren road, mumbling to himself. A mysterious robed figure watches him through a screen.

"Yeah, I wish I knew what it was all like. I need some answers, damn it. Anything will help; I just need a start."

The robed figure continues to watch for a brief moment.

"Enough time has passed. The time is now and ready."

As Alistor continues his walk down the road, he suddenly comes across a fortune teller stand. The robed figure kindly greets him.

"Seeking answers? I'll see if I can help. Come close and gaze into my crystal ball. Take a seat, Alistor boy."

He cautiously approached the table to take a seat.

"Who are you? And how do you know my name?"

"The names Rare. Mr. Rare and I make one-of-a-kind items. Allow me to read you."

The robed figure begins fiddling with his crystal ball. Then, finally, he takes a moment to look into his eyes.

"Yes, you are troubled. Indeed seeking answers to your origin. A desire for adventure. The thrill of reliving those legends. I see all."

Max Mathesius

"Are you serious? Tell me more. I must know."

The ball begins to emit a glow.

"I see a potential future. Opportunities, through a Labyrinth, you will rise up to a mechanized force. You shall cross paths with a silver maiden. A great conqueror will stand in your path to the pillar. All to end at Devil's Gate."

Mr. Rare's words continue to mesmerize him.

"And my past? Tell me! I must know." He demanded.

The crystal ball dims out.

"That is only half of it. The rest you must uncover for yourself. All will be revealed in due time."

"But wait!"

Alistor grabs onto his robe.

"The reading doesn't make any sense. What does this all mean?"

Mr. Rare pulls a mirror out from his pockets. A stylized mirror with serpents wrapping across. Five colored gems are fixed inside.

"What's this? A mirror?" Alistor asked.

"Are you ready to accept your journey? The adventure, the danger, the romance. This is where it will all begin."

He stares fixed at the mirror for a brief moment. Then, without hesitation, he reaches for the mirror in Rare's hands.

"I accept!"

The moment he touched the mirror, a great light emitted, blinding him. He takes cover as it immediately shatters into five pieces. He opened his eyes.

"Mr. Rare! Where are you? Hey, wait!"

Mr. Rare was nowhere to be seen. He suddenly feels a massive shake as the sky turns to pitch dark. Thunder roars down as a great labyrinth slowly materializes in the air.

"What the heck is that?"

Viper's Labyrinth

Somewhere high above, within a dark room... The Snake Emperor awakens from his deep sleep. The room was full of demons in the shadows behind.

"Ah! Finally free at last. Over the centuries, trapped under the tyranny of that Shrine Maiden's power, we can finally continue where we left off. But, oh, how long has it been?"

He took a moment to glance at the scene below. To the present day, many clueless kids are staring at the labyrinth above. The school ground catches his attention.

"How the times have changed. It's been so long. I can't hardly wait. But, oh, what monster to send first? I, Vilevelious, declare a grand-scale invasion on Mathias."

The crowd of monsters in the background begins to cheer.

"Now, to get to business. Our labyrinth needs energy, so who shall be the first to do the honors? Any volunteers?"

A general steps into the scene. Pounding the great flag on the floor, the room quickly fell silent.

"Allow me the honors to lead the battle. I shall gather lots of energy for the labyrinth."

"Mushogun, eh? Very well."

"I shall not fail."

Slamming his flag, Mushogun takes his leave, teleporting out of the room. In moments, monsters begin to deploy with a grand-scale assault.

Alistor ran back to campus to witness the terror. A horrified look on his face for the first time as he stood motionless.

"What happened here?"

Destruction was all around as he found many of his classmates incapacitated. He quickly finds Katty, taking cover behind the walls between a couple bushes.

"Hey, Katty! Are you alright?"

"Things aren't looking so good. These monsters just came from the sky. That labyrinth somehow. I don't know what to do."

They hear the sound of a student screaming. She trips over as the monster approaches. It begins to drain her energy away as they both witness the scene. Mushogun steps in.

"It seems that was the last one, general."

Max Mathesius

"Good, now return to base. Our job here is done." Mushogun commanded.

Both monsters vanished before their very eyes as they came out from hiding. Katty goes to check on the girl. Looking for a pulse, he could only hear a faint beat.

"It seems she's still alive but weak. Barely still breathing."

"So, what do we do now?" Alistor asked.

"I guess to check for any other stragglers in the building."

The two made their way inside the school building. Searching for any others they can find.

Meanwhile, back at the lair, Mushogun returns back victorious.

"The first batch of energy as promised."

Vilevelious abruptly broke the news to his general.

"It seems you've done a sloppy job."

"What? What do you mean? I cleared the school dry. No one else should still be left standing."

He takes a look back at the viewing screen below. Alistor and Katty are seen snooping around the corridors as laughter begins to echo across the room.

"What? Two stragglers. Well, I'll show them. I won't need an army of monsters; one will just do. Personally handpicked by myself."

"Then get down there," Vilevelious ordered.

Mushogun immediately deploys back down to the campus.

"No one makes a mockery of me!"

The general pounds his great flag on the floor. A monster begins sprouting from the cracks.

"Grass Horns! Seek out and take care of the remaining stragglers."

"With pleasure, general."

The monster makes a massive leap into the school building.

Viper's Labyrinth

Meanwhile, Alistor and Katty continue their search inside the building. Through a hallway entirely in ruins, they find nothing.

"No luck so far. We'll have to just abandon our search."

Alistor comes to a sudden halt.

"Hey, do you hear that?"

The wall suddenly bursts open from the side to their surprise. Through the smoke, Grass Horns appeared before them.

"What the heck is that?" Alistor jumped.

The monster immediately begins the attack. Swinging from one of its arms as they rolled to the side.

"I don't think I want to find out. RUN!" Katty shouted.

The two make a dash through the halls as Grass Horns begins pursuit. Back outside, Mushogun watches from below.

"Why bother running from the inevitable? Give up now! Your energy is as good as ours."

Katty quickly knocks down a row of lockers, hoping to slow the monster down. However, grass Horn easily slices through the barricade as they continue running.

"Any ideas now? We can't keep this up forever." Alistor warned.

"I'm trying to think."

They immediately come across a barricade with a small opening at the bottom.

"Get ready to slide under."

The two slipped through the bottom without issues as Grass Horns suddenly stopped. Then, unable to fit or breakthrough, the monster pulled back.

"Think you can hide from me? I'll just have to find another way around."

Katty and Alistor find their way to a door. Entering inside, they took a moment to catch their breath briefly.

"Looks like we made it to the cafeteria."

"No one's been in here yet."

Max Mathesius

They both suddenly hear a slight creeping sound in the room.

"It's coming from that corner over there." Katty pointed.

The two grabbed the nearest utensils as they approached a cupboard. Then, without hesitation, Alistor opens the door as Katty ready his weapon.

"Whoa! Wait! Hold it!" A voice screamed.

Katty halts his attack in the middle of the strike as a notable figure came tumbling out.

"Bamboo? Is that really you?"

A moment later....

"So you've been hiding here this whole time. Anything you can tell us?"

"Sorry, it just all happened so fast." Bamboo sighed. "I minded my own business till everyone bragged about that maze in the sky. Then, I decided to look for myself from the window, but the attack happened. The sound of explosions and monsters sent students panicking, so I quickly took some cover behind the storeroom."

They suddenly hear the cutting sound of the monster. Grass Horn's arms skid through the walls from the other side.

"So, any ideas? We need some plan to bring this thing down."

Katty took a moment to examine the things around the room. The gas stove quickly catches his attention.

"Wait a minute. What are you guys planning?" Bamboo asked. "WAIT! That stuff is fragile. It's expensive equipment you're messing with. My soufflé is cooking."

They make their way to turn the stove on. Unfortunately, a small fire began building up as they started tampering with it.

"If you got any better ideas. The monster is closing in on us."

Grass Horn sliced open the door, startling Bamboo.

"Oh, I hope you both know what you're doing. This stove is worth more than my salary."

The monster makes a leap onto the counter. But, drawing close to the stove, Grass Horn only finds Bamboo, shriveled up by a corner.

"Wait...where are the other two? Who are you supposed to be?" The monster confusedly asked.

Viper's Labyrinth

Under the counter's cupboard, Alistor and Katty emerge right from behind, pushing the monster to the burning stove. Grass Horn's arm blades pierced through the stove surface.

"What? Hey! That's not fair."

The monster is seen stuck. Katty quickly changes the dial to complete, causing the pressure to further build.

"You might want to make a run for it."

"Wait, what?" Bamboo stuttered. "My soufflé…."

Without further hesitation, the three make a run out of the room. Escaping as a big blaze begins to engulf the cafeteria. Grass Horn starts to slowly catch on fire. Breaking off one of its arms, the monster continues to struggle.

"Noooooo!"

The gas suddenly combusts, commencing in one big explosion. From outside, Alistor witnesses the explosion leveling down the entire half of the school.

"Well, we made it, at least." Katty dropped to the ground.

The flames quickly die out. Bamboo suddenly sensed something amiss. He goes to check the remaining debris while the other two rest. He immediately stumbles upon the gas stove. Opening up the oven compartment, he pulls out his cake. Burnt and black to a crisp.

"My soufflé… Huh?"

Bamboo feels a sudden shake from below. Grass Horns emerged, destroying the stove as it sent him flying to the other side.

"It's not over yet! A real dirty trick, but you won't get rid of me that easily." The monster laughed.

Fear struck Alistor's eye while Katty refused to turn around. Grass Horns emerged severely damaged with a missing arm.

A lightning bolt comes crashing down from behind as the monster intensely stares at them. Then, downright furious, it drew close to them.

"Now what…" Alistor was near to giving up all hope.

"I'm gonna slice and dice the energy out of you."

Max Mathesius

As Grass Horn begins to attack, a sudden energy force impacts the monster. Sparks began to fly as Grass Horns collapsed over in one incredible explosion. Smoke and debris scattered through the air as the two took cover.

From the other side of the school grounds, Mushogun witnesses Grass Horn's destruction.

"This isn't good. Better report back. Argh!"

The general quietly makes his leave. The labyrinth in the sky immediately vanishes, bringing the light back into the day.

"What was that?" Katty asked.

The smoke clears away, revealing a swordsman before them.

"Sairori? Is that really you?" Alistor asked. "How did you do that?" He was surprised with amazement.

The old man stares down intensely at both of them.

"Humph! You've all doubted me the whole time, but the time has finally come. I will teach you. So be ready."

Filled with motivation, the two decide to follow Sairori. Leaving behind what remains of the campus.

Chapter 2

The Five Demon Generals

Along the run-down schoolyard, Alistor and Katty follow the master down the path. Bamboo was nowhere to be seen.

"Just who are they? Where did these monsters come from? And why did they arrive?"

They had many questions while their master stood by.

"It's time you both know the kind of enemy you are up against." Sairori proclaimed.

"We're ready." Alistor nodded.

"The labyrinth you all witnessed above is none other than an evil waiting to be awakened from eternal imprisonment. That maze is none other than the Viper's Labyrinth."

"Viper's Labyrinth? Never even heard of it?" Katty nodded.

"It is believed to be timeless. Serving as a reminder for our founding fathers back when the times were bleak. The Aggerona Empire has emerged once more to continue their mission."

"What mission?" Alistor interrupted.

"I was about to get to that. Be patient!" The master snapped. "Yes! The Aggerona Empire. They acquired control of the maze shortly after the Hundred Hands Fall. They aimed to feed the maze by gathering enough negative energy from victims to awaken something deep within it."

"What are they trying to bring back?"

"We're not certain. Some believe it's a power catastrophic enough to end our days. Some say it housed a legendary treasure. Or some even believed the soul of an ancient evil rests within the very heart of the maze."

The both of them gasped for a brief second.

"An ancient evil?" Katty shook as he felt a cold chill down his spine.

The master smoked his pipe calmly.

"Then you have to teach us? Show us the way with your techniques and skills," Alistor begged. "We don't stand a fighting chance alone."

He removed the pipe from his mouth.

"So now you want to learn? Ha, and you all believe I was crazy before. You gave up when I was barely wrapping up the basics."

Alistor soon recalls scenes of his training at a younger age with a practice katana. However, he can barely wield a blade properly as he gets shunned repeatedly for every mistake.

"Yes, but over time with practice, I got it down." Alistor countered back. "I put up with your bullshit training, so don't hold back on us."

"Just show us how you made that move? That blast of light from your blade. We now believe, so please." Katty kindly asked.

They both were down begging on the field as the master took a deep breath.

"Sigh...enough already, your embarrassing yourselves. Before I even begin, you must know more about your enemy before diving in blindly. So don't get hasty."

The both of them stood right back up.

"The Aggerona Empire is led by five commanders. They are known as the Five Demon Generals. They carry out Emperor Vilevelious's orders."

"Vile, who?"

"I know...their leader's name is funky, but that's not important now."

Viper's Labyrinth

"Sorry, well, tell us more about it." Alistor apologized.

The master continued.

"After the fall of the Hundred Hands Emperor, nations competed for dominance and supremacy at the time. Thus, allowing an even greater evil to rise from the ashes of the Hundred Demon tribe. They are the Aggerona Empire."

His story goes back to a time and place.

The Five Demon Generals.

A silhouette of five generals appears above two armies clashing in the heat of combat.

"The Demon General's, personally handpicked by the emperor. Five tacticians that each specialize in a field of combat. They suited all his needs during the campaign. Ranging from offensive aerial to naval fleets, Aggerona was very flexible."

A massive pile of junk is seen detonating on the walls.

"Even on the defense, the demolition division proved one of their deadliest. Bringing down many walls as ground infantry broke through."

Mushogun is seen charging through the flames.

"Vilevelious success was due to each of his general's ability and leadership. One kingdom fell after the next, and all hope was nearly lost once Alandhite fell. They awakened the labyrinth and seized control of it as their own lair."

The labyrinth materializes before the emperor's eye's as his forces overtake it.

"So, how were they stopped?" Alistor interrupted once again.

"After Alandhite fell, a special imprisoning mirror was created by two priestesses. The priestess of light and the priestess of shadow. To counter Aggerona, they formed a band to combat the Aggerona forces. One by one, they sealed each general away within a quadrant of the mirror."

Mushogun is seen dropping his flag, unaware as the mirror pulls him right in.

"They eventually made it to Vilevelious, imprisoning him and the rest of Aggerona. Thus peace is finally restored thanks to them."

His story ends from there.

"To end this, we must obtain this mirror and lock them back?" Katty summed up.

"Easier said than done." Sairori nodded. "Vilevelious was unaware at the time, and with age comes wisdom. So falling for the same trick twice will be unlikely."

"Then, is there another way?" Alistor asked.

"Well…destroying him is another alternative. Maybe seek out a weakness if he has any. He'll most likely take more caution this time around. Getting through his generals will be the first step. For now, let us be on our way."

The two head back to the master place.

Meanwhile, high above, a dark fortress rests atop a great labyrinth. News of Grass Horn's defeat reached out as the rest watched its destruction on screen. A blast of energy finishes off the monster with an explosion. The video cuts off as Vilevelious presses the eject button on the VHS.

"Well? Explain yourself." The emperor demanded.

"It seems our enemies are quite capable," Mushogun muttered.

"You told me this would be a piece of cake. But, unfortunately, our labyrinth still needs more energy. We've barely even reached one percent."

Mumbling from the crowd behind the shadows begins to escalate.

"Not to worry, my lord. This was a minor setback. My next monster will get the job done. The humans plan to have their school back in session in a few days. My monster will gather plenty of energy by then."

They take a gander at the students returning to campus on screen. Slight reconstruction commencing all around.

"HoHoHo, a little repetitive, don't you think?"

"What?"

Another general step partially into the light.

"Attacking the same place twice? Not my style. These teenagers energy barely even sufficed to feed our labyrinth. If I were you, I'd go for the bigger ones."

"He does make a good point." Vilevelious pondered.

Steam begins to boil behind Mushogun.

"If I were you, you best keep your mouth shut, Shellshock." He threatened. "I'm still in command, so back off."

Viper's Labyrinth

He shoves the other general back into the shadows.

"Well, you sound pretty determined, general. Explain to us this plan."

"With pleasure."

Mushogun turns the station to showcase a garden center. An orchard filled with lots of flowers blooming in the pottery.

"I shall employ a tactic that proved successful in our past battles. These flowers symbolize this school, and announcements casually happen. The monster I've planted will ensnare the entire school with its pollen. The pollen will latch on hearing every word, thought, and many secrets."

"Wiretapping? And this will provide energy?" The emperor questioned.

"Even better! Exposing every gossip and skeleton in the closets will greatly amplify victims with negative energy. My monster Potty Mouth will be there to secure the energy needed."

"Potty what?" The emperor was lost for a brief second.

Mushogun attempts to explain his monster but is stopped from there.

"Never mind, just commence with the plan." Vilevelious approved as his general took leave.

Meanwhile, a few hours later. Alistor and Katty endure a tense training lesson with Sairori, practicing a new technique.

"You have to focus your thoughts altogether. Just time it right, and do not let your emotions cloud your judgment." The master rambled on.

Alistor and Katty are seen attempting to channel their energy together. But, unfortunately, their weapons could barely make a faint glow.

"Man getting the basic swordplay was fine, but I don't think I'm cut for this." Katty pouted.

"Come on! You can't give up now." Alistor pressed. "I can feel it. If we can master this, we'll be ready for anything."

Some energy formed around Alistor as he didn't hesitate to charge at the boulder. Diving his blade as it emits a spark of light. His attempt immediately fails as the energy dispels in midair. The master begins taking his leave.

"Keep practicing. The Star Breaker takes some discipline. But, once you achieve this technique, you'll be ready for the next step."

Alistor got back up to continue training as Katty placed his blade away.

"Where are you going?"

"Going to check back at the campus a bit."

"Fine, well, I'm not giving up."

As Katty left, Alistor continued alone. Hours passed, and then days as he endured sleepless nights with every attempt to master the Star Breaker, failing and getting back up with more determination than ever. Sairori watches from a distance smoking his pipe.

"I can do this."

He makes another attempt to break the stone but fails. The sun was beginning to set with darkness approaching.

"Call it a rest for today." The master hollered.

"No…not yet. I'm so close. I can do this." Alistor nodded.

"Suit yourself."

The master returns to his house while he continues to train throughout the night of a full moon. Many more attempts commence with him stumbling. Finally, he lies on the ground to rest for a brief moment.

"What am I doing wrong? I can feel it, but what is the answer."

Then the voice of Mr. Rare caught his attention. He gets up to look around, but no one is there.

"Am I imagining things? No…I can't waste any more time."

He then came to his senses. Staring tensely at the stone as energy begins to build up once more. Alistor starts to make a full charge at the boulder readying a strike.

"Star Breaker!"

A lightning bolt struck down as his blade impacted the hard surface with energy bursting out. The boulder slowly begins to crack as it shatters to pieces. He suddenly collapses to the ground, nearly drained with exhaustion.

"I did it…."

Viper's Labyrinth

The following morning, Sairori finds Alistor asleep outside.

"Three days to master, I see. Not bad at all."

A moment later, Katty is seen arriving at the master's doorstep, dragging Alistor away.

"Come on, wake up! You're gonna be late again."

The bell rang, and they were again back in class, enduring a boring lecture. Then, from a distance from the school, Mushogun arrives at the garden center. A group of gardeners panics as the general approach the flower pots.

"It is time to awaken. Potty Mouth, I summon you."

The general pounds his flag on the floor, causing one of the pots to shake up. Then, vines begin popping, forming a monster from the pottery.

"At your call, general. Burb! Boy, I'm starving."

The monster begins snacking on a bag of fertilizer. Mushogun slaps the load off the monster's hand.

"No time for snacking. Eat later; I have a job for you."

One moment later...

"Gah! Who are you? What do you want? Don't hurt me!" The announcer cried.

Mushogun and Potty Mouth arrive in an office. The monster begins entrapping the man with his vines.

"Good! Now work your magic." The general commanded.

Potty Mouth begins to mimic the announcer's voice before taking a stand. Then, with a mic on hand, a school announcement kicked off.

"Morning! Great for you to be all back at Emerald."

The monster immediately tossed the script aside.

"Oh, what the heck. Let's get direct here. You're all a bunch of stuck-up snobby students. I know all your very secrets. Been tuning in on you for the past few days."

Potty Mouth begins telling off the crowd listening. One after the next break down raged or moped in shame.

Max Mathesius

"Not such a bright crowd, huh? Don't think it's over because I'll leak something new every hour." Potty mouth mocked.

At the Aggerona hideout, Vilevelious and the others tune in on Potty Mouth's broadcast. Listening in on every group conversation in the background.

"This wiretapping is pointless." The emperor snapped. "We've been doing this for hours."

"Just give it time. We'll uncover something." Mushogun assured.

The sound of some school girls is heard in the background. All excited and talking about their hot date for Saturday night.

"If I have to listen to another teenage couple's pathetic sob story, I'm gonna wail."

Returning to the campus, Potty Mouth makes an unjust announcement to the school. Locking himself in the room while some argue and moan throughout the campus.

"I'm baaaaack! Hahaha. Ok, let's get down to business. Oh, Katty, I know you've tried hard to win some lucky dames heart. But that girl Natalie, really? She's soooooo out of your league."

Katty immediately breaks down briefly as the girl he admires pestered him from behind with names.

"But don't feel bad about it. Cause that broad has been sleeping with the last five only to get something. . It's a tough world. I feel for ya, brudda."

The crowd began laughing as that very girl ran out crying in shame.

"That's it!" Katty got up in a rage.

"Wait, where are you going?" Alistor asked.

He begins marching his way out the door.

"What do you think? I'm gonna strangle that announcer and knock some sense into him. I can live with being called a loser, but making a girl cry is very low."

He makes his way to the office as the crowd decides to follow him. The door breaks down, revealing the monster, to everyone's surprise. Potty Mouth bulls through the group, dropping the mic. Katty jumped in with his blade causing the demon to stumble back.

"Whoah, nelly! Watch where you point that. It can hurt someone." The monster warned.

"You've ruined my chance. Now I'll never be able to ask her out because she thinks I'm a freak." Katty raged. "Bring it!"

The monster continued to snack on some garbage as he was pumped and heated for battle.

"Burb....wait a minute, is this supposed to be a battle?"

Katty prepares to charge in, but Alistor intervenes.

"Allow me to take this one." He insisted. "I got a new move I wanted to try anyway."

"You don't mean...You actually mastered it?"

"Sit back and watch the fireworks. I'm gonna bring this monster down in one hit." Alistor assured the rest.

He pulled out his blade, focusing his power into one place as he charged at the monster. Potty Mouth stood by, confused as he got close. The energy from his attack suddenly fails as it completely fades once more. Awkwardly close, he looks up at the monster.

"What? No! How can this be happening?"

"Not impressed." Nodded the monster.

Potty Mouth drops the trash bin for a brief moment, lifting Alistor with his vines. Then, he gets tossed back into the watching crowd.

"That's it! I'm going in." Yelled Katty.

He charged right in, ready to impale the monster.

"Didn't I warn you?" Lectured Potty Mouth. "Bah! Kids these days! Gonna have to teach ya a lesson."

The monster easily dodged his attack, moving a little to the left. Katty begins mindlessly hacking away while Potty Mouth takes no effort to block with the top from a garbage lid. Finally, the monster disarms Katty and trips him over.

"Damn, I really need to find another weapon. Swords are not working for me." Katty muttered.

Potty Mouth begins twirling him in midair.

"And away you go."

As Katty got thrown back to the side, Alistor got back in, ready for another attempt.

"Ok, second try."

Max Mathesius

Alistor begins focusing his energy again, but Potty Mouth quickly catches on. The monster kicks the garbage bin over to him. It rolled down, knocking him down with a group of bystanders behind.

"Is that the best you got?" Chuckled the monster. "I have been in more fights than you can imagine. Standard human weapons are so crass. You're better off with a cooking ladle if you hope to stand a ghost of a chance."

Alistor begins doubting himself.

"Damn… he's right. I'm still too weak. Too exhausted to pull the Star Breaker off from that intense training. What do I do now?"

Katty quickly grabs a fire extinguisher on the side, spraying the monster from behind. Potty Mouth begins freaking out as Alistor gains some distance back.

"What should we do?" He asked.

"We'll have to improvise whether you can pull it off." Katty nodded. "We have to move somewhere fast. Too many bystanders in the way."

The extinguisher then dies out as Potty Mouth recalls something.

"Of course! Now I remember. I'm here to take all your energy."

"This isn't good." Alistor gulps.

Vines begin entrapping people all across the hall. Alistor and Katty soon became ensnared within Potty Mouth's grasp as energy began leaving their body.

"Haha, yes! Glory for our Labyrinth. Feed up!"

Meanwhile, back at the enemy lair…The sound of people panicking on the screen as Mushogun watched with Vilevelious.

"See what I told ya? Piece of cake." Mushogun smirked.

The emperor is pleased, witnessing life breathed into their base for the first time. However, a mass amount of negative energy is seen leaving the school as it makes its way to the mouth of the labyrinth.

"Excellent work, general. Some progress at last."

Back down at the battle, both continue to struggle under Potty Mouth's grasp. Finally, with all hope that seemed lost, Alistor was ready to give in. Suddenly from the cafeteria, the door sprung open.

Viper's Labyrinth

"Quiet!!!" Bamboo yelled. "Can you all keep it down?"

The scene was silent briefly, with everyone stopping in place. Bamboo expressed no reaction to the danger as he returned to the kitchen. The smell of food wafts through the air. Potty Mouth's belly begins grumbling.

"Boy… I'm famished. It smells so good."

The monster immediately released everyone from his grasp, heading to the kitchen. Potty Mouth receives a transmission from Mushogun on the other end.

"What are you doing? Who told you to stop? Go back and finish the job." Complained the general.

"Oh, put a sock in it. I'm eating first."

"What did you say to me?"

The transmission cuts off from there as Potty Mouth enters the cafeteria. He comes across Bamboo cooking up a large pot behind.

"Lunch special of the day. Ramen hot and ready." Bamboo announced.

A large bowl of ramen is passed to the monster.

"For me! Oh boy, thanks a lot."

Potty Mouth helped himself to a seat. Readying some chopsticks and begins eating peacefully. Alistor and Katty soon barge into the room.

"What is going on?" Alistor confusedly asked.

"You're just in time. Lunch is ready."

"But this monster. We have a score to settle." Katty said.

"Lunch first! Fight after." Bamboo ordered.

"But I'm not hungry. So we'll eat later."

"I said eat first! No fight in my kitchen."

A tense intimidating glare came from Bamboo, belittling the both of them. Flames from behind exaggerating the situation.

"Ok! Ok! We'll eat."

Max Mathesius

The two are seen dining with the monster by the tables, enjoying a brief moment of peace before a light crashes on the scene. Mushogun appeared before their eyes, firing a laser at the pot behind. Bamboo gets sent flying to the side as he pulls Potty Mouth away.

"Insubordination will not be tolerated. Now get back to work."

"Ok! Stop it! Geez, don't be a pushover."

Mushogun quickly takes his leave as Alistor and Katty finish their meal. Potty mouth once again stands off with them.

"Man, that food really helped. I'm feeling energized." Alistor jumped.

The two quickly notice the flame left from Mushogun's blast by the stove. Some propane tanks are intact on the side.

"Are you thinking what I'm thinking?"

"Let's do this." Alistor nodded.

Potty Mouth unleashed his vines once more, but then his stomach began growling. Finally, weakening as the two maneuvered their way to Bamboo's position.

"What? Hey, get back here. So hungry…."

The monster desperately charged in.

"I'll lure him in."

Katty successfully lures the monster close but gets quickly slapped aside. Alistor readied to fire some energy at the gas tanks. Bamboo regains his consciousness.

"Whoah! What do you think you're doing?" Bamboo wailed. "This stuff is fragile."

Without hesitation, Alistor shot out a flint of energy from his blade, causing the propane tanks to set the monster aflame. Fire begins to engulf the entire room.

"Noooooo!" Bamboo cried. "We must get out."

Without further ado, everyone quickly evacuates as the flame spreads across the halls. But unfortunately, an explosion soon leveled down the entire school once more as they watched the scene.

"No way…" Katty gasped.

They immediately spot Potty Mouth staggering through the remains. Smoked and nearly burnt to a crisp. Coughing out puffs.

Viper's Labyrinth

"Feed me! Feed me! Feed me….."

Potty Mouth immediately collapses to the ground in one incredible explosion. The crowd begins to cheer as the head of the school breaks through. He goes to give the breaking news to Bamboo.

"Bamboo… you're fired."

He was seen quickly heartbroken. Bamboo only gives off a dirty look back to Alistor and his friend.

"If you are gonna be using propane tanks, it's an endangerment to the campus. Plus, blowing up the school every time a monster attacks is inefficient."

At the enemy base, Mushogun witnesses his monster's destruction on screen. The sound of murmuring quickly escalates in the background.

"What?"

"HOHOHOHOHOHO! How priceless!" Shellshock laughed. "They took out your monster like it was some special Ed science project. Better luck next time."

Commander Shellshock pats Mushogun on the shoulder but quickly gets brushed off.

"Bah! No! This is ridiculous. Teenagers!" Mushogun went into a fit, pounding his flag on the ground.

Shellshock takes the stand.

"Hey, Vile man! Let me have a whack at it. I'll send a monster down that is way more efficient than Mushogun's plants."

Mushogun steps back in, pulling Shellshock out from the spotlight.

"No! I'm not done yet."

"Oh? Well, what are you going to do about it?" The emperor asked.

A severe look was now on the general's face. Raising his great flag with pride, he stares straight into the viewing screen at Alistor and company.

"Enough games! I'm going to put an end to this myself." Mushogun announced.

A sudden gasp followed throughout the room.

"Isn't this a little too early?" Shellshock questioned.

"Request to engage."

"Permission granted." The emperor answered.

Mushogun teleports out of the room, leaving with a fleet of Whoopers.

"Sometimes desperation is the best motivation to get things done. So let us continue to watch for now."

Back down below on campus, Alistor recuperates with the crowd as Sairori arrives on the scene by a recovery center. Bamboo suddenly notices a glint of light from above.

"It's not over yet." Bamboo pointed.

"What?" Alistor shook.

Mushogun appeared before them atop the bleachers with a wave of Whoopers behind. Holding his great flag with pride.

"What are those things?" Katty shouted.

Clay-like soldiers coated in purple and black intimidates the crowd.

"These are the Whoopers! Aggerona's finest soldiers for infantry." The general explained.

The soldiers are seen waving their arms in the air.

"Katty, you need to rest. We'll handle the rest from here." Alistor assured.

"I, Mushogun, declare war against Mathias. First, this school, and then the world. Whoopers attack!"

The crowd began to panic as the Whoopers came charging in. The master attempts to help evacuate the group holding the enemy off as Alistor passes Katty to Bamboo.

"Take Katty and leave."

"But I can still fight…." Katty said.

"No! You're in no condition to continue. You have done a good job enough. Now go!"

Bamboo leaves, dragging Katty out as he and the master battle against the crew of Whoopers. The enemy soldiers quickly surround him, prancing around in circles as punches are dealt to Alistor, blindly swinging his blade.

Viper's Labyrinth

"Gah! There's too many of them."

He lands his first strike on a Whooper. His blade stuck to its body like glue.

"Are these guys made out of dough?" Alistor asked.

"You have to break free." The master advised. "If you've been listening, use the Star breaker, dammit."

The master continues to hold his own against the wave of Whoopers. Alistor begins to concentrate his energy for a brief moment. Then, he focuses all his thoughts together as his blade emits a faint glow. Without hesitation, the Whoopers begin covering their face believing they are finished. Alistor unleashes his move in one great swing, but the light quickly diminishes in the middle of the attack.

"What? Still no good."

Six sucker punches commenced from the Whoopers, countering his failed attack. Sairori lets off a brief sigh as Alistor gets back up.

"You have to time it right. That was too early." Sairori nodded. "Try again!"

The Whoopers continue to dance around him.

"Damn, this is pointless. What good I am. I'm finished if I can't pull this stupid move off."

Mushogun jumps into the battle, causing the ground to shake from his heavyweight. The Whoopers cleared the way as the general approached closely.

"Ha! As I suspected. Nothing more than dumb luck keeping you alive. Well, now it's time to put an end to this. I will do the honors and end you."

Mushogun takes a sudden swing, but Alistor avoids his attack.

"So you're a demon general."

"And I'll be the last you'll ever face. Now stand still, and let me kill you."

Mushogun takes another big swing but misses.

"For a general, you're rather slow. Got ya!"

Alistor dives in with his blade with a few quick slashes. However, he had a confident look that was short-lived as Mushogun barely had a scratch.

"I may be slow, but my gut makes up for all the lost versatility. Think you can bust me?"

Max Mathesius

Mushogun stomps the ground once more, shaking things up. The Whoopers stumbled, cowering in fear as Alistor attempted to regain his stand.

"Take the battle to another ground," Sairori suggested. "I'll handle the remaining enemy soldiers."

Without hesitation, Alistor runs to another terrain field while Mushogun remains on the offensive.

"Think you can outrun me? I have other tricks up my sleeve."

Mushogun begins spewing acid, melting a few poles on the way.

"Youch!"

A part of Alistor's cloak begins to burn as some acid splashes on the tip of his leg. The battle escalates to a parking lot. Alistor came to a stop ducking and rolling from the burn. Mushogun was partly exhausted from the run.

"No more games!" The general panted.

Alistor took cover behind a vehicle, but Mushogun instantly impaled the car from its engine with his flag tip. Then, lifting the car midair, the general effortlessly tossed it aside. Explosions commenced with a crowd screaming on the other side.

"I'm going to bust that gut. If it takes all I have."

He begins hacking and slashing away at the general again with no progress. Finally, Mushogun stomps the floor once more, stopping everything.

"Face it! None of your moves are powerful enough to bust my gut."

Alistor begins to fall back for cover once more. Mushogun begins destroying all the vehicles in the parking lot. Lifting one car after the next as more explosions commenced.

"No use in delaying your end. Give up now. BWAHAHAHA!"

"He's right..." Alistor thought to himself. "Nothing is working. The Star breaker...no, I can't pull it off. Damn it! What now?"

Doubt was passing through his mind as the general finally uncovered him.

"Ah! Found you at last. Now standstill."

As he gave up hope, a sudden presence was felt. Alistor suddenly caught a glimpse of the robed figure from a distance.

Viper's Labyrinth

"Mr. Rare?"

The general goes in to deliver a final strike as he stays down.

"Victory!!!"

Mr. Rare's words came to his mind in a flashback.

"I see a potential future. Opportunities, perhaps, through a Labyrinth, you will rise up to a mechanized force. You shall cross paths with a silver maiden. On the way to the pillar, a great conqueror will stand in your path all to end at Devil's Gate."

Before the general's flag could impale him, Alistor quickly came to his senses with a counter. His blade now clasped against Mushogun's great flag resisting impact.

"I don't know what that reading means. But this potential future is something I must find out, and I'm not going to let you deny me."

Alistor pushed Mushogun far back with his blade just as he got back up.

"What are you blabbering about? Why all of a sudden are you resisting?" The general wondered.

Energy finally began to emit around his body as Mushogun stared.

"Bah! You don't scare me. None of your human attacks can hurt me. My gut is impregnable BWAHAHAHAHAHAHAHA!"

Mushogun begins charging directly at him without any hesitation. Alistor begins focusing his thoughts altogether.

"Now for the moment of truth."

Mushogun's body impacts Alistor, and they both suddenly halt.

"What? I can't move?" The general confusedly wonders.

He looks below directly at Alistor, blood slightly gushed out from below.

"My gut?"

"Star Breaker!"

A great blast of light burst through Mushogun's body, leaving a significant hole in his belly. The general stumbled a few steps back as he collapsed in place.

Max Mathesius

"This isn't supposed to be HAPPENING!!!"

Dropping the flag, Mushogun explodes dramatically, with sparks flying out. A piece from the mirror and a small orb are left behind from the debris. Alistor goes to retrieve the objects.

"A piece of the mirror, but what is this?"

He holds the purple gem in his hands.

"That contains the essence of Mushogun." Whispered a voice from behind.

Alistor quickly turns around, backing a few steps away. But, unfortunately, it was none other than Mr. Rare cackling from behind.

"What do you know about this?"

"Always the one with many questions, KeKeKe. A piece of Mushogun's power rest within that orb. Consider it as a complimentary gift."

"How do we use it?"

Mr. Rare turns away and takes his leave.

"Hey, get back here."

"That is for you to find out. KeKeKe."

In seconds, Mr. Rare vanished in the air, leaving Alistor only to wonder as he stared into the horizon.

Back at the enemy base…

"Look like Mushogun is out. Time for me to step right in." Shellshock declared.

"Very well! You are now in charge of gathering energy for our labyrinth." The emperor announced. "Do not repeat his mistakes."

The spotlight was now all focused on the following leading commander.

"Aggerona Aerial division at your service."

Returning to the Emerald campus, breaking news was in store for the company.

"What? You mean the school is permanently shutting down?" Alistor gasped.

Viper's Labyrinth

A serious look was on Katty's face. Bamboo was seen packing up in the background.

"Yeah…sucks, but the situation has grown dire with all these monster attacks. With the school exploding twice and Mushogun declaring war, Mathias is on high alert right now."

Katty suddenly picked up his bag to begin leaving on an empty road.

"Where are you going?"

A sudden moment of silence in the air.

"I'm leaving on a long journey away to hone my skills at the temple."

"What? But can't you stay here and train with us?" Alistor tried to reason.

He nodded back.

"Sorry, I just can't. I'm no good with a sword around these parts. Your master trained you well, but I must find my own path."

A sad look was on his face as Katty waved goodbye. Then, without turning back, they went their separate ways.

"Farewell for now. Till we meet again."

"Till we meet again…." Alistor waved back.

Chapter 3

Two Days Ago

"Come on! Please tell me. What's my next mission?" Alistor eagerly asked. "Will I learn a new move today? Or maybe something cool?"

He continues to ramble on while Sairori tries hard to ignore his every word. Enjoying a moment to himself by the table at an early morning breakfast. He has a coffee mug in his hands.

"Ahem…your next task is to secure some work. A local part-time job, one might say."

He stopped his rambling for a brief moment as the master drank.

"What? How will this help? Monsters are everywhere! And there's no time for that. I need to get stronger to take on every monster they got. Some new skill, a move, or something cool that can wipe out an army."

The master whacks him on the head.

"What was that for?"

"Don't get too cocky. You barely even perfected the Star Breaker."

"What! But I totally whooped that Mushogun guy at the last battle. Back at that parking lot, remember? I blasted him away. Even exploding!"

He attempts to use his previous victory as an excuse.

"Nay! You are not ready yet, and that one move is enough." Sairori assured as he tossed a newspaper over for him to catch.

Looking closer at the paper, he noticed it was filled with job openings.

"Are you serious?" He rejected. "Can't I be paid to fight monsters? Like, what you're doing? Mathias's local army or even a private defense establishment? A sword for hire, at least?"

Alistor continues to show disfavor in the master's decision.

"It's not as easy as you think…."

"How so?"

"Trust me, you don't want to bother. Long story short, you'll learn nothing from the local army. I've been there, and it will save you years." He explained. "Anyways, since your school is forever closed, a part-time job may be the next best thing for you. You'll learn way more than you think; now go."

"But…"

"Go! I have other matters to tend to."

Sairori quickly boots him out the doors. Then, with the paper clutched in his hands, he heads out to seek some jobs.

"Look like I'll have to give this a shot then. Hopefully…"

Meanwhile, back with Vilovelious and his forces... General Shellshock makes an announcement for the other minions to hear.

"Two days it has been. Mushogun was small-time, so I present my plan I've cooked up."

"Oh, goody! Do tell." The emperor jumped.

The general pressed a button projecting a busy street downtown. A local business with people shopping here and there.

"My newest monster, Decoma, shall take the sky at night. First, by stealing local valuables, my monster will replace them with duplicates that will drain buyers nonstop."

Max Mathesius

"And how will Decoma pull this? Sounds quite expensive." He questioned.

"Not to worry! Decoma specializes in replicating any object. May it be plastic, stone, wood, or even clay, it won't cost a single penny. The Whoopers will be there to secure the stolen goods."

"Pure forgery? I like the sound of it so far."

"Yes, imagine the looks on the shoppers' faces when they find their gifts were no more than replicas. A potential of negative energy for the labyrinth." Shellshock assured. "Even better, we get to keep the goods ourselves."

"Very well, begin operation. Deploy Decoma immediately."

Back below, Alistor arrives downtown. Focusing on the papers, he comes to the front of a local jewelry store as his first stop. A "Now hiring!" sign was posted by the window.

"Maybe this won't be so bad after all."

Alistor enters the shop, spotting an old woman tending the store.

A couple hours later....

"Youch! Stop it! Stop it! It was a mistake." Alistor wailed, taking cover.

He was getting whacked by the old woman with a broom.

"You sold that couple the wrong ring. I told you before, the discount section on the third right shelf."

The woman then takes a look at her inventory. She stood frozen in fear for a brief moment before screaming.

"AHHHH! You sorted these gems all wrong. You've been selling my most expensive gems for less. You're fired! OUT! OUT!"

He gets kicked out of the store. A moment later, the papers led him to an antique shop.

"Maybe this will work out."

Alistor entered without hesitation; a middle-aged man greeted him as he accepted the job offer. Then, in minutes, he found himself caught in a long lecture.

"I suppose I could use an assistant. As you see, all the items here are precious. I got artifacts from civilizations dating far back during the Alandhite reign. So they are centuries old blah blah blah...."

Viper's Labyrinth

Alistor quickly finds himself drowsy, leaning back against an object as the man rambles.

"With me, we'll explore and uncover lots of secrets. Discover the unknowns and learn about ancient pasts. But, of course, these items are fragile, so you have to be very...." The middle-aged man suddenly turns his attention to Alistor. "CAREFUL!!!"

He wakes from the tone of the man's voice as a large vase behind toppled over. It shatters to pieces, leaving the owner completely heartbroken.

"I'm so sorry...."

"Never mind, leave me be." The man cried.

Alistor quietly takes his leave, heading to the next job. But instead, he finds himself in front of a pizzeria that was now hiring.

"Third time a charm."

A few moments later, he biked fast in a pizza boy get-up. He was utterly stressed as he could barely make ends meet on time for each delivery. Boxes piled behind his back. Finally, he lost control of the bike as it came skidding to the side.

"Oh no!"

In seconds, he came crashing through a barnyard filled with hay. Pizza is scattered across as he returns with the bike nearly destroyed. Then, he is confronted by an oversized figure before him.

"WHAT! Twenty orders behind! Why do you do this?" The fat man yelled.

Alistor was being scolded by the manager of the pizza place.

"Look, I'm sorry. Just give me another shot. I'll get it right this time." Alistor promised.

The manager lets off a deep breath.

"Look...." He sighed. "You already had four tries and delivered them all to the wrong places. So sorry, kid, I will have to let you go."

Alistor walks out of the pizzeria with a long face. Disappointed with no will to look further. He goes and takes a seat by the bench nearby. A while later, he got up, bumping into a significant figure before him. It overshadows him, catching him by surprise.

"Oh, Bamboo? It's you!" He nervously stuttered. "How have things been going?"

A moment of tension and silence between the two. Alistor then takes a few steps back, intimidated by his glare.

Max Mathesius

"Look… I'm sorry for everything." He bowed. "I know you lost your job. I promise I'll make this up to you. With these monsters around and stuff, the situation is complicated. So no hard feelings?"

Bamboo begins lecturing back.

"Two days ago, monsters came a second time. Two days ago, you dined on my ramen. Two days ago, my kitchen was a battleground. Two days ago, you set my propane on fire. Two days ago, you blew up the whole school a second time. And TWO DAYS AGO, I got fired from my job."

"I'm sorry! So sorry, I didn't mean it to turn out this way." He continued to fuss.

Alistor was down on his knee, begging for forgiveness as he expected the worse yet to come.

"AND! I actually wanted to thank you for that."

Bamboo caught him by surprise.

"Say what? How so?" Alistor wondered as Bamboo began explaining himself.

"Two days ago, I nearly lost sight of why I cook. Working at a dead-end job in a cafeteria was not a good way to go. But seeing you dine with that monster gave me new hope inside. My passion for cooking and the joy of watching others scuffling food. Ever since I got fired, a new flame sparked inside. To follow my dream and finally open a restaurant."

Alistor turned around to notice some lights turn on. Witnessing the grand opening of a new restaurant in town.

"Well, congratulations, I guess... Oh, wait! Are you actually hiring?" He asked.

"Why, of course. Come on in!"

He enters inside with Bamboo to check the new restaurant. Chairs, tables, and fish tanks around. With a complete kitchen and some newly enforced floor tiles giving off a shine. Everything was set and ready for business. The two took a brief moment to converse quite a bit, sinking everything in.

A few minutes later…

"So you're not really mad about the school? How were you able to afford all this?"

"The students there were never really bright." Bamboo personally admits. "How I afford this? Let's just say I've saved enough. Plus, with some connections on the side. Nothing shady…Ahem!"

Viper's Labyrinth

Bamboo hands over a uniform. And so he begins training for the job. Commencing through quick lessons from taking customer orders to cleaning dishes and tables for the day.

"Now try this!" Bamboo ordered.

"What is that stuff?"

"Grass Jelly! My specialty on the house. Give it a try."

Alistor takes a spoonful in his mouth. A few seconds later, he is seen gasping for air in total disgust. Then, choking as he is unable to bear the taste.

"This stuff is awful….Such a foul taste. How can this be a delightful dessert?"

"Everyone's a critic…." Bamboo sighed.

Alistor then returns home after the long day. Utterly exhausted as the master greets him back at the house. A mysterious letter is seen in his hands.

"So, how was your day? Find any good work?"

"I don't want to talk about it, ugh…."

He caught a glimpse of the letter he was looking over.

"So, what's that letter for?"

The master puts it away.

"It's none of your concern. Ahem…"

Later that night, downtown…

Shellshock arrives with a team of Whoopers by the pizza place near closing as they approach a truck. He grabs hold of a big man from behind.

"Halt! I'm here to appropriate all the Pizza you got. So surrender!"

The fat manager is seen scared half to death by the general as he attempts to escape in the delivery truck.

"Lock on!"

Max Mathesius

The general fires a missile at the vehicle, causing him to break a fire hydrant and crash into a metal pole. Boxes of Pizza scattered across the streets as the Whoopers began collecting them. Shellshock helps himself to a slice as they take seats by the window.

"Now to sit back and watch. Decoma, you're up."

The monster arrives, swooping through the air. Pouncing down at the top of the first store, it sets sight on. Decoma materialized through the Jewelry store in liquid form. Moist and clay build up across the room as the power gets disabled. Finally, the monster sets sight on the inventory of gems displayed across.

"Finders, Keepers!"

Decoma's arm stretched out, encasing every gem in the display. Covered in a thick matter of goo as the stones are replaced with a duplicate. Finally, commander Shellshock arrives backdoors with the Whoopers.

"Good! Excellent performance! Next, we'll hit that gift shop nearby, followed by that expensive antique store."

"My pleasure, commander."

The following day…

Lines full of customers waited as Bamboo's doors opened. Tables packed in seconds as loads of work piled for Alistor. Bamboo is busy preparing various kitchen dishes while he carries them out. Meals from hot bowls of noodles with seafood are served across the tables.

"This is a lot of work. You need to hire a couple more workers." Alistor suggested.

"I'll put that into consideration," Bamboo noted. "Now hurry with this one."

Bamboo hands over an oversized seafood platter for him to carry out. Barely able to handle its mass as he stumbled on out. He then overhears some customers bragging by the table.

"Have you heard the pizza place got hit last night?" Some woman brought up.

"Yeah, I also heard my friend's boyfriend made a regrettable purchase today. His hard-earned money was wasted on a fake engagement ring."

Alistor then overhears a riot happening outside. A mob of shoppers across the street of another store with receipts. A store manager is seen refusing as a no-return policy gets posted.

"Looks like everyone's demanding a refund."

Viper's Labyrinth

"Much counterfeit stuff has been circulating the market today, and the merchant owners have no explanation for this."

"How so?" Alistor asked. "Can't they tell if it's fake through common sense?"

The customers inside continued to explain.

"Not from what I've heard. When her boyfriend first saw that ring. It looked so real and authentic when he held it in his hands. It wasn't until after purchase, minutes later, the ring magically turned to mud."

Speculation and theories begin making their way across the next couple of days. But, unfortunately, they could only watch as the other businesses fell victim.

"This is simply a matter of forgery," Bamboo stated.

"Forgery?"

"Yep!" Bamboo nodded. "Someone overnight simply replaced everything with an exact duplicate with such precision and accuracy."

Later that night, Bamboo was busy counting cash as the store got to closing hour. But, unfortunately, Alistor still remained after an hour.

"You're done for the day." Bamboo reminded.

"I know...but somehow it doesn't feel right. So I'm gonna go take a look around."

"Suit yourself."

He heads into the back of the kitchen to grab a quick drink. He suddenly hears a sound coming from the back corridor.

"It's coming from the storage room."

He checks the back, opening the doors quietly as he spots a robed figure taking leave through a back window.

"No way am I letting you get away."

Alistor pulls out his blade quietly, leaving from the back as he pursues the mysterious figure. He makes his way through the alley and down the street, keeping a distance.

Somewhere outside of the town perimeter. A marksman waits in the middle of a narrow path. Some bags of goods are on the ground.

"Dammit, Auroa. What's taking you so long? I'm tired of waiting."

Max Mathesius

Alistor continues to follow the robed figure through some shallow woods. Finally, he comes to a halt taking cover.

"Another one…so there's two of them."

The robed figure approached the waiting marksman.

"Well, about time! What took you so long? So you got the goods?"

"All here, Maigashi."

"Good! Now let's get out."

The two begin to leave as Alistor continues to quietly follow their trail. A slight breeze of wind passed by.

"Hey, Auroa…"

"I know…"

The two stopped as Auroa suddenly appeared behind Alistor, catching him by surprise.

"Peekaboo!"

Alistor reacted, jumping far back as he attempted to gain some ground.

"So you're the fiends who been stealing all those goods. Making forgeries for unsuspecting victims. Such low lives."

"We did no such thing?" Maigashi argued. "If we wanted something, we would have taken it normally."

He pulled his sword towards them.

"I don't believe any of you. Two days ago, the pizza joint got hit. And overnight, someone stole everything."

"Hey! Two days ago, we minded our own business."

Auroa suddenly stepped in the middle of their argument.

"I knew you were following back in town."

"What you actually knew?" Alistor stumbled.

"Of course! Think I wanted to attract attention? I can assure you we are not the foe you seek."

"I'm not buying it. Bring it!"

Alistor begins charging at both of them.

"Looks like this runt wants to play. He's even younger than us." Maigashi teased.

Alistor takes a swing but misses. The two easily dodged his next set of oncoming attacks.

"You must be a student from that closed school. How adorable." Auroa giggled.

"Shut up! And fight!"

A sudden gust of wind pushed him back, bringing him to a brief stop.

"Calm down; we're really not the ones you truly seek. You misunderstand!" Auroa repeated.

Alistor begins focusing his blade, building some energy around it.

"Don't underestimate me!"

"What! An energy user?" Auroa halted as Alistor attempted to strike.

"Give me a break." Maigashi nodded. "Enough games!"

The marksman quickly pulls out his bow, firing an electrical blast at his blade, canceling his technique. Alistor stood stunned as Maigashi knocked him back. He falls flat on his back.

A brief moment later...

Auroa is seen tending his minor wound as they reason out their differences. Finally, Alistor filled them in on everything that had happened so far.

"What? Do you mean you're not the real forgers? Why are you even helping me?"

Maigashi reveals the contents of the goods to him. Nothing but food and some leftover scraps from Bamboo's restaurant.

"A little kindness goes far." Auroa cheerfully said.

They suddenly hear the sound of an explosion.

Max Mathesius

"What was that?"

"That must be the culprit." Maigashi pointed.

Alistor immediately got right back up, rushing to the scene.

"Wait! You must rest!" Auroa hollered.

"No time! I must hurry back."

He leaves the two behind, making his way downtown. Commander Shellshock is seen blowing up the pizza joint a second time. The fat manager is seen popping from under the counter.

"Now, what do you want?" The fat man whined.

"I have a big order to make, and the emperor requests EXTRA CHEESE!" The general ordered. "Now get to work."

The man follows the Whoopers into the back kitchen.

"Stop right there!"

Shellshock turned around as Alistor appeared before his very eyes.

"So you're the little runt who bested Mushogun."

"What! A machine?" Alistor hesitated for a brief moment.

"Yeah! That's right! Straight from Aggerona's Aerial division! Mach-79, fully revved up and ready for battle. I'm the next demon general to run things, and Shellshock's the name."

He fires a small rocket at Alistor, forcing him to jump out of the store. The two made their way outside as the general began taking flight. Alistor had his blade gripped tight and ready.

"We'll see about that. Come on! Give me your best shot." He provoked.

Shellshock takes a dive swooping down at high speed. Alistor loses balance as the general glides past him.

"Hah! Never handled an opponent in the air before?"

Alistor begins charging his blade again, focusing all his energy as an aura emits around his body. He was immediately surprised as a metal chain burst out from Shellshock's chest, wrapping him.

Viper's Labyrinth

"What! You pop chains from your chest?" Alistor cried.

The general begins to haul him around like a yo-yo. Alistor lands hard on his bottom as the general laugh away.

"Ha! And to think Mushogun lost so easily. I can finish you right now if I want. In fact, maybe I will."

A Whooper grunt suddenly interrupts the battle.

"Oh, the pizza is actually ready?"

Commander Shellshock releases Alistor from the chain. Loads of pizza boxes are carried out from each Whooper as the general checks over the order.

"You're not even worth my time. I'll have my monster finish you. Decoma, you're up!"

A monster swoops into the fray as Shellshock and the soldiers teleport away. The fat manager is seen catching his breath, relieved.

"That's it! I can't take this abuse." He cried. "Too many monster attacks. I'm closing!"

Alistor got up, facing the new monster taking the sky. Decoma swoops down while he attempts to make a swing but misses.

"Gah!"

"Hahaha! Let's twist things up." Decoma chuckled.

Decoma begins flapping his wings hard. A dust storm begins encasing the entire battle concealing the monster from sight.

"What? A dust storm? I can't even see."

The monster continues to swoop down. Alistor gets knocked back and forth, taking every hit as he blindly struggles to figure something out.

"Damn! I don't know what to do." Alistor pounded. "He has a complete advantage while I'm a sitting duck. And to think I prefer fighting plants instead."

Decoma knocks him down once more. He was pinned to the ground as he couldn't get up. The monster took pity.

"Tell you what? I'll make this quick and painless, ha ha ha."

Max Mathesius

Just before Decoma can dive, he gets hit by two elemental blasts behind. The monster falls, crashing as Auroa pulls Alistor out of the battle. The two rogues stand against Decoma, recovering in the nick of time.

"Hey? Who do you think you are?"

Decoma takes the sky once more, creating another storm at high speed. The dust quickly collected in the air while the two remained stationary without hesitation. Alistor could only cover his eyes as the current escalated into a dust storm.

"Auroa, you ready? Let's show them how it's really done." Maigashi said.

Decoma swoops in close for the strike.

"Now I got you!"

Auroa immediately opens his eyes for a brief moment dispelling the entire storm. Decoma finds himself suddenly frozen in place.

"What? My storm! How is this possible?" The monster questioned.

Maigashi begins chuckling for a brief moment before explaining.

"My buddy, here's a wind channeler. You rely on keeping a distance from your opponents, but it's not your lucky day. We specialize in distance combat, and your little dust storm is of no threat to us."

"No! I'm not done yet."

Decoma forces himself further back, attempting to create another storm, but gets a wing pierced by an electrical dagger thrown by Maigashi. The monster stood completely stunned in midair. Then, Auroa creates a whip from thin air. Lashing out from under his long dark hair as it left Alistor speechless.

"Wind Whip Slash!"

"NOOOOO!"

A strong force of wind pierced through Decoma's heart, delivering the final blow to the chest. His body begins to crumble like clay before his very eyes. Finally, the monster came crashing down, creating a massive explosion on impact.

A while later...

"There! We're even now." Maigashi said.

Just before the two parted ways with Alistor, they sensed something behind a bush.

Viper's Labyrinth

"Bamboo?"

"Have you been watching this whole time?" Alistor asked.

Bamboo had a proposition to make.

"I'd like to hire you both. Come and work at my new restaurant." Bamboo offered.

Alistor's jaw dropped for a brief moment. Then, unable to believe what he just heard, he attempts to reason with Bamboo.

"What? No! Are you serious? You're seriously going to hire these low lives?"

"Hey! Who are you calling low." Maigashi beamed as he pulled Alistor up from his neck collar.

"But they're criminals."

Bamboo remained chill as a cucumber as Alistor broke out of his grasp.

"I'm heartbroken." Auroa sarcastically nodded.

"I know…" Bamboo admitted.

"Then why? Give me one good reason." He shouted.

Bamboo then whacks Alistor over the head with a frying pan. A smile cracked from the other two as they watched.

"Listen for one brief second," Bamboo explained. "They may be thieves, but they're not your everyday criminals. They worked together in harmony, and you could learn something from this. In fact, I can see you all working together."

"Give me a break." Alistor glared back at the two.

"It's a gut feeling, but I'm going with it. Plus, they're both around your age range. It's perfect!" Bamboo nodded.

The other two begin to privately converse.

"You think this is worth our time?" Maigashi whispered.

"Well…we do have nowhere else to go. But, unfortunately, food is scarce at the moment." Auroa shrugged.

"You'll be paid, of course," Bamboo mentioned.

Max Mathesius

Maigashi immediately accepts the offer sealing the deal as handshakes passed around. Leaving Alistor completely dumbfounded with two new members following back.

"No hard feelings. I'm sure in due time, we'll get along once you get to know us. We'll do our very best to help." Auroa smiled.

Alistor felt anxious momentarily, trying to distance himself from the two. Maigashi suddenly reached out to give him a noogie from behind.

"Yeah! You'll be just like an annoying little brother we never had."

"Get off me!"

He pulled away from his grasp as his hair was getting messed up.

A moment later, the party arrives back at the restaurant. Bamboo serves up a round of grass jelly for everyone, leaving Alistor again in utter disgust. Auroa and Maigashi simply helped themselves to the treat as he stood by.

"You guys can actually stomach that stuff?" He questioned.

"Are you kidding? This stuff is good." Maigashi pestered back.

"I've had worse," Auroa said.

"My gut was right." Bamboo wept as he happily watched.

The very next day later... Breaking news was in store for Alistor as Sairori came to the restaurant early morning with a sudden announcement. The mysterious letter from before was clutched in his very hand.

"There is a dire situation happening down in Lavendhite. Another great threat has emerged, and I'm needed elsewhere." The master said.

"Lavendhite? Where is that? And what is this other great threat?" Alistor hastily asked.

"It's a region halfway across the world," Auroa answered. "Surrounded by the Violet seas. I heard it also consisted of three islands protecting a legendary pillar."

The master begins to take leave, but Alistor immediately gets up, refusing to accept his decision.

"You can't leave now. There's so much I need to learn. I only know one move."

"The Star Breaker is enough," Sairori assured.

"But can't I come? And what is this new threat?"

Viper's Labyrinth

"No! That other threat is not of your concern. You must stay here and fight off the current threat in this land." He reminded. "Vilevelious has yet to appear, and four demon generals remain."

A slight look of worry was on Alistor's eyes as the master stepped out. He was completely unsure of himself while the rest bid him farewell. The master then pauses.

"Don't worry...You are in good hands."

Sairori's last words uplift his mood before disappearing into the morning sunrise.

Max Mathesius

Chapter 4

Spring Breeze:

Creature of the bottom well

Sometime early in the afternoon…

"Alright, Sword Monster! Stick it to them. Slice and dice em good."

Commander Shellshock is seen cheering for his monster from the sidelines as a battle commences in the middle of a busy street. Auroa and Maigashi are seen putting up a display of power while Alistor stumbles behind.

"Argh, Alistor! Get your head together." Maigashi pestered.

Explosions are seen setting off across the concrete pavement.

"I'm trying! You guys are moving too fast! We need to coordinate better."

The monster suddenly plunged through a car. Then, it hurls the scraps over to Alistor as he turns away.

"Watch out!"

Viper's Labyrinth

Auroa dashed in with his whip knocking Alistor out of harm's way.

"Ow! That actually hurts!"

"Oh, quite your jabbering."

Auroa quickly casts a burst of wind, pushing the monster further back. Maigashi then goes in for the finishing blow, leaving Shellshock distressed.

"Gah! Sword Monster! Don't just stand there! Do something."

The monster barely had time to react as it mindlessly jumped in the air with its point-tipped bottom. Aimed directly at Maigashi, an electrical surge of energy emits from his bow.

"The perfect shot!"

A bursting stream of lightning pierces through the monster, sending it crashing straight to the ground. Sparks quickly burst from the monster's eye as it bursts into a pile of flames within seconds. The team then quickly turned their attention towards Shellshock.

"Now it's your turn." Alistor pointed his blade.

He begins charging toward the general, but the other two unexpectedly intervene. Alistor falls to the ground as Maigashi jumps over his back to gain momentum.

"Leave this guy to me!"

He fires a few electrical bolts, but the General easily dodges them. Auroa suddenly appears from behind.

"Not so fast!"

Before he could strike, Alistor quickly intervened with a Star Breaker. Auroa was forced to fall back as a tiny glint was seen in the General's eye.

"Oh, this should be amusing."

Without hesitation, Shellshock hops over Alistor's head. Pressing both hands on top as Alistor fell flat on the ground once more. A mocking look was seen on the General's face.

"Such bogus! Your teamwork totally blows."

The other two attempt to fire some projectiles, but the General deflects them with his chain. Alistor quickly got back up with a fired look.

"Let me handle him! You guys stay out of my way."

Max Mathesius

A disbelieving look was seen from the other two as Alistor readied his attack once more. The General quickly turns away.

"I can't even take you seriously. You're not worth the time. But tomorrow's a new day, so I'll return with a new monster. So keep on, Wiggin!"

With one wave Shellshock immediately soars off into the skies.

"Damn, he got away!"

"Sigh…and that's a wrap." Auroa snapped.

A moment later, an argument escalates among the team upon return.

"Hey! What's going on?" Bamboo wondered.

"If it wasn't for us, you be mincemeat," Maigashi said.

Customers were seen watching in the middle of the background.

"Yeah! But you guys kept getting in my way. I would have had Shellshock if it weren't for you guys. And I'm not a platform."

"You should be more careful." Auroa reminded. "A careless move like that could cost you next time."

"Next time, give me a heads up! You didn't have to be so rough with your wind. That fall actually kind of hurt."

The argument continued as Bamboo was forced to intervene.

"Hey! We got customers eating! Take it out in the kitchen!"

Hours after the battle, the night begins to break in. Dinner was being prepared at the restaurant while Bamboo had a quick intervention with Alistor in the middle of cooking.

"So… what's the deal anyway? You needed some friends, so I found you a nice pair. They don't seem so bad."

A disagreeing look was on his face.

"Friends? We don't even have anything in common. They're criminals! And I don't approve them one bit."

"Sigh…Well, you can't be picky about everything. Things won't always turn the way you expect, ya know. Go on!"

Viper's Labyrinth

Bamboo continues to stir his pot while he rambles on.

"It's just… It's just the two work so well. Maigashi and Auroa are fast, and I can't keep up. Maigashi is a complete jerk the whole time. And Auroa…well, Auroa just plain gives me the creeps."

Bamboo placed his ladle down.

"Well, it seems you're rather intimidated. But that's ok because I'll figure something out. Maybe what you need is some good bonding experience."

"Give me a break."

He suddenly gets knocked over the head with a ladle.

"No, I'm serious! The first step is building a good relationship with the team. Get to know and learn from one another. Then, we begin with something called trust."

"Trust?"

Bamboo grabs some papers over by his counter.

"Just leave it to me. I'll have your next mission prepared."

"Really!"

His mood quickly shifted back right up.

"Now go! Back to work!"

Meanwhile, back somewhere above at the Aggerona fortress…

"Well, that monster was a bust. Do you have another plan ready?" The emperor questioned. "We need energy for the labyrinth."

Shellshock was seen waltzing back and forth.

"Give me a sec. I'm still brainstorming. My old Sword Monster didn't go as planned. So we need something fresh and new."

"Well, that monster was used plenty of times in our last war. But, your monster, how you put this lost its edge."

"Turn the channel." The General ordered.

Max Mathesius

A whooper grunt behind the scene pressed a button. The screen shifts to an area filled with forest and cabins. A great dam stands tall in the background.

"What is that object? Zoom in on that spot right there."

The screen begins focusing on an old well not far from a campsite. A dark presence is felt throughout the room.

"I got it! This is it! The answers we've been seeking."

"Oh? Do tell."

Shellshock begins elaborating as some files are presented.

"What we have here is not just an old broken well, but the sight of a monster sealed back during the glory days of the Great Moon. In fact, it's an ancient creature crafted by the Hundred Hands Emperor."

Vilevelious was puzzled for a brief moment.

"And you believe we can revive this monster?"

"Are you kidding? With my new tech on hand, this will be a cinch. In fact, with a little tweak, we can have this monster up to date and under our control. It will provide us with all the negative energy we need."

The emperor quickly gives the approval.

"Very well. You may proceed!"

The general look over the screen again, noticing boy and girl scouts are seen setting camp in the vicinity.

"So Camp Hazefall is it? No problem, I'll simply improvise. With that dam in place, this gives me an idea anyway."

"Whoopers! To Hazefall!"

The General exits the room as the scene shifts back to Alistor and the party. Bamboo presents the next mission to them.

"What? A camping trip! You can't be serious." Alistor questioned. "This was not what I thought you had in mind."

Auroa looks over at the pamphlets.

"Seems like more work for us." Maigashi pestered.

Viper's Labyrinth

"The director of Hazefall is in short supply of help this time of the year. So he needs a few helping hands to supervise these boys and girls." Bamboo explained.

An unmotivated look was now on Alistor.

"I won't even ask anymore."

"Good, then it's settled. We're off to Hazefall."

The party quickly packs, leaving in Bamboo's car. Meanwhile, somewhere in the middle of Hazefall, a fat man is seen rushing to a lone stall in the middle of a barren field.

"Woo, I need to go now."

Pulling out a newspaper, he quickly enters, slamming the door shut. In a matter of seconds, Shellshock and a group of Whoopers arrive down at the scene. A soldier immediately points to the stall.

"So the director's in here?"

A whooper grunt begins knocking on the door.

"One minute, I'm busy."

The whooper knocks once more, ticking off the guy.

"Dammit! Can't you see I'm busy?"

Without hesitation, Shellshock brings the door down, catching the director by surprise. He lets out a girly scream.

"Alright, tubby! Off with the clothes! I'm running things from here on out. Do it now! Or I'll fire my laser."

Fear struck within the director as he knocked his head to the back wall. His pants quickly flew off as the whoopers apprehended him. The man was seen tied up and gagged as Shellshock stole his outfit.

"And last but not least, your hat. I'll be needing this."

The director was seen stripped to his underwear. The General takes a look at himself in a small mirror.

"Hmm. this disguise doesn't match my red armor. Oh, wait!"

Shellshock begins tinkering with some buttons on his wrist. Shifting from a red-coated color to a jungle green for blending.

"Perfect! I now fit the part."

"Mmmmm mmmm."

The director mumbles on the floor as Shellshock shoves him back into the stall.

"Thanks for the cooperation."

With one kick, the stall tips over, trapping the man. A moaning sound is heard as the General walks off evilly laughing.

"Ok, guys! Head straight to the dam. Don't let anyone near."

The Whoopers immediately waltz off as the General approaches the campgrounds. A bus arrives on the scene, dropping off a group of kids.

"Excellent, heh heh heh."

Bamboo and the rest arrived on the scene in a matter of moments. Parking the car in the driveway as they quickly unloaded.

"Let's see, the director's office should be right here," Bamboo said.

The team enters inside, catching the General slightly by surprise.

"Who are you?"

"We're the help that you called for?"

Bamboo presents the papers to him. A confused look was on the General's face for a second, but he kept calm.

"Uh....Oh yeah! Of course! Of course! The help. Yeah, totally! Ugh, here's your helper's aid badges."

Alistor begins looking over at the director strangely.

"Hey? What are you staring at?"

The other two quickly bump his arm.

"It's not polite to stare," Auroa whispered.

"Oh, sorry. You seem rather familiar." Alistor speculated.

Viper's Labyrinth

Tension slightly builds within the General as a sweat slips out. Shellshock readies his blaster under the sleeve.

"Oh, do I now?"

"Hmm, maybe not. Oh well…"

Bamboo quickly boots the team out.

"We'll just be off to our designated cabins."

Within moments the team unpacked inside. Bamboo begins prepping up in the kitchen as Maigashi rests on the couch.

"Good! You three can begin to bond. I'll be in the kitchen if you need me."

Auroa begins reading a book quietly in the corner.

"Maybe this trip won't be so bad after all." Alistor thought.

"Time for some zzz's," Maigashi muttered.

Within a moment, Maigashi feels a force bumping from under the cushion.

"What the hell?"

A kid immediately pops up from under, forcing him to stumble back.

"Hey! What's the deal? This is our cabin!"

More kids begin to emerge from under various furniture pieces. The three are quickly overwhelmed. Then, finally, a little boy approached them.

"The name is Niko! You three must be the new aid the director sent over. Welcome to Hazefall, by the way."

The three are left dumbfounded for a moment. Unsure of what to do.

"Um…care to fill us in?"

"What? Do you mean you guys haven't gotten the drill yet? You're supposed to be our guide! Lead on activities and expeditions."

A tired look was seen on Maigashi.

"Yawn…Sorry. Just go and do whatever you need to do. I'm in the middle of a good nap."

Maigashi tucks himself back in, but the kids force him right off. Then, finally, a little girl approached him.

"Well, not with that attitude inside. I'm Miko, by the way."

"I don't care…." He mumbled.

"Come on! We need to get outside. Rise and shine!"

Alistor and the team are immediately forced out by the kids. Niko hands over the planner to them.

"These are the activities we have set for today. Just supervise and watch over us."

"You better!" Miko pointed. "My parents paid good money for this. So you three get yourselves together."

"Ok, what's the first thing on the agenda?" Alistor wondered.

Auroa pulls open a map as the planner points them to a river.

"Look like a small hike to the Hazefall springs. Followed by some arts and crafts. Then a boat rides down to the marshes for some games."

The three begin leading the pack through the forest. Following the tranquil streams as the kids got rowdy.

"Ok, we made it…."

A small tavern rest by the springs. Lined with arts and crafts as the kids quickly rushed towards it.

"Hey! Watch it!"

As time progressed, the three quietly watched as the little ones enjoyed themselves. Finally, Miko presents her painting to them.

"Well…what do you think?"

"Look's rather abstract." Maigashi shrugged.

The sound of a horn is then heard as Auroa cued the rest. Three disguised Whoopers pilot a boat downstream. The kids quickly dropped their brush to begin boarding.

Viper's Labyrinth

"Look like that's our ride."

The Whoopers quietly drove the boat downstream without speaking. The rest laid back to enjoy the scenery. Auroa rests peacefully on the side.

"Somehow, I feel I'm starting to understand you guys," Alistor said.

"Ugh... gag me with a spoon." Maigashi pestered.

They arrived at the marshes for some games in a matter of minutes. The kids are seen with nets catching various wildlife, from frogs to small amphibians. The team quickly spots some dead trees not far from the distance.

"What in the world is over there?" Alistor wondered.

"Is that a well?" Maigashi noticed.

"Looks like it." Auroa nodded. "How rather odd."

The three are drawn close briefly, but a dark presence sweeps past them. Alistor felt a cold vibe.

"I don't know...It doesn't feel right. It's as if there's a dark presence close by."

The others continue stepping forward.

"Come on! Don't be chicken. It's just some rusty old well." Maigashi muttered.

Before the two could get any closer, Niko's voice halted them.

"No! That area is off-limits!"

"What do you mean?"

Miko begins tugging the two away from the dead trees.

"Something evil is said to live in there. A big bad monster, I heard."

"Monster? Give me a break!"

Alistor immediately steps in, recalling something.

"Of course! It's coming back now. I may be familiar with this story."

"Oh? Please share." Auroa said.

Max Mathesius

Daylight began to diminish as night clouds in. The sound of stomachs grumbled as they began returning to the cabin. Bamboo prepares a full-course meal for the camp.

"So, what's the rest on today's agenda?" Auroa asked.

"Well…we still got roasting s'mores by the campfire. Oh, and sharing spooky stories." Niko mentioned.

A reluctant look was seen on them.

"Guess you can tell us about that later."

An hour passed, and the party was seen sitting by the campfire. Each kid shared a story while roasting s'mores. Maigashi is seen bored while Auroa pretends to listen. Alistor was the only one to stay interested.

"Yawn, do you guys have any stories that won't put me to sleep?" Maigashi pestered.

"Oh, you think you can do better?" Miko objected.

An unmotivated look was in Niko's eyes.

"Nah? It's just your stories bore me to death. I heard most of them already; some are just plain made up with bad twists."

"Maybe you can tell us about that well now?" Auroa reminded.

Alistor focused on the fire.

"Well, it's not what you would call spooky. But ok, here goes."

The Creature of the Well.

"It was during the last major war of the Zophian era. The battle was at its peak when the Great Moon led the final charge against the Hundred Hands army. The emperor sacrificing one of his many hands created one of the deadliest monsters known to man. A parasitic creature called Negmanite."

The kids were seen hooked in with Maigashi.

"This was one of the many trials placed in his path. The Great Moon's army was caught by surprise when it attacked. Craving the thirst for blood, it slaughtered countless victims. The casualties were great as it proved to be a match for Moon."

The Great Moon is seen holding his own against the creature while many bodies lie scattered across the marsh field. Then, finally, he draws his last breath.

Viper's Labyrinth

"So, how did he beat it?" Niko asked.

"Well, with the last stroke of power, he focused it all on a seal. Then, targeting a well, the monster was imprisoned for all eternity. And as we know, this makes Hazefall the burial grounds for many fallen soldiers."

The kids were now seen shriveled up near a corner.

"What? It doesn't seem so bad." Maigashi shrugged. "Now we know we were sitting over a bunch of dead bodies. Maybe we can catch a ghost or something."

"I don't think I can sleep ever again." Niko shuddered.

Alistor suddenly feels something sticky under his garment.

"What the?"

Auroa and Maigashi were seen giggling.

"Look like you got yourself dirty."

"Guys!!"

Alistor walks off into the cabin, slightly annoyed.

"So, what are the plans for tomorrow?" Auroa asked Niko.

"Beats me. That's up to the director to decide. We'll find out tomorrow."

"I hope it's some dollhouse and dress up," Miko muttered.

Meanwhile, back at the office, Shellshock is seen tossing papers about.

"Fishing? Hiking? Raft riding? Macaroni art! LAME!!!!"

The commander spun his chair around, thinking to himself

"What these kids need is some good labor! But, hey? Maybe I can start with that new base I want to build."

He begins looking over some blueprints but gets interrupted by an incoming transmission from a Whooper.

"What? You guys made it to the well. On my way!"

Max Mathesius

In a split second, the General arrives at the marsh field. Surrounded by whoopers dancing across the well.

"It's time to break the seal!"

The commander shot out his chains encasing the entire well.

"Come forth, Negmanite! Your new master calls!"

Within a moment, the blood-dried well shatters apart. A deformed arm first reaches out from the hole. Then, it slowly pulls itself up. Finally, the monster begins taking steps forward but stumbles to the floor.

"Man, you're a complete mess! Allow me to fix you up. You are no longer affiliated with Hundred Hands! You are now a property of Aggerona."

More chains begin to encase the monster. Then, repairing parts of its body with a new coat of paint and armor.

"You once craved blood. But now you'll go for power and water systems. Now go! Gather energy for the labyrinth."

The monster immediately jumps off into the nearest pond. The following morning the camp was awakened early for a surprise.

"Why is there so much garbage?" Alistor stumbled.

"Bamboo, did you forget to throw all your trash in the kitchen?" Maigashi asked.

"Hey! It wasn't me! I didn't cook that much last night."

A puzzled look was on the team as the director came forward. Handing off the agenda for today.

"A clean-up?" Auroa questioned.

Niko looks over the schedule.

"Let's see....Huh? Bridge-building, cutting trees, cement mixing, and assembling bricks and walls."

The disappointment was seen in Miko's eyes.

"But I wanted to play some dress-up in a dollhouse." She mumbled.

"Well, not today!" The director shouted.

Viper's Labyrinth

"These tasks seem rather odd?" Auroa replied.

The director begins to waltz off.

"I want this place squeaky clean by lunch. Then we'll talk."

The party begins grabbing bags for the morning clean-up while Bamboo is seen along with the kids assisting. Sometime later, the director hands over the blueprints to the team.

"Are you sure we can do this?" Niko asked. "It's huge!"

The group is overwhelmed by the blueprints set for Shellshock's new base.

"Get to work!"

The kids were seen unmotivated to begin. Then, objecting to his every command as whining begins to commence.

"I don't want to build a fort!" Miko yelled. "It's a boy's thing, and I want to go home."

The sound of kids begins getting into Shellshock's ears as Alistor and the rest stand by.

"Gah! I got to shut them up. But how?"

"I want to play dollhouse!"

From desperation, an idea struck the General.

"Of course! We ARE going to play in a dollhouse."

Miko and some others quickly calmed down.

"Really?"

"Yes! But instead, we need to build it first." Shellshock explained. "This is going to be a big dollhouse."

The children begin to get excited.

"Can we paint it pink?" She asked.

"What!!!"

"I want it pink!" Miko shouts.

"Ok, Pink? Fine! Just start!"

Max Mathesius

The kids begin to get to work as Alistor, and the others lend a helping hand. Then, finally, Bamboo makes his way back to the kitchen.

"Hmm, what to prepare for dinner?"

He spots a big bag of pasta.

"Ah! I'll just start boiling these, then. Now for some water."

Bamboo heads to the sink. He pulls the lever, but nothing but a drip leaks out.

"Huh? Is this thing broken?"

He begins tapping over the leaky faucet. Flames quickly burst in his face.

"That's not right?"

He turns his attention to turn on the stove; water quickly gushes on him. Then, the lights begin flickering in the room.

"What is with this place? It's haunted!"

Bamboo rushed out the doors.

"Hmm? What's cooking?" Maigashi asked.

"It's haunted! Something is messing with the power and water." He panted.

Maigashi goes to take a look back inside with Bamboo.

"Hm, I don't see anything?"

The two proceed into the kitchen. Maigashi approached the nob on the sink. Bamboo briefly backs away. Water is generally seen flowing out of the faucet.

"Works fine for me. Must be your imagination." He shrugged.

He proceeds to turn on the stove.

"But I saw something." Bamboo gestured.

Meanwhile, back outside, Auroa overhears the kids mentioning something obscure while construction commenced.

"What are you two bragging about?"

Viper's Labyrinth

Niko turned away in disbelief.

"It's true! My friends and I heard voices from the east side." Miko brought up.

"Voices?" Alistor questioned.

"When was this?" Auroa wondered.

Miko begins elaborating.

"Earlier, when we were cleaning. My friends and I decided to check the east field for any mess. That's when we spotted an unusual wooden compartment from a distance. We were tempted to check, but then we heard voices."

Miko and a couple girls were seen crouched behind a bush.

"Can you describe the voice by chance?" Alistor added.

"Well, it was like a moan. A cry for help or something. But we were scared, and it could have been a ghost, no doubt."

The camp continues with the labor for the remainder of the day. Nightfall soon arrived as everyone was ready for sleep. Auroa is seen reading a book by a small lamp while a group of kids is seen sneaking right out.

"Ok, Miko, I'll go. But you better not be making this up."

"Trust me! I know what I saw."

Miko is seen leading the way with a flashlight. The sound of owls hooting and crickets chirping as they walked by. Finally, the kids come to a halt behind a big bush.

"Ok, you got the camera? And you remember to bring the s'mores, right?"

"Of course, Miko."

Niko is seen pulling out the bag of marshmallows. The kids quickly spot the wooden booth nearby. They immediately hear the moans upon flashing the light over.

"Well...Go and check it out?" Miko ordered.

"What? Me! No! I don't want to."

The two quickly turned to the other kids, but they backed away.

"Ok, then how about we go together then. You hold the light while I get the camera."

Max Mathesius

Niko quickly agreed to her proposition. The two begin approaching the fallen stall as the sound grows louder. The other kids promptly came in to help turn the compartment around. Miko reached for the doors.

"Man, it smells so bad," Niko mentioned.

"On the count of three."

Without hesitation, the door flew open with a half-naked man emerging.

"EEEEEEEEEK!!!!"

Without a second thought, the kids quickly panicked as the man fell right over. The kids promptly rushed back to the camp, alerting everyone. Maigashi came barging out with his weapon in hand.

"Are we under attack? Speak to me!"

"Some fat half-naked bald guy jumped out at us." Miko cried.

The kids were seen shaking in their boots. He immediately fires a shot in the air to silence the situation.

"Oh really, eh?"

"Do you think your weapon is necessary?" Auroa questioned.

Bamboo's frying pan caught his eye.

"You're right! We have a potential predator, so drastic force is needed."

He grabs the pan right off of Bamboo's hand.

"Hey, I just washed that."

"Relax, I'll give it back right after. This is serious business."

Without further ado, the party heads to investigate the scene. Maigashi spearheads the front armed with the pan as Alistor flashes the light. Bamboo and Auroa followed from behind as the kids stayed close.

"Hey, is that chocolate I smell?" Bamboo said.

"Niko, did you remember to bring back our snacks?" Miko asked.

"Um…No, I sort of forgot."

They then hear a sound coming from the distance. Maigashi goes to take cover behind the bush.

"Look like something crawling our way. Get ready!"

Meanwhile, somewhere back with Shellshock, he overlooks the progress of the new base. Disappointment in his eyes. A charming giant treehouse was set in place.

"Leave it to child labor. This looks nothing like the new fortress."

He tears the blueprint to shreds.

"I can't even look at it. Pink!"

With Alistor and the team, Maigashi readies to strike as the figure slowly approaches. The figure is seen tripping over a bag left on the ground.

"Oh no! Our s'mores!" Niko gasped.

"Mmmm, can this day get any worse?"

Without hesitation, Maigashi goes in for the strike. The kids were seen cheering as he laid the beating on the intruder. Then, with a series of quick blows, he was down in a split second. Alistor shines the light over, revealing the half-naked man.

"Who are you?" Bamboo asked.

Completely smeared from the marshmallow and chocolate, he removes the rag from his mouth.

"Who am I? I'm the director! Who the heck are you?"

"Why we're the helper's aid, of course." Maigashi saluted.

"Wait a minute…The director is back in his office." Alistor pointed.

They continue to question the man.

"Yeah, how do we know you're not lying?" Bamboo pestered.

A furious look was seen in the director's eye.

"You morons! I'm the real director! That robot is a complete imposter. He took my clothes, and I've been trapped ever since. How can you be fooled by such a terrible disguise? Some aids you are."

Max Mathesius

"Is he red? Cause our director was coated in green." Alistor pressed on.

"Of course he's red!"

The children suddenly recognized the man's face in a matter of moments. A mistake of identity on hands.

"We're sorry. We were scared. We thought you were some creeper." Niko explained.

After a while, Alistor pieces all the facts evident from the start.

"I gave the sketchy director the benefit of the doubt when we arrived. Shellshock is behind this. We can't let him get away. Come on!"

Within moments the party came barging into the office. Their weapons were ready on hand for battle.

"So you finally figured it out."

The General removes his cheap disguise. The green coating on his armor shifts back to his usual red.

"You're through! We got you now."

A microwave sits behind the counter.

"Oh, I'm shaking under my metal boots. This camp really is starting to blow, and I'm getting bored. Negmanite! Get over here!"

Within a flash, the microwave explodes into bits and pieces. Negmanite emerges from behind the electrical socket. Kids begin to panic out of the room.

"I don't want my blood sucked." Niko cried.

"Me too!!!" Miko screamed.

Alistor takes his stand against the monster.

"It's too cramped in here. We need to take this outside." Auroa suggested.

The party rushes out of the office as the monster comes crashing through the window. Maigashi goes on to fire a few shots.

"Let me have the first hit."

Viper's Labyrinth

Three electrical arrows hit Negmanite, but the attack is seen getting absorbed within contact. The monster retaliates with a wave of beams sparking toward them.

"Damn, my moves will be useless." Maigashi nods.

Bamboo goes to take cover, shielding the children as Auroa goes in with his whip. The monster avoids his winds without effort.

"This one's fast. But, unfortunately, I can't get a lock on it."

Alistor makes a strike but misses. Negmanite is seen moving through the leaky pipes and power sockets.

"Ha! Ha! Ha! My monster won't go down that easily. Look around! We're surrounded by power and drain systems. Negmanite is made of energy."

Within moments the labyrinth can be seen overshadowing Hazefall. But, then, the power systems below blackout, leaving only the campfire in place.

"This isn't good."

The monster proceeds to the next faucet as Alistor attempts to land a direct hit. He continues to mindlessly swing, but Negmanite retaliates with a gush of water.

"Looks like you're all washed up." The General pestered. "Now finish him!"

Negmanite proceeds with a few stomps to the ground as Alistor dodges out of the way. Auroa intervenes with a few whips to stall but gets sent back by a blast of water.

"Watch yourself!"

Alistor makes his way to the director's position. The man, still half-naked, stumbled over as he slipped by. The monster immediately comes to a halt.

"Something disrupting it!" Maigashi pointed.

An astonished look was on General Shellshock's face.

A sticky substance lay smeared below the monster's feet. Its form begins to deteriorate from the bottom as Alistor goes in to make a cut. Slicing off part of its leg, the monster quickly pulls itself to the nearest drain.

"What? Argh! Of all the weakness."

Before the party could charge forward, the General takes to the air.

Max Mathesius

"A change of plans! We already drained the power! Now we need to fully contaminate the water. Negmanite! Get to the dam!"

The monster materializes into the leaking pipe as it reaches the Hazefall dam. Before the party proceeded, they quickly gathered some supplies in the kitchen.

"What are we looking for?" Bamboo asked.

"Anything sticky." Auroa pointed. "I got a plan."

Bamboo pulls out a massive jar of maple from the cupboard.

"Will this do?"

"Perfect!"

Back outside...

"So, what's the quickest way to reach the dam?" Alistor asked.

"Well, a big gondola can take us there in a few minutes," Niko mentioned.

"Then lead the way."

As Niko led the way, Negmanite arrived on top of the dam.

"Now get to work!"

The monster begins soaking its arms in the waters. Slowly polluting the system as negative energy flowed into the labyrinth.

"Good! In a matter of moments, nothing but a waste field will be left behind." Shellshock mumbled to himself.

"Sorry to rain on your parade."

Alistor and the team arrive at the scene.

"Argh! Whoopers, get them!"

Enemy soldiers begin rushing forward, but Maigashi jumps in.

"I'll handle these bogeys. Take out that monster!"

Bamboo begins setting the jar in place as Alistor charges at the monster.

Viper's Labyrinth

"Here goes!"

Negmanite halts with the draining as Alistor comes in with a Star Breaker. The monster dives into the waters, stopping him in place.

"Where did you go?"

Geysers began shooting from the dam as everyone rushed to higher grounds. Whoopers are seen getting swept away by the friendly fire. Negmanite came emerging from a geyser as Alistor fell back.

"Whoah, watch out!" Bamboo hollered.

Within a split second, the wind begins shifting the waters back.

"What? A change in altitude?" Questioned Shellshock.

Negmanite lands over the ground delivering a softer impact. The sound of a jar shatters from the crack of a whip.

"Oh no! Negmanite!"

The general retreats back as Auroa emerges from the shadow.

"Now, Alistor!"

The monster lies wholly covered in the syrup's sticky mess as Alistor delivers the final blow.

"Star Breaker!"

Negmanite's entire body begins breaking from the inside as sparks fly out. Shellshock starts to back away as the monster falls into the water, creating a massive explosion. Water rains over the scene.

"I'll get you next time!"

The general flies off into the horizon as the labyrinth fades away. Then, finally, a morning light begins to break in, with a rainbow appearing over Hazefall.

"Well, ya look at that." Bamboo smiled.

The camp looks over to admire the sight. Sometime later, the party was seen packing as the kids proceeded to bid their farewells.

"Well, it was a lot of fun," Niko admitted. "Hope you'll visit in the future."

Max Mathesius

"We'll never forget you." Miko smiled. "That dollhouse was fun!"

A distasteful look was seen on the director's face as the rest waved goodbye. Then, Bamboo takes off with the car into the horizon.

"And that was Hazefall," Alistor muttered.

"Too bad we couldn't stay longer." Maigashi shrugged.

"Yeah… Being let off is something." Auroa admitted. "I don't think we'll be back anytime soon. We're not what you call the ideal candidates in the director's eye."

The team starts to have a small laugh.

"See! Good bonding we have here." Bamboo noted. "If you guys keep up the hard work, I might take us someplace snowy next week."

The last sight of the Hazefall dam stands strong from a distance.

Chapter 5

Snow Business:

The Showdown at Snowpike Resort

Sometime early morning at the enemy fortress...

"Yawn, what is the meaning of this general?"

Commander Shellshock is eager to present his latest plan for the labyrinth. Fliers get passed across the room for Vilevelious to look over.

"What! A timeshare? For a ski resort?" The emperor questioned.

"The best plan yet! We will invest in this place, and I have a grand-scale attack ready for action."

Questions and some doubt through Vilevelious mind.

"I don't quite get this. How is a timeshare going to benefit the labyrinth?"

Shellshock presents a large picture for them. A large poster drops down from the window panel showcasing a new base. Everyone within the room steps back, astonished for a brief second. Large oversized weaponry with cannons to missiles all around. From heavy machinery, artillery, carriers, and gold-plated walls as well.

"This resort will be the grounds for a new base. I took the liberty of designing this all night myself. As you can see, it's Hip! New! And Cool!"

The emperor took a moment to fathom what he had just heard.

"New...Hip... Cool? I don't like the sound of this so far, general." He nodded.

Max Mathesius

"This may sound crazy, but I've been scouting Mathias for quite some time." Shellshock further explained.

The general then turns on the viewing screen, projecting a live coverage of the resort. Plenty of young people are seen enjoying themselves. Events from snowboarding to snowball fights happen as kids are seen running around and making snowmen. Some couples ice skate while some cuddle by a fire with hot chocolate.

"As you can see, ever since we arrived, many have fled their daily lives to escape the stress of monster attacks. All the young kids have been going to this place, and we need a change of scenery. A fresh new batch for our labyrinth."

The emperor continued to ponder whether to approve or not.

"I don't know. This sounds rather expensive. Do we really need a new base? This sounds rather unnecessary."

"That's not all! Now turn to the next page."

He turns to the next page, revealing an ad for a Ski Competition. "The Grand Ski off 79. Starring four-year winner Brenda Turnpike."

"Never even heard of her."

"From further research, she's some star many dumb teens are charmed over. So many guests are expected to attend and watch her perform in a matter of days."

"And you have a monster planned for this, general?"

"That will be taken care of later. Instead, I have this in mind. Whoopers, come forth!"

Commander Shellshock calls the Whoopers to the stand. The enemy soldiers enter the room, all dressed in gear.

"Such ridiculous attire. What is the meaning of this general?"

"I took the liberty to enter our soldiers into this race, taking half the roster. Phase one will begin by sabotaging the competition."

"And phase two?" Vilevelious asked.

"Rest assured. I'll have a monster ready to gather energy. But, then, if all else fails, my fleet will blow everything sky high."

The emperor gives his approval to the plan.

"I might regret this…but very well, commence with the invasion."

Viper's Labyrinth

"Onwards! To Snowpike!"

Meanwhile, back with Bamboo and the rest…

"We're closing for the day, and I have a special treat for you all."

"What is it?" Alistor asked.

Bamboo presents their tickets to the Snowpike Resort. Auroa and Maigashi rushed over to check it out.

"Hotel and reservation all prepaid. Sweet!" Maigashi jumped.

"My, how very generous of you. May I ask what the occasion is?" Auroa wondered.

Alistor lost interest quickly.

"Since you've all worked hard for the past few weeks, I thought we take a nice mountain trip."

"Count me out." Alistor nodded. "I don't have time for fun and games. I need to continue training."

He immediately takes his leave as the door shuts. A disappointed look was on Bamboo, nodding in disbelief.

"Not to worry." Auroa assured, "We'll convince him one way or another."

A moment later, the two came barging into Alistor's room.

"Hey! We're packing up, so you better not bail on us." Maigashi said.

"What? No! I'm not going." He refused.

"Come on, Alistor, this may be a perfect opportunity for us to bond. The resort has quite a few wonders to look forward to." Auroa promised.

He turned away from the two.

"No! I'm not going, and that's final. I must stay to continue training to get stronger. And you can't change my mind."

Maigashi immediately became irritated.

"Well, too bad. You're going whether you like it or not."

The two immediately grab him by force as he attempts to struggle.

"Hey! What are you doing? Let me go!"

The two begin dragging him out. Alistor attempts to pull out his blade to attack but gets knocked out cold by Bamboo with a frying pan at the door. They load him into Bamboo's food truck as they take off to the resort.

"Away we go!" Bamboo jumped.

They were on the road with Bamboo driving in a matter of time. Alistor soon regains consciousness in the middle as he felt a snowflake touch his face.

"Ah, you're finally awake." Auroa smiled. "You've been out for quite some time."

"How long?" Alistor grunted.

"About three hours," Maigashi answered.

"Ugh...I hate you guys."

"Don't feel discouraged. This trip will be good for you." Bamboo assured. "Let all your worries fade away. I'm even going to promote my Grass Jelly down there anyway."

"What else is new...." Alistor sarcastically mumbled.

Bamboo then passes a flier over to him.

"Who's this Brenda Turnpike?"

"Yeah, I hear this Brenda girl is expected to be there," Bamboo noted. "An annual Ski competition will go down in a couple days. Just imagine! If she likes my Grass Jelly, my restaurant will be an instant hit."

Alistor then shrugs, losing all hope as they arrive at their destination in a matter of time. Bamboo parks on the side of the driveway as the food truck gets set up. Bamboo then hands over the room key to Maigashi.

"Well, you guys go ahead and check in. I'm gonna sell some food for a while."

The rest quickly unloads the luggage, checking into the inn. After a few floors and stairways up, they arrive at the door. Maigashi inserts the key as the door clicks open. In a matter of seconds, the three were astonished for a brief moment. An entire suite was in front of their eyes.

"My goodness....how can we afford this?" Alistor dropped.

Viper's Labyrinth

"Who cares?" Maigashi said. "I can see the snow gears right over there."

He quickly went to the changing room as Auroa helped himself into the kitchen. Alistor was the last to enter.

"Free coffee and tea. Lovely!"

Alistor turns the TV on at the end of the room. Some live coverage from the resort is shown on screen. A lady is seen interviewing shady figures at the top of the mountains.

"And there you have it, folks! Some tense competition to expect this year for the annual ski-off. So what are your secrets?"

The geared-up enemy Whoopers are seen headbanging, mumbling back nonsense.

"Such competitive spirit! And oh, who do we have here?"

A poorly disguised Commander Shellshock enters the interview. A sizeable oversized scarf only covers a part of his face; Alistor hesitated for a brief second.

"No, it couldn't be." He thought.

The interview continues on the TV.

"The very sponsor of this great team, of course. As you can see, we trained all year round. So they are more than ready for this."

Some recap footage of the disguised enemy soldiers pulling off some tricks from extreme jumps to backflips.

"Ah, such a breathtaking view." The lady recalled. "And you're one of our judges this year, correct?"

He grabs the mic out of her hand.

"Yeah! And nothing is gonna stop us from winning."

She grabs the mic back from Shellshock.

"I wouldn't be too sure yet. Let's not forget our dear Brenda will be here in a few days. Well, that's all the time we have today, folks. Best of luck to everyone!"

Alistor then turns the TV off as it goes to a commercial break. Maigashi comes out all geared up and ready.

"Well, let's head out. I'm gonna shred those slopes." He announced.

Max Mathesius

"A grand idea. I think I'll try some ice skating." Auroa nodded.

And so the party heads outside. The group immediately breaks off as Maigashi runs to the gondola lifts. Everyone across the resort is seen enjoying themselves, except for Alistor, who leans awkwardly in the corner. Auroa soon caught up to him.

"Why the long face?" Auroa asked.

He was seen shriveled up, freezing.

"I don't know…." He nodded.

"Come on, you can tell me. If you stay in the same spot all day, you'll catch some painful frostbite."

Alistor begins speaking.

"Ok! It's just… it's just this was not what I expected."

"What do you mean?" Auroa wondered.

He begins to elaborate.

"My master completely ditched me. He only taught me one move, believing I was in good hands, but I didn't stand a close chance against the latest general. You guys were unsupportive, and Bamboo hasn't taught me anything."

"Don't take everything for granted." Auroa nodded.

A breeze of wind quickly passed by.

"But I need to get stronger. This Ski trip won't teach me anything. I need more power to stand a chance." He objected.

"Sometimes, power isn't the key to every solution. Maybe that was what your master believes." Auroa brought up.

"What do you mean?"

Auroa then made him turn around to face the horizon of the resort.

"Why did you think Bamboo brought us here?" He asked.

"I don't know. Just to profit for his own gain, what else."

"Wrong!" Auroa nodded.

Viper's Labyrinth

"Then what is it then? Tell me!" Alistor demanded.

"Retake a look. What do you see all around you? It's cold, right?"

"Isn't that pretty obvious? Tell me something I don't know."

"Think of it this way. You've only fought in a limited type of terrain thus far. To attain new levels, you need to work on sharpening your awareness."

Alistor became lost for a brief moment.

"Awareness? What do you mean?"

"Learn to adapt to different grounds in case of an attack wherever you are. The enemy likely has monsters suited for their every need, so diversifying yourself to a different environment is the next step."

He was speechless for a moment.

"I never thought of it this way. So maybe you're right after all."

Alistor then pulls out his blade for no reason.

"I'm gonna follow your words. Train like crazy and endure this cold." The ice immediately catches his eye. "And I'm going to start on that ice."

He makes a dash to the ice pond throwing Auroa off.

"Wait! You need skates first."

In a matter of time, Alistor was seen walking over the ice as Auroa watched. He then makes his way to the zone with a warning sign.

"No, wait! Don't go…."

Alistor then falls instantly for going over thin ice. Yelling for help as Auroa had to call a rescue team over. The day ends as the party is seen resting at the hotel. Alistor is seen covered in layers of blankets while the rest roast marshmallows.

"So, a good day for you all?" Bamboo asked.

"Hell yeah!" Maigashi gave a thumbs up. "I completely dominated those slopes. I even got an invite to enter the ski-off."

He shows off his ticket to the others.

Max Mathesius

"Well, congrats!" Auroa applauded.

"One day till the main event, and Brenda!" Bamboo clapped. "She'll be one tough cookie to break, so do you have any plans?"

"Don't know." Maigashi thought. "Not yet, to be honest."

"Hey! Maybe you all can train with him up those slopes tomorrow. So get ready the day before the competition." Bamboo announced.

"A splendid idea." Auroa agreed.

Everyone except Alistor cheered at the fire. The following day, the party geared up as they headed to the gondola lifts.

"I don't know if I want to do this," Alistor whined.

"Don't be a baby. You only fell due to your lack of awareness. Now come on!" Maigashi argued.

He was hesitant to enter, but the two pushed him in. The lift takes motion, bringing them up in a matter of minutes. They take a look at the breathtaking view of the vast mountains. Exiting out as they encountered a strange crowd by the corner. Commander Shellshock passed by them.

"Those guys are so hyped up."

The three took a look at the disguised Whoopers mumbling nonsense.

"From what I hear, those guys are foreigners," Maigashi informed. "Heard they're pretty good."

"Yeah, I saw it on the news."

As the three head off to start, Shellshock takes a glance back. He breaks away from the Whoopers, who continue nothing productive. The commander then removes his oversized scarf.

"They're actually here? This isn't good; I must proceed to the next phase."

The commander takes to the air, quietly leaving without anyone noticing. He makes his way down behind the inn. A bunch of kids is seen completing a snowman.

"Your snowman needs appropriation."

Viper's Labyrinth

The kids quickly fled the scene screaming as chains burst out from his chest. The chains softly make their way to the Snowman possessing it. The Snowman's face ultimately falls off as lips form around its body. It makes an artificial sound.

"Frost Lips! I have a job for you in tomorrow's race."

The scene returns to Alistor and the party racing down the steep hills. Auroa and Maigashi enjoy themselves as Alistor struggles to keep up. Finally, after a few quick jumps and tricks, the three returned in one piece. Alistor could barely catch his breath as the two dragged him back up for more.

"But I don't want to do it again."

"Come on!" Auroa pulled.

A few hours later, the party chows down back by Bamboo's food truck. A line of customers is seen waiting. The day soon comes to an end as night falls. The party is seen warming up by a hot tub. Maigashi takes one last look at the roster before tomorrow's race.

"A total of twenty-one competing."

Bamboo is seen daydreaming about Brenda on the other end.

The following day, Bamboo and the party are seen below with the audience. Maigashi is seen with the other contestants, ready and geared up. A limo approaches the scene, and the audience loudly cheers. The door opens, revealing Brenda Turnpike making her way to the stage.

"Oh, Brenda!" Bamboo waved.

She gives a kiss in the air to the crowd. The party immediately gets overwhelmed by the excited crowd.

"Are you people serious?" Alistor grumbled.

"Guess they all love her." Auroa shrugged.

She makes her way to the lifts as the audience cheers on. Brenda takes her place with the contestants above as Maigashi takes one last glance at the competition. Ten Whoopers are seen hyped and ready while the other contestants remain focused.

"Best of luck to you all." She kissed.

The bell immediately sets off as the contestants begin dashing off downhill. Maigashi rips hard through the snow for a head start. A few Whoopers are seen performing backflips behind as Brenda keeps calm. The other contestants are seen getting distracted by the remaining Whoopers.

"Not bad, but no one can beat me when it comes to these icy slopes."

"What...?"

Maigashi was suddenly caught off guard briefly as Brenda approached behind. Within seconds she easily glides her way past him.

"Oh no, you don't!"

Pressing his shins against the boots, he applied further pressure to pick up some speed. Two Whoopers, meanwhile, trip over an unfortunate contestant off-course. Then, the contestant skids out of control as he plows into three others below.

"Not far into the start, four of our twenty-one are down and out." The judge states as the crowd cheers below. "Our dear Brenda still got it."

Shellshock is seen among the judges behind the tables. Then, under his scarf, he quietly calls to signal the Whoopers above.

"As you order, general."

A Whooper is seen giving a signal to another colleague as they both closely approach Maigashi and Brenda from behind. One of them raises their sticks.

"What are these guys up to?" Maigashi suspiciously watched as Brenda kept her cool.

Without hesitation, the two Whoopers begin striking at them. Swinging their ski poles around as they were caught by surprise.

"Hey! That's against the rules." Brenda yelled.

The Whoopers continued the assault as Maigashi dodged their oncoming swings while keeping the balance.

"I've had it."

In a matter of seconds, their poles clasped together with the enemy. Using the sticks to counter back, Maigashi quickly pushed the two Whoopers off as they stumbled downhill. Brenda kept her focus as she continued the lead. A third Whooper suddenly jumps in from above to strike Brenda, but she quickly ducks. The third Whooper suddenly lost control in the air as it slammed into an oncoming tree.

"Man, she's good," Maigashi muttered.

Back from the audience below...

"Fourteen contestants remain, and Brenda is still growing strong." The judge announced. "YOU GO, GIRL!!!"

Shellshock makes another call from behind.

"Ready the second line." The general whispered.

The Whoopers above signal the fleet below. A vast hidden bunker emerges from the mountain. Positioned in place as one Whooper makes the call.

"Air fleet ready to fire. Commencing!"

Within moments missiles began shooting from below. Massive explosive fire commenced as sheets of snow began falling above. Three more contestants lose the will to continue as they panic from the pressure of an avalanche.

"This isn't good."

Four Whoopers surround the two as they begin locking the targets. Maigashi quickly anticipated their move and didn't hesitate to channel some lighting to stun the soldiers. A missile fires away as Maigashi and Brenda jump out of the blast range. The four Whoopers are blown out of commission.

"Now, only seven remain in this race. So we're getting close to the final stretch." The judge further updated. "Brenda fights on!"

The crowd below continues to cheer as Alistor does his best to cover his ears from the screaming crowd. Auroa remained calm while Bamboo continued to go with the flow. Finally, Shellshock begins to lose patience with his team.

"What's taking them so long? They're getting too close?"

Back above...

"Oh, give me a break." Maigashi objected. "Is Brenda the only one they care about? I'm still hanging on here. Hello?"

The avalanche comes to a stop as the contestants reach the final stretch of the race. Then, finally, the last three Whoopers begin planning something.

"Too close for missiles. Switch to the guns."

The bunker below shifts as the fleet replaces all the missiles with firepower. A Whooper gives off a smug look, but the grounds shake.

Max Mathesius

"What was that?" A Whooper confusedly asked.

In a matter of seconds, the entire course begins shifting. Walls and pillars of ice begin bursting right out in front of them. The remaining three Whoopers crash into the ice as the other two contestants lose their ground from the sudden shift. Maigashi and Brenda maneuver their way through the oncoming obstacles.

"Is this supposed to be a new twist?" Brenda wondered.

"No! I don't think this is even part of the race." Maigashi stuttered.

A massive explosion is then heard from behind. An avalanche is seen covering the entire bunker below. The audience below continues to cheer for Brenda.

"My goodness! We're getting close, folks! The final two left are just a mile from the finish line."

Commander Shellshock is seen crushing his radio. Banging on the table as the crowd remains too focused to notice.

"My entire fleet! Those Whoopers!"

Vilevelious suddenly contacts the general from the other side. Shellshock answers.

"Well, I'm tired of waiting? Where is the energy?"

"It's coming! Bring forth the labyrinth."

Brenda continues to give her all as the speed picks up downhill. Determined and focused on winning.

"I feel the need…The need for some speed." She muttered.

Then suddenly, the two stopped as the sky grew dark. A wall of ice caged Brenda and Maigashi from all sides. The audience below is lost, gazing at the sight of the labyrinth appearing before their eyes. The maze overshadows the entire resort within moments as Alistor and the party break from the crowd.

"We must find them right away," Alistor suggested.

"Oh dear, Brenda is in danger." Bamboo worried.

The party quickly heads off to find them both as Shellshock removes the scarf from his neck. The crowd began to panic as the commander took flight.

"Frost Lips! You're up!"

Viper's Labyrinth

Meanwhile, the two remain trapped within the layers of ice.

"Where are we?" Brenda asked.

"Trapped, no doubt," Maigashi said. "I could get us out, but it will take a while to channel enough force through these walls."

"Then get to it!" She yelled. "I don't want to spend the rest of my trip alone in this cold."

"And what's that supposed to mean?" He sarcastically pestered.

"Ok! Ok! I didn't mean it in that sort of way." She elaborated. "Just get us out!"

A sudden quake was felt as Maigashi was ready to get to work. She jumps back, holding his arm as it emerges from the snow.

"Is that a snowman?" She questioned.

The figure turns around, revealing a blank face. Lips begin to form across its body as it makes a screeching sound.

"I don't think it looks friendly."

She kept her grip tight on Maigashi as the monster moved towards them. Its mouths all open up, releasing a cold chilling breeze. The lips suddenly burst out to attack as Maigashi pulled her away from the danger. He cuts them down with an electrical dagger.

"Stay close."

More lips begin to form across the monster. The monster starts spraying an icy breath as lips continue to assault them. Chunks of ice plow into them as the monster suddenly make a jump.

"Brenda!"

He pushed her out of harm's way before the monster landed. Maigashi gets sent flying a few feet back from the impact.

"That's it!"

He quickly channeled lightning from his body. Maigashi then makes an attempt to impale the monster at close range. Frost Lips easily avoided his attack as the lips shielded it from harm. His arm became encased in solid ice.

"What?"

"Hahaha! Are you having fun with my latest monster?"

Max Mathesius

Commander Shellshock arrives at the scene. Maigashi takes a few steps back as Brenda tries to break the ice off.

"So…it was you all this long."

"Yeah! I'm running the show here. And once I take all the energy, this resort will be the grounds for my new base."

The two are displeased with what he said.

"You scoundrel!" Brenda cried.

Maigashi shatters the ice from his arm without hesitation as he readies his weapon at the general. Chains suddenly wrapped around his waist.

"What the hell?"

"I see you want to play? Have at it!"

Commander Shellshock begins twirling him around the air. Finally, slamming him into the walls as Brenda took cover. He then released Maigashi from his grasp to shift his attention toward her.

"And as for you. Frost Lips, take care of her."

The monster begins approaching as she lies helplessly on the icy floor.

"Oh, Noooooo!"

In a matter of seconds, the party came crashing in. Auroa shatters the wall with the flick of his wind whip.

"The party's here. Splendid!" The general jumped. "Now, we can destroy you all."

Frost Lip ignores their sudden appearance as it reaches for Brenda. Opening its cold frosty lips as she continued to cry.

"I'll protect you!"

Bamboo intercepts the monster as it releases an icy breath. Then, shielding Brenda from harm, he suddenly became frozen as Shellshock laughed away.

"HAHA! So much for your friend. My monster will put you on ice."

Shellshock begins getting away. Maigashi suddenly regains consciousness as Brenda takes cover behind Bamboo's frozen body. Alistor and Auroa huddled up by Maigashi to start quickly planning.

Viper's Labyrinth

"We'll handle the monster from here." Auroa agreed. "Take care of the general."

"No problem!" Maigashi said. "I have a score to settle anyway."

He heads off on the general's trail without hesitation while Alistor and Auroa face off against Frost Lips. The monster speechlessly stares at them.

"Are you sure he'll be fine?" Alistor questioned.

"He'll be fine. He can handle himself." Auroa assured. "All that matters now is the opponent in front of us."

Meanwhile, Maigashi quickly caught up to the general.

"Let's see how you handle this."

Maigashi fires a round of electrical arrows at the general. The lightning gets completely nullified upon impact.

"What? But how?"

"Is that your best?" The commander pestered. "My defense greatly surpasses any of the monsters you've faced."

"Then I'll just have to try something else."

Maigashi got back up, rushing to the commander as lightning began to channel across his arm. Taking Shellshock by surprise as he got close.

"If this does not work! Surging Thunder!"

His attack impacts the general at point-blank range. A burst of smoke commences as he jumps back to witness the fireworks, but Shellshock emerges completely unharmed.

"No way!"

Maigashi gets rammed by Shellshock's back shell. Then, he gets slammed through an icy wall as the commander taunts him again.

"Ha! Give it up! Your power alone is not enough. I can't take damage thanks to my natural tank armor, high caliber skin armor, and hip chest armor."

"How much freaking armor do you even need?" Maigashi irritably asked.

"Enough!" The commander assured." Now let's see you dodge my Comet Shots."

Max Mathesius

The general begins firing shots down below. Lasers rain across the snow as Maigashi is forced to duck and roll.

"This is not good...."

Meanwhile, back at the other battle...

"No, Alistor!"

Alistor makes the first strike at Frost Lips with his blade. Impaling through its soft snowy body as he stood fazed for a moment.

"Huh?"

One of the monster's lips made a smile. The snow from the monster's body attempts to pull Alistor in. Alistor struggles to pull his sword out. Auroa quickly shot a blast of wind from the crack of his whip in the nick of time. Alistor stumbled back rapidly. Frost Lip's head began to spin as copies of itself surrounded them. Vanishing and constantly reappearing as it obscured Alistor's mind.

"What is this thing?"

"It seems we're dealing with an Ice Apparition," Auroa informed as he kept calm and focused.

"An Ice Apparition?" Alistor nervously repeated.

"Yes, remember our talk about awareness and perception? But, unfortunately, power alone won't be enough to stop this monster."

Brenda still remained behind the frozen body of Bamboo, watching.

"Then how will we beat this?" He asked.

"We'll have to use our wits. It's attempting to confuse us, but remember, only one is the real target."

The monster began firing its lips once more. Ice-cold lips scatter through the air as Auroa shatters the oncoming ones with his whip. Then, the lips began targeting a bunch of bystanders outside. Kissing the victims as one by one became encased in solid ice for the labyrinth. A horrifying sight for Alistor to witness.

"They're frozen?" He gulped.

The crowd continues to panic as energy leaves in the air. The labyrinth above continues to overshadow the entire resort.

Viper's Labyrinth

"We can't let those lips touch us. So stay by my side Alistor."

Shifting back to the battle with Maigashi and Shellshock. The commander continues to fire his lasers at him. Raining down continuously as he was forced to take cover behind a wall of ice.

"Come on! This is getting old." Maigashi shouted.

The commander stops his firing for a split second. General Shellshock then takes a dive down as he breaks through the ice Maigashi hid behind.

"You were saying?"

"Me and my big mouth. Ugh!"

Maigashi takes a few steps back, regaining his ground as the commander flies back into the air. Then, aiming his bow, Maigashi fires two rounds of lightning arrows at the general again.

"Ha! Didn't you learn from before?" Shellshock laughed. "Your attacks can't penetrate my armor. You don't have enough power."

Maigashi remained quiet as the general attempted to fire his energy shots again.

"Huh? What! My Comet Shots!"

The general's weapons were damaged.

"I was never aiming for you." Maigashi snickered. "I knew I didn't have the power to break through you, but your weapons are another story. With all that heavy gear, you're a flying tank in midair."

"Curses!"

"And what goes up must come down."

The general removed a thick layer of armor, disposing of his guns. Then, armed with a twin claw and double-edged arm blades, he dashes at Maigashi.

"I'm not through yet!" Shellshock said.

Maigashi jumps back to gain some distance, but the commander takes him by surprise. His body gets wrapped by his chest chains.

"My reach and grappling ability have improved; as you can see, I still have a few tricks to show."

Max Mathesius

The general begins tossing him back and forth across the mounds of snow. Twirling him like a yo-yo before he had to use his dagger to break free. Maigashi suddenly barfs at a corner as he takes a moment to catch his breath.

"Cough! I think I'm going to be sick if this keeps up."

The general continues on the offense as Maigashi uses his dagger to clash. Thus, the two begin the battle in close combat.

Returning back to the battle with Frostlips...

"Auroa, Come on! We're sitting ducks." Alistor complained.

Auroa continued to shatter the oncoming lips as the two kept close.

"Patience! You must keep your eye on the real enemy at hand."

One of the copies begins to make the first slight move, and Auroa quickly notices it. Without hesitation, he used his whip at full force, striking the monster. The monster gets sent back, exploding as the fake copies disperse.

"How did you know?" Alistor wondered.

"Persistence and enough patience," Auroa replied. "Don't celebrate yet; our battle isn't over."

Frost Lips quickly reforms as the grounds begin to shift. Pillars of ice form, bursting out as ice-cold stalagmites scatter. The two promptly dispersed, avoiding the sharp ice.

The monster begins opening all its mouths as a blizzard quickly brews. Focusing all attention on Alistor as the cold air and snow mixed. He was barely able to hold his ground.

"What do we do? I can't hold on much longer." Alistor shouted.

"It's no good. The monster has the home-field advantage. If only we had a source of heat somewhere."

"Well, can't you cast any fire?" He sarcastically asked.

Auroa stumbled for one brief moment.

"If I did, I would have done that long ago." He slapped. "I can't channel fire, but we must find one for your sake. But where..."

Auroa thinks intensely as the monster continues to harass Alistor. Icicles begin to rain down, poking at him.

Viper's Labyrinth

"Auroa? Come on! Hurry up already!"

The monster then unleashed a giant snowball forcing him to make a run.

"Of course!" Auroa snapped.

Auroa turns around and quickly shatters the oncoming snowball with one flick of his whip.

"So you got something?" Alistor asked.

"There is a fire pit back at the inn. Outside, in fact. Where all the couples sit and enjoy their hot chocolate."

"But that's a mile away."

"It's all we got. Come on! Let's move!"

The two begin leaving for the inn as the monster gives chase. More bystanders are seen caught in Frost Lips' path. Frozen and encased in ice as the labyrinth feeds.

"Such horror…"

Back with Maigashi, his clash comes close as he disarms the general, breaking his twin claws. Shellshock takes a hard hit to the chest.

"Gah! Lucky shot." The general grumbled.

An electrical surge cracks through the general's chest.

"It seems I found your weak spot." Maigashi pointed. "With that armor gone, you're pretty much through."

"Don't count me out yet."

Shellshock takes to the air again, but Maigashi fires arrows piercing the general's body. Smoke and sparks commenced in the air.

"Heh...and you were saying?" Maigashi mocked.

The general was shrouded within layers of ice and rocks.

"Wait a minute. What?"

Max Mathesius

Shellshock emerged unharmed.

"My optical sensors attract matter and can condense into a shield." The general informed. "Not only does this excel my defense, but I can use it offensively. Have at it!"

Ice and rocks begin dispersing down at Maigashi. He takes further damage as he's forced on the defensive once again. Taking cover behind a wall of ice.

"Ha, haha! Nothing you can do to stop me now."

The general takes a dive down once more.

"Not this again." Maigashi jumped.

He emerged right out of cover to fire a shot at the general. Shellshock's sensors quickly reacted, drawing in whatever matter was around. Maigashi then jumps out, getting himself pulled close to the general. Then, channeling the power around his body, he readies his final attack.

"Wait, what?" Shellshock stumbled.

Maigashi got close, sending a charged punch in the general's face.

"Surging Thunder!"

The general gets sent crashing down on the ice, leaving a huge hole. Badly damaged, Shellshock emerged as Maigashi collapsed over.

"Come on!" Maigashi panted. "Let's call it a day. You got nothing left. We both played our best hands."

The general pounded in rage.

"A tie? No! But how? You had less power."

"Power was never a factor," Maigashi stated as he took his stand. "You had the advantage, but I simply used my wits. Nothing special, really. Just some common sense and perception to weather this storm."

"Perception? NO! I can't accept this." The general objected.

"Oh, come on! I'm tired." Maigashi wailed.

"Failure is not an option."

The general then takes one final look at the labyrinth above.

Viper's Labyrinth

"Vile, my lord....I did my best. That new base would have been nice, but I can still go with a bang."

Shellshock got right back up, taking charge.

"Huh? What are you up to now?"

"What I should have done first."

The general catches him off once again with his chest chains. Maigashi easily dodges the first chain as it backfires on Shellshock, but the second chain suddenly wraps across his waist. Commander Shellshock begins taking flight.

"We're taking this fight in the air."

The two deploy high up in the air.

Meanwhile, returning back to the scene with Alistor and Auroa. The two made their way to the inn's entrance. Couples are dispersed from the chaos as Frost Lips continues to freeze countless victims. Alistor made his way to the fire as Auroa stalled the monster.

"Now!" Auroa signaled.

Alistor knocks over the pit as Auroa lures the monster to the flames. Casting a heavy gust of air, the fire quickly spreads while Frost Lips struggle. The two suddenly hear a sound jetting through the air.

"Hey! It's them." Alistor pointed.

They watch Maigashi and Shellshock zip through the air, battling. Frost Lips attempts to move out from the flames, but the two keep it at bay.

"If I go down, I'm taking you with me." Shellshock laughed.

The two struggle in the air as Maigashi attempts to break free. But then, he suddenly catches a glimpse of Alistor and the rest down below.

"I must think of something fast." Maigashi thought.

The Jet pack quickly catches his eye as he pulls himself up Shellshock's back.

"Hey? What are you doing? Get off!"

"It's now or never."

Max Mathesius

Without hesitation, Maigashi takes a stab at the commander's Jet pack. Short-circuiting as Shellshock slowly lost control. The two began descending quickly as he broke free from the chains.

"Now to the finish line."

He approached Alistor's position with the monster using the general's metal chain. General Shellshock attempts to shake him off, but in the end, he gets tangled in his chains.

"And this is my stop," Maigashi waved.

"Whoah, Noooooo!!!"

Maigashi jumps right off as Alistor and Auroa move out of the way. Commander Shellshock came crashing into the fire pit where Frost Lips was. A huge double explosion commenced outside.

From the flames, two objects caught their eye. The glint from the fragment of a mirror and a red gem glowing. Maigashi goes to retrieve them.

"What is this?" Maigashi asked.

The second mirror piece and a red gem were obtained.

"That's the second shard of the mirror," Alistor said.

"And this red gem would happen to be Shellshock's essence, correct?"

The labyrinth above the resort immediately vanished as Frost Lips' power over the frozen victims wore off.

"And that's a wrap." Auroa sighed.

Bamboo was warming off with the rest by the fire a while later. Brenda was by his side, flattered as he bragged about his restaurant. But then, a disappointing feeling was in store for everyone as the committee made a sudden announcement.

"Due to certain circumstances. There will be no declared winner of this year's race. We hope you all had a good time, so enjoy the rest of your stay."

"What? You mean that didn't count." Maigashi objected. "I totally crossed that finish line."

"Yeah, on that general, of course." Alistor pestered. "You completely ditched your gear during that fight. You could have won if you still had it on?"

"Don't get smart with me."

Viper's Labyrinth

Maigashi got him pinned down to a chokehold.

"Yow! Let me go!"

"That general would have had your head already if it wasn't for me."

"Well, there's always next year." Auroa giggled.

The two stopped fighting.

"Sigh...I think one week is enough for this Snow Business." Maigashi nods. "I'm retired for good. So I'll just take this complimentary box of hot chocolate and call it a trip."

The scene ends with the party gazing into the bright moonlight.

Max Mathesius

Chapter 6

The Struggling Musician

"Scrap-Ram! Is your plan ready?" Vile asked.

From a viewing screen, the general's face materializes from a pile of garbage in a far corner. Lurking in the shadows, he spots a lone man approaching down an empty road.

"The target is ready as planned. This man is what we need."

Scrap-Ram eyes on a lone man carrying a guitar on his back. His hair covers nearly his eyes while the wind breezes by. He makes his way toward Emerald village.

"Who is this man supposed to be?"

"I've been watching this one for quite some time. This musician will provide the energy we need to nourish our labyrinth. My mark is already planted."

A faint glint appears from the side of the man's guitar.

"He will be the eyes and ears we need, haha."

A moment later, the man stumbles upon Bamboo's restaurant.

The door slides open.

"Oh, we have a new customer." Bamboo jumped.

The man drops to the floor the moment he steps inside.

Viper's Labyrinth

"Oh, my god? Are you okay?"

He goes to check his pulse. The man barely mumbled as he tried to explain what he was saying.

"So hu...ngry!"

"Someone help this man to a table. I'll fix something nice up."

Auroa and Maigashi go to help the man to a table. A moment later, he was digging down on Bamboo's cooking. Plate after plate while the others watch.

"Dude, you guys are a lifesaver."

"So, who are you again?" Alistor asked.

The man continues to chow down on the food.

"The names Axe. Axe Winston, I'm a musician."

"So what brings you to this boring place? What's your story?" Maigashi wondered.

He finished his plate before answering.

"I used to be an Ace Guitarist. A rising star on tour way before these monster attacks started happening. But my skills began to falter somehow after my last few sessions. My band kicked me out, I lost my pad, I dropped out of school, and my girlfriend even left. She took my car, and I lost everything, man."

"Your girlfriend? Who was she?"

"I wish to not talk about it...."

He grabs the next plate on the table.

"No, wait! You might not want to try that."

He reaches for the special dessert. Bamboo's plate of grass jelly. The others attempted to stop him, but it was too late. He quickly chomps it down in less than a few seconds. They stood speechless for a moment expecting the worse.

"Dude! This stuff is Bodacious."

A tiny teardrop ran down Bamboo's eye.

"Whoah! You seriously can handle that stuff?" Alistor was astounded with disbelief.

"Well, I'll eat anything," Axe replied. "Your cooking is excellent!"

The bill suddenly rang up.

"So, how is he gonna pay?"

Bamboo quickly figures out a solution.

"Not to worry! Any person who is a fan of my cooking is our friend. Especially for my grass jelly."

He hands a work uniform to Axe.

"What's this?"

"You have nowhere to go, right?"

Axe nods his head.

"Since you're a musician, my restaurant could use lovely music. You can even help in the kitchen, and you're welcome to stay as long as you want.

He suddenly reaches out to hug Bamboo.

"No way! Are you serious? Dude! Of course, I'll stay."

"Then it's settled. You can start tomorrow morning."

The very next morning, Axe plays, but the sound of his guitar sends a migraine through everyone else. Customers are seen covering their ears and leaving. Alistor falls over, breaking some plates. Bamboo came out from the kitchen.

"What are you playing? You're scaring all the customers away." Bamboo wailed.

He stops playing for the moment.

"When you said your skills faltered, I didn't realize you were this bad." Auroa honestly admitted.

"Was this the only guitar you ever used?"

They took a moment to examine his guitar. Old and slightly rusted with a few loose ends.

"This guitar holds a special place in me. Long story short, this was passed down to me."

Viper's Labyrinth

"So you have a family."

"Not anymore; they passed away before their time even came. Since then, I have never stopped playing this guitar. I take it everywhere with me."

"Well, for now, you can help clean up in the kitchen," Bamboo suggested.

The party continued their shift. Axe helps Bamboo in the back kitchen, cleaning the dishes.

A while later …

Bamboo presents them with their next job as Alistor, and the party looks over the paper.

"Hey, that's the old-school theatre. What's left of it, I suppose?"

"Don't tell me this is another cleanup job?" Maigashi showed distaste.

"Since Axe can't play this guitar, maybe finding a new one might work. You four will salvage what you can at this place."

"You think finding a new one will work?" Axe asked.

Bamboo grabs the old guitar right from his hands.

"I'll hold on to this for the time being. Any instrument you can salvage will reel us in some nice cash. So move out."

And so the four of them moved on out. Alistor and his friends head to the old-school theatre. Entering through the back door of what remains of the building. Through a dark hallway, Auroa reached out to find the lights. They entered the room, and the lights came on with the flick of a switch.

"Whoa, this place is totally trashed. Dudes, are you sure we can find something new? This looks like the aftermath of a wild concert."

"We can assure you it's not. So now let's just get this over with."

Behind the curtains, Scrap Ram lurks in the shadows. Vilevelious contacts from the other screen.

"What is happening, general? Why can't I see anything on the screen? Where in blazes is that guitar you planted?" Vile demanded.

Max Mathesius

"Look like we'll have to try something else for now. So a different monster will do for now."

Alistor and the party continued to salvage anything they could find from the back of the theatre. Scouring through the piles of broken instruments.

"A few broken harps, a piano, some violins. No guitars yet." Maigashi nods.

"Just my luck...when I thought things were turning up. I'll never find anything new to play at this rate."

Axe tossed a broken flute to the side. It rolls across the floor and into the corners as Scrap Ram grabs the object without notice. A monster begins forming in the back.

"Base Face! You will deal with them. Now go and gather some energy!"

Soon after, Axe finally stumbled upon an intact guitar. He begins to pull it out from the pile of junk.

"I finally found one. Dudes! Come help me out."

Auroa and Maigashi go to help.

"Man, this one is stuck in tight. Hey, Alistor, get over here."

With Alistor, they successfully pull it out. Axe Winston then held the guitar up in the air.

"Man, this one's a beauty."

The guitar suddenly shatters in his hands.

"What? Not cool, dude. Who did that?"

They turn around to find a monster before their eyes. Axe immediately jumps back from the sight of it.

"Ah! What is that thing?"

The monster gets close to him.

"Treat me like garbage, will ya. The names Base Face and my sound is gonna decimate your holes."

The monster begins to pick Axe up from the shoulders. Scared out of his mind, he was barely able to fight back.

Viper's Labyrinth

"What are you doing? Can't you fight back?" Auroa wondered.

"I'm a musician, not a fighter. This was not what I signed up for. Dudes! Help me out."

Auroa blasts a gust of air at the monster. Maigashi pulls Axe out of the way as Base Face tries to fire a screeching sound at them. Auroa's wind pushed the attack back at the monster as it lost ground. Then, he suddenly sensed something in the air.

"I feel another force at hand. Fall back!"

A pile of junk drops at the center as the four gain some distance. Then, finally, Scrap Ram materialized in front of them.

"Base Face! A change of plans. Stop wasting time and get some energy."

The monster begins to leave the scene as the four try to chase after it. However, a wall of junk blocks Alistor and his team's path.

"Just who are you? Are you the third demon general?" Alistor asked.

"You catch on very quick. Shellshock took you all so lightly; that was his biggest mistake."

"What kind of monster are you supposed to be?"

"I am composed of your everyday objects. From the trash, waste, and junk you humans take for granted. I am part of Aggerona's demolition division. The names Scrap Ram and I make monsters from your old trash."

They stare down face to face with the new foe at hand. Maigashi attempted to fire some shots at the wall, but it had little effect. The holes in the wall quickly repaired themselves.

"We can't let that monster escape outside. So what do we do?" Alistor asked.

"Just leave this one to me." Auroa insisted.

"Are you sure you'll be fine?"

Auroa blasts a big hole in the wall. His wind leaves an opening held from his power as Axe and Maigashi run off.

"Just go and take care of that monster. My wind will hold this one-off. You could use the training anyway."

As Alistor leaves, the hole closes. Auroa alone faces off with the general in the theatre.

Max Mathesius

"You think you'll be able to hold me off? You won't even last a minute."

"For some reason, this all feels familiar to me. Like I've already done this before."

"You're just delusional."

Auroa materializes a whip from his wind.

"Let's not waste any more time. My wind has been dying to break something all day."

And so, Auroa begins to clash with the general. Back outside, Base Face arrives at a park. The sound from the monster's flute drains the victims while Alistor and the others catch up to the monster's position.

"Stop right there! We have you surrounded." Alistor pointed.

"Ah! Just in time for my grand sonata. The sound of the century, and you'll have the honor of a front seat."

"I don't think so."

Alistor charged at the monster with his blade. Base Face effortlessly blasted him back with a wave of sound. He falls back flat on his face. Axe begins to cower behind Maigashi.

"Do you always mindlessly charge at the foe?" Maigashi asked.

"Well, we have to do something."

"No plan or strategy whatsoever. Just great; at this rate, you won't last long."

He continued to nag.

"If you know better? Show me! You always worked side by side with Auroa, so how would I know any strategy?"

"Have you ever used teamwork?" Maigashi asked.

"Teamwork?"

"Seriously? Have you never used teamwork? Do I have to explain the basics?"

Maigashi lets off a sigh.

"Uh, dude, I think you should totally explain." Axe suggested. "We could use some tips right about now."

"Sigh...fine. Just follow my lead."

"We're listening."

The monster begins to give chase as they follow his lead. Then, Maigashi begins to sarcastically explain the basics of teamwork.

"All levels of good teamwork rest on four foundational elements. The goal, roles, process, and relationship. High performance pays out for those who execute these successfully."

Base Face sends a wave of sound at them. The other two move out of harm's way as Maigashi blocks the brunt of the attacks, leaving smoke in the air.

"A goal is what we're trying to accomplish together."

The smoke clears away. Maigashi fires a couple shots from his arrows bringing the monster's attention toward him.

"The Role! Who does what, and how do we adapt? Who keeps the offense, plays defense, or even is the fool?"

Base Face continues to fire away as he makes a run for it.

"Process is how we roll and conduct things together."

Axe got behind, grabbing the monster by surprise. Base Face tries to shake him, but he keeps a tight grip in a piggyback position.

"Dude! This better work 'cause I don't feel comfortable doing this."

"And last but not least, communication. How we influence our skills... And get the job done!"

Maigashi turns around and throws a lightning dagger, piercing the monster's front. Axe loses his grasp on the demon as Alistor prepares for the finishing blow.

"Now finish him!"

Axe quickly stumbled, crawling away from the monster as Alistor got close. Base Face desperately fires another sound wave.

"Now jump!" Maigashi commanded.

Max Mathesius

He makes a leap in the air avoiding the attack. Then, making a quick dash, his blade slashed through Base Face, causing sparks to burst from the monster's body. The monster's body begins cracking up. Struggling to hold itself together, it grabs hold of him.

"What? Let go of me." Alistor struggled.

"My sonata! It is not done yet."

Base Face attempts to fire him from close blank range, but Axe suddenly intervenes, taking the shot behind. Base Face loses his hold on Alistor as Maigashi pulls them both back.

"Axe, are you okay?"

He is on the floor, barely able to budge.

"Dude…remind me to not do that ever again."

Relief was through both their eyes. They both got up to face the monster once more.

"We have to finish this monster right here and now. So what do we do?"

"A combination attack might just be enough," Maigashi suggested.

Base Face continues to taunt them as they both charge right in. The monster fires a sound wave in the middle, but they both break away to avoid the attack.

"Thunder!"

"Star Breaker!"

Lightning and energy impale Base Face from both sides.

"My sonata!"

Base Face shatters, reverting back to the original form it once was. Unfortunately, a broken flute was left on the ground pavement. They immediately go check back on Axe.

"Dude, is it finally over?"

He got right back up.

"Are you sure you'll be fine? Thanks for saving me, by the way."

Viper's Labyrinth

"Nah! No problem, I'll be okay. Just my back will be sore for the next few days."

The sound of a storm breezed by. Small debris of scraps drops on the park not far from the theatre.

"It's coming back from the theatre. Let's go check back up on Auroa."

From a distance, they witness the theatre tearing apart. The ceiling is completely ripped open as Auroa damages one of Scrap Ram's cores with his whip. The general begins to fall back as his pieces are swept away from the vortex.

"It seems Base Face has been totaled. You have quite a bit more power than I anticipated. For now, I take my leave."

Scrap Ram sinks beneath the ground, vanishing before his very eyes. Alistor and the party caught up with Auroa.

"He got away this time."

They took the time to check what was left of the building. Then, salvaging what Axe could, Maigashi loaded the instruments in Bamboo's car. Arriving back at the restaurant, Bamboo greets them with a nice meal.

"Is this really for us? Dude, thanks."

"A reward for a day of work."

They begin helping themselves with the food.

"Oh, and here's your guitar."

He hands the guitar back to Axe. All nice and brand new.

"Dude! You actually fixed it up. Awesome!"

"Well, I never knew you could fix things, Bamboo," Alistor commented.

Bamboo was flattered for a moment till Axe began to play once again. The sound of his guitar still hurts their ears.

"Huh? That's strange…it still sounds the same. I wonder why."

They continue to examine the guitar on the table. But, again, nothing was out of the ordinary to Axe.

Max Mathesius

"Well, beats me. I did what I could." Bamboo shrugged. "Tomorrow is a brand new day, so eat up and get a good night's sleep."

Meanwhile, back at the enemy lair, Vilevelious watched from the other screen as Alistor and the others enjoyed their feast. Then, finally, Scrap Ram is seen reporting back to the throne room.

"Today was not as expected. Axe's guitar is not ready and still requires time to collect enough energy to take form. But, once at its peak, our greatest monster will be ready."

"In the meantime, you better devise something else to feed the labyrinth. Now go! Don't come back till you have something new."

The general takes leave.

"Alistor…you foolish boy. You don't think I know. It's just a matter of time before the truth slips out."

The scene ends with the emperor focusing on Alistor through the viewing globe. He evilly laughs all alone in the room.

Chapter 7

Nursery Terror:

The Mystery behind the Weeping Cradle

Somewhere below the abandoned theatre, Scrap Ram lurks within darkness. He is contacted by the emperor from another screen.

"It's been almost an entire week. Have you got a plan yet? I'm tired of waiting."

"I took the time to set a base for operation. A good scheme requires an efficient amount of time and coordination. The guitar still rests on that man's shoulder as we speak."

"What! My patience is growing thin." Vile raged. "If you don't come up with something new, I'll have the next general take your place."

He continues to ramble on at the General from the other screen.

"I took the time to scope around. However, to quickly feed the labyrinth, we need to seek greater sources."

He presents the emperor with his next target on the screen, a small nursery not far from the city. A woman caretaker is seen bottle-feeding a child.

"Are you serious?"

"Hold the tongue for one moment. Such youthful energy is what we need. And the ones with the most are newborns clueless about their existence."

"I hate kids...Go on, explain further."

Scrap Ram laughs for a brief moment.

"Why yes! This nursery will be the next target. The babies' cry will be the key to our success."

"How so?"

"I have a monster that will amplify their cry. From an innocent newborn, no one will suspect a thing. The sound will be unbearable to the point that parents will suffer, producing the most negative energy we can imagine."

"Well, is the monster ready?" He cared to ask.

The monster was still under construction behind a large pile.

"When the time is right, the caretaker will fall. I have already infected her in advance. Once out of the picture, I'll obtain the last ingredient needed for my monster."

A while later, the caretaker is seen tucking a newborn in bed. She suddenly coughs; her vision becomes impaired as she goes outside. Finally, the woman collapses to the floor as someone calls for help.

Back at the restaurant, Bamboo hands Alistor's next mission. It was an urgent request, but it left a disappointed look on his face.

"How is this going to help with my training?" Alistor asked.

"Well....the caretaker is sick and unable to care for these children. No one else would take the job, so they need someone to watch them. We could use the extra money anyway."

"I'm no good with kids at all."

"Then it will be your first." Bamboo snapped. "Think of this experience as a head start if you decide to have kids one day. And remember, they are the future of our generation. So be a good role model."

Bamboo quickly forced them out. The four head off to their next objective. In a matter of moments, they arrive at the nursery. Entering inside was a room full of toddlers playing as a man went to greet them.

Viper's Labyrinth

"Finally, you guys arrived. So this was the best they could send? I couldn't stand a minute longer; phew. You guys are a lifesaver."

He hands the keys to Alistor and leaves.

"Hey, wait!"

Axe, Maigashi, and Auroa enter the room to watch over the kids. In a brief moment, the scene quickly got chaotic. Toddler's running amuck and making huge messes. Finally, Maigashi gets hit on the head with a toy.

"Hey! Get back here, you little runt."

They were soon drawing on the wall as Axe went to stop them. A few are seen pulling on Auroa's hair.

"This is going to be a long day…." He sighed.

Soon after, a baby was crying. Alistor covers his ears.

"Just great…What do I do now?"

"I think this one needs a change." Auroa pointed.

Alistor was then in the middle of changing a diaper. Unsure of what to do, the child stared at him. Then, it began kicking around as he removed the diaper.

"Hold still!"

The baby began to cry once more. He struggled to hold it in place, but it then pissed on his face.

"Argh! Somebody else, do this."

He turns to Auroa and Maigashi, but they are preoccupied. Axe suddenly steps in.

"That's not how you do it. Let me show you how it's done."

The baby immediately calms down once Axe takes over. Next, he places the child on a changing table.

"What you need first is a clean diaper. Wet wipes are next, but be careful and use mild ones. Newborns have sensitive skin."

He gently cleans the child while a new diaper is set in place.

Max Mathesius

"Next, some baby powder to prevent any rash. Then the optional lotion."

He finishes the change as the old diaper gets disposed of.

"There, good as new, dude."

The baby happily walks away to continue playing.

"I never knew you were good with kids." Auroa complimented.

"Ah, it's nothing. I used to babysit for my girlfriend back in the day. So if you need some tips and advice, I'll gladly help."

He gave a thumbs up to them.

"Hey, maybe I should play some music for them."

Axe suddenly reaches for his guitar but is stopped by the rest.

"Oh no, maybe that's not such a great idea. You can later play at the restaurant." Maigashi suggested.

A few hours later…the children were getting tucked into bed. Their shift ends as they hand the keys back to the other man. Axe Winston was rocking the last child to sleep as Auroa went to look for the remaining cradle with no success.

"I can't seem to find that last cradle." He sadly said.

The rest went to search but had no luck. Finally, Alistor stumbles upon an empty room with only a lone picture on the wall. The four go to take a closer look. The image contained a picture of a small child playing in this very room. A room that was once filled with stuffed bears and animals.

"Hey! There's a cradle in this picture. Why is this room empty?"

The man suddenly pops up from behind.

"Oh my, this isn't good. The cradle went missing. Could the lost child's soul have possibly departed?" The man muttered.

"What's special about this cradle? And what do you mean by the lost child?" Alistor asked.

"I guess you never heard the tale?" The man replied back.

"Then tell us."

He cleared his throat for a moment. The last child was still asleep, held in Axe's arms as he began to share a story.

"Let's see…where to begin. This was more than a decade back."

The room turns dark.

"Alright, okay, here goes..."

The Lone Cradle

Some say it contains the very essence of a child. The child's name was Anabel. Her parents were once wealthy in the world of business. They were always busy, so she was left in the nursery care daily.

She was a sweet girl, always smiling, and loved to play with her teddy bear. But, shy for some time, and it took her a while to adjust.

It wasn't till Rin came into her life. Our newest caretaker at the time was good with children. Anabel loved her.

Then one fateful night, Anabel's parent was involved in an accident. Their vehicle slid off the curb. Unfortunately, the bodies were never recovered.

Rin was heartbroken, but much to her despair, Anabel fell into a deep sleep. Days, weeks, and months passed, but the girl never woke up. Rin stayed by her side, day by day, hoping she would wake.

Sadly, that day never came, and so she moved on. Then, she disappeared on the day. Never to be seen again. Thus, to this day, some say they hear her voice playing in this very room.

The man's story concludes from there as the light turns back on. They all leave the room as Axe quickly finds another place for the child to sleep.

"Look like you'll have to share for tonight."

Axe places the child in the cradle with another; the party leaves for the night as Alistor hands the key back. They made their way back to the restaurant for a late-night meal.

"So, how was your day at the nursery?" Bamboo asked.

"Please don't mention it. Let's just say it's something I'm not used to doing." Alistor grumbled. "Anyway, Axe is the one who did the most."

"Wow, I never knew you were good with kids. Good to know." Bamboo nodded.

Max Mathesius

"So, how long will we be doing this?" Maigashi asked.

"Well, the good news is the caretaker is recovering. She'll be fine in just a couple days. So, you'll just have to continue watching these toddlers."

The party let off a slight groan at the table. Axe suddenly pulls his guitar out to begin practicing as they cover their ears.

Later that night...The cradle is seen pulled in, forming a new monster.

"Yes, complete at last. Now go and do your thing. Crass Cradle!"

The monster makes a gibberish laugh before leaving. By the nursery, Crass Cradle appears within seconds in the room where the babies sleep.

"Boo hoo hoo."

The monster pulls out a large rattle to cast an enigmatic sound wave in the room. Chuckling as the toddlers silently rest.

"Sleep tight. Cause tomorrow you'll be crying reeeaal good."

The following day, Alistor and the party take the children for an early stroll downtown. A bottle drops from one of the child's grips. The baby begins crying, a sound nearly unbearable to others' ears, as windows break.

"Such intense crying." Auroa grieved.

"Axe! What do we do?" Alistor asked.

"I don't know, dude. I never came across babies this loud before."

Soon after, the other babies cry, causing the concrete floors to crack as the ground shakes. Pedestrians are seen covering their ears while others inside panic to get away from the noise.

"We have to calm them down fast. Help me!"

Axe attempts to calm the babies as the others do their best to weather the storm. However, within minutes the whole street block was decimated entirely.

Back with Aggerona, Vilevelious follows up with General Scrap Ram on screen.

"Whoever knew sound can be such a destructive force." He complimented. "Their cry is fueling the labyrinth at an unexpected rate."

"Yes! And they suspect nothing. Everything is going perfectly." The general laughs.

They continue to watch Axe and the rest on-screen, struggling to calm another baby down. Laughter commenced across the room.

"General! I want you to send Crass cradle back down tonight."

"You mean to increase the wave frequency? That could be dangerous! The entire town will be in shambles if we go any louder."

"I don't care. We are going to double down." The emperor ordered. "I have something; hold one moment."

Vilevelious sends some coordinates over to the General.

"What's this? A new target?" The General questioned as he took a closer look. "The power plant? You don't mean...."

"Yes! We'll take this a step further. By shutting down the kingdom's main power source, towns, cities, and regions will be affected. Imagine hospitals without power. The doctors unable to care for their patients will cause distress, further amplifying negative energy produced."

"Very well... I'll send the monster back down tonight."

Returning back to Bamboo's restaurant...

"So, how was your day? Did you have fun strolling these youngsters around?"

"Even worse! I don't think I can last another day." Alistor moaned.

"The babies crying today were unnatural," Maigashi mumbled.

"How so?" Bamboo wondered.

Auroa was seen pondering at the table. The only one with his meal completely untouched.

"Something the matter, dude?"

"You don't think their unnatural cry could be linked to that missing cradle, perhaps." He brought it up.

"Good question." Axe thought. "Huh...I wonder too. Hey! Maybe we should stake out the place tonight."

"So you want us to investigate?"

"Yeah! We'll be sure to find something. Okay, let's do this." Alistor agreed.

Max Mathesius

Suddenly the power in the restaurant goes out.

"Hey! My favorite radio station was playing." Bamboo complained.

They go check outside to see the entire town completely blacked out. The fear of the worst quickly crossed Axe's mind.

"This isn't good. Without power, Rin won't be able to get well."

"You don't mean…."

"Yeah, dude! She could possibly die. We have to get to the bottom of this now."

And so they rushed back to the nursery with Bamboo following along. The city is shrouded in pitch darkness, yet they persevere through the night using the moonlight as their light source. Finally, they arrive within the nick of time, barging through the door.

"Gah! Getaway! Get away from me."

They spot the male caretaker crouched in fear as the monster laughs away. All the babies were now under a hypnotic spell.

"Boo hoo hoo! Just in time for the show. These kiddies are coming with me. And they'll scream reeeaal good when I bring down the kingdom's entire power supply."

The monster fires a laser creating a massive hole in the wall. Then, with one flick of the rattle, all the babies were afloat in a giant bubble as Crass Cradle fled.

"Hey, get back here!"

Alistor and the party begin chasing off the monster. Through the forest and into the open fields, Crass Cradle picks up the pace floating atop the great bubble. The babies inside remain calm and asleep inside their bubbles.

"We can't let that monster get to the power plant."

Maigashi quickly fires a shot from his bow, bringing Crass Cradle to a stop. They were now just yards away from the power plant's entrance.

"Hoo! You want to fight, eh? We'll give you a good whupping."

The bubble engulfs the entire party inside as they are transported into another realm of space. A domain with oversized toys and baby apparel floating around.

"Where in the hell are we?" Maigashi wondered.

Viper's Labyrinth

The monster materializes above them, laughing as the team ready their weapons. Bamboo and Axe kept a few steps back.

"You're now in mah territory. THE SQUARE ROOM! Boo-hoo!"

The monster fires a round of lasers breaking the group apart. Alistor makes the first move, charging right in. He pierced through Crass Cradle with his blade on impact.

"Now I got ya!"

He takes a second look as Crass Cradle instantly vanishes.

"Huh? What!"

"Hoo, miss me."

Alistor gets whacked by the monster's rattle. He then takes a beating, struggling to find a way around the monster's attack. The demon quickly disarms him, sending him rolling back to the others. A disappointed look was on Maigashi's face.

"Have you ever considered blocking, Alistor?" He asked.

"Huh, blocking?"

The others stumbled for a brief moment.

"You mean you don't know how to block? Seriously!" Maigashi slaps as the monster continues to laugh away. "At this rate, you'll never survive."

"Allow us to handle things from here." Auroa stepped in.

Crass cradle begins making multiple copies of itself, but the two quickly dispel the other targets. Whipping and blasting away as they got it close to a corner.

"Let's end this charade."

"Hoo! Before you do that."

Just before they got ready for the finishing strike, the babies began shielding Crass Cradle. The two immediately lower their weapons.

"Hoo! Just as I thought, you wouldn't dare hurt a sweet ol baby, would ya."

The monster unleashed two oversized beach balls sending Auroa and Maigashi flying back as Bamboo caught them. Lasers rain down on the group as they take cover.

Max Mathesius

"Gutless coward…" Maigashi pestered.

"Boo-hoo! You can't stop me. They'll follow whatever I want."

The babies are seen dancing around to Crass Cradle's command.

"Now, what do we do?" Alistor hopelessly asked.

Auroa's eye was focused on the monster's rattle, waving back and forth.

"The babies are under a hypnotic spell. If we can somehow disarm his rattle, we may be able to leave this place."

The group takes a stand against the monster once more.

"Hoo! Better yet! Why don't ya all rough 'em up? Attack!"

The babies were now seen charging toward the party. Axe and Bamboo immediately step into the fray.

"We'll distract these little dudes as much we can. Get that rattle."

The three make their way around within moments, avoiding the approaching toddlers. The toddlers quickly trample Axe Winston and Bamboo as Alistor charges in to attack the demon.

"Hoo! Back for more? I'll whup ya…Huh, what?"

Before the monster has the chance, Auroa disarms him with his wind whip. Then, pulling the rattle away as six electrical shots are fired by Maigashi.

"Whoah, Noooooo!"

Sparks fly as the monster takes amounts of damage. Crass Cradles realm pops within seconds, returning everyone to the power plant. Alistor quickly destroys the monster's rattle with the slash from his blade.

"Ah! Sweet Justice! I had enough with babies for the day."

"Boo! No! No! NO! Now you ruined everything." The monster cried. "Whoopers attack! Boo-hoo!"

Crass cradle begins running to the power plant as Vilevelious soldiers rush in to attack. Alistor unleashed his Star Breaker piercing through the pack of enemy soldiers. The Whoopers all collapse over, exploding upon destruction.

"Hoo! I must wreck that power plant. But, mess it reeeaal good!"

Viper's Labyrinth

Before Crass Cradle could go any further, Auroa trips him over with the flick of his whip. The monster stumbled over, struggling to regain balance as Alistor and Maigashi destroyed the remaining Whoopers. His whip pierced through the monster, and he took a dive unleashing a slashing vortex.

"Raizen Hurricane!"

"Boo Hoo!"

Crass-cradle gets engulfed within the vortex. Spun at high speed as it tore off the paint on the walls nearby. Then, completely dazed, intense sparks of energy burst out as the monster collapsed to the ground in an explosion.

Power is soon returned to the town from viewing distance. They find Axe and Bamboo playing with the toddlers. A baby is seen yawning as Axe checks the time.

"It's way past these dudes' bedtime. We better get them back."

The next following morning…

"Thank you all for caring for these little angels. It really means a lot." Rin sniffed. "Best of luck on your adventure."

After the team collected payment, they made their leave. Turning for one last look back at the nursery, Alistor and his friends wave goodbye to the caretakers. The babies are seen cheerfully smiling in the background. Bamboo then makes a sudden announcement.

"Hm. You say you don't know how to block. Well, I can teach you."

"Really!" Alistor jumped.

Bamboo happily nodded.

"We can begin when we get back. Work on building that stamina and learn defensive maneuvers." He assured.

And so the party head back to Bamboo's restaurant. The sound of a baby's last laugh echoes through the horizon.

Max Mathesius

Chapter 8

Violin day blues:

Axe unfortunate reunion

"Ow! Darn it!" Alistor yells as he gets sent flying back.

In the middle of a tense training session in the kitchen, Maigashi and Auroa watched Alistor takes a beating from Bamboo.

"Dude! You must not hesitate. When blocking, you have to anticipate your opponent's move. Now try again." Axe suggested.

He helps Alistor back up from the floor. Readying his sword, his eyes focus tensely on his opponent. Bamboo readies his frying pan once more.

"Now…feel the wrath and power."

Bamboo moves in for the strike. But, without much time to react, Bamboo easily overshadows him. With a stern look on his teacher's face, Alistor hesitates once more.

"OF MY COOKING!"

He gets hit in the face with the frying pan. Knocked back flat on the kitchen floor, Maigashi laughs from the other end. Alistor took a moment to rub the pain on his head.

"Ow…how is this supposed to be fair practice? A frying pan is not a common weapon; others try blocking. Can't we try something a little easier? Ow…my head."

"You can't expect every monster to use the same everyday weapons." Bamboo sighs. "There will be times when you'll have to adapt to certain situations."

He turns to the others for advice.

"You guys have any suggestions? Tips, at least." Alistor asked.

"Um… not really, but I can watch this all day." Maigashi laughed.

"So much for you..." He sarcastically glared. "Auroa, what about you? Come on! You have to at least have something. This training seems so pointless."

Auroa only gave a shrug back.

"Sorry, not much I can do." He slightly chuckled. "But learning the basics of good blocking can help you. Mindless rushing without knowing your opponent can cost you. Sometimes it helps reduce damage, but this training will help build your stamina and durability."

"Easy for you to say. I'm not the one holding the frying pan."

A sudden spark snaps deep within the glint of Bamboo's eyes.

"Is that a challenge, I hear?"

"What?"

"How would you like to try attacking back while I block?" Bamboo asked. "You can use your sword."

Alistor got back up.

"Are you sure?"

Bamboo had a stern look on his face.

"If you say so. Here goes."

Bamboo suddenly puts away his frying pan. Then, pulling another utensil, it throws Alistor entirely off for a brief moment.

"A ladle? You can't be serious? How can you possibly defend yourself with that? It's not a weapon suited for battle." Alistor argued.

"Don't question my methods. Just come at me."

Max Mathesius

As Alistor charged in with his blade, a sudden bell rang at the door. Bamboo turned away, avoiding his attack as he fell flat.

"Oh! Looks like we have customers."

Interrupted in the middle of practice, everyone halts for a brief moment.

"Don't worry, I'll get this." Axe insisted.

He leaves the kitchen to assist the customers. Then, as the bell continues ringing, he quickly gets the menu.

"Yeah, I'll be there. One moment!"

The moment he set eyes on the customer, a sudden chill ran down his spine.

"Axe? Is that really you? Oh my god!"

A crowd of girls suddenly laughs, mocking him.

"Cheryl? What are you doing here?"

Back from the kitchen, Alistor and Bamboo immediately halt training. The sound of an argument quickly escalates from the other end.

"Is that an argument I hear out there?" Maigashi asked.

"Must be Axe. Let's check it out." Auroa said.

The party leaves the kitchen only to witness Axe arguing with a girl at the table. Her friends continue to pester back at him.

"Axe! You are a sore loser! Of all the places, why are you even here?"

"As a matter of fact! I work here. You got a problem?"

"No! Just wondering who in their right mind would even hire you. Hahaha."

They continue laughing as pointless arguing continues. Finally, bamboo steps into the scene, hoping to break the fight.

"Enough!"

"Gah! Ew!"

The group quickly kicks Bamboo in the face, knocking him back.

Viper's Labyrinth

"Oh, give me a break." Maigashi slapped.

Maigashi fires a shot in the air. Everything in the room quiets down.

A moment later…

Cheryl and her friends were in the middle of eating their food while Axe kept a distance.

"What was with all that tension and heat? Do you know this girl?" Alistor asked.

Leaning one hand onto a wall, Axe lowers his head for a brief moment.

"Yeah… she's my girlfriend. EX-GIRLFRIEND!"

The rest suddenly stumbled for a brief moment.

"What? Really? Her…." He whispered back.

"Yep…"

The girls were done with their meals. The bell rings as Bamboo approaches their table.

"So you liked the food?" Bamboo kindly asked.

"So yeah….the food was pretty lousy. Mediocre at its best, if you ask me. You got anything better? Cause I demand something better if you don't say."

Bamboo suddenly crouched in the corner, depressed and wholly misunderstood, while Cheryl and the others pester him. Then, Axe suddenly steps in to confront her.

"Cheryl! I had had enough. If you don't like it, then take your business elsewhere." He yelled back.

"Oh, Axe! Trying too hard to be mad? Face it! You're not cut out for the music business. You'll never win me back!" She snapped.

As Axe is about to lose his cool, Maigashi immediately intervenes.

"We quite didn't get your full name. So who are you supposed to be again?"

She cleared her throat for a moment.

"The names Cheryl. Cheryl Faraday, but my friends call me Cher. I'm a renowned Violinist, and classical music is my forte."

She begins showing off to the crowd with an elegant performance. Finally, Cheryl closes her eyes, remaining calm and focused as the music plays in the restaurant.

"A classical music snob if you ask me," Axe murmured.

Her playing continues as the crowd watches. Auroa suddenly recalls something.

"Of course!"

"What is it?" Maigashi asked.

"There's a classical music performance expected this week in town. I read it in the papers a while back." Auroa noted.

She finishes up her session as the music stops. They begin to leave, but Auroa halts them from the door.

"You don't intend on leaving without paying, do you?" He threatened.

She did not hesitate as she tossed a twenty on the table.

"Keep the change."

Cheryl and the others immediately leave the restaurant. Things toned down as the room fell into an eerie silence.

"Huh? Axe, where are you going?" Maigashi asked.

"I need a moment alone."

He quickly left while the others stayed behind. Walking down some road, rain begins to pour into the scene. He starts looking back as memories of him and Cheryl escalate.

"Just why…did it have to end this way." He asked himself.

All their happy moments and times together flashed before ending in a breakup. Ending with her last words before turning away.

"You're just not sophisticated enough."

In cold blood, she leaves, taking off with his car. Axe Winston was hopelessly on the ground as he called out her name one last time. His flashback ends from there as rainwater continues to pour through the bangs of hair covering his face.

Meanwhile, back with Aggerona…

Viper's Labyrinth

Vilevelious contacts his general from the other screen while water leaks through the fortress. He holds an umbrella over his viewing screen.

"Scrap-Ram! Do you have your latest plan ready?"

The general presents a small pamphlet.

"There is a classical music act at the new theatre downtown tomorrow. So this girl will be my next target."

"A violin player?"

"Yes! A recent prodigy many is bragging about. Everyone has been dying to see her performance, and tickets are selling out. Her violin will be the perfect piece for making my next monster."

"Very well, you may commence." He approved in a displeasing fashion.

"Why the long face?"

Rainwater continues to leak behind the scenery. A hole bursts through the wall causing more water to pour in.

"In the meantime, you can call for some maintenance. Get a plumber!" The emperor commanded.

Back with Axe, rain continues to pour over him as he sits quietly on the hill. Looking back while he stares below at the new theatre Cheryl and her friends are staying in. A moment later, Maigashi appears from behind.

"Hey...."

He hands a spare umbrella over to Axe.

"Huh? Oh, hey."

Grabbing the umbrella, he got up and began strolling with Maigashi in the rain. They start chatting it up while Alistor continues his training with Bamboo.

"Yow!"

Bamboo deflects his attack from the tip of the ladle. Alistor is seen knocked back in the air. He lands on his bottom as his blade lands on the floor, nearly an inch from cutting him.

"Remember! Anything can be used as a weapon. Defense is the good way to go." Bamboo lectured.

"Whoever knew a ladle could be used so deadly." Alistor lies on the floor in astonishment. "This whole time, you've been holding so much back."

Bamboo helps him up. Before calling it a day, he begins lecturing with a few more tips and advice. Showing him more straightforward basics for timing and positioning his body from an attack.

A couple hours later…

"And one last tip. This is the most important advice I can give any student, man to man."

"What is it? I'm ready." Alistor said.

The moment grew tense as he eagerly waited.

"If you ever come across a woman. In battle…Simply just surrender."

Alistor immediately stumbled for a brief second. Unable to decipher what he just heard.

"What? How is that any help? Surrender? But why?"

He begins questioning his teacher for the sake of his logic and sanity.

"It's more of a moral code thing," Bamboo mumbled. "If you ever settle down or meet a woman in life. Simply listen, say yes, and do whatever she says. If provoked enough, they can be far more deadly than your average monster."

"Really? I never knew."

He slaps Alistor on the back shoulder.

"It's the manly way to go out."

The bell chimes at the door. Auroa got up from reading his paper on the counter to check. Then, he made his way into the back kitchen.

"It seems Maigashi and Axe finally returned."

A moment later, they are both seen drying off. Bamboo prepares some full-course meals as they begin closing for the day.

"So you're finally back from your slump?" Alistor asked.

Axe Winston was too busy to answer back as he was in the middle of chowing down.

"Let's just say we were able to sort things out," Maigashi stated.

Viper's Labyrinth

Meanwhile, they were in the middle of Bamboo's special grass jelly treat.

"So, how did you ever wind up with that kind of woman?" He wondered.

As Axe Winston gets ready to share his sob story with the rest at the table, Maigashi stops him.

"It's rather a long story best saved for another time." He suggested. "Why don't you play your guitar instead?"

"Alright, dude! If you insist."

"I had to endure two hours of this," Maigashi whispered to Auroa.

As Axe Winston prepares to play, Bamboo stumbles in on them with a sudden announcement. Clutched with some paper in his hands.

"Bamboo, what are those?"

"Since you've been making good progress so far. I thought I treat everyone to a little performance tomorrow night at the new theatre."

They begin to take a closer look at the tickets.

"Wait a minute? These are backstage passes." Maigashi slapped himself. "How in the world did you obtain these?"

"Tickets sold out since last week," Auroa recalled. "How were you able to afford this? Backstage passes cost a premium."

All eyes were on Bamboo for a brief moment.

"Ahem, let's just say I got connections," Bamboo stated.

"Wait...why are we even attending a classical concert anyway?" Alistor asked. "You know Axe and Cheryl despise...."

Before finishing his sentence, Axe stepped in.

"Don't worry. It's all cool now." He nodded to reassure him.

"Well, I suppose it wouldn't hurt to watch. Nothing has been happening in town for a while." He shrugged.

The next night later. A complete line outside as a vast crowd fills the newly built theatre. Alistor and the party tour the backstage, while Axe is nowhere to be seen with them. By the dressing room, Cheryl gets a knock at the door.

Max Mathesius

"Be ready in ten." She hollered.

As she finishes the final touch of makeup, a pair of eyes stare from above a vent. Adding the last tap of powder to her face, Cheryl reached to grab her violin case. Quickly exiting the door, she walks through a long hall to meet with the rest of her band. Cheryl suddenly hears a loud cranking sound from behind. She quickly turned around.

"Who's there?"

She continued walking her way through the halls. The sound continued to get closer as she increased speed. Then, a garbage bag suddenly drops in front, stopping her. The bag bursts open, revealing metal scraps inside.

"EW, someone forgot to take out the trash. I have no time for this."

Before she could go around, a face immediately formed from the small pile. Then, frozen in fear, a colossal figure rose before her.

"Not so fast, little girl."

"What are you?"

She suddenly falls back as the Scrap Ram intimidates her.

"Your violin is what I need. Now hand it over."

She didn't hesitate to scream out loud as she began to run for it.

"No! Not my violin! HELP! ANYONE!"

"AH! Why do they always want to do this the hard way?"

Her scream echoes through the halls as Scrap Ram gives chase through the narrow corridor. Cheryl quickly made her way backstage to her bandmates slamming the doors shut.

"Cheryl dear, why are you screaming, girl?"

Scrap Ram burst open the doors without hesitation. The band begins mindlessly panicking while the general corners her to a wall.

"I won't ask again. Surrender that violin." The general demanded.

She continues to cradle the case tight in her arms.

"No! I won't! You creep. Leave me alone!"

As she cowers helplessly by the wall, a voice from a man interrupts Scrap Ram in his tracks.

"That is far enough, dude!"

"Axe?"

Axe charged into the scene, swinging his jacket around like an idiot, confusing the general. Scrap Ram slowly steps back.

"Axe, what are you doing?" She asked.

"What do you think? I'm buying you some time to get away. Now go!"

"Oh, Axe...."

Cheryl quickly made her way to the other door with her bandmates. They continued to watch from a distance before Scrap Ram promptly caught on with Axe.

"Wait a darn minute! Why am I on the defensive? You have no fighting capabilities. Now be gone!"

Axe gets knocked back halfway across the room as Cheryl rushes to his side.

"Now, back to business."

She held onto his unconscious body as Scrap Ram continued to approach. Helpless as her bandmates could only watch.

"No! NO! It can't end like this."

"No point in weeping. That violin is mine for the taking."

As the general reached for the instrument, the doors burst open in the nick of time. Auroa came barging in with a few slashes of wind from his whip piercing through Scrap Ram's body.

"Gah! You again?"

The general fell back onto the defensive as the others caught up to Auroa. Finally, the rest of the party confronts the general in the very room.

"This is as far you go. Ready for round two?" Auroa pointed.

"Damn you...blew parts of my vitals again," Scrap-Ram grumbled. "If I can't have that violin, I'll just have to use something else."

Max Mathesius

The general quickly locates the closest object in the room. Scrap Ram makes his way toward a man trying to move his harp. The man quickly jumped out of the way as the general got a hold of the instrument. A monster instantly forms before their very eyes.

"AH-HA! Harpona at your service. How may I be of assistance?"

"Destroy them! And steal all the negative energy you can find in this theatre. Clean them dry." The general ordered before leaving.

The others try to go after Scrap Ram, but the monster steps in.

"Hey, what's the hurry? The night has just begun. My good time debut is about to air, so none of you are leaving."

"We have no time for this." Auroa cracked his whip out for an attack.

Harpona's strings suddenly bind across his weapon, catching him by surprise.

"What?"

The monster begins swinging Auroa high up in the air while the others ducked for cover.

"Around and around and away you go. Where shall you drop? No one will know?"

Auroa is sent flying out off the stage, knocking down the curtains. The monster makes its way to the stage filled with a half-scared audience.

"Ladies and gentlemen. The delicate tranquil sounds of a timeless masterpiece are about to begin.

A lousy harp begins screeching through the room, hurting everyone's ears. Then, thousands of strings began slithering across the entire theatre encasing everyone as chaos commenced. A crowd is in terror as energy is drained from their body.

"Yes! More for the labyrinth. HA HA HA!"

"We can't let this go on. I'm stopping this." Maigashi rushed in.

A few electrical bolts hit the monster from behind. Finally, Maigashi rushed in with a charged bolt of energy, ready to impale the demon.

"You want a piece of me too, eh? Well, come and get it."

Harpona countered back, firing its wrapping strings, but he quickly moved to the side, slashing through the line. However, Harpona didn't hesitate to fall back.

"Now I got ya!"

Viper's Labyrinth

As he got close and ready for his attack, strings immediately burst out from the ground, altogether canceling his attack.

"MWAHAHAHAHAHAHAHA! Once again, it seems you got the short end of the stick. Or is it the string? No matter!"

Harpona quickly encased him with strings as he began to levitate him up.

"Oh no...not again." Maigashi groaned.

Harpona slams him to the ceiling, then to the ground and back up. Swinging him back and forth, followed by the walls. Alistor quickly ducks to avoid getting hit.

"And away you go!"

Maigashi gets sent flying straight into Bamboo as Alistor stands frozen in fear. Alistor hesitates on what to do as the monster approaches.

"The last one standing? Tell you what? I'll make this quick by giving you a half discount." Harpona mocked.

"I don't think so."

As Alistor got ready to fend for himself, Axe's words came to his mind.

"Dude! You must not hesitate. When blocking, you have to anticipate your opponent's move. Now try again."

Harpona begins to charge in, ready with the strings, as Alistor focuses deep into thought. Bamboo's training flashed through his mind.

"No hesitation...Anticipate your opponent's move. I already saw what you can do."

Harpona got close, ready to incase Alistor but was suddenly blinded by an unknown object. Confused, the monster begins bumping into things.

"What is this sorcery? I'm blind! Blind! I say!"

Axe finally regained consciousness as he found his jacket covering the monster's face.

"Dude...my jacket?"

"A nifty trick Bamboo luckily taught."

The monster blindly attempts to ram into Alistor, but he counters back. He blocks the impact immediately, bringing Harpona down with the edge of his blade.

Max Mathesius

"Star Breaker!"

Harpona finally removes the jacket trapped within its strings, only to be finished with Alistor's finishing attack. Sparks begin flying out as Harpona runs back to the stage, collapsing.

"But the night is still young...."

Harpona explodes on stage, leaving nothing but debris as everyone within the theatre evacuates.

Ten minutes later, Axe is talking with Cheryl. The rest is seen patched up from the battle.

"Look, what you did was brave but stupid. What were you even thinking?" She coldly turned away. "The show is canceled, so we'll have to reschedule. But thanks anyway. We'll call it even for now. See you again, Axe."

With a smile, she went her separate way.

"Heh, sure thing." Axe nodded.

He made his way back to Bamboo and the rest.

"So...how did it go?" Maigashi asked.

"Not so bad," Axe smiled back. "Dude! Bamboo, can you whip up more of that bodacious jelly?"

"Sure thing." Bamboo jumped.

And so the party heads back in the still of the night.

Chapter 9

Fast Outcome:

A Half-Baked Battle

One fateful morning…

"Another day for business."

Inside, Bamboo opens the doors to his restaurant on an early Saturday morning. Taking one fresh breath of air, he gazes at the blossoms across the street. Then, something quickly catches his attention.

"NOOOOOOOOOOO!!!!!!!!!"

Alistor and the party come rushing to the scene. Axe helps Bamboo right up in the middle of a state of shock.

"What's the matter? Are we under attack?" He asked while readying his blade.

"Yeah, dude! Speak to us."

Bamboo points his team's attention to a new building across the street. A new restaurant ready for business. One moment later…

"So what? A new restaurant in town can't be this bad." Maigashi shrugged.

Auroa returns with some gathered insights on the situation.

"A hotshot chef named Rondo has opened up in this town." He informed.

"Well, I don't like the sound of this." Bamboo beamed. "This is going to affect the income. Competition not good for business."

"Well, there's a chance the food might not be good?" Maigashi debated.

Alistor sees a huge line across the street from a window while Axe returns with some news.

"Dude! You guys aren't going to believe this."

Bamboo and the party checks the scene outside. Catching a glimpse of the new restaurant ready for its grand opening. Female waiters are seen handing out pamphlets to the crowd.

"It seems Cheryl and her friends have taken up jobs at this place."

Tension further builds within Bamboo's spirit.

"New Steel Plated Floorings, V Powered Gas Stoves, Sushi Bars, Live Fish Tanks, and Sexy Waiters! I can't compete with this." He further scowled.

A pamphlet gets handed to Alistor's group. They take him back inside to his business. Bamboo is seen waltzing back and forth in places.

"Get a hold of yourself." Maigashi pestered.

"Yeah, it can't be really this bad?" Alistor added. "Maybe everyone will just forget about it the next day."

"Not going to happen." Bamboo nodded. "This is serious business. And your pay from last week is ready on the other side of the counter."

They collect their payroll from the counter. Maigashi suddenly grabs the pamphlet off Alistor's hand, leaving for the door.

"Where do you think you're going?" Bamboo asked.

"Where do ya think? I'm gonna give that new place a try."

Bamboo immediately stumbles over.

"Relax...If the food is bad, I'll let you know. Plus, I can give immediate insight if I catch anything fishy."

He quickly got back up.

"Hmm, actually, that might not be a bad idea. Get close to the enemy and strike when the iron is hot."

Bamboo then turned his attention toward the others.

"It's settled then. Your next mission is to investigate this new restaurant. You'll use your money to sample some of the food there. Now go!"

Alistor stumbled for a brief moment.

"What? But I don't want to."

Maigashi and the others immediately pull him straight out the doors with them. Then, jumping into the long waiting line.

"This might not be so bad, dude."

Meanwhile, back with Vilevelious...

"Scrap-Ram! What is the meaning of this?"

The emperor is seen conversing with his general on another screen.

"What is the problem?"

He turns to the screen showing the new restaurant opened across the street. The general is clueless about the situation.

"Did you send a monster without my approval? What's this new plan that I haven't heard of?"

Scrap Ram takes one glance at the restaurant showing Rondo cooking.

"Not that I know of? In fact, I haven't given any orders for him to open up? Is this a monster gone rogue for the first time?"

"Well, I'm going to get to the bottom of this." The emperor announced. "My personal monster chef Rondo was supposed to make breakfast. Now I'll have to get takeout."

Back down below, Alistor and the company are getting seated at the tables. High-end chandeliers light the table as the menus get passed out. A man comes strolling into the scene, making a flashy entrance.

Max Mathesius

"AHHAHA! I am the Great RONDO! The one and only beautiful! I traveled the world far and wide, seeking the greatest ingredients known to mankind. With one taste, you'll be mesmerized by the enchanting flavors. Your tongue will swirl and twist. You'll never stop coming back for more. So what will it be today?"

The party was utterly astounded. Speechless for a moment before proceeding to the menu. The rest were deep into planning, while Alistor remained uncertain about what to order. Maigashi starts the order.

"Okay, we'll start with some Sashimi and Deep Fried Tofu for appetizers. Then some Chicken Katsu and Beef Teriyaki combos."

"Okay, dudes! We'll take the Rock n Roll, a Spider, and a Rainbow for the rolls. Then the Dragon, Unagi, and Viper. And top it off with extra ginger."

The waiter takes the orders down.

"As for drinks, give us some Hot Tea." Auroa closed.

"Splendid!" Rondo clapped. "Your food will be ready in a split. You won't be disappointed."

The chef spun his way back into the kitchen. Meanwhile, Bamboo peeps through a pair of binoculars on the other side. Rondo is seen in the middle of cooking. Preparing many dishes as the sound of water drips in the sink. Then, he suddenly hears a voice.

"RONDO! What is the meaning of this?"

He comes to a halt.

"That voice…"

Rondo turns his attention toward the water. The emperor's face materializes in the sink beaming at him.

"Vile, my lord."

"What is that awful human disguise? You have some explaining to do."

"I confess…I acted on my own without a superior's notice. But I have a plan that will heat things for our labyrinth."

The emperor became intrigued.

"Go on."

Viper's Labyrinth

"This new restaurant will gather all the energy we need for the labyrinth. With this concoction, my food will keep them spending and returning for more. With a simple drop just like this."

He is seen pouring something into the sashimi.

"I see...But why go through the trouble on your own?"

A small flashback pass through Rondo's mind.

"I'll tell you why. It was Mushogun's fault. He took my glory that very day. I never had the chance to become a general. I was so close, but favor curried to him. So by cruel fate, I lost by a mile. But now that he is long gone, I want to prove what I can do."

"Interesting..."

Rondo takes his stand.

"Promote me, and I'll have them on your knees."

"Well, you seem rather determined. So fine, I'll give you a chance. Dispose of Alistor and his nuisance group, and I'll give you that promotion. I've grown tired of waiting on Scrap Ram's countless failures anyway."

"They will not stand a chance against my Dynamo-style techniques."

Vilevelious face disappeared into the waters.

In a matter of time, the food arrived at their tables. Presented in fancy plates, sparkling under the light.

"Hot damn... Didn't see this coming." Maigashi admitted.

"Well, let's dig in," Auroa said as they pulled out the chopsticks.

The party digs in as Alistor takes the first bite of the sashimi. A sudden sparkle lit within his eyes.

"Wow! This stuff is good."

"Yeah, dude, this stuff is excellent."

An hour later, they are back at Bamboo's restaurant.

"Well...So how was the food?"

Maigashi was seen cleaning his teeth with a toothpick.

"Yeah, you're pretty screwed." He broke the news.

Bamboo crouched up in the corner, depressed.

"With unbeatable prices, Rondo could drive you out of business."

He gets right back up.

"How much was the bill?" Bamboo hastily asked.

"Just five hundred yen for every item." Alistor jumped.

Bamboo suddenly froze in place.

"I didn't even get to try the sashimi, thanks to him." Maigashi bops Alistor over.

"Ow! But it was so good."

"Though…I did sort of notice something off." Axe noted.

"What? Then spit it out." Bamboo shouted.

A flashback shows the four in the middle of eating while Rondo returns to the kitchen. Axe Winston is seen placing his plate down.

"Gonna wash up, be back in a sec."

He heads right off to the men's room. Axe immediately hears Rondo laughing as he sees him pouring something into a plate. But, unfortunately, the scene fades from there.

"He was using some sort of small bottle. I thought it was like nothing, but the food began to sparkle. Like it's some sort of secret ingredient."

Something sinister suddenly catches Bamboo's mind.

"Hmm…This actually gives me an idea."

"Like what?" Alistor asked.

"If we steal this secret formula, my food will taste better."

The party immediately stumbled over.

"What? But I can't take part in any criminal activity." He objected. "No! I won't do this. Even if it means risking your business."

"Not to worry!" Bamboo assured. "This plan will not fail."

He begins drawing out a plan at the tables. And in a matter of hours, everyone was lined up for dinner. Alistor was again in line with Maigashi and Auroa, waiting for a table. He was nervous for the first time.

"Stop, with your shaking," Maigashi whispered. "You're making us look suspicious."

"But I can't. I've never done something like this before. How can you guys stay so calm?"

Auroa was seen reading over the menu outside.

"Look, he gave us the easiest part. We have free money to spend, so keep it together. After that, it's up to Axe and him to pull this off. We'll be on the lookout, so don't mess this up."

The three are soon seated at the table once again.

"Hey? Where's your other friend." The waitress asked.

"Um, well, he's occupied with his music. You know, guitar practice."

"As if." The girl snobbishly said. "He can barely strike a single cord. Other than that, what can I get for you today?"

Maigashi began making the orders while two figures crept past a window behind. It was none other than Axe and Bamboo sneaking past the unnoticed crowd.

"Okay, dude, the back kitchen should be right around here."

"Good, all good. Everything going to plan." Bamboo rubbed his hands. "When Rondo makes his way out, we'll break in."

The three were in the middle of ordering.

"While Maigashi makes the big order, Auroa will signal when he comes right out."

Maigashi concludes with the order as Rondo spun out from the kitchen, again making his flashy entrance. Auroa opens out the chopsticks tapping them on the table lightly.

"That's the queue," Axe whispered.

The two slipped through the window panes arriving in the back storage room. Axe gently opens the door leading to the kitchen. A waitress is seen taking a dish out.

Max Mathesius

"The coast is clear."

The two scoured around for the secret formula.

"Do you remember what it looks like?"

"Yeah, this will only take a minute." He pointed. "Right there!"

The bottle was seen located inconveniently high above a cabinet.

"Dude, there are no chairs around."

"Then we'll have to do this the hard way. So I'll give you a boost."

Axe got right on Bamboo's back, reaching for the bottle. Some pots and pans begin to dangle over.

"Hold still, man."

"I'm trying!"

A waitress begins to notice the noise.

"Hey, Rondo, I think something fell over."

"What?"

The staff begins turning their attention back to the kitchen.

"Oh shit!" Maigashi snapped. "They're gonna be discovered. We need a distraction to bide some time fast."

Auroa quickly reached for the wasabi. Maigashi immediately stuffed a whole chunk in Alistor's mouth. His face was red in seconds, and his mouth caught fire. Then, screaming, coughing, and gagging for some water.

"AHHHHHHH!!!"

"What is going on?" Rondo turned back. "Someone get that kid some water."

The waitress goes to pour some water over him. He was seen soaking wet while the others laughed. The sound was still heard from the kitchen.

"Got it, dude!"

Viper's Labyrinth

Bamboo then loses balance, forcing them to fall over. Finally, the two begin to make their escape through the back window. Axe successfully slips out first, but Bamboo struggles to pull himself up.

"Grab my hand."

Before Bamboo had the chance, a loud scream forced him back down.

"EEEEEEEEEEKKK!!! We got an intruder!"

"Wu, oh!"

Axe flees from the scene as the waitress hurls things at Bamboo.

"Oh, NO!!!!"

An army of waitresses soon barged in, pinning him to the ground. In a matter of minutes, Bamboo was seen handcuffed as the authorities took him away. Rondo looks back at him in utter disgust.

"Anyone in the mood for dessert?" Auroa asked.

"I'm not amused," Alistor grunted while Maigashi continued to laugh.

A few hours later, the party caught up with Axe. Bamboo was quickly let off with a warning for breaking and entering.

"So you got it?"

"Right here, dude!"

He hands the formula over to Bamboo.

"Perfect!"

A few days later, the line was still packed by Rondo's restaurant. Bamboo's business was empty, with not a single customer.

"I don't understand...Even with this formula, my food hasn't improved one bit. Everything on Rondo's menu is the same as mine."

"You can try lowering the price?" Alistor suggested.

"Are you crazy? I can't go any lower."

Bamboo suddenly crouched back down into his sad state.

Max Mathesius

"It's hopeless… We're through."

Then, unexpectedly the bell rings with two customers' insight.

"Are you open for business?"

"No way!"

The man from the nursery and the middle-aged owner from the antique shop enter.

"What are you guys doing here?"

"The food at Rondo's may be great, but the line is too long to bother the wait. Plus, all the young kids eat there, and it's rowdy."

Some hope was restored back to them.

"Indeed, Rin and her lady friends are gossiping away, so I don't want to be there. Your food, however, is more like home cooking."

"So, what can we get you?"

Two orders of noodles were placed. Bamboo heads right off into the kitchen to prepare the dish. He stumbles, looking for the secret formula, but an unexpected ingredient slip in.

"OH…"

The pot for the soup base quickly turns red, letting off a ghastly smoke. Choking up, Bamboo looks over the unexpected ingredient dumped in.

"Atomic Wasabi?"

He remained conflicted for the moment about whether to feel guilty or not but let off a shrug as the noodles were served. Axe hands the food to the customers as they take their first slurp into the noodles. Their face immediately burns red within seconds.

"Uh, dudes? Ya feeling okay?"

Fire immediately bursts aflame from their mouths as they spin in circles. Gagging for some water as Maigashi quickly goes to pour it over them. Bamboo backed away, fearing a refund.

"So I take it you don't like it?" Alistor asked.

"Are you kidding? We love it!" The middle-aged man cried. "This reminds me of the food back in my childhood."

Viper's Labyrinth

In a moment, a large crowd flocked to the front doors. Looking over, the two men were satisfied with the new hot dish.

"We got a whole bunch of hungry customers at the doors." Maigashi pointed.

"Let them in!" Bamboo ordered.

In a matter of minutes, the line at Rondo's was deserted. Auroa quickly placed a new poster advertising their unique dish. Atomic Wasabi Noodles. Rondo can be seen snapping a pair of chopsticks from the other side. The waitresses stood on the sidelines, curious.

"Maybe Bamboo's not so bad after all." One girl thought.

"That new dish sounds interesting. I want to try it." Another girl said. "What do you think, Cheryl?"

"I don't know...I don't trust Bamboo one bit. Axe and the others must be up to something." She merely nodded.

Rondo took his stand cooking up a new plan.

"If it's hot, they want! Then hot they will get."

In an hour, Rondo's place had a new dish ready by the windows. Kamikaze Curry. Customers begin to flock back to Rondo's restaurant.

"We will fight fire with fire!" Bamboo ordered.

The next moment Bamboo quickly created another dish to lure the customers back. Scorching fried Gyoza. Double the Spice!

"Take that!"

Rondo immediately retaliated with Blistering Fried Tofu. Triple the firepower. Both restaurants were at war, creating one new dish after the next till Rondo finally had enough. Both chefs stared down at one another from across the street.

"This is the last straw!" Rondo snapped. "I didn't want to do this."

He takes a marker to write up something as they attempt to figure out his plan. Then, in seconds, he placed the sign on display, causing Bamboo to fall over.

"What? Buy 1, get 1 free! FREE!!!"

Rondo let off a burst of jeering laughter as he entered back inside. Alistor goes to help him back up while the customers flock back to Rondo's restaurant once again.

Max Mathesius

"Can't we one-up him with a free deal as well?" Alistor asked.

"What? NO!" Bamboo objected. "My cooking has more dignity than this, and I refuse to go low with all you can eat."

A moment later, Rondo can be seen eyeing the customers in the middle of eating. Then, he lets off a creepy grin.

"The time is now right. Time to fuel energy for the labyrinth."

With one wave from his hands, energy begins to drain from all the customers across the tables. The waitresses all stand clueless as he maniacally laughs.

"Hey, dudes! Something is up on the other side at Rondo's." Axe pointed.

"This is not good. We should check it out." Maigashi thought.

Bamboo takes the lead in opening the front doors. Bamboo takes the first steps in while the rest follow behind. Proceeding through the receptionist hallway.

"I hear a sound."

In seconds, a group of waitresses was seen running away. Bamboo was caught by surprise, getting trampled in their path.

"Hey, Cheryl." Axe waved.

Auroa goes to check over Bamboo, who is knocked out cold. The party placed him on the side of the tables.

"Good grief..." Maigashi nodded.

The party proceeds into the dining room. There Rondo stood in wait for them. A sinister look was on his face.

"Who are you? Show your true form." Alistor demanded.

Rondo steps into the center, and smoke sets loose from under his garment as the rest back away. Then, in seconds, his true face was revealed as he burst into laughter.

"It was a monster this whole time."

Rondo begins to bang his pan like a drum. Alistor stood fazed momentarily, distracted by the getup while the others pulled their weapons.

"I, the great Rondo, will defeat you here and now. After that, you shall fall to my Dynamo-style techniques."

Viper's Labyrinth

"What is he doing?" Alistor dropped his guard.

"Wouldn't want to find out."

Maigashi makes the first charge with an electrical dagger. A sly look was on Rondo's face as he made the first strike deflecting the attack with his pan. Next, Rondo unleashes a rapid series of punches, sending him crashing into the tables. Auroa and Axe then stepped in.

"We must end this quickly."

"I got your back, dude."

Auroa lashed open his whip with a force of the air.

"Wind? I got an answer to that."

Rondo immediately pulls out a bag of wasabi to chug down. In seconds, flames spew from his mouth, dispelling Auroa's wind in the air.

"No way!"

"Gah!"

Axe immediately falls back as the crowd begins to evacuate the scene. Auroa gets slammed back by his pan.

"HAHA! Did I mention I was also the Wasabi-eating champion back then?"

Alistor attempts to jump in but is kept back by Rondo spewing more flames.

"We have to do something about that fire," Maigashi said.

"As long the flames are around, my attacks are useless." Auroa nodded.

Axe caught a glimpse of something on the corner as the others quickly huddled to plan. Bamboo still lies unconscious at the other end of the table as Axe crawls under. The two make a stand against Rondo once more.

"Back for more?"

Rondo didn't hesitate to unleash another round of flames. The two maneuvered their way around using the tables as cover. Maigashi fires a few shots, but Rondo quickly blocks the oncoming attacks.

"Is that all you got?'"

Max Mathesius

Axe quickly gets him from behind with an extinguisher on his face. The fire soon dies away as the others charge in to strike Rondo. Auroa and Maigashi then unleash a series of ranged attacks, damaging him while Alistor charges in with the Star Breaker. Finally, a spark lit within Rondo's eye.

"DYNAMO!"

Rondo hurls his wok over at Axe, knocking him away while he charged head-on to their attacks. Next, he hurls his utensils at Maigashi and Auroa, stunning them. The two get sent back with fast kicks and punches while Alistor continues his charge.

"Your reign of cooking ends here and now!"

Alistor dashed into the air, ready to finish the unarmed monster. The fire was still burning in Rondo's eyes. Within a split second, Rondo grabbed a pair of chopsticks from the tables.

"What? You got to be kidding me."

Alistor's Star Breaker was stopped midair as Rondo held him by the blade's tip with the sticks. Then, he tossed him aside with a series of quick punches.

"What is with this guy?" Alistor raged.

The rest held him back from charging in.

"This might be a fight we cannot win." Auroa nodded.

"But we can't just give up now?"

Rondo retrieves his wok and bangs it like a drum once more. Alistor begins to lose his mind as the monster taunts away.

"His Dynamo style is hard to read," Maigashi admits. "Might be best to call a retreat. This guy is unpredictable."

Alistor refused to stand down.

"Enough chit-chatter. You're not escaping, so I will end this right now." Rondo snickered.

The door closed behind them. Alistor attempts to charge once more, but Rondo, this time, pulls out ingredients. Pineapples and Kiwis were sent exploding in his path. His pan begins to expand in size, pulling the party in.

"Is he really gonna try to cook us?" Axe jumped.

Rondo tossed more ingredients into the pot.

Viper's Labyrinth

"Onions! Bell Peppers! Cucumbers and Tomatoes."

He starts shaking them up back and forth as the heat readies.

"See Vile! I am worthy enough to be general. Victory never tasted so good."

Just as Rondo starts the flames, a sudden force knocks over the entire pan. It rolled, crashing open the doors as it freed Alistor and the party.

"It's you again...." Rondo muttered.

It was none other than Bamboo, armed with a ladle. A serious look on his face.

"Bamboo?" Alistor stuttered.

"Stay back. This one is mine." He insisted.

Fire lits between both chefs' eyes as the battle move outside. Rondo charged in with his utensils delivering a series of punches as Bamboo matched him move for move.

"Look at them go." Maigashi dropped. "I have never seen him like this."

Rondo spews another round of flames, but Bamboo easily deflects it from one twirl with his ladle. The sun was now setting as both chefs stood off.

"I am the great Rondo! No one's cooking can compare to mine. My Dynamo style will not fall."

"You have dishonored my cooking. I cannot let you live. You will feel the wrath of my Bamboo style."

Like a samurai showdown, both chefs make the final charge. Putting everything, they got into one final move. One last clashing sound commenced as both stood hand in hand.

"Hmm."

Bamboo's body suddenly falls back as the others hesitate. Rondo takes one look back.

"Dy...Na...mo Sty...le.........."

Rondo immediately collapses to the floor, exploding in one great puff of smoke as Bamboo emerges victoriously. The party goes to help him back up as the scene cuts back to the enemy lair.

"No!!!!" Vilevelious pounded.

Max Mathesius

"So Rondo has failed." Scrap Ram nodded.

"With him gone, I'll have nothing to eat but instant noodles." The emperor sadly expressed. "I'll need to find a new chef."

The general look over the progress of Axe's guitar.

"Well, look on the bright side. The good news is Axe's guitar is almost complete in collecting energy. So my brand new monster will be soon ready."

The following day, Rondo's restaurant completely vanished overnight. Bamboo's restaurant was back to its usual business. Large orders of Atomic Wasabi Noodles were flying off the counters.

"Bamboo, did you have to keep this on the menu?" Alistor complained.

"Hey! It was the best mistake that ever happened. It's new, hot and everyone wants to try it. Now shoo! Don't leave them hungry and waiting."

He scoots him out of the kitchen as he delivers the bowls to the tables.

In a matter of minutes, customers' mouth was burning away while Axe Winston went to extinguish them. The sound of gold coins and hard cash was only on Bamboo's mind.

"At this rate, I'll be rich if I keep making stuff like this. Maybe I should start adding wasabi to all my cooking. Even grass jelly!"

"Oh, give me a break...." Alistor sighed.

The scene closes with Bamboo stirring his big pot.

Chapter 10

Dark Emissary:

The Emperor arrives & the hour of Discordus

Sometime in the middle of the afternoon…

"Dude! Where did it go?"

"Where did what go?" Bamboo questioned.

Axe Winston was in the middle of searching for his guitar. Looking under every table and top cabinet. He then checks by the desk counter.

"Maybe you misplaced it, perhaps?" Alistor said.

"Nah! I swear I had it last night. I left it right by the cabinet before locking up last night."

The rest of the party begins searching the entire perimeter of Bamboo's restaurant.

"You don't think someone could have broken in, do you?"

"Not that we know of." Bamboo intensely thought.

Maigashi suddenly hollered to the rest. They all head out to the backside of the restaurant. An empty guitar case was left on the scene.

"Oh no!"

Axe stood fazed for a moment. Then, shocked with disbelief as he speechlessly fell into despair. They recovered the case back inside.

"A mystery for us yet to unfold. Who or what could have taken this guitar."

The party begins searching for any clues left at the scene. Auroa suddenly uncovers a bag left by the edge of the storage room.

"Does this happen to be yours?"

He hands the bag to Axe as the party checks through the contents, from spare dirty clothes to old pictures. Finally, a cassette tape catches their eye.

"What do we have here?" Maigashi wondered.

"Oh, that's just my old demo tape. Back when I was on top." Axe clarified.

"Well, can we hear it?" Alistor asked.

"Ugh... Sure, dude."

Bamboo popped the tape into the music player. The sound of an electric guitar begins rifting through the roof. In seconds, the rest starts rocking out to the track. The sound of the drums and synthesizers followed along.

"Man, this isn't half bad at all," Maigashi admits. "You sound completely different."

"Were you in a hairband?" Auroa asked.

A guitar solo begins playing in the middle of the track.

"Yeah, this song was my grand debut." Axe nodded. "Back when my band was still around."

"Exceptionally tolerable." Bamboo agreed.

"But sadly…We never got any airplay on the radio. I used to be an Ace guitarist before my playing went downhill."

"Well then, they're missing out," Alistor added.

Viper's Labyrinth

Meanwhile, back at the Aggerona lair, the Emperor is seen composing a song through the glass in a recording studio. The sound of an organ plays as it echoes through the labyrinth. Scrap-Ram reports on the other side of the screen.

"Our monster is now ready."

"Bring it forward!" The Emperor commands.

"May I present to you! DISCORDUS!"

A guitar monster emerged from behind the general. Taking the spotlight on the screen as the Emperor continued his song.

"Ah, Splendid!"

"Discordus is our most powerful monster yet. It will ensure the energy for our labyrinth, plus dispose of Alistor and his pitiful party.

Vilevelious then completes the final chorus of his song. A cassette pops out from the recorder as the tape hovers above his palm.

"I have an assignment for you." He pointed to the monster.

"Do tell!"

"Your mission is to break into the local radio station. Once you do, ensure that this tape plays."

He sends the tape over to the monster on screen.

"What will this do?" The general asked.

"Anyone that listens to this song will produce negative energy. Further speeding the process for the labyrinth."

Discordus and the general begin evilly laughing on screen.

"Now go!"

The scene shifts back to the abandoned theatre as Vilevelious exits on screen. Scrap-Ram prepares the location for Discordus to deploy down.

"You do know where the radio station is, right?"

"Of course!" The monster quarreled.

"Now, this will just take a moment. I just have to adjust the previous coordinates."

The general readies the teleportation device, but Discordus quickly rushes without patience.

"NO, WAIT!"

Discordus teleport out of the room without any further ado. The monster arrives, crashing down behind a familiar building.

"Oh, hey? It's the restaurant."

Discordus enter the back door, finding himself in the kitchen. Bamboo was seen thoroughly occupied cooking while customers were seated at the table. The monster attempts to stealth its way past the kitchen but knocks over some pans.

"Can you pass over the salt?" Bamboo ordered. "And then the pepper."

Bamboo was too focused on his cooking to notice as the monster hands over the requested items without question. Discordus take leave, stumbling out of the kitchen doors. Alistor and the rest were not around as it crept past, ignoring customers. The monster then trips over a chair, losing the tape as a few things drop to the floor.

"The tape!"

Bamboo's music player is seen on the ground as Discordus stands confused with two cassette tapes on the floor. Discordus quickly grabs the closest tape before rushing out. A moment later, Bamboo came out, noticing his things knocked over.

"Darn, kids!"

He placed the tape player back on the counter. Picking up the tape on the floor, Bamboo then pops the tape back inside.

"Don't want Axe's tape to get lost. Maybe it wouldn't hurt to listen again."

Without hesitation, he pressed play, and an unbearable sound started playing within seconds. The customers were seen in pain as Bamboo stumbled back for a brief moment. He covers his ears as he reaches for the stop button.

"What was that?"

Bamboo then turns around to notice all his customers lying flat-out unconscious. Meanwhile, Alistor and the rest are seen making fliers for Axe's lost guitar downtown. The monster Discordus slips past them without notice. The demon then bumps through an oncoming crowd. A small child is suddenly seen crying over his ice cream.

Viper's Labyrinth

"Watch where you're going!"

The crowd, confused, stares back as the monster readied its guitar. Then, with one flick of its finger, Discordus unleashed a booming sound dispersing the traffic. Windows completely shatters all around as an explosion commences. The monster then takes one look at the map on the side.

"Got to get to that station."

The monster pressed on, leaving the entire block destroyed. Sprinting through downtown while others staggered. In a matter of minutes, the radio station came into view. A secured gate stood in Discordus's path.

"Objective reached!"

Without hesitation, Discordus fires a shockwave destroying the metal gate. The monster storms through the doors while bystanders begin to panic. Explosions commenced across the whole building as Discordus went through the floors without retaliation.

"It's time for a new song!"

The monster arrives at the very heart of the station. The radio host quickly bolts out of the room as Discordus inserts the cassette tape.

"Mission complete!"

Meanwhile, Alistor and the others observed the destroyed block downtown.

"Did we miss something?" Maigashi asked.

"Dunno…Dude, this block is totally wrecked."

They find a man still barely conscious on the sidewalk. Auroa goes to help the man up as Alistor questions him.

"Do you know what happened here?"

The man quickly explains the situation to them in a few words.

"A monster attack, you say? Figures…"

"By the way, have you seen this guitar?" Auroa presented a flier to him.

"Hey! I've seen it!" The man pointed.

"Yeah, where?" Maigashi asked.

Max Mathesius

"The monster was carrying it around during the attack."

They leave the man in peace as they huddle up for a plan. Then suddenly, a familiar song begins playing through the radio.

"Dude...Am I tripping? Or is that my song playing on the air."

Back at the Aggerona fortress...

"What is the meaning of this?" The Emperor pounded as he contacted his general from the other screen.

"Is something wrong?"

"Your monster played the wrong tape!"

Scrap-Ram stumbled for a brief second.

"Well, this is no good. What should I do? Shall I commence action?"

"One moment!"

The Emperor was deep in thought as the general kept an eye on Alistor and his team's movements on another screen. Then, Vilevelious suddenly takes a stand.

"Oh! So you have the orders?"

"Scrap-Ram! Prepare the red carpet."

"Wait, what?"

"You heard me!" The Emperor snapped. "It's time I make my grand debut. I won't tolerate any further failures. My tape must be played."

Within moments, Vilevelious arrives at the station alongside the general. A platoon of Whoopers surrounds the entire vicinity. Axe's song comes to a stop.

"Discordus, you happen to remember where our tape went?" The general asked.

The monster attempts to recall its step.

"Oh yeah! I remember now. I bumped into a few things back at that Bamboo joint. The restaurant by the very front corner." Discordus answered.

"Well...then get over there!" Vilevelious shouted.

Viper's Labyrinth

Discordus immediately left as Alistor and the crew approached close to the station. However, the monster came bolting out as it crossed the path with the party outside.

"Dude! That's my guitar." Axe pointed.

"You wanna piece of me?" The monster replied back.

Discordus readied the guitar as the party entered the battle. Maigashi and Auroa start with a few lightning and wind attacks at the monster.

"Careful! My guitar is on the line." Axe reminded.

Then suddenly, with a smug look, the monster unleashed tremendous pressure. A force of sound stops their attacks in midair. The two were astonished as the monster sent it back at them. The four are sent flying as Discordus laughs away.

"Right back at ya."

"Star Breaker!"

Alistor came rushing in with his attack, but Discordus countered back with a shockwave. Axe suddenly came from behind, attempting to take his guitar back. A struggle that only lasted seconds as his fingers touched the keyboard part on Discordus's forehead.

"Gah!"

Axe got sent back by the wave of sound. Discordus unleashed a further pressure of sound slowing things down. Finally, the pavement begins cracking up.

"Hahaha! With my state-of-the-art defense, your ranged attacks are worthless. My 360-degree sound is impenetrable."

"Then we'll just have to get close and personal," Maigashi said.

"What?"

The monster suddenly stumbles as Maigashi and Auroa get close, avoiding some lightning while Auroa's whip trips the monster over. Discordus began rolling across the pavement as Vilevelious watched from the window.

"Our monster is struggling!" The general informed.

"I'm aware! Looks like we'll have to get involved. The time is now!"

Back outside the station, dark clouds poured across the sky as sunlight became eclipsed. A more tremendous pressure begins raining down in the middle of battle.

Max Mathesius

"What is going on? Such great force. Is this all coming from the monster?" Alistor questioned.

"No! It's something else." Auroa sensed. "We should step back."

As the party steps back, a red carpet roll in as Scrap-Ram emerges from the floor. A platoon of Whoopers followed from behind.

"It's the general again."

"Wrong!!!"

A different voice came from behind as the general moved out of the way. Emperor Vilevelious appeared before them.

"Who are you?" Maigashi pointed.

"The one and only. Yours truly, Vilevelious!"

The party stumbled back for a brief moment.

"Oh snap! Dude, it's really him?"

"You've meddled with our plans long enough. Our labyrinth must feed!"

The Emperor turned his face to Discordus, getting back up.

"Now go! Retrieve that tape!" He ordered. "Whoopers! Go and create some havoc downtown. And general, do not let anyone inside the station. Go!"

Vilevelious forces began spreading out as the party stood, fazed briefly. Finally, Discordus leaves the scene as Scrap-Ram walls off the building with his body.

"Dude! They're everywhere; we must think of something fast. And my guitar! Alistor!"

A sudden surge of confidence sparked through Alistor's eyes.

"Just leave the emperor to me...."

"Come again?" Maigashi asked.

"You heard me! The Emperor's all mine! You guys take care of the Whoopers downtown."

"Dude! You'll get destroyed out here. And what about the monster?" Axe reminded.

Viper's Labyrinth

His attention turned towards Auroa.

"Auroa! I want you to take care of the monster." He pointed. "Now go!"

"It's your funeral." Maigashi pestered.

The party dispersed, leaving Alistor to face the Emperor alone. He readied his blade, pointing it at Vilevelious.

"It's about time you showed your face. You've hidden behind your generals long enough."

"So...little boy wants to play?"

The Emperor begins to levitate in midair.

"Little!!!" He snapped. "I'll show you I'm not little."

He charges straight at the Emperor to unleash a swing, but Vilevelious easily avoids it by moving up. The Emperor begins leaving the scene.

"Catch me if you can."

"Hey, get back here!"

Alistor begins following the Emperor to the outskirt of the city. Meanwhile, Maigashi and Axe attempt to halt the Whooper's mischief downtown. Finally, Auroa pursues Discordus downtown as bystanders get drained on the way.

"Get tape! Get tape! Get tape!"

Auroa commenced downtown as the monster unleashed its pressure upon victims. The labyrinth is seen overshadowing the streets above. The Emperor continues to lead Alistor away from town. Pursuing through the woods, followed by an empty path. The Emperor then comes to a sudden stop.

"So you finally ready to fight?" Alistor pestered.

An extraordinary summit rests far from a distance.

"Like what you see?" The Emperor asked.

"What is this place?"

Vilevelious lets off a slight chuckle as he slowly descends down.

Max Mathesius

"The Shooting Star Summit, of course. This place may serve some significant importance one day, heh heh."

"What do you mean?"

"I know what you are." Vilevelious pointed. "You may be able to fool anyone, but not me."

Alistor draws out his blade.

"Enough talk! Shut up! You don't know me."

He charged at the Emperor.

"Hit me with your best shot."

Meanwhile, Axe and Maigashi arrived at a busy shopping center. The Whoopers are seen causing chaos in a women's clothing store. Finally, the two come across Cheryl and her friends.

"Hey, Cheryl!" Axe waved.

"Gah! Creeps! Give back my purse!"

She is seen tugging a purse back and forth with an enemy soldier.

"Sigh… Didn't expect to come across Cheryl's group." Maigashi groaned.

"Well, we got to help them."

The Whoopers are seen flamboyantly dressed as they jump in to surround the two. Axe and Maigashi stood side by side, ready to throw down.

"Whenever you're ready."

One block just away from Bamboo's restaurant, Auroa continues to chase Discordus down the streets.

"I can't let that monster get the tape."

Auroa took a detour through an alley. In seconds, his whip came lashing before the monster, taking it by surprise.

"You're getting on my nerve. If that's the way you want to play channeler. Then have at it."

Viper's Labyrinth

Discordus begin sending shockwaves toward him. Auroa rushed, dodging a few shots and attempting to get close, but the monster jumped back.

"Trying to get close? Think again."

The monster unleashed a wave of pressure, slowing Auroa in his tracks. The pavement around begins to crack as the foe charge back in. Discordus knocks him right down as he attempts to counter with a wind blast.

"You're more cunning than I thought."

"Ha! As I was saying. Your ranged attacks are useless." Discordus reminded. "My soundproof defense is impenetrable. And if you think that's all I can do, think again."

Discordus begin emitting gravitational pressure once more. Auroa attempts to anticipate the move but gets caught off guard. The monster starts absorbing the tension within its mouth.

"What are you up to now?"

The monster held its breath for a brief moment. Then, within seconds, vast cannonballs spew from Discordus's mouth. Auroa attempts to take cover behind a dumpster, but it gets destroyed within seconds. He tries to counter the attack with his wind but gets blown around in the open. A shock gets sent through his system as he lies paralyzed briefly.

"You like that? That's my special Shock Cannon."

Auroa slowly got back up. Slightly shaken up as he kept his ground.

"And I thought Maigashi's thunder was strong."

"You still want more?" Discordus asked.

The monster attempts to unleash its pressure again, but Auroa gets close to fire some wind from his whip.

"What did I tell ya?" The monster pestered.

Auroa suddenly disappeared for a brief moment.

"Wait, huh?"

He reappears right from the opposite side, lashing a secondary round of wind. Discordus's defense attempts to respond, but he takes damage by surprise. Sparks and smoke in the air.

"Just as I thought. A flaw in your defense." He figured.

Max Mathesius

"What! But how?"

Auroa begins briefly explaining.

"Normally, my first attack would have been deflected, but I increased the speed of my second wind to match the timing with my first."

"Come by that again?"

"You're so-called defense may have repelled any of our attacks from earlier. But if two attack lands simultaneously, your defense won't protect you. That split-second gap, in other words, means you're only capable of blocking one indirect attack per second."

Discordus hesitated for a brief second.

"Lucky shot! It's not over yet."

The monster attempts to unleash the Shock Cannon once again. However, Auroa didn't hesitate to continue his strategy rushing close to the creature.

"I must end this quickly."

As he jumps to the other side to fire his second wind, Discordus makes a slight grin. Both attacks impact, but Auroa soon becomes trapped in a paralysis state. The sound of a bone suddenly cracks as blood drips on the floor.

"Heh Heh! Bait and sink!"

The smoke clears away. A blade of lightning came right out of Discordus's mouth as it's seen pierced through Auroa's right shoulder. He let off a scream in pain before getting tossed aside the ally.

"Wasted enough time. I got a tape to get!"

Discordus leaves off as the scene cuts to Maigashi and Axe. The two are seen in women's clothing and makeup. A cold chill was felt as they wrapped the battle with the Whoopers.

"Yeah! We totally cleared them out. Ugh, something the matter, dude?"

"Something's not right," Maigashi muttered. "This is taking too long. We need to find the others and regroup."

He leaves in a hurry as Axe follows behind.

"Hey! Where do you think you're going?" Cheryl pouted.

Viper's Labyrinth

He halts for a brief second as her friends are seen emerging from under the pile of merchandise. But, unfortunately, their hair was completely ruined.

"Ugh, Cheryl. Now's not the time."

"Some help you guys are. It's all your guys' fault. I just finished my hair, and you ruined my new dress."

Axe suddenly grabs a perfume bottle right from her hands.

"I'll need to borrow this."

"Hey! Get back here."

As Axe leaves the scene, Discordus arrives at the entrance of Bamboo's place. The sound of a bell rings.

"Oh, another customer." Bamboo smiled.

Discordus spots the tape still intact within the player. Without hesitation, the monster jumps over the table. He makes a grab for Bamboo's radio. Pulling it right off the wall as Bamboo reacted.

"What? My radio!"

Bamboo intercepts, grabbing hold of the player from the other side. The two are seen yanking it back and forth.

"It's mine!"

Meanwhile, back with Alistor...

"Heh! Your attacks are so predictable." The Emperor pestered.

Alistor is seen swinging his blade mindlessly as the Emperor continues to dodge without effort. He then resorted to his final attack.

"Star Breaker!"

Alistor rushed in with the energy surging from his blade. Vilevelious didn't hesitate to move out of the way. With one hand, the Emperor quickly reduced his attack to nothing within seconds. Then, holding the tip of his blade with one finger, Alistor got sent flying back.

"Is that the only move you got? Don't tell me. It's true, isn't it?"

"No way! My Star Breaker...."

Max Mathesius

"Face it!" The Emperor laughed. "You're no match against me."

He quickly got right up to attack as the Emperor turned his back.

"I'll never give up."

Before Alistor can fight back, a root suddenly trips him over. He falls flat on his face as the Emperor continues to laugh away.

"I wasted enough time with you."

Vilevelious fires a set of lasers as Alistor quickly takes cover behind a tree. Unfortunately, some roots and branches begin grabbing hold of him.

"What the heck!"

He slashed away the roots stumbling back into the open.

"Now, to show what I can really do." The Emperor grinned.

More roots emerge from under the ground. Snaking its way as he struggled to hack them down. He was entangled within a matter of seconds.

"What kind of power is that?" Alistor questioned.

"I hold power to manipulate Wood. The life-giving element. An essential foundation in nature."

"Then why are you trying to destroy it?"

"Hmm, I never did such a thing."

"Liar! How do you explain those monster attacks?" Alistor objected back.

The Emperor continued to laugh for a moment.

"Hahaha. Just like your father, but with the stupidity of the reckless mother. Mr. Rare had this set from the very start. But why in this timeline?"

"What? You know something about my parents. Tell me!" Alistor demanded.

"Whoops! Almost slipped that one right there. So soon, you'll be joining them."

Before the Emperor can continue, a bottle explodes by them. A pleasant scent expels through the air.

Viper's Labyrinth

"What is this? This smell."

Vilevelious loses his grasp on Alistor as he backs away to cover himself from the smell. It was none other than Maigashi and Axe arriving at the scene.

"Gnarly, dude! Knew that perfume would come in handy."

"I did not expect that to work." Maigashi shrugged as he lowered his bow.

Vilevelious starts to back away from the smell.

"Too nice!" The Emperor gagged. "You'll pay for this! Till next time."

He immediately teleports away as Alistor regroups with them. He gives a strange look at both of them.

"Um…Why are you guys dressed in girl's cloth?" Alistor asked.

"Don't ask…." Maigashi mumbled. "Let us head back to that restaurant."

Meanwhile, Bamboo continues to engage in a tug-of-war against Discordus over the radio at the restaurant. Alistor and the others made their way back quickly downtown. They immediately spot Auroa by the ally.

"Auroa!" Alistor gasped.

The party was stunned as blood seeped through Auroa's shoulder from an open wound. He struggled to maintain balance as Axe and Maigashi quickly helped him.

"We need to get you to the hospital." Axe suggested.

"Not yet! The monster!" Auroa muttered.

Maigashi temporarily reseals his wound with a cloth.

"Where is it? Back at the restaurant?" Alistor pointed.

The party arrives at Bamboo's restaurant in a matter of time. The tug of war escalates outside the front street of the restaurant.

"This is my radio. Get your own!"

"That tape is mine!"

Max Mathesius

Maigashi suddenly fires a shot destroying the radio. The cassette tape was reduced to nothing as Discordus stood fazed in Shock. Axe jumps in to disarm the monster knocking it down.

"Awesome! I got my guitar back." Lights suddenly shot out from his instrument. "Whoah! Gnarly, this thing can now shoot lasers."

"That radio cost me $29.99." Bamboo cried.

The party quickly surrounds the monster as Auroa explains the situation to them.

"Discordus can only repel one attack within a given time. However, it should be enough to finish it if we all attack simultaneously from multiple angles."

"No problem!" Alistor said.

"Remember! At the same time and not a second too short." Maigashi reminded. "On a count of three. ONE! TWO!"

The four ready their weapons as the monster got right back up.

"THREE!!!"

Discordus get impacted from four sides. First, massive sparks burst right out from its body with smoke. Then, an explosion commenced sending it flying through the air. Leaving only a tiny twinkling glint in the sky.

"We finally did it...." Auroa whispered as he got to the ground, losing consciousness.

"The wounds open!" Axe shouted. "We need to get to a hospital. Fast!"

Moments later, the party was waiting by the medical center. Alistor nervously walked back and forth. A feeling of guilt on his hands while the others were patiently seated. A nurse then opens the doors.

"So...Is he going to be ok?" Alistor asked.

Auroa emerged right out from the doors behind. An enormous cast wrapped around the right side of his shoulder.

"My battle against that monster left my right arm completely dislocated. Sorry for being a bit careless."

"No! It's not your fault." Alistor nodded. "It was me. Things got out of hand today. With the Emperor arriving, I wasn't thinking straight."

Auroa let off a brief smile.

Viper's Labyrinth

"Well, the good news is Discordus didn't hit my good arm. So I may still be able to battle, but not effectively."

"No!" Maigashi objected. "You get some rest for now. We weren't prepared this time, but we'll be ready next time."

"Yeah, dude! No worries."

Axe's demo tape suddenly airs on the radio once more. Their mood lifted back in seconds as they rocked out to the song. Forgetting all their troubles as they head back to the restaurant.

"Tonight! Dinner is on the house." Bamboo jumps.

Meanwhile, back at the abandoned theatre…

"Discordus may be down but don't count it out just yet. In a matter of days, we'll be back."

General Scrap-Ram is seen repairing the monster while Vilevelious contacts from the other side of the screen.

"That plan worked better than expected, general. So when you finish the repairs, I have a new monster for you to try out." The Emperor announced.

"A new monster? How so?" The general questioned.

"Let's just say. It will amp up the situation!"

The silhouette of a new monster appears behind the Emperor.

Later that following night, Alistor is seen sitting on the top balcony. At home, reflecting back on everything that has happened so far. From his fateful encounter with Mr. Rare to his first victory against Mushogun. The Emperor suddenly crossed his mind.

"Vilevelious…What do you really know?"

A peaceful breeze of wind passes by. The scene ends with Alistor gazing upon the crescent moonlight. Pondering with many questions still left to be answered.

Max Mathesius

Chapter 11

Eternal Performance:

Lovers of the Moonlight Sky

Early morning downtown on the opening hour, Bamboo and Axe barge into the restaurant to make a sudden announcement.

"What are you guys so excited about?" Alistor asked.

"The best plan yet!" Bamboo jumped.

"This sounds shady. Well, keep me out of this."

Alistor turned the other cheek around.

"No, dude! This one's legit."

"I'm all ears." Maigashi entered.

Axe begins explaining to them.

"Ever since my demo tape played on that radio, I became an instant hit overnight. My bandmates even contacted me the other night. So we're totally gonna be hosting a big rock concert."

Alistor stumbled for one brief second before objecting.

"What!!! But Bamboo, you promised you guys would train me this weekend. So this is not going to help me at all."

"A concert sounds like a splendid idea." Auroa agreed.

Viper's Labyrinth

He continues objecting to their decision while Bamboo passes fliers to them. Then, finally, Maigashi goes over to knock some sense into him.

"Come on, don't be a killjoy."

"We even got the paperwork all filed here." Bamboo presented.

The rest of them in the room was excited, except for him.

"Well, I'm still not going. It's a waste of time." Alistor refused.

"Hey! I paid a premium to rent this spot. You're gonna help whether you like it or not." Bamboo ordered as he felt belittled.

"Ok! Ok! Fine, I'll help. Where will the concert be held at?"

He began looking over the content of the papers.

"The concert will be held at the Kabuki Coliseum."

"Kabuki Coliseum?"

"Yep!" Bamboo nodded. "A place that holds a significant amount of history. Tell you more about it later."

Meanwhile, back with Aggerona…

"It's done! Finally! At last." The emperor announced.

General Scrap Ram appears on the other screen.

"The repairs are complete, my lord. May I present Discordus 2.0!"

A different color variant of Discordus emerged from behind the screen. Vilevelious applauds for his finished work.

"Now, to get to business."

He presents a new cassette tape to the monster.

"Didn't we try that plan before?" The general questioned.

"I'm aware, general. But that was our first time, so they won't expect us to try the same plan twice."

He sends the tape over to the monster.

Max Mathesius

"I'm not sure if this is the best idea. Discordus nearly failed last time attempting."

"But he was able to injure one of their friends." The emperor reminded.

"True, but still. Maybe we should try something more passive?" The general suggested.

Vilevelious heard his general out for a brief moment.

"Not a problem. I have something that will cover our monster's weakness this time."

"Oh?"

The lights dimmed out.

"Amp Master! Come forth!"

A new monster enters the spotlight. Clunking back and forth, the room suddenly shook up. A metal sound screeched in the air.

"I nearly forgot."

"Yes! With Amp Master, Discordus power increases by tenfold." The emperor announced before catching a paper sent by the general.

He looks over the ad for the concert.

"I wanted to bring this up before you announced the plan. Thanks to Discordus's last slip-up, many have become intrigued by Axe's song. So many are bound to show, and the tickets are selling out fast."

"Even better! Our monsters will play this tape at the event. So we better get ready."

Meanwhile, back with the rest, the party sells concert tickets while Axe chats it up with Cheryl.

"Two thousand and counting. At this rate, I'll be rolling in the money." Bamboo spun.

"So, tell me something about the Kabuki Coliseum," Alistor asked.

Bamboo went into deep thought for a brief moment. Then, clearing his throat as he began to recall the story.

The Kabuki Coliseum…

Viper's Labyrinth

"Many battles have taken place on those very grounds. It was said to be where the Great Moon and Hundred Hands Emperor clashed. Also, rumor has it, he proposed to some lucky gal under the stars."

"Ok."

"I'm not done." Bamboo snapped. "Other than that. This place was known for its great performances. There was said to be once a great performer. No one knew his name, but they said he lived for the spotlight."

"The spotlight?"

"Yes! He would put on many shows daily. He would take the stage with his puppets and reenact famous battles such as Moons."

"Tell me more."

"Not only did he perform, but he was an exceptional battler during his time." Bamboo continued. "Offering his service to the highest bidder."

"What kind of weapon did he wield?" Alistor asked.

"Puppets....ahem. Kabuki was known for using poison to his advantage. He would concoct them himself. A warrior by day and performer by night. He had it all, but sadly...he had plenty of heat on his shoulder."

Things suddenly turned quiet.

"What happened in the end?"

"In the end, he fell by the poison he used slipped into his drink. So he passed before his very time came."

"I see..."

Just as Bamboo wrapped up the story, three figures approached them. A surprised look was on Axe's face.

"Dude! You guys came."

It was none other than his former bandmates. Reunited once more as he introduced them to the rest of the party.

"Long time no see, Axe."

"Hey, guys! Uh, so yeah, these are my bros. Blade, Lance, and Bow."

Max Mathesius

Each member of the band begins introducing themselves to the party.

"Blade Tempest, Bass guitarist."

"Lance Yamada, group's Drummer."

"And I'm Bow Kaito, the Keyboardist."

Axe and his bandmates then huddled up for a brief second. Then, in a matter of seconds, the group begins to pose.

"Power Hair Metal Band, Steel Specters!"

Alistor was lost for a brief second.

"With Axe as our leading vocals, we'll rock at the Kabuki Coliseum tomorrow night."

"The grand opportunity we've been waiting for. Our big Break."

Bamboo abruptly breaks up the conversation.

"Back to work! We've got more tickets to sell."

"Yes, sir!!!"

Axe's bandmates leave the scene with a handful of tickets.

"How many more are we supposed to sell?" Alistor asked.

"About 8000 more."

"Say what?"

"You heard me! Get moving." Bamboo ordered.

"And we're selling these for less than 700 yen." Maigashi nodded. "Come on, let's get this over with. I'm starting to get hungry."

Alistor hurries off with Auroa and Maigashi to sell the remaining tickets for the rest of the day. Hours later, the party is seen checking out backstage. Meeting up with Axe and his band the night before the performance.

"Man, why are there so many puppets back here? It gives me the chills." Alistor shook.

"Come take a look outside." Auroa pointed.

Viper's Labyrinth

Two giant Kabuki statues are seen fixed within the center stage. An astonished look was on their faces as they took one glance at the massive arena. The stage lighting suddenly turns on. Fog from a smoke machine begins flowing through the ground.

"Getting a preview?" Axe entered.

"You guys actually did all this?" Alistor marveled.

Layers of equipment, from Amps to sophisticated soundboards, occupy a part of the stage. The band members are seen setting their instruments in place.

"Tomorrow night is gonna be something, dudes…."

"Hey! Let's warm up with a practice jam." Blade suggested.

"Just like the old times."

Axe and his band begin a session while Alistor and the rest watch for the remainder of the night.

Later that night…

"Good! It's all clear."

Vilevelious arrives with Scrap Ram at the empty coliseum. The Whoopers tamper with the equipment on stage.

"Now, plant that amp right over there." The emperor points out.

Four Whoopers carried over the amp backstage.

They placed it down gently, and it immediately began to emit a dark aura. Then, negative energy starts infecting the arena.

"Tomorrow will spell the sound of their demise." The general laughed.

Back somewhere at Alistor's home, he is asleep. Visions of the emperor appear before to torment him. Roots begin grabbing hold of him once more.

"No! Not like this again."

He slashed his way out with his blade, but more roots continued to sprout from the ground. Snaking its way as he struggled to hack them down. He was entangled within a matter of seconds.

"Just like your father, but with the stupidity of the reckless mother."

Max Mathesius

"What? You know something about my parents. Tell me!" Alistor demanded.

"Soon, you'll be joining them."

The roots quickly wrapped him up to his neck. He begins to lose all hope.

"I just don't have what it takes...."

"Face it! You'll never have what it takes. Now be gone!"

The roots suddenly cover his face as he screams in agony. Then, in a split matter of seconds, he finds himself awake.

"What a horrible dream...."

He opens the window for some fresh air. Looking out at the stars above, he ponders again about his past.

The following night later, the concert was underway. Lines from all across packed the entrance, filling the arena within minutes. Bamboo was seen selling food at the corner, while Alistor and the rest were seen backstage. Finally, Axe makes his way to the stage while the opening music starts playing.

"Dudes and Dudettes! Let's get started."

Axe and the Steel Specters began performing their song. Rifts from the electric guitars start playing as the crowd cheers. The sound of the drum thundered as the keyboard followed along. Axe began singing.

"Man, look at him go." Maigashi pointed.

A guitar solo begins playing.

"I'll be sure to pick up an album later," Auroa assured.

As the first song ended, the audience cheers roared through the air. Then, Axe goes to make an announcement.

"Looks like we're having a good time tonight. You ready for some more?"

The cheer continued on.

"This next song is for all you ladies out there."

Just before the next song had the chance to begin, familiar laughter was heard through the speakers. Alistor hesitated momentarily as it was none other than Vilevelious making his way to the stage. He grabs the mic right from Axe's hand.

Viper's Labyrinth

"You may have won the battle, but the war is far from over."

The labyrinth materializes in the air above the Kabuki Coliseum. The sound of booing commenced all around.

"Insubordination will not be tolerated."

The emperor responds with a blast of lasers dispersing the audience. Panic soon commences as the audience attempts to escape, but a wall of junk seals off all the exits.

"Escaping is useless." The general pestered.

Alistor and the party confront the emperor on stage.

"Not this again. Can't we ever enjoy something without you guys bothering?" Maigashi asked.

The emperor called for his monster to the stage.

"Discordus!"

Discordus arrived down on stage with the cassette tape in hand once more.

"You again? But didn't we already beat you?" Alistor recalled.

The monster quickly inserts the tape into a ready player nearby. Large wires connected to an amp nearby. The sound of the emperor's song played through the arena. The audience in the background is seen drained as the unbearable sound plays. The band members covered their ears in pain as Axe made his way to the party.

"Dude! This monster is ruining our show. We have to put a stop to this."

"Do try." The emperor pestered.

Axe, Maigashi, and Alistor surround Discordus once again.

"Just like last time. On a count of three, we'll fire simultaneously." Maigashi ordered.

As the three readied to fire, Discordus stood in place without fear.

"Three!"

The attacks impact the monster, but a surprise is suddenly in store for them. In seconds, Alistor witnessed their attacks wholly absorbed, leaving Discordus unharmed.

"What happened?"

Axe suddenly spots something emerging from backstage.

"Dude! It's coming from over there."

The large amp begins taking shape in the background. A second monster formed before Alistor's very eyes.

"What the heck is that?" Maigashi hesitated.

Three large power cables are attached to Discordus from this new monster. In addition, a battery pack is seen attached from behind.

"I introduce to you Amp Master."

The monster takes the stage intimidating the party with its mass size. But then, things begin shaking up from the sound of Discordus as the general rams through them, unexpectedly knocking them back.

"Damn! One of us has to handle this general."

"These numbers aren't looking good." Maigashi hesitated.

"What do we do now?" Alistor asked.

"I don't know...."

The three found themselves cornered as the emperor laughed from a distance. General Scrap Ram begins spreading his junk-like body across the arena. Just before the general can make the next move, a burst of wind magic suddenly halts him in his path.

"I'll handle the general," Auroa said.

The party regains its ground as Auroa steps in.

"No! You can't be serious," Alistor said. "You're still injured from the last fight."

He attempts to pull him back, but Auroa continues to step forward. Confronting the general without any hesitation.

"Do not worry. Go and take care of the monsters and that song. I got a score to settle anyway."

"No! You can't!!!" He objected.

He continued being persistent, but Maigashi suddenly pulled him back.

Viper's Labyrinth

"It's ok...."

"No, it's not. I can't bear another guilt if something worse happens."

"I know, but this is his fight. You'll just be getting in his way."

A focused look was now on Auroa's face.

"Are you sure?"

"Yeah... Auroa will be fine." Maigashi assured. "I know that look on his face, but now all we can do is focus on these monsters. In fact, I have a plan."

The scene focuses back on the two monsters. The general begins leaving the stage as Auroa pursues after him.

"You do?"

Maigashi suddenly points his bow toward Amp Master.

"If we can't hurt Discordus. Then we'll have to focus everything we got on the source powering it."

"Locked and ready, dude."

"Let's do this."

Meanwhile, Scrap Ram makes his way toward the outer perimeter of the coliseum. Face to face with the injured wind channeler as bystanders around cleared out. A large fountain sits gently at the center while the two Kabuki statues stand firm from a distance.

"Hahaha. With that broken limb, this fight will be a piece of cake."

"I wouldn't be so sure yet."

Auroa pulls out his whip from his left hand as the general build a junk ball. Within moments a wave of scraps and debris is sent flying toward him.

"DIE!!!"

The debris impacts Auroa, but he emerges unscratched. Instead, a barrier of air is seen tossing the scraps aside.

"Are we ready?" The general smirked.

"I'm just getting started." Auroa pestered.

Max Mathesius

Back with Alistor and the rest, the three fire their best attacks at Amp Master. But, again, smoke and explosions set off from the impact.

"Right at the core!" Axe snapped.

Amp Master emerged utterly unscratched.

"No way!" Alistor gasped.

"Not even a single dent. Even from our best attacks!" Maigashi pounds.

The three continued to feel intimidated by Amp Master as the song played on. The emperor further mocks them.

"Ha, haha! Fools! Amp Master's defense is composed of state-of-the-art Moon Titanium. Greater than any shields imaginable."

Alistor begins backing away.

"Give it up! Amp Master with Discordus, having their powers in conjunction with one another, increases their total by tenfold. You can't win."

Discordus unleashed tremendous pressure on them. Within seconds, Discordus absorbs it once more, holding its mouth shut. Maigashi and Axe got into a defensive stance anticipating the monster's move.

"The Shock Cannon again?"

Discordus faced his head upwards, spewing his attack this time in the air. Then, to their surprise, a great ball of lightning begins dispersing into pieces across. Hundreds of Shock Cannons came raining down at the three as Alistor stumbled in panic.

"Ha, haha! That's Discordus Neutron Shock Cannon technique." Vilevelious bragged. "Face it! You've lost."

The three were seen down but not out, barely with some power left to fight. The emperor continues to laugh away as the music plays on, draining energy from countless victims across while the labyrinth feeds above.

"It can't end like this...." Maigashi struggled.

"I know, dude...Total Wipeout."

Just as Axe got right up, he glanced at the battery attached to Amp Master. The monster is seen fixed in place as steam smokes out from a power box.

"I got it!"

Viper's Labyrinth

"You do?" Maigashi asked.

"Yeah, dudes!"

Axe reached for his guitar once more. Connecting it through a stereo device as his bandmates regain consciousness. The three made their way to the sound equipment.

"You know how to beat it?" Alistor wondered.

An assured look was on his face.

"If we can't break them from the outside, we'll have to hit them from the inside." Axe pointed.

An astonished look was on the rest as questions began getting up.

"So, how will we pull this?" Maigashi wondered.

"Through sound, of course. Through my years of rocking, a smoking amp only means one thing. When the music continues to play hard, the battery will leak. Imploding everything on the inside. So just follow my lead."

Axe readies his guitar as his bandmates take their position on the stage, setting the wires by the equipment. Alistor and Maigashi got in place as he made the cue.

"What are you fools up to now?" The emperor questioned.

Meanwhile, back at the battle with Scrap Ram…

"Ha, haha! What's wrong, channeler? You've been on the defense this whole time."

Auroa deflects another round of junk hurled towards his way. Tossing the debris far aside from the flick of his whip.

"In due time, general. Due time…"

He grips tight to his wind whip as another round of junk impacts his barrier. Then, bracing on by the skin of his teeth, the general brought forth his next wave of assault.

"Ha! You've got nothing. With that bad arm, you're only delaying the inevitable." The general mocked. "This next wave will end you!!!"

The general unleashed his second wave at Auroa as he embraced the worst. Piles of junk begin crashing down like a tidal wave.

Back with Axe and the rest, the party had everything set in place. Alistor and Maigashi are given the cue to press a couple buttons.

Max Mathesius

"Blade! Lance! Bow! LET'S ROCK!!!"

Axe and the Steel Specters begin playing. Two forces of sound collide in place, shaking the entire coliseum up. Vilevelious starts covering his ears as the labyrinth is no longer feeding.

"Gah! They're interfering with my sound. Amp Master! Make it louder."

The monster begins cranking the volume up. Absorbing all the sound Axe and his group unleashed.

"Dudes! We got to play louder."

Axe gives Maigashi the cue to increase the sound. Thus, the labyrinth stops draining energy once again.

"Maximum Power!" The emperor commanded.

Amp Master was seen smoking up as the song played at the max.

"We need to go all the way."

Axe's guitar begins to crack as the smoke spews from the intense playing. Then, finally, he gives Alistor the cue for the final push.

"But your guitar might not be able to take this." Alistor feared.

"It doesn't matter. It's now or never. Do it, dude?"

Without hesitation, Alistor pressed the final button bringing Axe's guitar to the max. Pink and blue lightning rain across the arena as Amp Master pushes on. Ultimately, the battery pack gives out as it explodes, short-circuiting the fuse on Discordus.

"What?" The emperor's jaws dropped as his monsters mindlessly stumbled in confusion.

Both monsters' insides crash as circuit boards and wires spark out. Axe's guitar suddenly catches on fire as he makes the final note.

"SHAKA BRAH!!!"

Axe hurls his flaming guitar toward the monsters as it explodes in place. Two great explosions commenced bringing Vilevelious's song to an end.

"Curse you!"

Alistor steps up to confront the emperor once again.

Viper's Labyrinth

"You're done!"

"As much I would like to stay for idle chit-chatter, I have pressing matters to attend to. So, general! I leave the rest up to you."

With one step back, the emperor leaves within a split second. Axe Winston was seen lying flat on the floor, completely wiped out, as his bandmates gathered at his side.

"You did good, Axe...."

"Blade....Lance....Bow...We totally did it."

The bandmates go retrieve what's left of his guitar.

"You end up sacrificing your guitar. The one thing you treasured most." Alistor sadly felt.

Everyone was bummed out briefly, but Axe's spirit quickly lifted as he stood right up. Then, holding the only piece left, he tossed it aside.

"It's alright, man...Because the music was with me this whole time. Dudes! We totally rocked!"

Axe makes a big jump in the air.

"Hey! We need to check back with Auroa." Maigashi reminded.

"Let's go then!"

The secondary wave of scraps gets tossed aside. The general attempts to fire another round of junk but suddenly pauses. Scrap-Ram's hand blindly traces across the floor for any material but comes empty-handed.

"Wait a minute...."

The general desperately searched his body. Salvaging for any material, but was now left with a skeletal frame. His cores are exposed in the open.

"Just as I suspected...." Auroa gestured. "Your power's limited to the amount of substance around you."

"But how? I had the advantage."

"We've been battling since the day Axe came along. The ruins, the nursery, the theatre, and now the Kabuki Coliseum."

Auroa suddenly lowers his barrier as the wind quickly shifts in his favor. Then, a tornado begins spinning, pulling the general in.

Max Mathesius

"What? NO!" Scrap-Ram shouted.

"You've exploited your last resource. Now it's time to end this."

He summons his trusty whip to unleash a massive tornado. The vortex escalates, engulfing the general's body as Auroa takes one final dive.

"Raizen Hurricane!"

"WAAAAAAAHHH!!!"

An explosion commenced bringing the battle to an end. The labyrinth above immediately dissipates, bringing the sky back into place. Auroa finds himself by an open field outside the coliseum. Lying by a haystack, he spots the third piece of the mirror nearby.

"The third one finally, at last. Huh? A green gem?"

He retrieves the shard finding the gem right under it as Axe and the rest quickly arrive at the scene in moments.

"We're more than halfway there."

Bamboo is seen fiddling with the gems.

"Well, we still haven't figured out what these gems do?" Maigashi reminded.

"Maybe the generals are into jewelry. It could be something like friendship bracelets." Bamboo thought. "Very pretty, after all."

"I highly doubt that's the reason."

The rest of Axe's band finally catches up as the group celebrates their successful performance despite the attack.

"Dinner on the house tonight," Bamboo announced.

"Can't wait, dude! Whip up more of that bodacious jelly."

The following day, the party waited outside as Axe packed his last bag. His bandmates were seen loading the truck right up.

"So...I guess you're leaving," Alistor muttered.

"Yeah, dude. It's time I hit the road again. Got another gig in the next city thanks to this concert. You've been all so good to me. I'll never forget this."

He turned away for one brief moment, silence in the air. Bamboo is seen wiping a tear off his eye. Unable to hold back, Axe turns around to hug the party.

"And I'll miss your cooking." He cried.

The sound of a car beeps, breaking the moment. His ex was seen waiting in a particular vehicle along with the others.

"Come on! Axe, hurry up!"

"Uh. Coming, Cheryl."

Axe stumbled his way into her car. Jumping into the backseat as he took one final glance back at them. The sound of the engine sparked.

"I'll be sure to visit."

"Take Care!" Bamboo waved.

Axe and Cheryl's band disappear into the setting horizon.

Max Mathesius

Chapter 12

Enter Admiral Bombshell

By a distant realm someplace far out of the way... A reunion between several evil forces gathers at a banquet. The majority of the guests were only visible as a silhouette. Emperor Vilevelious mingles with a couple dark figures before him, chatting it up.

"Oh, Vile dear, you must come out from that maze more often. Destroying is soooooooo last season. I shall make the world fabulous, Hun."

"Well, you haven't even done much or even succeeded in capturing a pure target in your turf. You got nothing." He argued back.

The dark figure brushed his hair while the Snake emperor ranted back.

"Ah hush, true art takes time and planning. My fashion will one day be top-of-the-line in Lavendhite. And once that happens, I'll send a memo."

The other dark figure steps in. A man was barely visible, with long dark hair and tentacles slithering behind.

"And you're having any success stealing energy for your labyrinth? From what I see, more than half of your generals are already gone; hoo hoo."

A chart appears behind the emperor, showcasing his progress. Gossip begins to quickly spread across the room.

"Only 45% towards your goal? That's kind of embarrassing; hoo hoo."

"Shut up!"

Viper's Labyrinth

He pounds on the table.

"Vile dear, you're barely even halfway feeding that labyrinth. It's too slow, even if you did collect enough energy. Have you considered another strategy?"

The snake king got right up.

"The last three generals were a minor setback. Especially Mushogun! This time I have a real general that will get the job done."

The crowd was skeptical of his claim.

"What will make this next one any different compared to your last? Who, by the way?"

"Admiral Bombshell. Come forth!"

Moist fills the room and a dampened mist of energy bursts into the scene. Admiral Bombshell appears before them. The room suddenly became silent. His anchor drags across the ground with the sound of the chain dangling.

"You called my lord?"

A jealous feeling is expressed by the other figures.

"What? Him? It can't be."

"I couldn't even get him to stay on my side."

"Admiral Bombshell! You are now in charge of gathering energy from where Scrap Ram left off. You have a plan ready?" The emperor asked.

"Already set in motion."

The Admiral takes his leave, vanishing from the mist in the room.

"Don't let me down."

Meanwhile, back at the restaurant, Alistor arrives with a bunch of mail. Finally, Maigashi and Auroa took a break from their shifts while Bamboo skimmed through the letters.

"Let's see some bills, junk mail, and more junk mail. My catalog and, oh, a letter for you."

Bamboo hands the letter over to Alistor.

"It's from Sairori."

Max Mathesius

"Well, what are you waiting for? Open it." Maigashi orders.

He opens the letter, and Sairori's voice comes to his mind.

To Alistor and his new companions...

Hope you are faring well with your battles. As your master, I'm sorry to say I'll be gone much longer than anticipated.

I wish I could have stayed to further train you, but I'm needed elsewhere now. Lavendhite is a complete war zone; you are still young and unprepared. Aside from that, hopefully, you are learning some things with Chef Bamboo.

I'm aware you expressed distaste for training under a chef. I know it's difficult, but please, you have to understand. No matter where you train, you must make the best of it. Remember, you can learn from the best but won't be guaranteed a job.

P.S. By the way, I have an old friend who just came back from his journey. I have informed him, and he may greatly help your team. Please check his calling card attached below this mail.

Yours truly: Sairori.

The letter ends from there. Alistor took a moment to look over the calling card clipped at the end. A skull insignia marked with a number on the card.

"Mr. Tannen. Top class Detective for hire. What?" Alistor became lost for a brief second.

"Well, give the number a call," Maigashi suggested.

He took a moment to make the call. A silence occurred for a brief moment, but no answer was on the line. He tried once more.

"Sorry, but the number you called is no longer in service."

Auroa took a close look at the card. A date is set on the card.

"It seems there is a date set right below for his service. From the years 69-75. The number expired, it seems?"

"Well, so much for that. Now what..." Alistor sighed.

Just as Alistor is about to leave, Bamboo suddenly brings out a package to present to them.

"It's a package for you guys."

Viper's Labyrinth

They didn't hesitate to open it. Filled with confetti, Alistor finds a small pumpkin, a candy box, and a card attached.

"It's an invitation. To a costume party of some sort?"

"In the middle of July? But it's not Halloween." Maigashi said.

"Well, you can count me out."

Alistor loses interest in the invitation, drifting away as Bamboo looks over the card for himself.

"It's settled then! We are all going." Bamboo announced.

The party stumbled back for a brief moment.

"What? You can't be serious. How is this going to benefit my training?" Alistor abruptly asks.

A severe look was in Bamboo's eyes. He suddenly felt belittled.

"Well, sometimes you need to enjoy some of the fun things offered in life. Don't take everything too seriously. It's not good to strain yourself. Plus, parties are nice! I never get invited to any, and this is a first. I'll just close for the day. So this is your next mission."

"What choice do we have?" Maigashi sighed.

"Come on! This might be fun." Auroa cheered.

And so Bamboo closed for the day. The party leaves town for the event. A few hours pass, and the night quickly falls. They arrive in costumes at the entrance of an abandoned manor. A crowd of guests waiting outside.

"Is this really the right address?" Maigashi checks over the flier.

"No one seems to be entering? Is there something wrong?"

Bamboo didn't hesitate to approach the front. He knocked on the door, but there was no answer. So he hits once again, and the door suddenly creeps right open. They enter the house, and the light turns on. Music begins playing in the background. A line of waiters in ghost outfits greets them.

"What?"

They were lost for the moment but quickly blended in a matter of minutes. Then, finally, they stumble upon a section of barrels filled with apples. A mysterious man in a barrel outfit approaches them.

"Come over and dunk them. Give it a try! A free prize!"

Neither of the three wanted to try, as the party only noticed the host's fancy mustache.

"Sorry, but I'm not in the mood to get wet." Maigashi pestered.

"I'll go!" Bamboo volunteered.

They watch as he takes a dunk into one of the water-filled barrels. The barrel suddenly explodes, shattering to their surprise. After that, everyone got wet and doused.

"What just happened?" Bamboo confusedly asked.

"Ah, sorry, but not a winner. But here, take this complimentary prize for playing."

He hands a cheap lollipop over to Bamboo. The party heads right to the tables with food and drinks. They mingle with the other crowds in costumes as the man in the barrel costume takes cover behind a curtain.

"All is going according to plan, Admiral. The room is filled. When will the monsters be ready?"

The Admiral was on the other side of the screen.

"In due time. Continue to entertain our guests. Keep them busy."

"Will do, Admiral!"

The music then got louder as the crowd danced the night away. The smoke of fog fills the floor as the neon lights shine on. A giant disco ball is fixed at the top. As the hours passed, Barrel man kept the crowd busy with cheap games and karaoke.

One moment later....

"What do you mean we can't leave? We had enough, and it's getting late." One person yelled.

"Who do you think you are? I'm getting tired."

Alistor and the other three overhear a small crowd complaining by the doors. The barreled one laughs at them mockingly.

"Who am I? I'm Barrel Man! And the party just started."

They suddenly hear a big shaking sound in the room.

Viper's Labyrinth

"Ah, just on time."

All the exits inside the manor were sealed shut. Then, a colossal ship comes crashing through the roof. The disco ball shatters, revealing a skull draining energy away from the crowd as panic commences.

"What is the meaning of this?" Alistor asked.

"Huh ha! Your very demise! The names Barrel Man! And don't forget it."

The ghostly waiters removed their disguises.

"Just as I figure...enemy Whoopers," Auroa said.

"And yet another trap we fell into. Sigh...just great." Maigashi nodded.

Alistor pulls his blade out at the Barrel Man.

"Oh no, I'm not your opponent for today. I'm just the mere host." Barrel Man explained as he geared their attention toward the ship above.

A massive monster with a witch hat plows on them from above. Taken by surprise, the party is knocked down by the sudden entrance. Bamboo goes to take cover from behind a table.

"The name is Kinetica. And your energy is all mine."

Maigashi and Auroa got right back up. Unfortunately, Alistor was injured as the monster got close.

"Damn you. I'm getting sick of this." Maigashi fires an electrical blast at the monster but suddenly loses his breath.

"What's wrong?" Auroa asked.

Barrel Man laughs at them.

"Haha, you fools have exhausted yourselves from too much partying. Just as the Admiral planned."

He could only watch for a brief moment resting to regain some will to fight. Kinetica grabs hold of Alistor and begins sapping his energy away.

Auroa quickly breaks Kinetica's grasp on Alistor with a wind blast. He pulls him away from the battle.

"You're still able to fight?"

Max Mathesius

"I happen to take a five-minute break every hour. So I still have some energy left." Auroa briefly explained.

Kinetica began firing a ray of beams at them. Auroa blocks her incoming attacks with his wind shielding them.

"Well, look at the time. That's my cue! And I got to get going." Barrel Man announced. "Sorry to say I must leave, but here's a parting gift."

Barrel Man presses a switch causing all the barrels in the corner to explode. A huge gaping hole is revealed before teleporting away from the scene.

"You can't keep playing defense forever. We need a plan." Alistor suggested.

"At this rate, we're at a disadvantage the longer we stay inside. We need some open space; our best bet is to get outside from that hole left behind." Auroa pointed out.

"We got nothing to lose."

The three of them make a run outside as Kinetica follows them. A fog begins to build around them as they lose sight of the monster for a brief moment.

"Just where are we?"

They took a moment to study their surroundings. Finally, the smoke slightly clears away, revealing a row of tombstones.

"Looks like some sort of cemetery. We must be somewhere behind the manor. So keep your guard up."

Auroa took a few steps behind the graves. His leg suddenly bumps into one of them, causing the ground below him to shake. The tombstone below bursts out from the ground before he can react.

"What the hell. Don't worry, I got this." Maigashi fires a few shots at the object behind him. "Yes! A direct hit."

The smoke from his attack clears away, revealing a second monster.

"What is that?"

A monster composed of tombstones stares down at them. Levitating in the air, the demon grips tight around Auroa's body to drain his energy.

"Zeus Geist at your call."

Kinetica reappears in the scene.

Viper's Labyrinth

"No use running, haha. Just give it up."

Alistor and Maigashi were surrounded by two monsters. Auroa continues to struggle while the monster drains him away.

"We have to do something."

"Yeah, but what?" Alistor wondered.

"Just attack me now. Don't hesitate. Just do it." Auroa suggested to them.

Alistor rushed in while Maigashi kept Kinetica busy for a brief moment. Then, he leaps into the air as his blade fills with power.

"Star Breaker!"

His attack came towards Auroa. Zeus Geist immediately loses control in the air as the winds shift significantly in Auroa's favor. Changing how it faced, the attack rams straight behind the monster forcing it to let go. The beast came crashing down to the ground.

"Are you okay?"

Auroa took a moment to hold his neck, regaining breath.

"The battles are not over yet."

Zeus Geist was back up. Maigashi came stumbling back from his battle with Kinetica. Both monsters circle around them.

"I'm losing ground. So we have to pull further back."

Zeus Geist suddenly pulls out its scythe, intimidating Alistor. Lightning rains on them as they fall flat to the ground.

"This is pointless. We need a way out of this."

Before Zeus Geist could attack, Auroa breaks open a fog sphere to confuse both monsters.

"Hey? Where did they go?"

The three make a run for some cover. The party stumbles into a ditch to regain breath. Both monsters continuously scout around. Finally, they hear the sounds of unsuspecting victims from the party being drained.

"Nothing we can do for those people at the moment." Auroa nodded.

Max Mathesius

"Well, we can't hide forever. The enemy will eventually find us." Maigashi noted. "So, any ideas?"

Auroa took notice of the card in Alistor's pocket. So he brings up the calling card once again.

"Are you serious? You want to make a call at this time?" Alistor asked. "If no one answered before, how will this work?"

Both monsters continue to attack any suspecting guests that they stumble upon. Auroa continues to explain things to them.

"Well, I recall a phone post somewhere when we came outside. So if you have some spare change, that would help."

None of them had any spare change. Auroa suddenly hears a sound; as their boss Bamboo catches up to their position. Somewhat breathing hard, he takes a moment to sit back.

"Those monsters … they're attacking the guests."

"You happen to have any spare change by chance?" Auroa asked.

"Yeah, why?"

He begins explaining his plan to them. A moment later, Bamboo finds himself by the phone booth. He gets ready to make the call on the card. Inserting the coins while Kinetica chased down other victims.

"Let's see 111-111-1111."

The phone begins to ring, attracting Zeus Geist. There was no answer; Bamboo redials the number once again. Finally, the operator came on the line.

"Yes, I would like to make a long-distance call."

"Please hold and wait one moment."

Still with no answer, Bamboo abruptly hangs the phone. He sensed Zeus Geist directly behind but didn't dare to look back. The phone suddenly rings. He answers the call for a brief moment.

"It's for you."

He passes the phone to the monster. But, unfortunately, Zeus Geist soon became lost, distracted by the voice from the operator.

"Now!" Maigashi yelled.

Viper's Labyrinth

Auroa emerges right from behind the booth. Bamboo ducks and covers as the wind shatters the windows inside, catching Zeus Geist by surprise. Maigashi rushed in to disarm the monster with a couple ranged attacks.

"Now I got you."

His wind materialized into a long whip piercing through the monster. Zeus Geist's body begins to erode from the impact. Auroa pulls the whip out, unleashing an explosive storm and tearing the demon away.

"Rip Tide!"

Zeus Geist crumbles apart, exploding with the phone still in his hand. Kinetica suddenly reappears on the scene, firing lasers at them. Her attacks cause Bamboo to stumble back, falling flat on his face.

"Okay, Auroa, do you have a plan for this?" Alistor asked.

"To be honest, not really."

The other two stumbled for a brief moment. Alistor got back up to quickly grab Auroa by the neck sleeve.

"Are you serious? Nothing for the second monster. Just great." Maigashi sighed.

The three continue to run while Kinetica follows them.

"We'll just have to improvise somehow," Auroa said.

"I'm tired of running."

As they venture more deeply through the cemetery, they stumble upon a dark-cloaked figure through the fog of smoke. The three come to a halt. The cloaked figure turns, revealing a skeleton. Alistor hesitates for a moment, pulling his blade out.

"A third monster; this isn't good."

Kinetica caught up to them as she got ready to blast them away.

"You're all finished." She snickered.

A reaper card suddenly hits the front tip of Kinetica's hat. Paralyzing her as the party turns their attention back to the cloaked figure.

"What? I can't move."

The three kept their guard upon the cloaked figure.

Max Mathesius

"Friend or foe? Who are you?" Alistor asked.

The cloaked figure springs in the air to pose. A scythe in one hand while giving a brief introduction.

"You called, of course; it is I, Tannen. How can I be of service?"

"Didn't expect you to be a skeleton. Well, better late than never."

They turn their attention back to the monster, unable to move. Maigashi readies his bow, a surging rush of energy focused on one big attack.

"I had enough running for one day. Surging Thunder!"

"Noooooo!"

Kinetica gets blasted at point-blank range. A thunder pierced her body, causing her back to lose balance. Then, the monster collapsed, falling flat in one big explosion, leaving her hat behind.

"Phew…and that's that."

The ground suddenly begins to shake once more.

"Now what?"

"It's coming from back inside." Auroa pointed.

A massive pumpkin deploys down from the ship and plows through the manor. Two giant pendulums swing out from the sides as they take the form of a tank. Revealing a face, it stares down at the party.

"A third monster?" Alistor gasped.

He fell flat back along with the rest, tired and completely exhausted. Tannen immediately steps in.

"Leave this one to me." He insisted.

Pulling out a long staff, it turns to a scythe as they watch him in action. He rushes towards the giant monster. The Pump Tank opens its mouth, blasting flames, but Tannen quickly jumps into the air.

"Haha! Now watch my masterful art in action."

The monster throws its two massive pendulums in the air, but he easily dodges them. Alistor and the others fell back for cover as the two pendulums came crashing by them.

Viper's Labyrinth

Darkness quickly emits from his weapon as he slashes through the oversized Pump Tank. Tannen's scythe pierces through its shell, causing sparks to burst from the demon's body. Tannen takes one big jump back as the rest watches the tank explode in fireworks. A moment later, they returned back to the scene inside the manor.

"Hey! There's the item that was stealing everyone's energy." Auroa pointed.

From the remains of the Pump Tank, they spot the skull. The party goes to check it out, but an anchor suddenly comes crashing down on them before they can look at the dome. Alistor and the rest jumped back to avoid the damage.

"Who's there? Show yourself right now." Alistor demanded.

Admiral Bombshell materializes right out from the smoke before his very eyes, standing atop his massive ship in the air.

"I'll be taking what's mine."

The skull falls right into the general's hands.

"Who are you?"

"For now, that does not matter. Till we meet again...."

The Admiral disappears with his ship from their very sight. Light begins to break in as they help the victims back outside. They looked back at the old manor. A complete total mess was left behind.

"Well...so much for the party." Maigashi shrugged.

"It couldn't be helped." Auroa nodded.

"Not a bad night at all. We had enough fun for the day. At least it all ended with a bang." Bamboo nodded.

Returning back home, an apron gets handed over to Tannen.

"What? A restaurant? Is this the training ground? Wait, I work here?"

"Don't worry; you'll get the hang of this. I was surprised just as much as you." Alistor assured him.

"And you can start tomorrow. Here's some grass jelly. It's on the house."

Bamboo hands a plate of grass jelly to Tannen. He tried the jelly while Alistor and the others backed away briefly. Seconds later, a disgusted look was on his face. He was close to barfing but took it all in one hard swallow. He reached for the glass of water, his head bent entirely down.

"Sigh….no more. Never again! How can anyone eat this?" Tannen gasped.

He took a moment to regain his posture as Bamboo slapped him on the back.

Meanwhile, back at Vilevelious lair…

"My, you've collected a great deal of energy today, Admiral. Keep up the work. We'll be needing much more."

"My next plan will be ready in due time, my lord. More energy will be on the way." He assured him.

The Admiral takes his leave.

Chapter 13

Cruise Dilemma:

Bamboo's possible romance and enter detective Tannen.

"So, Admiral? Is your next plan ready to go? My labyrinth needs more energy." The Emperor demanded. A flier is presented to him. "A couple's cruise line? You can't be serious. How will this gather us more negative power?"

"These luxury cruise lines will be my next targets. Humans are passionate about love, romance, and time off with their dear ones. My ship is in position and ready to take one over." The Admiral explained.

Vilevelious was skeptical. "And you have a monster ready with you? Couples produce positive energy, so how will this work?"

"True, my lord, they produce positive feelings, but I have a monster specializing in ruining relationships. Known for breaking couples, turning all that positive feeling into anger, hate, emptiness, etc." He explained.

"Very well, as long it works, do as you must." Vilevelious returned to the shadows.

Meanwhile, Alistor and the company gathered at the table for their next job at the restaurant. Bamboo was all happy.

"This next job will reel us in the big bucks. My restaurant has recently been selected to cater to the S.S Lavi. A love boat for couples."

The company took a glance at the flier with no amazement.

"Here we go again...sigh. For a moment, I thought you would drag us on another ski trip. Fine, let's do this then." Auroa sarcastically remarked.

"Just give us a moment to pack."

Max Mathesius

"Already taken care of." He brought their bags out from under the table. The group was slightly astonished.

"Hey, what's the idea? So you actually had the time to go through all our stuff in our rooms?" Maigashi asked.

Bamboo nodded without guilt.

"Rather creepy if you ask me," Alistor replied.

"Well, you're all on my payroll anyway. So think of this cruise as a nice little treat for doing a good job. Plus, Sairori approved me to pack all your stuff anyway. We're set to board next week, so I'll need you all to help load my supplies into the cart."

"Sairori, you bastard." He mumbled to himself.

A while later… On some ship away at sea. A riot breaks out as a crowd of couples is seen arguing. Chairs tossed, tables flipped, and food everywhere. Yelling and shouting all around.

"You bastard! I know you were eyeing that other woman. Admit it!"

"It's over! All over, we're through."

"You lost our engagement rings? How could you."

"You're not man enough for me."

From above, a dark spectral figure emerges through the walls to glance at the scene. Chuckling and laughing at the fools below.

"Heh, my power is working just like a charm. All is going as planned, master. Their energy is ready for the taking."

"Excellent, Patched Specter, time for the ship to move in."

The air begins to dampen, moist filled amid the barren sea. The Admiral's ship materializes before the oncoming boat heads its way. A massive skull emerges from the mast of the vessel opening its mouth. The energy was being sucked away from the enormous cruise ship. The fighting on board dies out in seconds as the crowd lies unconscious on the floor. The Admiral drops in to take a gander.

"So shall we dispose of them, master?" The monster asked.

"That won't be necessary." He replied.

"What do you mean? They are no use to us further."

"Indeed, but we'll leave them stranded on this island instead. When they wake, they'll be even more traumatized. Since they're already broken, they'll continue feeding our labyrinth hypothetically."

"Very well, this ship is now ours for the taking."

"Prepare to round up the next batch."

One week later, Bamboo and company were seen waiting outside by a hotel. A concerned look from Tannen as the others stood by.

"Something the matter?" Alistor asked.

"The previous guests that boarded this ship miraculously never returned. It's been happening a few times already. A little shady, don't you think?"

"Yeah, I heard about it as well. It's been going on this past week." Maigashi nodded.

"The cruise claimed all those couples found true happiness on some distant land. However, once you have boarded, you never want to return." Auroa explained.

"Well, that's not our problem if these couples feel like never coming back. We're here for the money and promotion for my restaurant." Bamboo reminded them. "And maybe they'll all love my grass jelly."

"Ooh, don't get started," Alistor mumbled.

Moments later, the party arrives at the docking bay, ready to board the Lavi. A large crowd waits in line. Bamboo presents the documents with five special boarding passes to a crew member. A confused look suddenly appears on the ticket man's face.

"I'm sorry, but I don't remember our cruise requesting any catering service at all? So, who are you supposed to be again?" He asked.

Bamboo immediately puts on his chef hat and pulls out a frying pan. Aprons get tossed on the faces of the others as he spins around.

"You mean you haven't heard of me? I am Bamboo! The great gourmet chef. I have ventured into distant lands, sailed turbulent seas, dwelled in gloomy caves, endured molten chambers, and climbed towering peaks for the freshest ingredients."

"I'm sorry I quite didn't catch that? Are you sure you're on the right ship? Cause you must be mistaking us for another cruise line?"

Bamboo continued to ramble on as the rest of the company kept quiet from the embarrassment. Then, finally, the crowd behind begins complaining as the line comes to a sudden halt.

Max Mathesius

A lady with dark green hair suddenly appears behind the ticket man.

"Do we have a problem here? What's the hold-up?" She asked.

"Oh, captain...This nut job claims they're part of some catering service we didn't order? He is a great master chef. He keeps rambling on about it. But he refuses to leave; what should we do?"

The lady immediately gives off a nasty grin to them. Then, a tense stare-down begins between her and Bamboo while the others wait.

"Who is this odd one?" She mumbled to herself. "I can feel a vast amount of energy coming from this idiot. Maybe this could be the boost we need to fill our labyrinth."

The rest continues to watch them both stare down. The frying pan was clutched in their boss's hands as the lady gave a welcoming smile.

"Sorry for the inconvenience. You all may pass through."

Bamboo rushed to the kitchen without hesitation.

"Well...that was easy. I can't believe we actually made it through somehow." Alistor wondered.

"For a minute, I thought security was gonna boot us off for holding up the line," Auroa said. "No time to waste; Bamboo needs us in the kitchen."

As the party goes to assist Bamboo, the ship takes sail in a matter of time. Hours later, dinner was in the middle of preparation. Guests are seen dancing in the ballroom. Finally, the captain appears from behind the doors. A grin on her face.

"Time to begin the first phase of my plan. Heh heh heh...."

Moments later, Bamboo was distressed while the crowd grew tense waiting for their meals. Finally, Tannen and the rest rushed back to the kitchen to sort out the situation.

"My whole pot of stew I've prepared is missing. My bacon as well!" Bamboo weeps.

A magnifying glass immediately pulls out from a pocket as Tannen steps in.

"Someone must have taken it then. This looks like the time for some detective work. What we have here is a mystery." Tannen said.

"A mystery?" Everyone in the room wondered.

"Yes, a mystery. We must find some clues that will lead to a culprit."

Viper's Labyrinth

The group begins to follow Tannen as they investigate the ship. Leaving from the kitchen through the ballroom, they spot a trail of drips leading through a hallway. Bamboo dips his finger to take a taste.

"This is my stew!" Bamboo confirmed.

"Ah-ha! These drops will lead us straight to the culprit. This way!" Tannen said.

"My only question is, who in their right mind would bother stealing a pot of stew?" Maigashi wondered.

"We'll soon find out."

The trail ends in a closed room labeled VIP. A couple was arguing behind the door while Alistor and the rest took caution. However, Bamboo didn't hesitate to kick down the door before them. Next, they witness a couple fighting over food as a woman tries to pull him away from a pile of bacon. The pot of stew rests on the side of their bed.

"What the hell is going on?" Maigashi asked.

"My boyfriend said he loves bacon more than he loves me. I can't take this." The woman cried out.

The man couldn't resist engorging his face into the pile of bacon. He immediately began to stutter before speaking out.

"BACON! Can't stop the feeling. I love bacon, but I love you too."

"How can you say that?" She cried.

The couple continues to argue endlessly as the rest take a moment to digest what they just saw. Auroa and Maigashi couldn't resist laughing at the sorry sight.

"It's clear this man is delusional." Auroa nodded.

"I just want my pot of stew back. You can keep the bacon." Bamboo said.

He tries to take the pot but is quickly pushed back by the couple. Bamboo started to feel bad for them.

"I love bacon, I love you, I love bacon, but I love you too. My mind hurts."

"Then you can love them both." Snapped Tannen.

The situation quickly cools down as Tannen resolves the problem for the strange couple with advice and ideas. In a matter of time, the couple was soon in each other's arms once more as Bamboo reclaims his pot.

Max Mathesius

"Yeah, you can love each other while smothering in food. I guess..." Maigashi repeated.

"We'll try that out." The woman agreed.

"Okay, mystery solved. I think it's about time we take our leave. Sorry about the door, by the way."

The party returns victoriously to the ballroom as the captain peeps from the shadows. A distasteful look on her face.

"Argh, they ruined my plan. I'll just have to try something else, then. Heh heh."

A while later, another problem soon immersed on the ship. In moments, Alistor and his team investigate the situation as couples are seen blaming one another for lost possessions.

"We have a case of missing valuables this time, it seems. A pair of shell earrings, a pink brooch, and an engagement ring. The list goes on." Auroa read.

"So, detective Tannen, do you have a lead on where to start?" Alistor asked.

Things begin to quiet down as Tannen is in the middle of intense thinking. They took a moment to wait for his words of wisdom. A brief moment later…

"I have no clue, to be honest." He said.

The party quickly stumbled. The situation continued to heat up with the crowd as the rest began covering their ears.

"QUIET!!!" Bamboo shouted.

"It's not our problem if guests misplace things. So you all can afford this cruise, I'm sure you can always repurchase the items again. We're just about to serve dessert, so relax."

Bamboo's words allow Tannen to come up with a solution.

"Ah, of course!" Tannen snapped. "Love cannot be replaced by mere trinkets. Never forget these are just possessions clouding your judgment against another's trust. Your love for one another is something special. Remember, you're all here and now. Live for the moment and ask why you are here in the first place? To be together in each other's arms, right?"

The couples quickly come to their sense, forgiving one another and cuddling in the ballroom. Bamboo gives Tannen a pat on the back.

"A job well done! Now we can bring out the dessert."

From a dark corner, the captain is seen biting her thumb. Then, finally, she quietly leaves the room.

"Argh! These guys are ruining everything. I must try something else."

Her communicator begins to ring as she heads into the lady's room. Closing the door behind a stall, she takes a seat before answering. The Admiral's image appears on a small screen.

"So, are the next set of victims ready yet?"

She turned her eyes away for a moment.

"Sorry to say, we're experiencing just some minor setbacks."

"Well, then, you better pick up the pace. My ship will arrive at your position tomorrow night, so you better not fail."

The call ends immediately as she quietly mumbles to herself. She hears a slight knock on her door but ignores it. The setback continues as she tries to lose herself in her own thoughts. A third knock happens.

"Can you see I'm busy minding myself? Go away!"

The moment she leaves the lady's room, Bamboo pops right in front of her by surprise. She quickly stumbled back before kicking him in the face.

"Ow....."

"Oh? It's you? I'm sorry, are you alright? Wait a minute, were you spying on me? You peeping pervert!"

"Oh no, it's not like that." Clueless he was.

"You didn't hear anything, did you? Cause you better not." Her eyes glared down as he felt belittled.

He continues shaking his head.

"Then what were you doing knocking?"

He was shy for the moment but regained posture before presenting her with something. A plate of grass jelly.

"I noticed you were the only one not around for dessert. So I felt obligated to search high and low this entire ship just for you."

Max Mathesius

There was a slight blush on her face.

"Ooh… what do you mean by that?" She quietly asked.

He placed the dish in her hands.

"I couldn't bear seeing someone missing out on my greatest creation. Especially a pretty gal like you who has never been hard to forget. You must try it!"

"Well, thanks, I guess? I'll just save this for later. I'm not hungry at the moment."

He brought a spoon out for her.

"No, I insist! You must try it now."

"But I'm not hungry." She repeated.

"Just one bite!"

She turned her face away as he tried to spoon-feed her. The spoon entered her mouth as the taste of the grass jelly melted across her lips. Taking a quick swallow, she immediately became ill within seconds and rushed back into the lady's room.

"She must have loved it." Bamboo carried on his way.

She is seen barfing in the sink in the lady's room. A toothbrush in one hand, trying to brush the bad taste out of her mouth.

"That stuff is nasty. Ugh… I'll make Bamboo pay for this if it's the last thing I do. Argh!"

The next night a loud scream was heard on board. Alistor and the party rushed to the scene to check what it was. They stumble into a bathroom where a man sits in shock.

"What happened here? Explain!" Alistor asked.

"I minded my own business on the toilet when some guy jumped out and surprised me. It was that chef. Bamboo! I'm sure of it. Plus, he left something which belongs to someone."

A shell earring was picked up.

"Hey, that looked like something one of the guests lost the other night?" He mentioned.

"Yeah…you guys don't think Bamboo could have done this?"

"Well, he's the only one not with us now," Maigashi mentioned.

Viper's Labyrinth

"It just doesn't add up. Bamboo was in the kitchen the entire day, and there are security and cameras throughout this ship." Auroa thought.

"Sounds like it's another mystery." Tannen brought out his magnifying glass. "Take a close look at this earring. You can see there is a stain left on it."

They took a closer look at the clue and were amazed.

"You're right. Our boss couldn't have done this. Something is amiss, and we must uncover the truth."

Another scream was heard, and they rushed to the next scene. More theft occurred across the ship as missing items began popping up in the kitchen. Soon all eyes were on Bamboo back in the ballroom.

"We have to head back to the main room. Bamboo is in trouble." Alistor was worried.

"Go on ahead. I'll continue to search the ship for clues." Tannen explained.

Alistor and the party make their way back to the main room. Bamboo defended himself as the crowd continued to label him a suspect.

"I told you! I don't have anything to do with your case. I was in the kitchen all day preparing your meals. So how would I have the time to pull that off?"

"That's creepy, and you should be ashamed of yourself." One pointed out to him.

The party came to the scene to defend their boss, but the crowd did not favor them.

"Then we'll have to find a way to claim he is innocent," Auroa suggested. Before they could build a case, Bamboo suddenly got right up to admit to something he was guilty of.

"Okay, I admit it!"

Everyone was struck cold for the moment, as he further explains.

"I forged the documents to get us on this ship. The tickets used to get us on were counterfeit, but I didn't steal anything, and I don't stalk people in bathrooms because that's just creepy."

The party was relieved to hear the news strangely.

"You mean we couldn't get on this ship in the first place?" Maigashi asked.

"I thought you paid for these tickets." Alistor thought.

Bamboo nodded to them.

Max Mathesius

"What $800.00 per ticket? Do you think I'm out of my mind to pay that much for a trip? That's $4000 down the drain."

"Ah-ha! Indeed." Tannen makes a dramatic appearance in the room. "That leads us to the final answer to our investigation. It's all clear now."

"How so?" Maigashi wondered.

"Think back; why would we even be on this ship? If we couldn't get in the first place, the crew should have had us booted off before the ship left."

"Oh yeah, that sweet captain allowed us on board," Bamboo remembered.

All eyes were now on the captain. She came out from the shadows.

"So? What differences does that make? I must have mistaken your documents due to the heat. Yeah, that's right. We'll be sure to report you back to the local authorities."

"Cut the chase; there's no use denying it anymore. There's something you want from us." Auroa pointed.

Tannen suddenly throws a reaper card cutting open her lower pockets. The missing valuables slipped from her pants and were scattered on the floor, causing the captain to stumble back in disbelief.

"What? No, he must have planted these in my pockets."

Tannen presents the final clue to the audience by pressing a button. Video footage rolled back to last night's events with her and Bamboo.

"But how....I was so close."

"I had to compromise with a little force against your security. Your crew is nothing more but a sham. Reveal yourself!"

She looked down with a gloomy look on her face. Then, smoke starts to emit across her body.

"Very well...heh heh. I was getting sick and tired of this form anyway."

Her disguise materialized away, revealing a monster. Multiple appendages begin popping out of her back.

"If I can't take this crowd's energy, I'll just have to take this dope face. Whoopers attack!"

Viper's Labyrinth

She takes a dive at Bamboo, wrapping herself around him. The crew members turned into enemy soldiers as the crowd began fleeing. Tannen and the rest of the party start clashing with the grunts approaching them.

"Ow, wow, get off me." Bamboo struggled as energy began leaving his body.

"I'm not letting go. After what you pulled. It took me all night to wash out that taste from your dreadful sweet."

A loud crashing sound immediately commenced shaking up the room.

"What was that? Did the ship hit something?" Alistor asked.

"Sounds like it's coming from the front deck," Maigashi replied.

"The Admiral just arrived on time for the fun. Once I'm done with this idiot, I'll gladly take the rest of your energy."

They faced ready against the monster, but Tannen stepped in.

"Leave this one to me. The rest of you handle the situation upfront."

The three of them leave to the front deck taking out the remaining enemy grunts in the way. Tannen brings out his Scythe to begin charging toward the monster. Two massive limbs stretched out to retaliate, but he sliced them back. He moves close, ready for a direct hit, but she takes cover behind Bamboo's bulky body. His Scythe bounced back upon impact knocking him halfway across the room.

"Your friends are fools if they think they can take the Admiral on. The name is Patched Specter, by the way."

Bamboo continues to feel drained.

"You coward...."

"Your friend here makes a nice big shield for me. Just look at him. So hopeless to do a single thing. Heh, this is all too easy."

"Damn, Bamboo, you have to break free from her grasp. It shouldn't be too difficult for someone big like you."

"But she's a woman. I don't hit girls; ooh. Ow, stop it." He complained.

"You got to be kidding me...." Tannen nodded with disbelief. "This fight is going to take a while."

Max Mathesius

Meanwhile, Auroa, Maigashi, and Alistor went outside to the front deck. Moist and mist fills the air as they spot a massive ship rammed into the S.S. Lavi. The Admiral appears before them on board.

"We meet again."

"Tonight, we'll defeat you here. Just like the three who came before you." Alistor rushed in to start the attack.

"Hey, wait! Damn it!" Maigashi yelled.

The Admiral quickly vanished within the smoke, appearing right behind. He sent Alistor flying back from the strike of his anchor.

"Don't take me too lightly, unlike the previous three generals who came before you. I am Admiral Bombshell, Veteran commander of the Aggerona Naval division. You have interfered long enough."

As the rest moved back, a high burst of wind began building from Auroa. Objects across the deck start breaking apart. The Admiral stood his ground, barely budging an inch.

"Ah, the wind channeler. You've displayed quite some power despite Scrap Ram's demise. But your wind cannot hold me back."

He launches his anchor at Auroa, forcing him to jump back as it crashes through the wooden deck. Maigashi runs to the sidelines as Auroa materializes his whip out of the air.

"If we're going to beat him, we must work together. I can sense a water-based aura coming from this guy. Maybe I can stun him." Maigashi said.

Maigashi fired five rounds of bolting daggers, impacting the Admiral from the side as Auroa charged at the Admiral with his Riptide technique attempting to slice through. Smoke and debris scattered across the air, but the Admiral stood unharmed.

"What?" Surprised Auroa.

He backs away from the Admiral, retaliating with some blasts of air, but the general remains unharmed.

"You both rely on distance combat, I see. Well, I can play that game too."

The general pulls out a small cannon blasting them. The walls across the S.S Lavi begin to crumble apart. Maigashi runs, avoiding the fire as holes are made through each exploding shot.

"Okay, now what?" Maigashi asked.

Viper's Labyrinth

Alistor suddenly came from behind Bombshell in the air, catching them by surprise. His sword impales the top of the general's head.

"A direct hit. That has to hurt."

The Admiral was stunned for the moment, but victory was cut short as he tossed Alistor aside, breaking his sword.

"You got to be kidding me? Is this guy a brick wall?" Alistor asked.

The general removes the blade's broken part on his head while the three maintain distance. Then, moisture begins building up, forming walls of liquid around him.

"You are right about sensing a water-based aura, but my body is composed of high-grade titanium dating back to the late Zophian period."

The Admiral relaunches his anchor, forcing the three to jump further back.

"Auroa…can you think of something. We can't keep this up much longer."

"I don't know…this might be a fight we cannot win. Hopefully, Tannen is faring better. We'll have to wait and see."

Back with Tannen, the monster continues to drain Bamboo's energy. He continues to do nothing till Bamboo comes to his senses.

"Seriously, just do it."

Bamboo continues to whine.

"Ooh, I hate this, but fine."

He takes a bite at Patched Specter's hand, forcing her to break free.

"Ouch! Ooh, I think you broke a nail. I'll have to get another manicure." She cried.

Five reaper cards are thrown at the monster.

"What? I can't move."

Tannen rushed in with his Scythe at full power. Darkness bursts out, plowing through the monster's entire body.

"Submerge into darkness."

"Noooooo!"

Patched Specter falls back to explode as Bamboo runs to take cover under a table.

"Well, that's a relief. Now let's check on how the others are doing." Bamboo gave him a pat on the back.

They both make their way to the deck.

Meanwhile, the Admiral unleashed a water vortex, forcing the party to fall back. Maigashi immediately recalls something.

"Now I remember. I heard about you long ago from a story somewhere but didn't believe it was true. You were a prestige war hero. A valiant commander who went mad after a sudden military discharge."

The Admiral further explains.

"True, I have tried everything to fill the void. Worked my way into a position of greater power and influence to fight for what was right and wrong. But, there was a time I used to be just like you, seeking the thrill of adventure."

"What do you mean?"

"You'll one day wake up to realize the harsh reality. Fighting for an impossible dream while a government forces you to do horrible things, participating to ensure cover-ups. Then, the same government will turn and eventually abandon you."

"We're nothing like you. You serve under Vilevelious, a fiend bent on destroying our world. You are no different from the rest." Alistor pointed out.

"Believe what you want. I'm too trapped in a war to be at peace. Vilevelious was the only one who recognized my worth. His goal is my mission, and nothing will stop me from bringing this labyrinth to your world."

Tannen and Bamboo finally catch up to the party. They watch as the sunlight begins to break in. Then, finally, the Admiral starts to step away.

"It seems Patched Specter has been vanquished. No need to continue leaving her efforts in vain. She has gathered quite enough energy. Time for my leave."

"Hey, get back here," Alistor demanded.

"Till we meet again."

The Admiral disappears into the horizon along with his ship. The fog of battle clears as an island comes into their view.

"Hey! I can see a bunch of people waving." Bamboo points out.

Viper's Labyrinth

"Wait a minute; they look just like the crew members and missing guests," Maigashi said.

The ship stops at the island as the party encounters the real ship captain. The guests who were missing were finally found.

Back at the enemy base, Admiral Bombshell reports back to Vilevelious.

"She may have failed, but you accumulated a mass amount of energy over this past week." He was pleased to say.

"I'll have another plan ready in no time, my Emperor. Your labyrinth will rise in due time. Your goal is my dream."

A while not too later, everyone was back on board. The ship captain was busy telling off Bamboo as the others kicked back to enjoy the breeze.

"The captain said we'll be let off with a warning this time," Auroa explained. "Maybe Bamboo can finally work out his affair, hopefully."

"Yeah… Bamboo's been crushing on a monster this whole time." Maigashi teased.

"So, Tannen, how long were you in the detective business?" Alistor cared to ask.

"I used to own a detective agency back in the day. But that was long ago."

Bamboo immediately pops up from behind them.

"Okay! Back to work. We got another feast to prepare for the trip back. And she is even interested in trying my grass jelly." He smothered.

He hollers and dances joyfully into the kitchen as the ship sails home through the horizon.

Max Mathesius

Chapter 14

Ding Academy:

A week of Traffic Safety

"No! Stop; you're going the wrong way. Hit the brakes!!!" Maigashi yelled.

The car slides and skids off the side of the road. A sudden crash suddenly stops the vehicle's momentum ramming into a big tree. Outside in the middle of the rain, the four of them exit. Food and supplies were scattered everywhere.

"Hot damn! You have done it now." Tannen muttered.

"Bamboo isn't going to be pleased with this. Look at it; completely totaled. You should have let me take the wheels." Maigashi warned.

Alistor had a guilty look on his face. The look of disappointment and worry for the others.

"Hopefully, he's got good insurance."

One hour later...

"What! My car! What happened?" Bamboo wept.

Back at the restaurant, the other member's eyes were on Alistor for the blame. A facepalm was the only thing their boss expressed at the moment.

"I'm sorry, I just couldn't control it any further. It was raining, and if it wasn't for Maigashi's backseat driving." Alistor explained.

Viper's Labyrinth

"Take that back! You obviously never had any prior experience on the road. Plus, I'm a better driver." Maigashi argued back.

Arguing between the members commenced as Bamboo left the room to think about it momentarily. He returned back after a quick breath of air.

"That was my good car. I paid good money for it."

"Don't you have insurance?" Auroa asked.

"No, I don't. I never even bothered. I left you all for a simple pick-up mission, and you destroyed my car. Mathias is a wide-open road, so I never expected this to happen."

"So what happens now?" Alistor asked.

"Well, this must come from all your paychecks for the next two months." He shrugged.

"What!" Maigashi had the sudden urge to snap. "If it's anyone's payroll, it should all be his. How could it be our fault?"

The party continues to argue with Bamboo trying to reason the situation out. Meanwhile, from another screen, Vilevelious watches them. Then, finally, an idea comes to his mind.

"That is it! Admiral Bombshell. Come forth!" Vilevelious hollered.

The Admiral appears in the room behind the shadows.

"My next plan is not ready yet. What did you call for?" He asked.

The emperor presents him with a driver's handbook. A confused expression on the other lesser minions in the room.

"I want you to oversee and carry out my next plan in gathering energy. We are going to open a school to promote safe driving and traffic safety."

An astonished look was on the general's face.

"An odd plan, don't you say? How will teaching the ways of traffic safety benefit the labyrinth?" He further questioned.

"Young drivers are practically more reckless and likely to be in accidents during their first year behind the wheel. When teens get into accidents, insurance rates get high. When insurance gets high, parents get stressed; when parents get stressed, negative energy is made and ready for the taking."

"Very well, is there a monster ready?"

Max Mathesius

"Not to worry, Admiral. Professor Ding! Come forth." The emperor called.

A short, stumbling professor appears in the room. Carrying a large book in one hand. He trips and stumbles down a small step of stairs. Then, he quickly got back up to regain posture.

"You rang Vile, my lord?"

"Professor Ding, you will carry out my plan. He is a well-informed instructor with a Ph.D. in traffic safety. You shall educate the young minds occupying them with loads of homework."

"And how will we have control over the insurance?" The general asked.

"As for the insurance, I have plenty of inside informants planted and ready to take over at my command. So we'll have a complete monopoly on time, and it's your duty, Admiral, to keep the rates high once accidents commence. Now go!"

The professor and Admiral take a bow before teleporting away.

One hopeful night later, a new building appears out of nowhere. When morning came, Bamboo offered a deal the party couldn't refuse.

"What? You're kidding me? We have to take a class on traffic safety?" Maigashi yelled.

"How will this benefit their training?" Tannen asked.

Bamboo nodded with a serious look.

"Yep! It's a new school that opened in Emerald, and all the parents are enrolling their kids. It's been a while since a school was really around. This might be a skill that would come in handy one day. Young adults are taking this course, so I might even consider taking it one day, but now I have a business to run."

"Traffic safety…Why us? At least, Alistor, I can understand. Don't we have a say in this?" Auroa complained.

Bamboo continues to nod.

"Look, if you don't want to go without two months' pay, you'll all enroll in this program. It's only five days a week for a few hours. Plus, I even heard the instructor was a driving guru." Bamboo further explained.

The party couldn't refuse the offer.

"Looks like we don't have a choice then." Alistor shrugs.

Viper's Labyrinth

A bell rings, and a mass of people is gathered at the new school. The four check the facility out as the crowd waits below the stage. Finally, a short professor heads up to the front step. He walks forward and reaches out for the speaker that is too high. He grabs a small stool to help reach.

"Dear fellow students: I am Professor Ding. Whether you are a new or experienced motorist, I hope my course will enhance your road experience and promote safe driving in the future. So without further ado, follow me."

Alistor and the party follow the crowd into the building. A standard classroom with tables, chairs, and chalkboards is all set. They all took a seat as the professor began his speech.

"I'm here to help drivers prepare for exams. First, the five most common reasons for motor vehicle accidents are speeding, driving recklessly, running off the road, driving in the wrong lane, and DUI. We will look at each category fully, so pay attention."

A few hours later…after a long lecture.

"You even listening to half the things this guy is saying?" Maigashi yawned.

The party was snoozing at the back while Alistor was taking notes. The professor immediately passes out fliers to the class.

"What's this?" Auroa wondered.

"By law, you must be financially responsible for your actions wherever you drive. Having a reliable insurance policy ensures responsibility. So here are a few trustworthy programs you may find. Look at them over and choose before tomorrow." Ding explained.

"Well, there's only three known in this kingdom." Alistor boasted before noticing something amiss. "What? Did they all have a sudden change of name?"

"Who cares anyway?" Maigashi pestered. "Let's see, we got Shogun, Admirals, and Meister Insurance?"

Everyone was looking over at the choice they had for coverage.

"That's a low price! So cheap!" Tannen snapped.

"Why yes, great auto insurance for as little as a cent a day. Flexible payment options offered, including low down payments." The professor stated.

The bell suddenly rings.

"That concludes our lesson for today. As for tonight's assignment, consider one of the three options you'll sign up for. Have a nice day."

Max Mathesius

Back at the restaurant, Bamboo looks over at the given insurance offers.

"Wow, these are good deals. I think I'll go with Shogun insurance whenever I have free time." Bamboo picked.

"Admiral for the rest of us, it seems. Meister seems a bit strange for our taste." Alistor replied.

The next day of class…

The students all turned in their choices from the flier Ding passed.

"Today, we will watch this video on the dos and don'ts of safe driving."

The professor pops in a VHS tape, and colorful logos appear on the screen. Then, a speeding car on a racetrack zips through with cheesy music playing.

"At least it's not another boring lecture," Maigashi whispered.

The video begins…

"The Dos and Don'ts of safe driving: Smoking when a minor is present. Dumping abandoned pets or loitering on the highway. Leaving a child unattended, following too close such as tailgating."

A while later…

"And most importantly, do not let your emotions interfere with safe driving. Good judgment, common sense, and courtesy will lead to successful driving."

The video comes to an end. Then, the professor begins handing out the next assignment.

"For tonight, I want you all to write a ten-page essay on what you learned about safe driving. What will you do to embrace this experience?" Ding announced.

"What ten pages?" Maigashi yelled.

"Yes, due tomorrow, and you must all write it up on my specially marked paper provided? You must also study the first two chapters from the textbook for tomorrow's test." He said.

"Can't we use normal paper?" Auroa asked.

"No! It doesn't have my stamp of approval. Sorry, but it's either credit or no credit. So be ready for a test tomorrow." The professor took his leave.

Later that night…

Viper's Labyrinth

"You guys are seriously bothering with this assignment?" Maigashi asked.

No one in the room paid attention to him. The rest of the party was studying as he glanced at their papers. Erase marks here and there.

"You're done?" Auroa asked.

"Whatever, you guys can stay up all night. I'm gonna head to sleep."

As Maigashi headed to bed, the rest continued studying through the night, pushing their limits. Then, finally, the stamp on the marked papers begins releasing a faint glow as energy slowly leaves them.

The following day: Day 3 of class.

"It seems most of you have done your assignments. Get ready for a test now!" The professor announces.

Everyone except Maigashi was exhausted and too drained from concentrating or focusing as the test was handed out.

"Multiple choice; this should be a breeze." Alistor thought.

A while after the test…

"You need good vision to drive safely. If you cannot judge distance or spot trouble, you may be unable to make the best judgments." The professor lectured.

Nearly half the class was awake to listen as he rambled on.

"When driving in the rain or snow, it's best to slow down so your car won't skid off or slip off-road. If you can't see more than 100 feet ahead of your vehicle in a heavy rainstorm, you cannot drive faster than 30 mph. You may have to stop repeatedly to wipe any mud or snow off your windshields."

The bell rings.

"Well, look at the time. Unfortunately, I got a little carried away. I'll be sure to mail in your results later this evening. Class dismissed!"

A while later in the evening…

"What! You all flunked your first exam." Bamboo yelled.

An astonished look was on nearly everyone except for Maigashi.

"How can this be?" Alistor wondered.

Their scores were all below forty as they had their heads down. They then took a look at Maigashi's paper.

"You didn't even answer a single question."

The look of disappointment was around as Bamboo lectured them.

"What to do with you...sigh."

Maigashi immediately steps in with a reminder.

"Hey! Do you remember our deal? You said we must take the class but never mentioned we had to pass it." Maigashi pointed out.

His claim enlightens everyone in the room for a brief second.

"Oh...you do have a point." Bamboo agreed. "At least try putting in a little effort to learn something."

"Plus, I didn't bother with last night's assignment because I sensed something fishy was up."

"What do you mean?" Alistor asked.

"The feeling of life energy sapping away from your very soul. So when I wrote my name, I quickly stopped and crumpled my paper." He further explained.

The party begins to recall the professor's words from the day before as Maigashi brings them to their senses.

"Let's take caution and see what happens tomorrow."

The very next morning...The professor briefly cuts to the chase.

"It seems you've all struggled with the test." He coughed.

The look of disappointment was on Ding's face.

"But I'm sure you'll get the hang of it. I won't give up because I believe in every one of you. Cause today we are going outside."

Outside behind the school, a surprising look for the class. An entire practice course for driving was ready for them.

"I figure a more hands-on experience would help embrace your understanding of traffic safety. So I'll be by your side as you drive, and by the end of the day, you'll all receive a certified license."

Viper's Labyrinth

"So, who wants to go first?" Ding asked.

Alistor steps in first, entering the vehicle with Ding. He reached for the ignition key to start the engine but was slapped on the wrist with a ruler.

"Not so fast! Safe practices always begin by checking your rearview mirrors. You must also signal when turning left or right, changing lanes, or even slowing down and stopping. Can you demonstrate signaling?" He asked.

He rolled the windows down. Then, before he could answer, Ding used him as an example.

"From the left, stick your arm out; to make a right, you raise your arm, and to slow or stop, you leave it raised down. This will allow motorists or other pedestrians to know your intention."

"Right…Can we begin?" Alistor grumbled.

"Proceed!"

The car begins to accelerate and stop constantly.

"What are you doing? Shift to drive and accelerate. Do you know which one is the brake?" Ding nervously asked.

After a brief moment, he finally got the hang of the controls, thanks to Ding's assistance. Then, he proceeded through the track, making a left and right around the set cones. The practice continues with Alistor making signals and stops at red lights. Finally, the lesson ends with Alistor parking the vehicle.

"So, how did I do?" Alistor nervously asked.

"Well…I suppose I can pass you with a C."

The feeling of relief through his eyes.

"So, who's next?"

From that moment, everyone was motivated to drive with Ding. As the hours passed, Tannen proceeded next, followed by Auroa and the rest of the class. The entire morning was spent driving. Finally, the afternoon came, and the professor checkmarks the remaining students.

"And last but not least, Maigashi. Will you please enter the vehicle?"

Max Mathesius

He entered the vehicle, and the professor sat flat on the front passenger seat. A cup of coffee is clutched in one hand as he waits for Maigashi to start the ignition. A brief moment of silence commenced as Ding turned to face him.

"Um…anytime now. You may proceed?"

A glint sparks in Maigashi's eyes.

"If you say so."

He steps hard into the acceleration bursting the exhaust as the vehicle dashes at high speed. The professor stumbles over his chair, and coffee spills over as cones outside begin flying.

"Ahhh! What are you doing? 70 miles? Are you mad! Too fast! Too fast!" Ding panicked.

He knocks Ding back.

"I'm driving! Just sit back and watch. You saw nothing yet."

Alistor and the rest of the crowd speechlessly watch from a distance with amazement. But unfortunately, the professor continues to panic.

"Let's ditch this small track."

The speed increases up to 90mph. Finally, the car bursts through a fence, out of the school premises, and into an open field.

"Hit the brakes! Watch out for those open trees." Ding cried.

"Heh."

Maigashi maneuvers around the row of trees without effort as they approach a steep hill with a ramp. Then, without hesitation, Maigashi drives off the ramp as the car zips through the air.

"Waaaahhh! Mommy!!!"

The car lands on the ground as Maigashi makes a fancy U-turn back to the school. The car arrives in one piece, and smoke streams from the tire tracks left behind. Ding exits the vehicle, dazed and ready to barf.

"So, did I pass?" Maigashi grin.

Ding took a moment to regain his breath.

"You want me to go again? Sure, I don't mind."

Viper's Labyrinth

Ding began waving his arms around.

"Oh no! No need! Yes! You passed! You passed! You all passed." Ding hastily said. "Your license will be in the mail later this evening. So to conclude this lesson, keep your eyes moving and scan your surroundings to avoid hazards."

The professor began to hurl once the bell suddenly rang.

Later that evening…

The Admiral contacts the professor from another line.

"All the students have just received their license in the mail as instructed, general."

"Good; now we can proceed to the next phase of the plan."

Back with the party, they wouldn't hesitate to open their mail. Finally, a valid license was issued to them as they rushed out of the house to see Bamboo.

"Well, at least you all learned something. I'm so proud of you all." Bamboo snuffled.

"Hey, there's a short message at the bottom." Auroa pointed.

"Well, read it out then," Maigashi replied.

He begins reading aloud to the group.

"Congratulations on passing the driver's test exam. With this valid license, you are now certified to drive. It's been a grand time and honor to instruct you all about traffic safety. And never forget to buckle those belts."

Be ready in the following hour to receive your diploma. 7:00 pm sharp.

Yours truly: Mr. Ding.

Not a moment sooner, a loud sound could be heard from the distance. The sound of an engine roars recklessly as it grows louder.

"What's that sound?" Tannen turned.

Bamboo takes a quick glimpse out the window and starts to panic.

"Fall back!"

A car comes crashing through the restaurant, knocking everyone behind the counters. A huge mess of tables and chairs scattered across, leaving a gaping hole in the wall.

Max Mathesius

"What? Who dare crash my business." Bamboo yelled.

Alistor goes to check on the person inside. They pulled him out of the wreck to see if he was ok.

"Hey! This guy was a classmate of ours."

"We need to get him to a hospital. His insurance better covers this." Bamboo frowned.

The man regains consciousness at the hospital later that night. Then, he begins explaining himself to Bamboo and the rest.

"I don't know what came over me. At first, I was driving, but then I had the sudden urge to speed up. My parents are gonna kill me for this. Ugh!"

As Bamboo wrote down his insurance information, Auroa closely examined the license issued.

"Hey, take a look once more. That's the same marking as the papers Ding provided." Auroa pointed out.

"You're right...Something is not right here." Maigashi nodded.

More patients begin arriving through the doors as Tannen goes out to investigate. He quickly returns to give the news.

"Six more accidents have just occurred across town. The same case with all of them." Tannen explained. "We should get to the bottom of this."

They all left the room and headed to the school. The Admiral's ship was nearby, sucking energy away from a crowd of victims. There Ding waited for all of them with the general by his side. The mouth of the dark skull closes.

"The insurance rates are skyrocketing." Ding chuckled. "Just look at all the families suffering. The rates have increased tenfold!"

"Be ready to round up the next batch of students." The Admiral ordered.

"No problem! Just give me another week to rack 'em in."

Ding was getting ready to file the papers, but Bamboo and the party arrived at their door.

"We meet again." The Admiral greeted.

"So you fueled everyone with the false sense of safe driving. Those tests, the driving, and this license were all a setup." Auroa explained.

Viper's Labyrinth

"Of course…Who else would you think?" He laughed.

Alistor pulls out his blade at the professor.

"So you finally caught on," Ding smirked. "Not that it matters, Whoopers attack!"

Enemy soldiers begin charging towards their way while Bamboo falls back for cover.

Tannen destroys the oncoming wave of Whoopers with one quick slice. The professor begins stepping back. He turns around to notice the Admiral no longer at his side.

"Hey! Where are you going?" Ding trembled.

"You go handle these fools. I must return back with the energy collected."

"What? Fight? But this is not part of my job. I didn't sign up for this. Oooh, don't leave me here."

The professor grabs onto his leg, getting dragged across the floor momentarily.

"Then improvise!" Bombshell commanded.

He immediately kicks him back to face the rest. Then, as the professor begins cowering in the corner, Auroa and Maigashi rush in to attack the Admiral.

"We're not letting you get away."

Bombshell quickly sends them both back with a blast from his cannon. Bamboo watches from a distance squinting his eyes. Maigashi loses consciousness.

"I have no time for this."

Tannen immediately tosses three quick reaper cards at the Admiral, but his attack is nullified by a wall of water.

"Ding! Destroy them." He ordered.

The Admiral scares Ding with an attack from his anchor, leaving a hole in the floor. The professor regained his attention.

"Yes, Admiral, I'll do it."

Alistor then jumps in with his blade, clashing against the chains from the Admiral's anchor. Easily outmuscled, Bombshell sent him flying back toward the others.

"I know this guy from somewhere," Bamboo whispered to himself.

The Admiral's ship immediately vanishes, leaving them with Professor Ding to face. They follow the professor outside the practice course.

"You have nowhere to run," Alistor confidently said.

The professor begins chuckling.

"I have no intention to run. So give me your best shot." He provoked.

"No problem. This is going to be a piece of cake." Alistor rushed in, ready to swing.

The professor immediately pulls out a stop sign, instantly stopping his attack in midair. Tannen and Auroa then attempt to move, but a red light flashes from the professor's head. The three could not move as he placed a large table before them. Then, the light turns green, causing them to slam against the object.

"A Dirty trick!" He grumbled.

The professor continues to provoke them by slapping his butt in front of them.

Alistor then readies the Star Breaker from his blade; Ding simply turned the light yellow slowing his attack down to easily dodge. Finally, a large mirror gets placed, deflecting his attack back at the three.

"Haha, none of you can touch me. You are bound by the laws of traffic safety."

"What? Explain!" Alistor demanded.

The professor pulls out their test results.

"You may have failed to answer all my questions, but you had the common sense to correctly guess the basics. From green to go and red to stop, you sealed your fate with this test ha ha ha."

A lightning arrow immediately hits the professor from behind, shocking him.

"What? Show yourself." Ding demanded.

Maigashi appears before them.

"You're finally awake." Auroa smiled. "Get us out of this mess."

He slowly begins to walk towards Ding, his weapon locked and ready to fire.

"I just about had enough with your school. Class is canceled."

Viper's Labyrinth

"Argh, I'll show you! You can join the rest of your friends." Ding grinned.

He faces Maigashi and turns the light red to stop, but he continues forward. He quickly changes the dial to yellow, followed by green. Flicking back and forth between the lights as he got close. Finally, Ding pulls out a yield sign.

"By the laws of traffic safety Yield?"

Maigashi quickly sends him stumbling to the ground. Then, a burst of high lightning begins channeling around him.

"Sorry, but I never answered any of your questions. None of it applies to me, so good riddance to your traffic safety school."

"Uh oh…." Ding gulped.

"Surging Thunder!"

The professor gets impaled and sent flying from an electrocuting blast from his attack, crashing into the school. The entire school explodes, leaving nothing but the bell intact. They go to watch the fireworks.

"We still have to deal with Admiral Bombshell. Damn, we're still no match for him." Alistor mumbled.

Bamboo creeps up behind them.

"I might know something about the admiral," Bamboo claimed.

Everyone was all open ears, ready to hear what he had to say.

"Well, spill it. Any time now."

"This might be a little complicated to explain. So I'll tell you back home after a glass of grass jelly." He nodded.

The scene ends with them leaving the ruins of what remains of Ding's school. A full moon brightly shines as they never look back.

Chapter 15

The Admiral's Lament

Returning home, Bamboo takes his time sipping hot tea by a fireplace. Alistor and the party patiently wait for him to begin. Finally, he places his cup down, halfway finished.

"It's about time I tell you what I know. So heed my words, if you choose to believe or not. It's a rather depressing tale." Bamboo warned.

"Well, we're ready for anything. We can take this." Alistor requested.

"Very well then...."

There was once a renowned sailor. His name was Bombshell, and he spent most of his days traveling on the open seas. An adventurer like you all at one point. He was a hero who worked his way up to fame and glory during the late Zophian era.

And, of course, there was a woman once in his life as well. Her name was Kimi Taranaka of the Taranaka household. So naturally, he became infatuated when they set eyes and eventually fell in love, only to be matched by his passion for the sea.

Serving under the late king of the Zephrite kingdom, they were at war with Magval. Two powerhouse nations competing for dominance at one point, and unfortunately, he always had to leave. Still, Kimi would always patiently await his return.

When there's a war, there have always been casualties, and the losses are significant.

He was up against a nation that employed hundreds of thousands of wyverns at their disposal. Magval was renowned for striking fear within the hearts of their opponents.

Viper's Labyrinth

Many commanders were either overwhelmed or swarmed by their sheer numbers. The most tremendous Aerial force to be reckoned with during that time.

But he did not allow that fear to discourage him. The Admiral had the Superior Naval fleet, and with his trusted anchor, nothing stood in his way of battle. He was a maniac who would stand between the lines of a dragon's gunfire.

As a skilled navigator, Kimi was the source of power and inspiration that allowed him to fight. He was a ruthless warrior, taking on countless swarms as many fell to his anchor. He was the one to lead the way toward victory.

Eventually, this sparked an outburst toward his enemy. A slayer who soon became an adversary worthy of a bounty. A great enemy towards Magval.

But with victory came a price, and one day he stood from the sideline witnessing from another perspective. He was responsible for bringing grief, pain, and sorrow to many. Baring tremendous guilt towards the many widows and orphans he created.

One fateful icy winter, Kimi fell ill while at sea. Unfortunately, her condition rapidly deteriorated, and she passed before he could return. Struck and deeply saddened, Admiral Bombshell could only blame himself for not being at her side.

The Admiral eventually discovered he had been discharged from the service and that she could have been nursed back to health by her people. But, furthermore, they wanted him disposed of as well. Enraged, he took matters into his own hands.

Storming and blasting his way through the palace, he made his way toward the throne room and eventually took the king's life. From one thrust of his anchor, nothing was left of the king's head. And so he was on the run, an enemy to both nations. The Admiral had no place to go.

He was a hero, yet many things were done that he was not so proud of. Some say he's still tormented by nightmares and hallucinations of Kimi. And so, he vowed to never look back from his guilt and perceived failure to his beloved.

This war gave rise to an even more significant threat. The Aggerona Empire emerged, and it wasn't before long he got recruited. Leaving both Zephrite and Magval to perish from a blind ambition. And the rest was history...

Bamboo's story ends from there. The party didn't know what to further ask, as they all took a moment to sink it in.

"Well....I don't know what to say." Alistor replied.

Bamboo goes back to sipping his tea.

"And that's why dragons are no longer much relevant this day," Auroa noted. "The admiral nearly wiped them all out."

"With the help of Aggerona, of course." Bamboo nodded. "With his experience, they easily overthrew both nations putting them in their place."

"Okay, so we got some backstory on this guy. But how will this help us beat him?" Maigashi asked.

"Yeah, we got three pieces of the mirror. But, unfortunately, the Admiral has the 4th piece, and we have no idea how to approach this guy." Alistor reminded.

Bamboo finishes his tea.

"I was about to get to that," Bamboo said.

Scouring through an old suitcase, he brings out an old unopened letter to show them. It was addressed to Admiral Bombshell.

"Are you serious?" Maigashi sarcastically remarked.

"This was a letter before Kimi Taranaka's death," Bamboo explained. "Her very last words that were never delivered to him."

This astonished everyone in the room for a moment. Then, hard to believe the very moment, Tannen got him back into a corner.

"And how did you happen to stumble upon this?" Tannen skeptically asked.

"Whoah! Wait a minute! This letter was passed down through generations of master chefs." Bamboo further explained.

"I was a student once learning the way of good cooking under the wings of Master Shimi. Originally Kimi's best friend was a great cook during her time, so she requested her to deliver this letter to him. She agreed but could not do so after seeing how depressed the Admiral was. Nonetheless, she believes it was best things were left unsaid after hearing the news of the monster he became."

The party took his word.

"So no one bothered to ever deliver it? Not even take a quick peek?" Maigashi asked. "At least you should have been tempted to look inside?"

Bamboo started to feel the jitters. A cold feeling creeps from behind him.

"Hey, I don't go snooping into personal letters. It's like bad luck."

"Come on, you can't be serious." Maigashi pressed on. "How do you know it's not some kind of fake?"

Viper's Labyrinth

He snaps the letter right from him.

"No! No! My master told me that's like a curse right there. Never open letters not addressed to you. Especially from dead ones. And that's what his master told before to him as well. It's like a burden for each chef who came before me. I had to be the unfortunate one to take it. You don't want spirits haunting you."

"What, are you scared?" He further teased him.

Bamboo snatched it back.

"Just don't open it. I'll keep hold of this until your next encounter with the Admiral."

"Whatever." Maigashi shrugged. "Not that it would make a difference."

"Even if it's real or fake? Fine then..." Tannen shrugged.

"So our plan is to give this letter to the Admiral. But where?" Alistor asked.

Bamboo nodded.

"An event is coming up in a few days. The Bon festival." He suddenly announced.

"What's that?"

He begins explaining.

"It's an event dedicated to honoring the spirits of one's ancestors, including fallen ones who died in battle. It lasts for a few days and concludes with Toro Nagashi. A ceremony in which participants float paper lanterns down a river."

"Oh yeah. I may have passed through there several times during my early days." Auroa recalls.

"But over the years, it became a fairground and a tourist attraction. So most likely, the Admiral won't miss the chance to plan an attack, I assume."

"So you assume? Great..." Maigashi sighed.

"Well, it's worth a try. Plus, I have a stand set up every year at this event. So your next mission is to accompany me to make sales in this festivity."

The party gives off a moan.

"More work? Don't worry; you can all take turns in shifts. I only need one of you. So you can all enjoy the festival." He assures them.

Max Mathesius

Back at the Aggerona's lair, the Admiral announced his next plan.

"Ah, the Bon Festival, you say? This may be the best opportunity to feed the labyrinth further." Vilevelious was pleased to hear.

"Thousands will gather for this event. I have already ensured a monster within the festive supplies."

The emperor was skeptical for a moment.

"And that will be enough? What makes this monster any different than the last failures sent?"

"I place my entire fleet on the line. They will be ready in case things fail. This monster will be just the bait needed to cause a riot. Once things are set in motion, I'll personally take the battle." Bombshell declared.

The Admiral took a bow.

"A desire to go all out already? This brings back such sweet memories. The very day you became one of us, and how I later stole your loyalty away from him."

He had no response.

"Yes, I still remember the reaction on his face. In fact, you never explained why you desired to serve under me? Our force has a very minimal concern with the sea."

"It doesn't really matter. Your goal is my dream and nothing more."

The Admiral takes his leave, vanishing from the room.

A few days later, Alistor and the party arrives at the event. They assisted Bamboo with the setup as crowds flocked within hours.

"So, Tannen is taking the first shift," Auroa said. "Where should we head first?"

"Hey! There's a house of mirrors and a wax museum over there." Maigashi pointed. "Let's check them both out."

The three enter the house of mirrors. Meanwhile, Admiral Bombshell arrives from the other side of the festival. A lady in the woman's apparel section suddenly screams and faints at the sight of the Admiral.

"Heh, such a loud nuisance."

Bombshell walks through the clothing racks before stopping at a section of overpriced purses. He raised his hand out.

Viper's Labyrinth

"Higabon! I summon you."

A monster suddenly begins to materialize from one of the purses on the wall. A headless knight wielding an extravagant purse.

"Go and do some damage. Use any means of force necessary."

"At your command, Admiral."

Higabon teleports out from the store.

Meanwhile, the three continue their tour through the rooms within the house of mirrors. Then, they suddenly hear a loud noise outside.

"Was that the sound of someone screaming outside?" Alistor wondered.

"Nah, you just hear things," Maigashi said.

"Are you sure? It could be the Admiral attacking."

"Just relax; things are not what it seems when you're in this kind of place." Auroa took a moment to gaze in the mirror.

Back outside, the monster can be seen mingling with the public crowd. People in costumes here and there.

"Hey, Mr., What's with the purse?" Some random guy asked. "You carrying some nice load in there?"

The monster reacts back, swinging him hard. The man gets sent flying into a food stand. Security immediately comes in as the three exits the house of mirrors. They stood by to watch the scene.

"Do we have a problem here?" A security guard asked.

"Ooh, this pervert tried to mug me. He got so close, I just had to whack him." The monster explained.

"Uh...sorry, Mr. uh, I mean mam, or whoever you are. We'll take care of it from here."

The security takes the man away while Higabon leaves to continue more nuisance.

"What a weird costume. Must have come out of that wax museum." Maigashi thought.

The party goes to check out the wax museum next.

Max Mathesius

Meanwhile, Bamboo is busy cooking dishes to serve the crowd at the food court. Higabon goes to take all the samples offered at the stands. Shoving food into its headless body.

"Oh, we have a hungry one right here." Bamboo smiled. "Care to try my dish?"

The monster grabs the whole plate from his hands, shoving it all down. Bamboo only claps with joy.

"Bravo! Now try some grass jelly."

Higabon shoves the whole block of grass jelly into its body. Then, a few seconds later, the monster hurls it all out on the crowd. A woman gets traumatized by the mess on her.

"My dress! My beautiful dress! It's all ruined." She screamed to the monster. "You're gonna have to pay for my dry cleaning, ya know."

The moment she got close to lay a finger, Higabon shocked her with the heat-ironing piece from his arm. She gets flung back into the crowd.

"So much for the appetite." Bamboo pity.

"My shift is over." Tannen couldn't care less what happened.

The three return to the food court only to notice the mess in the middle. Higabon casually walks away.

"Looks like it's my turn." Alistor volunteered as Tannen left to join Maigashi and Auroa.

The three heads by the game corner. Stuffed animals lined the shelves as they noticed a crowd of disappointed kids in the shooting gallery.

"Sorry, kid, not a winner. Try again?"

"I'll have a go." Maigashi steps in. "So, which one do ya want?"

The kid pointed to the animal on the far right. He takes a shot hitting the target as the man relinquishes the prize.

"Now, which one next?"

The kids pointed to the larger one on the top. He successfully lands another perfect shot as the kids happily jump. He continues to play on.

"Since when did he take a liking to these games?" Tannen asked.

"He can go on for hours. So we may as well find something to talk about." Auroa said.

Viper's Labyrinth

As Maigashi continues to play, Higabon can be seen passing through the background. Then, finally, the monster approaches a game.

"Knock the bottles! The winner gets a prize! You there! Want to give it a shot?"

The man gives the ball to the monster, but instead, it throws its purse, knocking the stack down.

"Hey! Hey! That's not what you're supposed to do. No prize for you."

Higabon immediately knocks over the game stand, shattering all the bottles. Maigashi and the party took a moment to look back but ignored the situation.

"Who do you think you are?" The man pointed. "You ruined my business. But, hey, wait...what are you doing? Put me down."

The monster lifts the man up, throwing him into a cotton candy stand. The kids at the shooting gallery continue to cheer Maigashi on. Hours passed as all the stuffed animals nearly cleared away on the shelves.

"No more games for the day. No more! I'm losing money." The owner of the game refused to stay open.

"Well...that was riveting." He sarcastically expressed.

Auroa took a look at the time.

"Seems like it's my turn to take the next shift." He leaves as Alistor rejoins the party to the fair rides.

By the rides, the three took a moment to browse their choices. But, unfortunately, they cannot decide which ride to go on first.

"There's always the Swing Carousel and a Ferris wheel," Alistor suggested.

"Nah! Too slow for my taste." Maigashi nodded.

"Can't we just pick something to go on?" Tannen sighed. "Hey, something's not right over there."

They finally notice a crowd panicking. Security gets tossed aside as they spot the monster attempting to tear down a Ferris wheel.

"Hahaha, I'll start with this Ferris, then move on to the next attraction."

"Stop right there." Alistor points his blade toward the monster.

Higabon ignores him completely.

"Ouch… That's a cold shoulder right there." Maigashi chuckled.

"Shut up! I'll show this monster not to ignore me." He rushed in with blinding rage.

The moment he got close, Higabon turned around to knock him back with a purse. Alistor gets sent crashing into a hot dog stand.

"A purse? You got to be kidding me?"

Maigashi and Tannen rushed in but got whacked as well.

"Gah! That actually hurts." Maigashi complained.

"It's even deadlier than my scythe." Tannen hated to admit it.

"Maybe a ranged attack might work."

The two immediately attempt to fire back from a distance, but the purse absorbs the attacks. Higabon sends their attacks right back at them as Alistor gets back up.

"Okay, now what? Any ideas, Tannen."

Tannen turned his back away from the battle.

"This fight is not worth our time."

"What? You mean we're gonna ditch this monster?" Maigashi asked.

He nodded.

"We're not getting paid enough for this." He reasoned.

They suddenly hear the sound of cannons firing from the other side of the festival. Their priority quickly shifts, turning their backs away from the monster.

"That must be the Admiral's ship. Come on!"

The three of them decide to ditch the monster. The Ferris tips to its side as Higabon is left dumbfounded.

"Hey, wait! Wait a minute? Where are you going?" Higabon was puzzled to ask. "What, I'm not a good enough monster to destroy you? Get back here!"

Higabon gets irritated.

Viper's Labyrinth

The monster attempts to chase after them but can't keep up. It trips over a whip as Auroa enters the battle, stunning the demon from behind.

"Now!" Auroa yelled.

Alistor goes in with his Starbreaker attack as the monster tries hard to get back up. His attack plunges through the monster's armor. Sparks of energy burst out from the headless knight.

"But I didn't have a chance to try the coasters." Higabon cried.

The monster drops its purse before collapsing in one big explosion. Nothing but debris was left from the flames.

"I can't believe that plan actually works," Alistor said.

"If the monster ignores you. Just simply ignore it back." Tannen suggested. "Plus, it didn't seem capable of running in the first place."

"Let's go take care of the admiral."

Alistor and the party make their way to the shorelines of the festival. An entire fleet of battleships awaits them. Each with skulls latched on the mast draining energy from the crowd panicking.

"Just on time for the finale," Bombshell announced to them.

Their jaws dropped at the sight of the Admiral's army. Thousands of Vilevelious whoopers aboard each ship.

"There must be at least over a hundred ships." Auroa estimated. "We're outnumbered."

"Yes! And this battle will be your very last. Fire away!" The Admiral commanded.

Cannons begin firing at the party as they immediately fall back for cover. The Admiral laughs at their attempts trying to get close.

"None of you can reach my fleet at this rate. So just give up already."

The fleet continues to drain energy from traumatized crowds at a fast pace.

"Well, this is just great. How are we supposed to fight the Admiral if we can't get close." Alistor asked.

Meanwhile, back at the food court...

"Oh, Auroa, you left in such a hurry. This letter! I must give it to them."

Max Mathesius

Bamboo closes the shop early and makes haste to the battle.

Auroa takes a moment to look back at the massive fleet studying the cannon's blast and range patterns. He spots a flaw.

"Have you noticed none of the fleet's shots are even aimed at us? It's as if they're missing on purpose." He pointed to them.

"Yeah, I wonder why?" Maigashi intensely looks at the fleet's cannons. "Of course!" He slapped.

"What do you mean?" Alistor asked.

"Simple, those cannons are equipped only for anti-aerial purposes. I know weapons pretty well." Maigashi claimed. "Just think back; why has the Admiral been collecting energy with those skulls? And we can clearly see all the victims being straight-up drained. So it's a crazy amount of people, right."

Alistor nodded.

"If his fleet kills any of them, they won't have the energy to steal."

"In other words, this is all just a meaningless scare tactic." Tannen figured.

The party emerges from hiding, charging toward his fleet. They make their way, boarding the closest ship. Admiral Bombshell suddenly pauses; as Maigashi starts destroying the skulls on each pole of the boats with his lightning arrows. The party easily plows through the waves of Whoopers on each ship. The vessels began losing energy as each skull shattered from the blast.

"How did they know?" Bombshell pounded against the wall. "At this rate, we'll have nothing left to bring back. So I'll just have to destroy them first."

The Admiral immediately calls his fleet off. The remaining ships disappear into the darkness, leaving only his ship to confront them.

"He called off the majority of his fleet?" Tannen pointed.

"I wonder why? We only took out thirty, and he still had another seventy-five." Maigashi counted.

Admiral Bombshell's flagship rams down the enemy ship they were on.

"Abandon ship!"

The four of them board the Admiral's ship to confront him. A stand-off commences briefly between them as the boat suddenly stops by the shore.

Viper's Labyrinth

"It all ends right here. We'll take your mirror piece and be one step closer to stopping Vilevelious. That labyrinth will never see the light of day."

"Round three, then? Come at me." The Admiral taunted.

Auroa and Maigashi went in with a combination attack, but a blast of his hand cannon split them apart. Alistor got close to disarm his weapon but was hit by his heavy anchor. Tannen goes in, hacking away with his scythe but gets caught in a tug of war. His scythe pressed against his anchor.

"This is just like last time. We need to try something else." Maigashi stated.

The Admiral overwhelms Tannen forcing him to break free from the struggle. However, he gets sent flying back. Tannen quickly counters with his reaper cards. It hits the Admiral this time, but it has no effect.

"What? But how. That's just crazy."

"My will to fight is stronger than any demon employed under my command. But, great power comes slow and steady."

Tannen gets damaged from a strike by his anchor. Alistor jumps in with his special attack aimed straight at Bombshell's chest.

"Starbreaker!"

"A direct hit!" Auroa snapped.

Alistor's attack slowly pushes against the Admiral as he attempts to break through him. Bombshell had close to no reaction. His attack dies out as he quickly gets tossed aside from the mere chains of Bombshell's anchor.

"Damn it! I can't tell if this guy is really taking damage."

Auroa attempts to bind the Admiral with his wind.

"We cross again, wind channeler." The Admiral softly spoke.

"I got you where I want this time."

The Admiral remained calm without any hesitation.

"Your technique…How powerful will it be when perfected? I can sense a great amount of untapped potential."

Moist builds inside the vortex as aquatic power shrouds the Admiral's body.

Max Mathesius

"What?"

The Admiral suddenly turns the vortex against him with his very own.

A tornado composed of water begins swirling rapidly in the ship's center as Auroa loses his grasp and gets thrown back to the rest.

"Plutonic Turbulence!"

The Admiral's vortex breaks down to a tidal wave gushing through the whole deck. The party takes the brunt of his entire attack. Auroa, Tannen, and Alistor are down for the count.

"Where's that other one?" Bombshell asked.

"Over here!" Maigashi yelled.

He turns around to notice his ship's cannon aimed directly at him.

"Hope you like a taste of your own medicine."

Admiral Bombshell suddenly gets blasted by his ship's gunfire. Cannonballs impact the general making a deep hole in the boat. Explosions set off in the burning pit as the Admiral gets engulfed in the debris.

"Yeah, that has to leave a mark. We got him this time."

"I simply recalibrated his cannon while you three kept him busy," Maigashi explained.

An anchor suddenly comes flying straight at them. Maigashi jumps out of harm's way as it destroys the ship's cannons. The Admiral emerges right out from the smoke unharmed.

"Nice try, but you'll have to do better."

"Unreal..." Alistor thought.

"This is just like last time. We're getting nowhere in this fight. This guy is like a brick wall. Not even a single dent." Maigashi ranted on.

"I have enough strength for one more attack," Tannen announced.

"Well, it might be a good time to do it now. We're running out of options."

Admiral Bombshell continued his approach toward them.

Viper's Labyrinth

"But we have to make this one count, and this guy won't let his guard down for even a brief second. So one of you needs to make an opening somehow."

They didn't have time to plan as Maigashi shook his head with disbelief.

"Hold it!"

Bamboo enters the scene with a letter to the Admiral amid battle. Maigashi took a glance back at him. Then, the conflict comes to a sudden halt.

"Are you serious? Now's not the best time for this."

The Admiral suddenly lowers his guard.

"Wait, that's Kimi's handwriting. Hand it over!" He demanded.

He hands over the letter without hesitation. The Admiral opened it right out and began reading it. The sound of Kimi's voice resonates through his mind.

My dear love, I am no longer of this world if you are reading this. Fate struck, and I've unexpectedly fallen ill, but I can only guess you'll blame yourself for it. Although you'll mourn, never lose touch with what you love. No matter where you go or what you do. You have already given me a lifetime's worth of dreams.

You have crossed oceans to find me, and I'll never regret our short time together. Crazy but true, I promise to wait for you beyond this life. Even in your darkest hour, never forget who you are. You're not alone and will always be special in my heart. Maybe in the next life, we'll have another try.

Yours truly,

Kimi Taranaka

The thought of Kimi only flowed through his mind at the moment. But then, he suddenly has a flashback. To a point and time, confronted by a dark figure before him. An unknown man with long dark hair approaches him.

"Sometimes, this world doesn't need a hero."

"What do you mean?" The Admiral confusedly asked.

"You are lost, seeking answers. What is right or wrong? Who is good or evil? I'll tell you there's no such thing."

"What do you want then?"

He presents him with a crystal orb.

Max Mathesius

"An enemy of our enemy is a friend of ours. With this, you'll have the power to destroy those who took her away from you. A new purpose is what you need."

The Admiral gladly accepted the offer; from that day, his human self was lost. Turning into the demon, he is now today.

"Ah yes, little brother is going to be jealous once he hears." The unknown man laughs.

As time progressed...

"What? You're leaving already?"

"I'm transferring to your brother's army. I have a purpose of fulfilling." Bombshell broke the news.

"But he doesn't have anything to do with the sea. Just a musky old labyrinth. You will regret this."

The Admiral turns his back away from the man who gave him power. The flashback fades from there. The thought of Kimi only crossed his mind as Tannen rushed in with his big attack.

"Symphonic Darkness!"

Darkness surrounds and wraps across him, crashing down with a vast force. An explosion commenced leaving lots of smoke in the air. The Admiral emerges right out from the smoke, still able to stand.

"What? He actually lived through that?" Maigashi was astonished to say.

The Admiral raised his anchor once more for another attack but suddenly paused. He collapsed right to his knees as the boat top of his head dropped right off, revealing an empty shell with a soul trapped inside.

"And this is what brought me to my final mission. To be close to Kimi. This is the reason I fight on. To gather energy for the labyrinth." He confessed.

"What? How absurd." Alistor said.

Bombshell gives some last words with the letter still clutched in his hands.

"I've lived long enough to know how to kill, and I know how to do it, so there is no pain. You're still young with a whole life ahead. So don't be like me."

The headless Admiral leaves himself open and ready for the final blow.

"Kimi...please wait for me."

Viper's Labyrinth

With one final swing, Tannen frees the Admiral's soul. Energy bursts out into purple flames dispelling the evil contained deep inside. His body slowly fades away on a starry night. A mirror shard and a blue orb were left behind.

"So his body was nothing more than a shell of what was left of him." Auroa realized.

Alistor goes to pick up the mirror and sphere left behind.

"This sphere contains the essence of the admiral's power."

Bamboo suddenly senses a ghostly presence in the air. Then, light emits, clearing the darkness away from the open seas.

"It's a lady."

A ghostly woman smiles while the spirit of a man in uniform appears before them. Reunited at last, the rest took a moment to watch. The couple stares down at them.

"Thank you…"

With one wave of goodbye, the couple happily departs.

One hour later, Bamboo and the rest of the party gathered by the shore with everyone else. The closing event to bring a close to the Bon Festival.

"So why are we lighting these lanterns again?" Alistor asked.

"It is believed that this guides the spirits of the departed back to the other world," Bamboo said.

They release the lanterns into the water, lighting up the night.

As the paper lanterns drift away into the open night, Vilevelious watches from the other end back at the base.

"The admiral had his way; it looks like you're up, Meister."

The silhouette of the final general appears behind the emperor. Two yellow eyes are visible within the darkness.

"Leave it to me! Nya ha ha ha ha."

With four mirror shards in Alistor's possession, the party draws close to reaching the labyrinth. But, with the final showdown with Vilevelious on the way, one lone fragment remains. So, what will the last general have in store for them?

Max Mathesius

Chapter 16

Grand Encounter:

The Final General Triumphs

"Hurry up! The last part is gonna unfold." Shellshock hollered. "I don't wanna miss any of it."

Mushogun and Scrap Ram's spirits appeared before him.

"I got the popcorn."

"About time. Hey, I think those kids are talking about us."

Shellshock peeps through the window as the other two struggle to get a view.

"Let me get a look." Scrap Ram pestered.

Alistor and the party reflect on their adventures so far at the restaurant. Gazing at the mirror fragments and essence collected at the table.

"One general remains." Alistor repeats. "The biggest and worst of them all. The strongest one, Vilevelious, saved for last. So I should be the one to lead the final battle."

He suddenly gets knocked over the head.

"Hold one minute!" Maigashi snapped. "Don't get too full of yourself. You wouldn't have made it this far without us. Plus, I was the one who handled Commander Shellshock, remember?"

Scenes from his battle at the Ski Resort flashed back to them.

Viper's Labyrinth

"Shellshock was the most versatile one. So I should be the one to take the last guy. You can have your fun with the emperor."

"But I defeated Mushogun!" Alistor objected.

The others begin to laugh.

"Mushogun, who?"

"He was the guy you finished back at the parking lot," Bamboo recalled.

Back outside, Mushogun was belittled as the other generals laughed away.

"Well, at least I didn't go down at a parking lot." Shellshock shrugged. "I went down someplace eventful."

Returning inside, Auroa had a say in this.

"If you're speaking about eventful, it was Axe's concert where I finished Scrap Ram when I was injured. He was the most troublesome."

Tannen then steps in.

"Troublesome? The Admiral was the one who had you all running for your money. He was the most calculating one. If anyone, I should be the one to first have a shot with the last guy. My scythe will be enough."

The party continued to debate while Bamboo returned to the kitchen. Outside, a cold wind drifts past the lurking generals by the window.

"We meet again...."

The Admiral appeared before the others to join them. The three stood fazed for a brief moment.

"Can it be? Admiral, but how? Didn't you turn good?" Shellshock questioned.

"Fools! That spirit was the weak human trapped within me. I am the evil that fueled him."

The others didn't question further.

"Makes sense, I suppose." Mushogun shrugged.

Somewhere back at the enemy lair, the emperor gazes at the labyrinth from someplace high above.

Max Mathesius

"We're getting close. Thanks to the Admiral, we now have 79% of the energy needed. I leave the rest to you to complete our mission."

The final general remains behind the shadows. His yellow eyes and top hat are barely visible.

"NYA, HAHA! No fret! I've studied every one of their moves. I cannot lose."

"Where shall you begin?" Vilevelious wondered.

A big screen appeared in front of him.

"Mathias city shall be the final place to collect the remaining energy needed." Announced the general.

"Good! Now go!"

Returning to the party, Bamboo comes up with a solution to end the dispute. Some straws are seen in his hands.

"We can draw straws to see who fights the next general. Whoever picks the one with the red tip gets to fight first. Followed by the rest from tallest to shortest. The one with the tallest fights second, and so on."

"Fair enough." Maigashi shrugged.

Each member of the party begins picking one of the five straws. Finally, four are pulled, revealing plain white ones.

"Hmm, then that means... I get to fight the general."

Bamboo pulls the final straw in his hand, revealing the red one. The disappointment was in Alistor's eyes.

"It seems you drew the smallest." Auroa giggled.

"Ah, no fair!"

"Seems you'll be fighting last. Just leave the rest to the adults here." Maigashi pestered.

Bamboo had a sly look on his face.

"This is my time for some screen time. With my cooking, I shall pounce the final general like an action movie star. Just wait and see."

He continued to object as the straws were tossed aside.

Viper's Labyrinth

"No! This isn't fair."

Bamboo whacks him over the head with a ladle as the rest of his friends begin laughing. Alistor suddenly gets fired up at the table, causing a couple plates to fall over.

"No! I'm tired of feeling small. Being belittled and treated like some helpless kid."

He barged right out of the restaurant.

"Should we go after him?" Auroa asked.

"Let him be." Bamboo nodded. "He needs to cool off. Right now, I have some preparations to do."

He leaves into the kitchen, giving a quiet chuckle as he disposed of the straws.

"What they don't know is all of them are red-tipped. Just a matter with the sleight of hands."

Meanwhile, Alistor continues to run off into the distance downtown before coming to a stop moments later. Lying the back of his head on the wall by some electronic store. He closed his eyes to collect his thoughts.

"Hey, he's right over there." Shellshock pointed.

The four general spirits passed through the wall. Their heads peep right out of solid glass, watching over Alistor.

"So cocky, don't you say?" Scrap-Ram whispered.

"If I had my body again, I could easily destroy this chump." Mushogun blabbered.

"As if..." Shellshock sarcastically remarked.

"Hey! That fight was a minor setback. If I had a second chance, I could pummel him."

Nearly an hour passed as Alistor stood in one place while the generals continued rambling. Then suddenly, some breaking news appears on the T.V, catching his attention.

"A massive explosion just occurred off a refinery by the coast near Mathias City. In addition, we've experienced a major power outage due to some unseen disturbance."

A picture is handed to the reporter.

"This is just in. A picture of the alleged suspect, appearing to be cloaked in yellow with a large top hat."

Max Mathesius

An explosion suddenly sets off behind the reporter. The news crew panics as the camera focuses on the mysterious figure swooping down. He grabs the mike off the reporter's hands. His face is still extensively covered on screen.

"Nya, haha! It is I, the one and only. The final demon general. Your city is as good as done. The labyrinth draws close to its completion. So challenge me if you dare!"

The transmission cuts from there. A sudden burst of motivation was seen in Alistor's eyes. Alistor begins to rush off in a new direction as the generals continue to follow.

"Yes! This is my chance to prove myself."

He is seen leaving town in the distant sunset. Passing by the Kabuki Coliseum and slipping through the Power Plant. His path is set on a course to the city of Mathias. Within an hour, he arrives at the pier in the town. The weather quickly became cloudy as he spots a cloaked figure sitting comfortably by a café. Without hesitation, Alistor approached the man with his blade.

"So you're the general? I will end you right here and now."

The figure turned his chair around.

"Grand, you could make it. Would you like some tea?"

He takes one step back, fixated on the general.

"Heck no! I came to fight."

The general placed his napkin down before getting up.

"That's no way for a gentleman to behave. A proper introductory greeting is how to begin things."

"I don't care!" Alistor pestered.

The general remove the sheet covering part of his face. A great mustache set before his very eyes.

"I am known as the Mustache Meister. General of the 5th platoon of the Aggerona army. As long I have my mustache, I am invincible. So surrender now!"

Surprised and speechless for a moment. Alistor started to crack as his worries began to slip away.

"What's so funny?"

Viper's Labyrinth

"At first, I thought Vilevelious saved the strongest for last." He pointed. "But you're not so intimidating. With such a ridiculous getup, Vilevelious must have run out of quality followers by now."

The general cracks open his cane.

"Better be watching your mouth, boy."

Alistor continues to act cocky as he makes the first move.

"About time!"

Making one quick hard swing, the Meister dodges with little effort. But unfortunately, his blade gets stuck on the wooden plank.

"A predictable strike to avoid by 30 degrees to the left."

The general retaliate back with a cane slap knocking him back. Alistor gets right back up to strike again but gets tripped over.

"Ow!"

He falls flat on his face as the Meister follows up with a beam of lightning, sending him off to the side.

"Give up, boy! You are no match for me!"

An annoyed look was now on his face.

"I'm just getting started."

He recklessly continues his charge but quickly gets stopped by a door appearing in place. Bringing him to a brief halt.

"What the heck?"

The Meister's fist burst through an open hole punching him hard. Blood begins to drip under his nose.

"My door summoning technique. Think I'm messing around?" The Meister snapped.

Alistor got right back up, determination still in his eyes.

"I'm not through yet."

Max Mathesius

He begins charging for the Star Breaker attack. Bursting with energy as he makes a significant jump toward the general.

"A simple countermeasure." The general nodded.

Before he can land his attack, the Meister kicks the door in midair. The Star Breaker impacts the door knocking him down.

"Are you serious?" Alistor furiously yelled.

He continues to fight on blindly swinging, but the general easily avoids his attacks. But then, the Meister suddenly slapped him back.

"Give it up! I know your moves. You cannot win."

The thought of the rest belittling him slipped through his mind.

"Don't underestimate me!"

Alistor goes in with the Star Breaker once more as the Meister nods.

"Enough games!"

The general pulls out his whip catching him by the leg as he gets stopped once more. The Meister slams him across the wooden planks as an electrical surge shocks his body. Blood begins to cough out from his mouth as he lies helpless, struggling to stand up.

"I won't give up. Not yet."

"Foolish boy!"

The Meister kicks him back down. He then sends a Shockwave through his body once more as he screams out in pain. Rain begins to pour down.

"It's over…." The general snickered.

Alistor desperately grabs onto his boot but loses his grasp from a simple shake. Blood continues to drip out from his body as he loses consciousness.

"It's getting late. The tea has gotten cold."

The Meister catches a glimpse of an approaching figure not far from a distance.

"This will do."

Viper's Labyrinth

The general reached his pocket for a calling card, placing it by Alistor before taking leave. The rain continued to pour as the four generals watched under a large cabana.

"Oh golly! The Meister sure messed him up good." Shellshock jumped.

"Hoo! It was a rather quick fight, I have to say." Scrap-Ram replied.

Some tears were seen on Mushogun's face.

"My glory was taken away…."

"Quit your whining." The Admiral nodded.

"Hoo, look! Someone is coming."

The figure approaches Alistor's body as the scene fades from there. Moments later, at Bamboo's, an unexpected face showed by the doors. The bad news was in store for them.

"DUDE!!!"

"Axe, is that really you?" Maigashi said.

"What? You mean Alistor's been badly hurt?" Bamboo gasped. "We have to hurry!"

A while later, the party arrived at the hospital. There, Alistor was undergoing treatment in critical condition.

"Who could have done this?" Auroa asked.

Axe hands over Meister's calling card to the group. Tannen examines it over with the lens.

"Someone by the name of Mustache Meister. The final general."

The mystery quickly cleared in the room.

"Alistor, you cocky idiot." Maigashi nodded. He then turns his attention to Axe. "So, how did you round up finding him."

"Yes, I'm rather curious as well." Auroa wondered. "Aren't you supposed to be on tour?"

Axe begins to explain himself.

"Yeah, my bandmates and I are on tour. We're supposed to perform in this city. But the concert has been delayed due to the recent power outages."

"I see…"

Max Mathesius

"Yeah, dudes! Cheryl and the others are staying by the hotel near the pier. I pretty much have plenty of free time on my hand. So we can hang around for a while."

The mood begins to brighten as the party catches up.

Meanwhile, back at the Aggerona hideout…

"Splendid job!" Commented Vilevelious. "Such a brutal beating delivered. Now his life is lingering on edge."

The Meister takes a bow.

"My pleasure!"

"So? What will you do to obtain some energy?"

"Already done. At this moment, my monster has infested the city's people in their sleep."

Visual footage is presented on screen.

"I present to you Wizjin. This monster will feed on people's dreams within the dream realm. A monster not of this very world."

"I like the sound of this so far." The emperor gestured.

"In a matter of days, our labyrinth will have all the energy we need."

Two days later…

The party is seen gathered at the table, planning for an approach. The Meister's calling card sits in the middle.

"It's been two days. Alistor has been diagnosed with a coma." Auroa lectured. "We have to do something, Bamboo."

"We don't know when he'll wake up. So we can't remain as sitting ducks." Maigashi pressed on.

Tension and sweat seeped through Bamboo's eyes.

"Make the call…." He whispered.

Tannen inputs the numbers contacting the Meister on the other end. Within moments a form of negotiation was underway. The Meister sets a time and a place for the meet-up, as Tannen wrote it down.

Viper's Labyrinth

"So? What did he say?" Bamboo nervously asked.

"We'll meet him at the Café pier. Two o clock by the city."

The party begins to leave for the city in Bamboo's car. Axe makes a jump into the backseat.

"Axe, you don't have to do this," Maigashi said.

"Nah, Dudes! I got your back. I owe you guys a favor. Who knows what could have happened if I hadn't found him."

"You're a true friend," Auroa replied.

"You can return the favor by giving us free backstage passes to your concert when this is over." Maigashi requested. "Well, Bamboo. Hit on the gas!"

And so the party takes off at high speed to the city.

"We won't let you down," Bamboo whispered to himself.

The party arrives in the docking bay within minutes. By the front of a café, they spot a striking figure sipping on a hot cup of tea.

"A lovely day, don't you agree?"

The Mustache Meister turns his attention towards them.

"So, you're the final general?" Maigashi asked.

"Mustache Meister's the name."

The general placed his cup down as he got up from his seat. He pulls out a large parchment. A quill pen dipped in a bottle appears before them.

"Grand, you can make it. So are we going to address your terms of surrender?"

The party was speechless for a brief second.

"Surrender?" Tannen questioned.

"I'm feeling rather generous today." The Meister announced. "All you have to do is sign on the fine print here."

The general skims past the long words. Bamboo first grabs hold of the quill pen, thinking intensely.

Max Mathesius

"And if we don't?" Maigashi pestered.

"Then you'll wind up like your dear friend." The general snickered. "If you do, there are free cookies."

Bamboo didn't hesitate to begin signing.

"Free! Sign us up."

Auroa and Maigashi quickly pull him back.

"Are you serious?" Maigashi slapped. "We can't just give up yet."

"Same here." Auroa agreed.

He tossed the quill back into the bottle.

"You're right!" Bamboo nodded. "You have to offer a better bribe than that."

The rest of the party stumbled.

"Well…How about a free color-screen T.V?"

The general pulls it right from under his cape. Bamboo grabs hold of the quill once more. Mesmerized by the colors before him.

"Free?"

"Yes!" The Meister snickered. "Features high grade 8 track quality sound."

Bamboo begins having second thoughts.

"Hmm, I don't know…Alistor did work hard for those mirror shards."

"Would a free microwave close the deal?"

A microwave oven drops right out of the general's cape. The party was slightly astonished for a brief moment.

"How does this guy carry all those things?" Maigashi asked.

"I don't know, dude!"

"Oh, why the heck not."

Viper's Labyrinth

As the pen touches the parchment, a sudden force breaks the ink bottle splattering over the papers. Bamboo quickly dropped the pen as both sides backed away.

"What? Who dares interfere?" Meister demanded.

From a distance, a figure in a ninja getup is seen hiding behind some boxes. Maigashi and Tannen immediately act, destroying the parchment in Meister's hand.

"The deals off!"

Bamboo quickly comes to his common sense as the general stomps over what remains of the parchment.

"Fine! Have it your way then."

The general pulls out his cane. Auroa readied his weapon along with the rest as Axe and Bamboo took a few steps back.

"You'll pay for what you did. We'll avenge Alistor if it takes all we got."

"Once you're done, Vilevelious is next." Maigashi pointed.

The three faced off with the Meister as bystanders began clearing from the café. Then, the general starts waltzing back and forth.

"Fools! You have no idea what you are dealing with. I represent a force far greater than you can imagine."

"Oh yeah? Who?" Tannen questioned.

"That is not of your concern." The general snapped. "I've memorized all your moves from your previous battles with my colleagues. None of you stand a chance, and as long I have my mustache, I am invincible."

The party immediately felt less threatened by his words. Axe and Bamboo didn't hesitate to step back in.

"This guy is so sure of himself." Maigashi pestered.

"Yeah, dude! Totally whacked."

"Let's end this quick." Tannen agreed.

The Meister stood his ground against the five as a battle was underway. The spirits of the four previous generals watched from a distance.

Max Mathesius

"Look like another show is about to begin." Shellshock pointed. "You brought the popcorn?"

A big bag of popcorn was attached to Mushogun's flag.

The Meister takes his first step toward the group. Observing them as they stood fearless and ready to go. Maigashi makes the first move sending a shot of lighting hitting the Meister.

"A direct hit!" Maigashi snapped. "Huh?"

Within moments the Meister stood unfazed as they witnessed his body absorbing the lightning.

"Nya ha! Thanks for the free charge."

An electrical aura begins flowing across his cape. Finally, the general fires the attack back at Maigashi.

"Another lightning user? Damn, this won't be a good matchup for me."

"Now it's my turn." Auroa stepped in.

He pulls out his wind whip.

"Ah, the Wind Channeler. I'll even the field by matching you up with my own."

The Meister pulls out his own whip, matching Auroa's attacks move to move as an electrical surge sends him back. Tannen then rushed in with his scythe.

"Allow me!"

The Meister avoids all his swings with ease. He then waves darkness, but the general opens his cape, forming an interdimensional door. The darkness disappears within seconds as Tannen gets sent back by a beam of lightning.

"He can absorb darkness too."

Bamboo and Axe Winston suddenly rushed in from two sides.

"I got your backs, dude!"

"Feel the wrath of my cooking!"

Before they even have the chance to strike, a ladder gets summoned from under the Meister, pulling him straight up. At the same time, Axe and Bamboo crash into one another.

Viper's Labyrinth

The party got right back up as the general got back down. He suddenly pulls out a handkerchief.

"Five on one? A bit excessive, but do I want to get dirty?"

"We're not done yet." Maigashi fired another shot.

The Meister jumps back, avoiding the shot as the others charge in.

"Fools! Let's see how you like this. Muskers!"

From the flick of his finger, enemy soldiers emerged from the waters catching the party by surprise. A line of energy fires, sending the group back.

"Who the heck are they?" Axe stammered.

"Not the usual Whoopers, for a fact." Maigashi jumped.

Coated in yellow and black, the new soldiers quickly surround the team. The general explains the details to them.

"These are my personal elite super soldiers. The Muskers!"

The party begins to clash with the enemy soldiers.

"They feel no pain. And they are far superior to your standard Whoopers."

A group of Muskers suddenly pulls out their rifles, intimidating the party. They lined into formation to begin firing energy at the group. Axe and Bamboo are sent flying back as the rest attempt to put on a fight.

"Man, these guys are brutal," Auroa commented.

Maigashi and Tannen counter with lighting and dark waves, bringing a row of soldiers down. Still, they quickly got back up within seconds.

"They defiantly take more hits compared to a Whooper." Tannen agreed.

The soldiers rushed in with their sword-tipped rifles. Maigashi and the rest clash with the Muskers while the other generals watch in envy.

"Since when did he have his own personal soldiers?" Shellshock asked.

He turned to the other generals for answers, but the Admiral only gave a shrug.

"They're putting up a better fight than our Whoopers." Mushogun sighed.

"We should have had our own personal soldiers, to begin with." Scrap Ram yearned.

"I know, right?" Shellshock agreed. "Working for minimum wage was bad enough. We should file a complaint or something."

The three generals write on a ghostly paper while the Admiral remains indifferent.

"If the emperor would even allow it." The Admiral nodded. "Knowing our budget, he's too cheap to even bother."

"Yeah…We sort of did exceed our expected budget," Scrap Ram reminded.

As the general spirits continue to fool around, the party struggles against the Muskers. Finally, they were backed into a corner while the Meister laughed.

"Surrender now! You don't stand one shred of a chance."

Bamboo started to whine while Tannen tried to think of a way out. Then, a sudden force quickly swoops down, knocking a group of soldiers down.

"What was that?" Maigashi sensed.

"I don't know. Here it comes again." Auroa pointed.

The soldiers stood, confusedly lost, as the force knocked the next group down. Then finally, the Meister skims the entire perimeter.

"Fools, he's right over there. Fire away!" The Meister commanded.

The soldiers stumbled back up, attempting to shoot but fired blanks.

"It looks like they need to reload?" Maigashi laughed.

Within seconds, a cutting sound swiftly pierced through the soldiers. Sparks are sent flying as ninja stars rain down on the group. The Muskers collapsed in place, vanishing as the Meister hesitated briefly.

"Who are you?" The general pointed.

The masked figure quickly swoops down to the scene. Pointing a short katana at the Meister.

"The one to stop you, of course."

The general didn't hesitate to step back.

Viper's Labyrinth

"This was not in the plan. Argh! Consider yourself lucky, but you'll never defeat my monster in the dream realm."

Within seconds, the Meister summons a door, taking his leave. Bamboo and the rest approached the figure before them.

"And who might you be?" Bamboo asked.

"Yeah, dude! Who are you? And thanks for saving us, by the way."

The figure quickly unmasked himself. It was none other than Katty.

"Hey! It's been a while, Bamboo."

Bamboo quickly filled the rest in as they returned to Alistor at the hospital. Katty was quickly outraged within seconds but kept his emotion under control.

"Yeah, he's been in this coma for the past few days." Auroa nodded. "He was determined to face the Meister alone."

"A really dumb move if you ask me," Maigashi said.

"We don't know when he'll wake." He further noted. "The Meister's monster has been terrorizing the town in their sleep for quite some time now. But unfortunately, none of us had the luck to confront it."

Within minutes Alistor's condition begins to worsen. A feeling of pain as the rest rushed for some help. A doctor attempts to lighten the situation, but his condition continues to escalate. Tannen takes a glance through his lens, revealing a dark presence.

"This must be the work from that monster." Tannen snapped.

Back at the enemy base, the Mustache Meister is seen holding a black crystal. Fueling energy for the labyrinth as he watches Alistor struggle.

"Yes, Wizjin! Destroy him from the inside."

Deep inside, Alistor finds himself in a distorted dimension. A barren wasteland with nothing but rocks floating across. Four demonic spirits begin to circle across him.

"Go away!"

He swings his blade around, but it has no effect. Instead, the spirits begin to laugh.

"That voice...Mushogun, reveal yourself." Alistor demanded.

"We meet again!" Mushogun laughed as he first materialized. "I got a bone to pick you."

Max Mathesius

The general slams his great flag at Alistor, knocking him down.

"I must gain some space."

He rolled out of the way, avoiding Mushogun's next strike, but the other spirits blocked his escape. Shellshock, Scrap Ram, and the Admiral appeared before him.

"How is this possible? We've already beaten you guys."

The other generals did not speak as Mushogun continued his assault. Alistor avoids the next attack, gaining enough room to counter back.

"Still slow as ever. If I can best you before, I can do it again. Star Breaker!"

Alistor plunged his blade through the shogun's stomach popping his spirit. Then, within a moment, the general reform.

"Nice try, but your attack is useless. We're already dead."

"No way!"

He begins to hesitate as the other generals laugh away. Finally, Mushogun pins him to the floor.

"Give it up. You can't win!"

Meanwhile, in the waking world, Katty quickly steps in, rushing to Alistor's side. Placing his hand on the top of his forehead.

"What are you going to try?" Bamboo asked.

"Something I learned back at the temple. I'm gonna reach Alistor through my voice."

Alistor suddenly heard a familiar voice in a matter of seconds.

"Katty, is that you?"

"If you can hear me, you have to try and wake up. You are in a dream fabricated by Meister's monster. None of this is real."

Mushogun continues to pressure him.

"But it hurts so much."

"The more you fight, the worse it will only get. It's not real! Trust me!"

Viper's Labyrinth

He then breaks free from the shogun's grasp. Standing his ground as Mushogun readies for a fatal strike. Closing his eyes, the general pierced through his body.

"I trust you...."

He opened his eyes, and in a matter of moments, Mushogun vanished. The other generals leave the scene as Wizjin appears before him, caught by surprise.

"Go ahead and take him out. We'll be waiting for you."

Katty gave his final words before leaving. Alistor readied his blade at the monster.

"You no longer have power over me. Time to end this nightmare."

With one leap, Alistor unleashed the Star Breaker vanquishing Wizjin within seconds. Then, the realm begins to fall apart as light appears before him to follow.

"Time to come home."

Back with the Meister, the black crystal shatters in the palm of his hands.

"Argh! Curses, I'll get you next time."

At the hospital, Alistor finds himself awake in bed. Surrounded by friends while Bamboo and Axe jump in joy.

"Hey, it's good to have you back." Katty greeted.

Somewhere outside, the general spirits watched in disappointment.

"So much for my screen time." Mushogun pouts. "I was having fun."

"So...what now?" Scrap, Ram wondered.

"Dunno..." Shellshock shrugged. "Peace is starting to return to their world. Come on! We'll be waiting for the final battle. Let's see how the ending unfolds."

Chapter 17

Arcade Madness:

Barrel Man and the wrath of Columnbrutey

"On the count of three, I want you to strike at me again."

Alistor is seen in the middle of training with Katty by the shores near the city. Axe watches the two go at it.

"Ow!"

Alistor is seen falling over as Katty swiftly dodges without effort.

"Is that really all you can do? I know you can do better." Katty pestered.

"Hey! I'm trying to keep up. You're just a little too fast."

The two come to a brief stop to catch their breath. Alistor quickly reflects back on his battle with the Mustache Meister. A discouraged look on his face.

"I just don't stand a chance. He's just too good."

"Not with that attitude, you won't." Katty pointed. "The Meister only won due to your lack of discipline."

"Yeah…I was cocky at the time. Caught in the heat of the moment. If it wasn't for Axe, I would have died."

Axe hands some drinks to them.

"Yeah, dudes! Even with our team effort. The general has the advantage. It's like he knows our moves."

The three gaze at the shores.

"He may have seen you fight, but he hasn't seen what I can do yet." Katty reminded.

"Hey! Come to think of it, you're pretty fast. How much training did you have to endure at the temple?"

"Tell us about it."

Katty goes to recollect his thoughts as they make their way to sit at a nearby table. Flashback from when they parted after Mushogun's defeat came back to him.

"It's a rather long story, but if you insist."

The two were focused.

"Right after we've parted ways, it was one tough road ahead. It took a month to reach the temple. On my way, I took many detours. Crossing raging rivers and rocky hills. But, the worst of it didn't come till reaching the Hydra Desert."

"The desert?" Axe questioned.

"Yeah, I had to actually pack adequately. Spent nearly all my cash getting hints or even a map for directions. The sandstorm was an even bigger thrill. As days went by, my supplies slowly diminished. With the tense heat rising, I wasn't sure if such a place existed."

A flashback of him was seen struggling on the sand.

"I was close to giving up. Down to my knees and crawling through the dust. Then finally, a shadow eclipsed me. It was a figure of a man, but I was tired and couldn't tell if he was real or not."

He is then seen losing consciousness.

"The one who took me in was Abotemous. That was when I knew I arrived at the temple."

"So what kind of training did you have to go through? Was it enjoyable?" Alistor asked.

Max Mathesius

"Are you kidding me? The training was total hell." Katty slapped. "To be exact, it was in the art of the ninja. Learning to be swift and agile with cat-like reflexes. In fact, there is a quick history lesson I can give on the temple and its history of Ninja and Cats."

The two quickly nodded.

"No! Just continue on," Axe said.

"Well, for the training, let's see…I had to hang upside down for seven hours daily for the first three weeks doing sit-ups. Then the next two weeks, I did nothing but keep my balance on some steep cliffs. Followed by some stamina workout."

A quick flashback shows him swimming.

"It wasn't till after two full months I got to work with weapons. Metal stars and Katanas were flying everywhere. Abotemous nearly ruined my good looks from this mad training."

"So, what was he like?" Alistor asked.

A quick breeze flew past them.

"Abotemous? Well, he's got this sort of disfigured look. A little bulky with pale skin and long dark hair. He may not look it, but he's fast."

"I see…"

"After four months, the remainder of my training was spent in isolation. I was thrown into the Cave of Deception. Forced to endure whatever came at me."

A scene shows him climbing out as he reaches for the light victoriously. Abotemous stood waiting before him.

"In the end, all his training paid off. In fact, I learned quite a few tricks thanks to him."

His story ends from there as the three head upwards.

"Let's go check on the others. I'm sure Tannen finished retrieving the supplies for Bamboo."

After a quick stroll, they find the car parked near a crowded building. The three check out the commotion.

"What's going on?" Alistor wondered.

They quickly spot Tannen fixed at some screen. Auroa was seen focused in the middle of a game while Maigashi cheered from the side.

Viper's Labyrinth

"I see you dudes haven't checked the new Arcade yet. Video games are starting to be on the rage."

The two are seen lost in the middle as they joined with Axe to watch. Auroa continues pressing buttons as meteors are shown blasted on the screen.

"Come on! You can do this." Maigashi said.

He continues to tensely focus with not even a single blink of insight. Then, in moments, the last wave of meteors explodes, causing the machine to ring loudly.

"Yes! A new high score!"

A small stuffed prize is given to them.

"Well, onto the next game?" Maigashi asked.

"Think I'll take a break from here." Auroa requested. "Axe can take things from here. I require a cold drink."

Axe heads with Maigashi to the next game as Alistor and Katty follow them.

"What are you guys doing?" Alistor asked.

"Playing video games, of course."

The two are seen inserting a couple coins. Then, picking up a pair of light guns as a game suddenly begins. A recolored scheme of Whoopers is seen being blasted away.

"Isn't this a waste of time? We can't keep Bamboo waiting."

"Chill out; we got plenty of time," Axe assured.

The two continue blasting away a pack of Whoopers on screen. Finally, a giant Mushroom monster appears on the screen.

"But you guys promised to help me train." Alistor reminded.

"Yeah, yeah, in a minute. We got a boss to beat."

The two were too focused on the game to bother listening. So instead, a mopey look was seen on Alistor's face as Auroa and Tannen joined to watch the game. Then, a game over was shown on screen in moments.

"Damn, we were so close!" Maigashi raged.

Max Mathesius

"Another go?" Axe said.

Alistor steps in between the two.

"Argh! No! I want to go home."

"Hey? It's not our fault you lost to Meister. Stop being serious. You need to kick back for once." Maigashi suggested.

"But this is a waste of time. Games won't help me."

Katty suddenly steps in on the topic.

"Actually, games could possibly help."

"What do you mean?" Alistor wondered.

He begins explaining the details to him.

"Remember earlier with our reflex training? You struggled to dodge my simple attacks. Even when you came in, I read all your moves."

A puzzled look was now on his face.

"So, where are you getting?"

"Maybe…Just maybe if you want to improve on your reflexes. Video games could be the answer we are seeking. To begin training your eyes against the unexpected."

An astonished look was now on Alistor's face.

"Really? Then let's begin."

Maigashi hands the light gun to him as Axe begins inserting the coins.

"Ok, dude! When I press the middle button, that's the cue for us to begin firing. Lock onto the target and blast away. And don't forget to reload; just hold the gun back and quickly step back."

"Right! Got it!"

As Axe presses the button, Alistor begins blindly firing at the screen. A Whooper is seen jumping over their player. A game over on the screen quickly commenced.

"Dude, what was that? You got to be a team player and coordinate."

Viper's Labyrinth

"Then let's go again."

Maigashi inserts a couple coins for both of them. Meanwhile, from another screen, Vilevelious and the Meister watch from above.

"So this is your latest plan to gather energy? Video games fuel the youth's mind with false hopes and dreams." The Emperor chuckled.

"Nya, yes! Games are now in demand. With this newly placed Arcade as a base of operations, nothing will stop our Labyrinth from feeding."

They oversee the many youths hooked to the machines.

"Hmm, but still. You need to dispose of Alistor and his brittle team." The Emperor reminded. "You had them on the run, but why did you retreat?"

"True, but they have a new player. I need to read his moves first."

"So what? This boy shouldn't make much of a difference. I want them destroyed as soon as possible."

The Meister begins calculating. He then looks over a kid on-screen playing a game. A game shows a man jumping over a barrel.

"I have our next candidate." The Meister announced.

"Oh? Who is it?"

The Meister calls forth his next monster.

"Barrel Man! Come forth!"

The monster arrived in the room within a matter of moments. Fully armored in wooden plates, Barrel Man makes an entrance.

"You rang, Meister?"

"Nya, yes! I need you to test the waters against this new player they got."

Katty's image was seen focused on the screen.

"This pretty little boy?"

The Emperor begins expressing doubts about his monster.

"Are you sure you're even competent enough? You abandoned your last mission with the Admiral during that Monster Bash."

The sound of a whip cracks between the Mustache Meister's hands.

"Hoo no! I won't run away this time. I promise! In fact, I have something to show you."

"Well, then bring it out!"

Barrel Man brings in an object covered with a large sheet.

"During the time off, I took the liberty to program this new game."

He pulls off the sheet, unveiling a new Arcade Machine. Flanked with Greek Columns and neon lights.

"I present Columnbrutey! The next hit game programmed by yours, indeed. This bad boy will bring more energy to the Labyrinth."

The Emperor was puzzled.

"But we already are gaining energy. So I need someone to destroy Alistor and his pesky team ."

"HOO! No worries, vile man. When enough energy is gathered, a new powerful monster will emerge to battle. Then I will jump in to take out this new player you speak of."

A transmission abruptly interrupts the room. The Emperor answers the call.

"Rare? Well, it's about time. You say we have a business to discuss? Excellent, we'll be there."

He turns his attention back to Barrel Man.

"Very well! Do whatever it takes to destroy them. I don't care how. We got a crucial meeting with Rare."

Barrel Man gets dismissed from the room.

"Hoo, I will. I will! I got plenty in store for them."

The following day later, the party cashes in on their paychecks. Bamboo goes to check the cash register.

"Hey? Where did my change go? Why are the coins all gone?"

Viper's Labyrinth

"Sorry, Bamboo! But we need it for the Arcade."

Alistor rushes out the doors as the party drives off with his car. Bamboo looks out into the horizon.

"Sigh…the weekend comes, and they're in a hurry to spend. Back to the kitchen."

Within the nick of time, the team arrives in the city. Axe Winston was seen waiting by the front entrance of the Arcade as Tannen parked Bamboo's car.

"Well, here we are!"

They enter inside. Alistor immediately grabs the nearest light gun as Katty joins by his side. The coins get inserted.

"You ready?" Katty said.

"More than ever!"

The game starts with them shooting at waves of discolored Whoopers on screen. Next, the rest of the party is seen playing various arcade games. Meanwhile, a door slightly creeps open from behind the counter. Barrel Man is seen taking a glance behind.

"Good! All the kiddies are here. Time to roll out my new machine."

As the party remains focused on the games, Barrel Man slips by the unnoticed crowd. With a push of a button, a top compartment opens up. He begins rolling out the new game machine by chains.

"Ok! We're at the boss. We can do this."

The two begin firing away at a giant mushroom monster. Barrel Man quickly plugs his machine and leaves for the back door. Alistor is seen intensely focusing.

"Just one more hit!"

The mushroom monster quickly explodes on the screen, and the victory screen pops up.

"Alright! We finally did it!"

The two quickly enter their names in the high score charts.

"Let's see what other games we can play."

Hours began to pass as the team went on to play countless other games. Then, finally, the group noticed a strange machine fixed at the center stage.

Max Mathesius

"What is this game?"

Maigashi goes to inspect the big machine. Neon lights flicker across as gems begin to roll out on the screen.

"Columnbrutey, it looks like some sort of puzzle game."

Alistor reached into his pocket for some coins.

"I'm down to my last coin."

"Well...give it a shot then." Maigashi shrugged.

He inserts the coin to begin the game, and a wrecking ball slams across the screen. He quickly jumps back. A timer appears as the gems start rolling across the screen.

"Quickly! Line three or more gems to break the columns."

He reached for the buttons to begin moving some gems across the screen. But, unfortunately, the timer quickly hit zero as the wrecking ball came smashing in with a game over.

"Over already?" Alistor gasped.

"Man, they don't give you much time." Axe nodded.

He then pulled out some bills.

"I'm beaten, but I still want to play more. Maybe I should cash in for more coins."

Katty immediately halts him from going any further.

"I think that's enough games for one day. After that, I think we're ready to resume our training."

"You mean it?" He jumped. "Let's go then."

The party exits the Arcade, leaving Barrel Man feeling salty behind the counter. The team begins splitting up.

"So, where are you guys heading?" Alistor asked.

"Just going to check the music store nearby. We'll be seeing you guys around." Auroa waved.

The two head back to the shores to resume training. Katty begins by throwing a few swings with his practice katana. Alistor's eye quickly catches on.

"Good! Now let's see you dodge these next attacks."

Katty goes in with more kicks and punches. Ninja stars are seen scattered across the smooth sands. Alistor swiftly avoids them without any problems.

"Boy, you've improved. Your reflexes got a bit better. The games really did sharpen your eyes."

Bamboo arrives at the scene, exiting from a taxi cab.

"Bamboo? What are you doing here?" Katty asked.

The taxi quickly drives off.

"Business was slow, so I closed early to check what you were all up to."

The three take gaze at the ocean. A dreamy look was on Bamboo's face.

"Such a view. The weather is fine, and I like this. Maybe I should relocate here."

Meanwhile, Axe and Maigashi leave the music store, searching for a bathroom.

"Man, what kind of place doesn't have a bathroom. This is annoying." Maigashi muttered.

The two find their way back to the Arcade once again.

"Maybe this place might have one." Axe pointed.

The two enter right inside. Maigashi and Axe go through the back door and stumble into the basement. Axe flicked on the lights.

"Whoah, look at all the machines."

"Yeah, but not a stall in sight. But man, I have to go."

Maigashi quickly finds some barrels fixed by a giant statue. He approached close to the object.

"Ok, Axe, I'm going to take a quick leak right over this corner. So you keep on the lookout."

As Axe turns away, Maigashi begins removing his belt buckle. The statue's eye begins to glow red, making a loud sound.

Max Mathesius

"What the hell?"

Maigashi and Axe immediately stumble back as barrels topple over.

"An alarm statue? Dude, we got to bolt!"

Back at the enemy lair, Barrel Man looks over the security monitor.

"What! My Barrels!"

As Axe and Maigashi ran for the doors, Barrel Man rushed off his chair. The two quickly slip by an unnoticed crowd playing. A group of kids is seen playing Columnbrutey in the background. As the two draw close to the exit Barrel Man drops in from above.

"Oh no, you don't. Think you can get away from breaking mah barrels?"

"You seem familiar?" Maigashi recalled. "Oh crap! You're that guy who bolted back from the Admiral's party."

He reached out for his bow as Axe got into a battle stance.

Barrel Man takes a good glance at the two.

"Neither of you is the new player the boss speaks about. But you can have some fun with this."

He pulls out a remote pressing the red button. From behind, the Columnbrutey game machine begins shaking up. The kids around quickly backed away as the machine formed into a complete monster. The crowd starts panicking out the doors.

"Ha Ha Ha! This bad boy will wreck things up."

Columnbrutey takes a few steps towards them.

"This monster is huge!" Axe gulped.

The two take a few steps back as Barrel Man endlessly chuckles.

"Let's take the battle outside. That will lure them. Columnbrutey, destroy them."

The monster launches a wrecking ball from its head. The Arcade entrance quickly shatters as the two make a run for it. They quickly spot Tannen across the street purchasing a drink from a vending machine.

"Yo, Tannen!" Maigashi yelled.

Viper's Labyrinth

Tannen quickly rolls to the side as the monster destroys the vending with its ball. Barrel Man takes a stand atop a nearby balcony.

"Bring out your new player. I want a piece of him."

"Is he talking about Katty?" Axe mumbled.

The monster begins shooting gems at the group. Maigashi and Tannen launch an offense against the creature while Axe attempts to strike Barrel Man.

"Eat Barrel!"

Axe gets knocked away by a barrel, comically falling to the floor as his teammates battle the enemies.

Meanwhile, back with Bamboo and the others...

"What is that commotion?" Alistor wondered.

"Must be a monster attack. Let's go!" Katty shouted.

The two left Bamboo's side to join the battle. Meanwhile, Barrel Man and Columnbrutey made their way to a populated area in the city.

"Surging Thunder!"

"Dark Enigma!"

Tannen and Maigashi's attacks impact Columnbrutey at full force, but the monster emerges unfazed.

"No way! Not even one scratch."

"Then we need to try something else," Tannen said.

The monster fires another round of gems again as the two begin taking cover. A gust of wind shatters the attack as Auroa arrives on the scene with his whip.

"In need of assistance?"

"About time," Maigashi muttered.

Axe returns to the team to plan as Barrel Man openly mocks them from above.

"You're not the new player the boss wants. Columnbrutey! Do your thing!"

The monster pounds its staff shaking the grounds. Then, columns begin bursting from the ground as a structure slowly forms.

"What are you up to now?" Auroa asked.

"Ha, haha! It's a surprise."

Alistor and Katty arrive on the scene. Barrel Man jumps down to greet them.

"Just on time! Oh! Do we have a new player? I'm gonna mess you up real good."

Barrel Man points to Katty.

"Hey? I've seen you before. You're that guy that bailed from the party."

"So what if? I'm back and better than ever. I'm only interested in this new player, so beat it."

Alistor quickly draws his sword.

"You don't look so tough."

"Try me!"

Without hesitation, he charged at Barrel Man, readying his Star Breaker. A barrel is hurled towards his way, but he dodges.

"Too easy!"

A second barrel comes crashing at his face, bringing him to a halt. He gets up for a few quick slashes, but Barrel Man kicks him back hard. A spark suddenly lit between Katty's eyes.

"I'll handle this guy from here. You guys handle the monster."

Barrel Man jumps up to the building to gain some elevation. Stairs and ladders are seen fixed across the structure.

"I don't need to take the stairs."

Without a sweat, Katty jumps up to the structure, surprising Barrel Man.

"Well, this changes things?"

Barrel Man leaps into the next floor of the structure as flames and traps get activated. Barrel Man begins tossing a few barrels at Katty.

Viper's Labyrinth

"You'll never catch me! I'm Barrel Man!"

Back down below, the party faced Columnbrutey...

"Watch out for that ball!" Maigashi shouted.

The monster fires its wrecking ball as the team disperses. It quickly retracts back into the monster's head.

"That mustache doesn't make it look any prettier." Maigashi pestered.

"Couldn't agree more." Tannen nodded.

Alistor took cover with Auroa and Axe from a distance.

"So, what do we do?" Alistor asked.

"The first thing is getting rid of that ball," Auroa suggested. "Then we can find a way to topple him over."

Meanwhile, Katty swiftly avoids the wave of barrels hurled at him. Barrel Man continues to proceed upstairs.

"Time to kick things up a notch. Muskers, come forth!"

The yellow-coat soldiers begin charging toward him. While down below, Maigashi and Tannen fire away at Columnbrutey.

"There should be a weak spot somewhere. But, we got to keep trying."

The monster begins to fire the wrecking ball at Alistor but misses. The ball starts to retract again, but Axe intervenes with a distraction from the sound of his new guitar.

"Now, dude!"

Auroa attacks with his whip, tearing the chain attached to the ball as the monster wobbles back. Next, Alistor goes in with his Star Breaker.

"I got this!"

The attack impacts Columnbrutey at point-blank, but within a split second, the attack bounced right off. The monster emerged unscratched.

"What's with this guy? For a broken column, he's durable."

The party dispersed from another wave of gems.

Max Mathesius

"We'll need to figure something out." Auroa nods. "Pure force won't bring it down."

As the rest of the team begins brewing another plan, Alistor sees a familiar robed figure walking casually down the alley. He decides to follow.

"Rare!"

Alistor confronts Mr. Rare.

"We cross once more."

Mr. Rare froze for a brief moment. Then, turned away as he clasped onto a watch in the back of his hand. The sound of ticking commenced.

"Hold it right there! I have questions."

He readied his blade at him.

"Adventuring been treating you well?" Rare quietly scoffed.

"Very funny! But now I need to know something. Why me?"

Rare turned towards him.

"It's rather simple, of course."

He briefly recaps the moment they met on the side of a road.

"You were yearning for something missing in life. The thrill, the excitement, the adventure? I answered your call. Wasn't this what you wanted?"

Rare is seen presenting the mirror in a flashback.

"True…but still, you're the source behind this evil. If I had known, this would have never happened."

"I'm just a simple being who crafts one-a-kind works of sentimental value. I gave your fortune and fulfilled someone's promise."

Something quickly catches Alistor off.

"A promise? Whose promise? Answer me!" He demanded.

Mr. Rare takes a few steps back.

"Now, I can't answer that. I uphold a policy of keeping clients' information confidential. It wouldn't be fun if I told you everything."

"You think this is a game? I should destroy you now."

An explosion sets off from the other battle.

"Tisk! Tisk! Time is running thin. I have an important date I can't miss."

Rare begins walking away.

"Hey? Get back here!"

Alistor attempts to stop him, but Rare simply floats off, directing his attention to the other side.

"The time is not right. You have a battle to finish. Till we meet again, heh heh heh."

Mr. Rare fades away into the darkness. Alistor returns back to his fight against Columnbrutey. The monster is seen crashing through a brick wall.

"About time? Where the heck did you go?" Maigashi asked.

"Yeah, dude! Did you have a long bathroom break?"

Alistor was hesitant to answer.

"Nothing…It was nothing."

The monster charges in with a ram, but Auroa trips it over with his whip.

"No time for talking. Are you guys ready?"

The rest gets into position as Alistor is left clueless.

"Wait? What's the plan? I wasn't here?"

Auroa quickly gives him an overview of the plan.

"Sigh…here goes. Since Columnbrutey was a game, we couldn't damage him. The monster revolves around color-coated gems. If we play by the game rules, three or more matching colors should break each monster's columns away."

"Oh! I see."

Max Mathesius

The monster begins firing its gem at the team. Axe and Tannen got into place, slamming the first two gems back at the creature. Then, two yellow gems impact a matching indentation on its right leg, freezing it in place.

"Now it's my turn!"

Maigashi redirects four green gems onto the monster's right arm shattering it. Auroa whips the red pieces back on the left leg, bringing Columnbrutey to its knees. Smoke and sparks burst into the air. The blue gems are seen directed toward Alistor.

"Ok, dude! You can do this."

Without hesitation, Alistor readies his Star Breaker sending the blue gems slamming into the monster's torso. A glowing inner core gets exposed.

"It's time to end this," Tannen said.

Maigashi and Tannen readied their final attacks.

"Surging Thunder!"

"Dark Enigma!"

A stream of lightning and darkness impales the monster's core shattering it. Columnbrutey instantly collapsed, exploding in place.

"Now the rest is up to Katty." Auroa glanced.

The rest of the team looks back at the high structure above. Meanwhile, somewhere atop a great building, two forces rally up. Mr. Rare patiently sits perched against the ledge as the Emperor arrives. A massive clock stands between them.

"Just on time."

He is seen shutting a small gold watch. Vilevelious steps forward and immediately dismiss Meister.

"Go oversee the situation below. I have some matters to discuss."

"As you wish."

The Meister teleported away as the scene focused on the two.

"Well, Rare? I'm sure you didn't call to discuss the weather. What insights do we have on that Prophecy?"

The robed figure is seen tinkering with the watch.

Viper's Labyrinth

"So…What do you think of this timeline? Have you grown accustomed to the cultural craze yet?"

"Very funny... Now get to the point! Time is wasting."

A not-amused look was on the Emperor's face as he pressured Rare on.

"Fine…but you won't like what I have found. We have an anomaly upon us."

"An anomaly? Explain!" The Emperor demanded.

Tension was building as Mr. Rare pulled out his crystal ball.

"There is an outer force that will soon arrive within a year from now. So far, your forces have failed to overtake Mathias with the Labyrinth."

"Who is this force we're speaking of?"

The orb begins to slowly materialize an image.

"Not far from the furthest stars of our system lies another empire. They call themselves Baronia and will soon set course to this world."

An army of monsters consisting of machines is seen marching before the great shadow of a king.

"So we have a little competition? Not that it would change things?"

A worried look was seen on Rare.

"Are you serious? Their army far outnumbers us with such industrial strength. We need to act now."

"Then what do you propose?" The Emperor asked.

The great clock continues to tick between the two.

"Alistor and his team have hindered your forces from taking this region. As a result, your forces have dwindled to nearly nothing. As a safety precaution, I suggest we contact your brother to allow our armies to merge."

Vilevelious immediately objects.

"No! I refuse!" He pounded. "If you think I'm gonna seek help from that half-rate brother, think again. We'd be a laughing stock."

"Then what do you suggest?" Rare wondered.

A quick breeze passes between them.

"We continue on course as planned. This Baronia is not among us, so we still have time. The Labyrinth will be complete, and when the time comes, I shall emerge victoriously."

Mr. Rare begins chuckling quietly.

"Hmm, very well…In two weeks, a new moon will rise. Begin to move to the final phase of the plan."

"Good! And as for the anomaly, I'll leave it to you. Make an item or do whatever it takes to hinder them. I have no time for this."

The two give a parting handshake as the Meister arrives back on the scene. Mr. Rare is seen tinkering with his watch once again.

"These one-of-a-kind items take eons to masterly craft. I can't be rushed!"

"Just do it! Good day, Rare!"

Both sides part ways as the Emperor descends with the general below. The two go to oversee the battle against Barrel Man.

"You'll never get to me! I'm Barrel Man!"

Another barrel is seen hurled towards Katty, dodging the impact.

"I won't let you get away!"

Katty engages him in a clash. Barrel Man attempts to throw a punch but is too slow to keep up with his speed. Katty is seen kicking him away.

"You're too slow! Give up already."

A smug look was seen on Barrel Man.

"Ha! We're twelve stories up already. My Barrels are the finest they can get. In fact, I got another surprise."

"What do you mean?"

Barrel Man presents another remote to him. Explosive barrels are now seen set in place across the structure.

Viper's Labyrinth

"I rigged this whole place with my explosives. With a push of this button, it will bring it all down. Taking you with it."

"You're insane!" Katty gasped.

"If I can't get you, then I'll just take you down with me. But not till I leave this doppelganger."

A burst of smoke sets off, blinding Katty briefly as Barrel Man is seen getting away. A dummy of Barrel Man attempts to attack, but Katty quickly kicks it off.

"Ha, haha! Here she blows!"

Barrel Man presses the button ditching the remote as he is seen pulling out a massive kite. Katty catches a glimpse of Barrel Man from the upper stairs.

"Now for my master escape."

As Barrel Man readied himself at the edge, Katty landed above him. The two are seen in a struggle as the Barrels slowly set off.

"What the? Get off me!"

"I won't let you get away!"

The kite quickly knocks off.

"No! My kite!"

Barrel Man attempts to swing another punch, but Katty again dodges it. In seconds, he countered back with a barrage of metal stars causing Barrel Man to lose balance.

"I got you now!"

Without hesitation, he kicks Barrel Man off of the structure as it begins to collapse in place. Katty quickly makes his way down, jumping onto each platform in place. Barrel Man was seen rolling across the pavement on impact.

"Yow! Why I outta! I'll show you. I'm Barrel Man!"

Katty makes his way back to the other's position. The team confronts Barrel Man reinforcing himself.

"Muskers! Get 'em."

The yellow coats are seen charging toward the team, but Auroa and Maigashi quickly topple them with ranged attacks.

Max Mathesius

"You have no place left to run!"

Barrel Man pulls out another barrel.

"I'll get you this time! This one's stuffed with a chunk full of bombs!"

Katty begins charging at him as he hurls the barrel.

"What is he doing? Katty, get out of the way." Alistor shouted.

A surprise was in store within a split second as he kicked the barrel back in midair. Then, the barrel explodes back on Barrel Man, stunning him in place.

"Time to end this!"

Katty pulls out his katana. Flames spark out.

"Flashfire!"

A wall of white flames impacts Barrel Man causing sparks to burst.

"Meister!!! I FAILED YOU!!!!!!!!!!!!!!!!!"

Barrel Man collapses, exploding as Bamboo returns to the team. Katty is seen putting his katana away.

"And that's a wrap."

"Whoah! How did you do that?" Alistor asked.

"The training, of course!"

The rest of the party is seen chuckling. Meanwhile, back above, a displeased look was seen on the Emperor's face.

"Both our monsters were destroyed. Ugh…"

"I'll get them next time. Next time!" Pestered the Meister.

The two quickly teleport away, leaving the scene. Back below, the party is seen strolling past the Arcade once again.

"Well, it seems everyone is back inside? Want to go again?" Katty asked.

A tired look was seen on Alistor's face.

Viper's Labyrinth

"I think I had enough games for one day. Let's go get a drink or something."

"A good idea!" Auroa agreed.

The party leaves off into the horizon. Leaving the wind to carry off the dust from the barrels.

"Tonight! I'll make great grass jelly." Bamboo said.

"Give me a break." Alistor sighed.

Chapter 18

Mines and Mimes:

The Shrine Mirror Prophecy

"What's this? An eviction notice?"

Bamboo was seen removing the notice on the front door of his restaurant.

"You mean you forgot to pay your rent?" Katty shouted.

The party was seen stranded outside by the food truck as Bamboo quietly loaded his supplies.

"Look, I'm not perfect. It's been three months, but I got a plan to relocate. Somewhere far and out of town. The city would be a good start. Business should be good over there."

He crumpled the notice beside him.

"That means it leaves us both with more time for training." Alistor excitedly jumped.

The team helped load the final crates of supplies as they set off to the city. And in a matter of time, Alistor and Katty were seen training together by the shores.

"Come on! You guys are boring me. When is this combination technique of yours gonna happen?" Maigashi pestered.

The rest of the team was slouched back on the chairs under an umbrella.

"It's getting there!" Alistor yelled. "Just be patient."

Viper's Labyrinth

"Alistor, stay focused. We can do this." Katty assured him.

He readies his kunai in the air as the two begin coordinating, preparing their attacks. Meanwhile, Bamboo can be seen converting his food truck into a noodle stand from a distance.

"Okay! It's time for your Star Breaker. On my mark."

The scene suddenly shifts to the Mustache Meister watching from a viewing screen. The Emperor is called into the room.

"What have you devised this time, general?"

"Watch and see! My greatest monster will take them by surprise. Mine- Golem, come forth!"

Back below, the two are interrupted by a shaking sound.

"What was that?" Alistor wondered.

"The sand! It's coming from under the sand." Katty pointed.

The two jumped out of harm's way as a monster emerged, overshadowing them. Then, armed with large mines, it begins chucking explosives toward their way.

"No need for an introduction. Let's go!" Maigashi shouted.

"No! You guys sit back," Katty demanded. "Let us handle this one."

He tossed a couple kunais destroying the incoming mines.

"But we might need all the team power we can get," Alistor questioned.

A worried look was in his eyes while the monster slowly approached them.

"We have all the team power we need right now."

"You don't mean…."

"Yes! I think we are ready to test our new combination. Just get that Star Breaker ready, and I'll handle the rest." He assured.

As Katty takes charge, the monster begins laying out explosives through the sand.

"Here goes!"

Max Mathesius

One explosion commenced after the next as he swiftly dashed through the sands. Destroying one after the next as he closed in on the monster. Finally, the creature makes one big swing but misses.

"Too slow! Flashfire!"

Within seconds the monster became stunned as its feet sank into the sand. Alistor came in with the Star Breaker attack, but the enemy began to shoot mines taking aim at him.

"What?"

He begins to hesitate, but Katty stands by his side.

"There is nothing to fear! Ninja Dispersion!"

With one strike, Katty dispersed Alistor's Star Breaker, scattering it across and destroying the mines. The monster gets impacted by a barrage of beams raining down as it explodes in seconds.

"Whoa! Did we actually do that?" Alistor couldn't believe his very eyes.

The other members of the party came to join them.

"Whoah, dude! That was fast." Axe slapped. "You guys totaled that monster in under a minute."

Back above, a displeased look was on Vilevelious's face.

"What? It's over already. You call this your best monster?"

Pieces of the Mine monster lay scattered across the sands.

"Nya! It's all part of the master plan." The general assured.

"A master plan? Do tell, Meister."

The general presents a recent article to the Emperor.

"What's this? The Shrine Mirror?"

Flashes of the past begin ringing through Vilevelious's mind. Sending back a cold vibe from memories filled with a grudge.

"Nya! Yes! An event is to be held soon regarding the Shrine Maiden's prophecy. It's about time we eradicate a past nuisance and destroy the sealing scrolls for the mirror."

Viper's Labyrinth

An eager look was now on the Emperor's face.

"So, how shall we proceed? Security is bound to be tight. We won't be able to destroy the mirror till it's whole. We can't even get near the sealing scrolls."

An assured look was on Meister's face.

"Today will be a good day. Alistor and his petty team already possess four of the five mirror shards."

"And you have the last piece in your hands. What do you propose?"

The viewing screen changes channel, focusing on a circus troupe.

"Security? Nya! They're nothing compared to a circus troupe. At this moment, my soldiers are salvaging my monster's remnants. After that, we'll be able to create a new monster far destructive enough to gather energy from the entire city."

"And for the sealing scrolls?" The Emperor repeated.

"For the scrolls, just wait and see. I got something in store for them."

Back at the beach, Alistor and his team are seen hanging by Bamboo's new noodle stand. Chowing down while Auroa informs them of some upcoming events. He presents a pamphlet advertising the Shrine Maiden set to perform a song.

"The shards we've been collecting have led us to the Shrine Priestess. Whoever she is, she may know how to reseal the Emperor."

The image depicts the Priestess holding a mirror resembling the one they've been gathering. Alistor begins reflecting back on their adventure so far.

"It all comes down to this. Whatever Vilevelious knows, the answer may lie with her. So where is this taking place?"

Bamboo is seen cooking some noodles in the background.

"So where is this taking place? And what time?" Alistor asked.

"Relax, it's just a block down by the hotel at the Theatre of Arts. We've still got a few hours." Auroa assured.

Alistor begins setting right off in a hurry.

"That kid…. He'll never learn to sit still." Maigashi nodded.

"Hey! Wait up!" Katty followed.

Max Mathesius

The four remaining members continued on with their noodles. Bamboo was now seen making some doe in his cart.

"This noodle stand was the best idea yet. Soon we'll be rolling in the money."

Money signs were seen sparked within his eyes for a brief moment.

"So you won't need any help for a while?" Axe asked.

"I can manage the cart fine on my own for now. In the meantime, you kids go and have some fun. Up north, there is a circus I hear coming by."

The four finished their food as they set off in another direction. In a matter of moments, they stumble upon a great tent.

"He wasn't really kidding when he mentioned circus." Tannen glanced. "This tent's huge."

"Then let's check around," Auroa replied.

Axe and Maigashi followed from behind. As they enter the tent, the team gets confronted by a strange-looking mime within seconds.

"Whoah, Dude!" Axe jumped. "Don't scare me like that."

Billboards of acts are seen highlighted above. For example, an opera singer, along with a magician depicted among other performers.

"HAHAHA! Welcome, all!"

A flamboyant man in an oversized green coat appears.

"I see you got a chance to meet our mute Kotaru."

"And who are you?" Maigashi asked.

The man tosses a rose high up in the air and twirls around in motion. Then, he dances across the stage as a trio of performers drops down on them.

"The Names Doe!"

"I'm Rei!"

"And I'm Mii"

The party continues to stand by, speechless.

Viper's Labyrinth

"We are Do Re Mi!"

The man in the green coat stops as he catches the rose with his mouth. Then, he goes to shake each one of the member's hands.

"Pleasure to meet you all. I am Marvo! Marvo the magnificent. Singer in the arts of all that is opera."

Maigashi began to feel weirded out while the others casually felt flattered.

"Okay....So yeah. I think we'll just be going right now."

"Not so fast! You four are our first customers in days! Our show is going to begin! So please take your seats and sit back and watch."

"I don't know." Maigashi hesitantly nodded. "Circus acts are not my kind of thing."

Marvo suddenly got down to the ground kneeling as Doe, Rei, and Mii joined to the floor with him.

"I'm begging you! Please stay and watch." He cried. "We are a traveling circus troupe hoping to make it big in show business. But, unfortunately, we've been struggling to get a solid gig. We will be out on the streets if we don't get any viewers."

He begins to feel slightly sorry for them.

"Sigh... Okay, we'll stay."

"Splendid! You won't regret this. So sit back and feast your eyes. Beginning with our opening act, a magician unlike ever before."

Smoke began to fume through the stage as the four took their seats. Then, finally, a sorcerer emerges right out of a large black top hat.

"I present to you. MAGIC MAN!"

"Dude, this is tubular!"

Meanwhile, with Alistor and Katty...

"It's been a long time, but we made it this far."

The two are seen side by side on the fence, waiting outside the theatre.

"You came a long way since we last parted. Although I must admit, you have grown a little." Katty said. "The journey may be almost over, but somehow I feel this is just the beginning."

Max Mathesius

The two look over the 4 gems and mirror pieces collected.

"What do you mean?" Alistor wondered.

The recollection of Mr. Rare begins to resonate in his mind.

"It wasn't just by chance or fate. Mr. Rare was the one truly responsible for starting this. He came to you on purpose."

The two then recall the day the labyrinth appeared over the school.

"So…when Vilevelious is through. Rare will be next."

"Exactly!" Katty snapped.

Back at the tent, Marvo is seen ending the show with a high-pitched voice. Then, all the performers are seen gathered on the stage to make a final bow. Axe and the others applauded before taking leave.

"Come on! We got to get to that theatre." Axe said.

"No worries! We still got time." Tannen assured.

The four reunite back with the two for the Priestess's arrival.

"Man, look at all that security." Alistor pointed. "We'll never be able to get close for questions."

"I know… It's pretty tight." Axe agreed.

The Priestess makes her arrival on the stage.

"Hello, all! I am Nayuki. 48th descendant of the Shrine Carrier line. Long ago, my ancestor Yoko sealed away the dreaded forces of Aggerona within the sacred mirror."

The Meister can be seen watching from a distance high above.

"She, along with her fellow band of warriors, fought bravely against Vilevelious forces. In the end, Yoko gave her life to seal the Emperor away. We have for generations looked over this mirror, protecting it along with the sacred scrolls used for the sealing spell."

Bamboo is seen making rounds of sales in the noodle cart.

"But now that it is gone, evil has been scattered ever since. A dastardly fiend known as Rare has stolen it from our grounds."

Viper's Labyrinth

She suddenly turns her attention toward Alistor and his team.

"But now that most of it is back. Come forth! Chosen ones! Bring the pieces you collected over here."

All eyes were now focused on the party as they stood awkwardly. A path was immediately cleared for them.

"Don't fear! Allow me to help bring this mirror back together."

The party hands over the pieces to her as she places them together. Then, the Meister flies off in the other direction.

"The time is right."

The Meister comes to a stop by the circus tent. He then fires a hole through the top of the tent catching Marvo's attention.

"Who are you?"

The Meister descends upon the performers chuckling at them. He points his cane toward them.

"Nya! From now on, you'll be working for me! Your voice! It's what we need to destroy that mirror. So surrender now!"

"And if I refuse?"

Marvo draws out his card tip blade, but the general snaps his finger, calling out a platoon of Whoopers and Muskers from the stands. The performers quickly find themselves outnumbered.

"You don't have a choice."

Remnants from the Mine monster begin dropping over them. The parts start circling around the performers. Marvo attempts to resist but ends up on the floor as the heart piece locks for him.

"Whoah, Noooooo!"

The opera singer closed his eyes as he couldn't watch. Only to hear a clunking sound from another force.

"Kuuuu......."

"Kotaru? You saved me...."

The mute falls to the floor. Then, leaving only a faint heartbeat to be heard, parts of the monster begin latching on, creating a new monster.

"What? You're not the monster I wanted?"

Back to Vilevelious watching…

"What! A Mine-Mime? This is your great monster?" He questioned as the general broke a sweat.

The monster pulled itself right up.

"Nya! I'll have to improvise. Now Mine-Mime! Go and destroy the mirror. Ensure its destruction and gather energy from anyone you see."

The Mime jumps in the air with one bow, bringing the entire tent down. And within moments, a tiny glint was spotted in the air.

"What in the world is that?" Maigashi questioned.

"I don't know…." Axe shrugged.

The Priestess Nayuki continues to repair the four mirror pieces back together. The glint within moments impacts the stage like a meteor.

"We're under attack!"

Mine-Mime emerged from the debris as royal guards swarmed across the theatre, taking action to protect the Priestess. The Meister appears above, clutching the final piece of the mirror in his hands.

"You! You have the final piece." Nayuki pointed.

"Got a mirror to destroy, so don't delay."

He tosses the final piece into the other shards, completing the mirror. The party begins to race for it against the general.

"We have to get it now." Alistor rushed.

The Meister quickly pulls it towards his way from the force of his aura. A sinister look was seen on the Mime's face. Security begins to retaliate as the Mime starts to set in motion. Mines started to scatter across as it spun its arms in midair catching everyone by surprise.

"No! We must get that mirror back!"

Viper's Labyrinth

"Aim at the general!"

The royal guards begin to shift their focus to the Meister.

"Think I didn't come prepared?"

With one snap, a platoon of Muskers appeared right over the building tops. Armed with their guns as they readied to fire.

"Not the yellow coats again!"

Explosions begin to commence as fire scatters the group below. Katty attempts to snatch the mirror from behind but forces the general to drop it.

"We must protect the Priestess."

The mirror was now on the ground, still intact.

The Meister immediately calls his forces to a halt as the labyrinth materializes over the city again.

"Here's how things will go. This shall be an all-or-nothing battle. If you want the mirror, you must defeat my monster."

Alistor and his team stepped up to accept his challenge.

"You're on!"

"Good! Very good! Now Mine-Mime, do your thing."

A cold chilling fog begins to shroud the city. A siren-like scream is then heard as Axe starts to chicken out.

"Dude! What is that sound? It's giving me the creeps."

"Above us! Watch out!" Auroa pointed.

The party avoids an immense spirit swooping down on them. Instead, more ghosts lock onto them as Alistor takes the front stand.

"I'll handle this!"

"Get back!" Tannen warned.

He pushes Alistor out of the way.

Max Mathesius

"Hey! What's the deal?"

He directed his attention toward the danger. The energy was seen being sucked out of countless victims across the city.

"These aren't just any spirits." He further informed. "They exist on a different plane of a nether existence. They drain the life of any existing soul coming in contact."

"Then what can we do?"

The Mime continues to spew countless souls from its exhaust pipe.

"A direct approach on the controller will stop them. I'll cover you from here. My powers flourish in darkness, so my scythe is enough to counter the dead."

The labyrinth is seen being fueled with energy above.

"Well, you heard him. Let's go!" Maigashi commanded.

The party begins to direct their attention towards the Mime as Tannen counteracts against the dead souls.

"Mine-Mime! They're getting close! Do something." The general ordered.

The monster launched a wave of explosive spikes, but Maigashi and Auroa took them out with ease. Then, Katty and Alistor rushed in.

"Now we got you!"

Axe power kicks the monster from behind to knock it off balance. The fog quickly dispersed as the spirits faded away. Katty and Alistor unleashed a wave of attacks at the Mime, but it promptly threw them all back.

"Don't just stand there. Get those fools!" The Meister further ranted.

The monster took its time to regain some posture while Auroa and Maigashi went in with a wind and thunder attack, knocking it back.

"Nya?"

The Mime got back up, ready for more.

"Man, this guy is durable. Not even a scratch." Maigashi said.

An idea suddenly catches Meister's attention.

Viper's Labyrinth

"Impressive. You're a better monster than I expected. Maybe this can work to our advantage."

The general pulls out a door handing it over to the Mime.

"What is he planning now?" Alistor wondered.

"Don't know, but I wouldn't want to find out." Katty nods.

The two charged straight at the monster as it let off a cunning smile. The door immediately opens, pulling Alistor and his team into a dimensional gateway.

"It's a trap! Dude!!!"

Axe, Maigashi, and Auroa are then pulled in. Finally, the door shuts, leaving Tannen to face the monster alone.

"What did you do with them?"

The general points into the sky, directing his attention toward the labyrinth. The Emperor immediately contacts his general from the other side.

"What is the meaning of this general? What are they doing in our base?"

"Nya? Not to worry. I sent them straight into the middle of our labyrinth. They'll never escape as long you hold the key."

Axe, Maigashi, and Auroa are seen dropping over Katty and Alistor in a pitch-dark room.

"Where in the world are we?"

Auroa finds a window on the far end.

"I think we're up. Somewhere very high up."

The screen zooms out, showing the entire labyrinth floating above the city. Katty spots a door at the very end.

"Look like we have nowhere else to go."

The team opens the door, revealing a hallway. Time begins to slowly pass as they continue forward.

"How long is this hallway? It's like it's never-ending." Maigashi complained.

Vilevelious can be seen watching over them through another screen.

"So you want to play? Let's see how you like this."

Multiple paths open up for them at the very second. The party stood confused for a brief moment.

"So…which one do we take?" Katty asked.

"Let's try the one on the far left." Alistor points.

The team enters through the door, finding themselves in a school setting.

"Why does this all seem familiar?"

The party then proceeds through a hallway of lockers. Classroom doors at every corner. Alistor opens a room number familiar to him.

"Are we back in school again?"

"This can't be? It's impossible." Katty recalled.

The party then proceeds to the kitchen.

"So this is where all the goods are stored." Maigashi pestered.

"The food isn't half bad," Auroa noted.

A creeping sound is then heard.

"What was that?"

A garbage can falls over, alerting their attention to a figure behind the shadows.

"Reveal yourself!" Alistor demanded.

Potty Mouth appeared before them unexpectedly.

"Boy! I'm starving. You guys got any food?"

The party quickly draws their weapons.

"You again?"

"Let's end this one quickly."

Alistor and Katty charged at the monster pulling off their team combination without hesitation. The Star Breaker attack gets dispersed, raining down on the demon.

Viper's Labyrinth

"Woo! Not too hard. Easy there! Hey, that tickles." Chuckled the monster.

The monster emerged unharmed.

"What? Not even a single scratch. Has it gotten stronger?"

"A retreat might be best." Katty hated to admit it.

The party leaves the room as the monster stumbles around.

"Hey? Where are you going? I'm hungry!"

The team exits the room, dashing through the halls as more paths open. Finally, the group finds themselves by the corner of an ally.

"Hey! I see the pizza parlor right over there." Maigashi pointed.

Before they could proceed any further, Decoma emerged before them.

"We'll beat you just like before."

Maigashi prepares his bow.

"Surging thunder!"

His attack quickly slips through Decoma, leaving it unaffected. The monster swoops down on the team.

"Man, no good. We have to get out."

The party makes a run to the next door stumbling into a nursery. Auroa begins to have second thoughts.

"This is a recollection of the trials we've already endured."

"Well, it seems these monsters are out for revenge. Think fast!" Axe shouted.

Auroa quickly reacts as Crass Cradle comes swooping down for a strike. He pulls out his whip to strike, pushing the monster back as they enter the next room.

"It's no good." Auroa agreed. "We have to find a way out. These are the monsters we've already defeated. So they must not be real."

"Of course! Just like with my incident against Wizjin." Alistor recalls.

Max Mathesius

The party now arrives at the Kabuki Coliseum. Amp Master waited before them as it began shaking up the ground.

"So if they're not real. These monsters can't hurt us, right?"

Amp Master fires a Zap Cannon at the team, sending them back.

"You were saying?" Maigashi sarcastically expressed.

The party continues on the run. Back outside, the labyrinth feeds on energy as the Mime disperses dead souls across the city.

"We need to get out of this."

Amp Master continues to pursue after them through the maze. Finally, three doors opened, bringing the three other monsters to the chase.

"Decoma, Potty Mouth, Crass Cradle, and Amp Master. They're gaining on us." Axe yelled.

"It's as if…this place is actually alive." Maigashi thought.

An idea suddenly caught his mind. Coming to a halt, he reached for his bow to fire a shot at the floor. The monsters come to a stop as their body begins to slightly fade. A sudden shake was felt back in the Emperor's room.

"What was that?"

Looking over the screen, the party begins attacking the labyrinth from inside.

"No! They're attacking the maze. It's losing energy."

Auroa whips his wind across the walls as the rest begins covering the surrounding area. Alistor's Star Breaker leaves a hole in the wall as Vilevelious's voice yells in rage.

"Enough!!! Out! Get out!"

The team instantly teleported away as the four illusions dissipated. Alistor and his crew find themselves back with Mine-Mime.

"About time! What took you guys this long?" Tannen asked.

Nothing but destruction commenced across while the Mime began taunting. Finally, the general begins to back away.

"Nya? The mirror! The scrolls! It needs to be destroyed."

Viper's Labyrinth

Nayuki was seen hastily placing the mirror back in its pedestal along with the scrolls as the Meister gave chase.

"The girl, you fool! Get the girl!"

The Muskers charged right in, but Auroa and Maigashi intercepted.

"Do I have to do everything myself?"

A few royal soldiers attempt to stop the general, but they get crushed by a wave of doors. The Mime begins twirling his body once more, targeting the Priestess. Alistor and the rest jumped in to redirect the attack.

"Dude! Hold on!"

The spiked explosives get redirected toward Bamboo's noodle cart.

"NOOOO!!!!"

The noodle stand explodes within a second, sending Bamboo flopping back. A distressed look was in his eyes.

"My Noodle cart!"

The Mime continues to spin out of control. Randomly sending waves of bombs as it impacts countless vehicles.

"My Car!!!" Bamboo cried.

Axe then latched on behind the Mime. Grabbing hold of its exhaust, but quickly loses grasp. Nayuki begins chanting some words from a scroll as the mirror glows.

"Nya! No, she's actually performing the sealing curse."

Her words bring all the enemies to the ground in a pressuring bind.

"I have no time for this. Next time!"

The Meister escapes from his cape.

"The mirror! Bring it to me." Nayuki ordered.

The Mime lay flat on the floor as Katty handed over the mirror to her.

"Hope this works!"

Max Mathesius

As she attempts to perform the seal, the same cunning smile is seen on its face. The Mime caught her by surprise, forcing its body back up as she dropped the mirror again. Tannen swoops in with one slash, stunning the monster.

"It's open! Now finish it!"

Alistor and Katty took a look at one another.

"You ready?"

"Let's do this."

Alistor readies the Star Breaker technique once more while Katty performs his Ninja Dispersion. The Mime gets impacted by a barrage of beams bringing it to the floor.

"That should do it." Tannen snapped.

As Nayuki goes to retrieve the mirror, the monster turns its head, locking on her. In one final attempt, the Mime persistently shoots out his most excellent mine latched on its back. An oversized ball land near her direction.

"Get back! It's gonna blow!" Maigashi yelled.

Nayuki fell back, hesitating as Katty had to pull her away from danger. Then, in a split second, the mine explodes, destroying the mirror and sacred scrolls in flames.

"Oh no…The sacred mirror."

The Mime loses consciousness reverting back to his original human form. Marvo and the other performers came running to his side.

"Kotaru….Hold on! I know you never really talked but stay with us. You can't leave us just yet." He cried.

The performers mourned alongside their fallen comrade. The mute man looks over them with a smile.

Marvo closed his eyes before a storm of royal soldiers came marching in. The performers are seen being taken away.

"Unhand us!"

Meanwhile, Nayuki is saddened by the loss of the mirror. Thus, disappointment commenced among the team.

"Oh great! Everything that we worked for is now gone." Alistor pounded.

"I know…but now our battle may be harder. Vilevelious is at an advantage." Katty stated.

Nayuki approached their side.

"I'm…. I'm so sorry. Now that the scrolls, along with the sealing mirrors, are gone. I don't know what we can do."

Hope was now far from reach.

"Hey! Stop blaming yourself. We'll just have to defeat the Emperor the old-fashioned way," Maigashi assured.

"Hey! We still got the gems, remember?" Auroa reminded.

A small breath of relief was seen through them.

"Then I guess that's something we can look forward to. If only we knew how to use these gems, though." Katty wondered.

"Let's hope it will be enough," Tannen said.

The party begins looking over the essence collected from the previous demon generals. But then, something suddenly caught Alistor's mind.

"Hey? Where did Bamboo go?"

Somewhere downtown on the other side of the city. Bamboo is seen alone, searching for some work. A flier catches his attention.

"Hmm, what's this?"

He grabs hold of the paper.

"Part-time private chef needed."

A wide smile was back on his face.

"High pay! No questions asked! Apply today! Good enough for me."

Bamboo quickly bolts off in the other direction. In minutes, he arrives by the back alley behind the arcade building. He looked over the paper one last time.

"The Arcade? This doesn't look right."

Max Mathesius

Without hesitation, Bamboo enters through the back door. Making his way down a small step of stairs. He finds himself wandering through the basement floor filled with nonoperational arcade machines.

"Someplace."

He continues to mindlessly wander. A dimensional portal was soon within his sight.

"Hey! What are you doing here?" Questioned an enemy soldier.

Bamboo barely jumped back as a couple Muskers drew their weapons at him.

"Whoah, hold it! I came here for the job you guys listed."

He hands the paper over to them.

"So you're interested in filling Rondo's position?"

Bamboo quickly nodded. Seen eager to start as they took one good look at him.

"Hey, you seem rather familiar? Do we know you?"

"I'm a master chef! Top class! And I whip up a mean Grass Jelly!"

They didn't bother to have second thoughts as they moved out of the way.

"Very well, you may pass through."

Within seconds Bamboo enters, and the portal vanishes, taking him to a dark room. The fire quickly emits through the room as a fantastic set of stairs stands before him. Vilevelious can be seen occupied reading behind a chair facing away.

"So I heard you're our new chef. Go and cook up your best dish. I'm busy right now."

Without further questions, Bamboo made his way into the kitchen. A pile of ingredients was set before him.

"Oh boy! My luck has to be turning around now. This is the best job yet! I'll make my best killer jelly ever to celebrate."

An hour later…

"Dinners ready!"

Bamboo sets his dish on the table by the Emperor's chair as he reaches for the utensils.

Viper's Labyrinth

"Hmm? What a peculiar dish do we have here?" The Emperor questioned as it jiggled from one tap with his fork.

"It's my special Grass Jelly! My hottest item on the menu. Just try it and see. It's a total killer."

The Emperor takes his first taste.

"Hmm!!!!"

Anger sparks through the Emperor's eye as he gasps within seconds. He then spits out the jelly as the table flips over.

"Wuh oh?"

Bamboo takes a few steps back.

"What's this atrocity?" He pointed out. "Ahhh!!! So unsanitary!"

"Just give me another chance," Bamboo begged. "My next dish will be a great knockout."

"Away with you!"

Without further questions, Vilevelious unleashed a blast sending Bamboo flying straight out of the room.

"No!!!!"

He is then seen booted out from the fortress by a couple Muskers. His frying pan lands over his head before the gateway closes.

"What! My food is not good enough for ya. Hmph! Critics these days."

He made his way back upstairs from the basement. Opening the door and waltzing past the arcade floor. He makes an exit through the front door.

"FREEZE!!!"

"What?"

A surprise was in store for him as he was surrounded by a fleet of police cars. Armed and ready as he gets brought to the ground.

"What's going on? Hey!!!"

He is seen getting cuffed.

Max Mathesius

"You have the right to remain silent."

Later the following evening, Alistor and the team are dining by the hotel Axe was staying at. A news flash suddenly came on the air from a nearby T.V.

"This is just in. Authorities recently apprehended an alleged tax evader involved with Aggerona forces."

The party quickly stumbled back in shock as they found mug shots of Bamboo on screen.

"The arrest was made early right outside of the Grand Arcade. No further details are available on the suspect being detained for questioning at the station. We now go to commercial break."

The disappointment was seen through Alistor's eyes.

"This can't be happening."

Chapter 19

Vipers Labyrinth:

The Final Battle for a New Tomorrow

"The time has come! Rally all of our remaining forces. The time is right."

The emperor was seen giving direct orders.

"What? But the labyrinth is not at full power yet? It's only 90% there!" Stated the Meister.

"I am aware, general. But it is good enough."

"Nah? Maybe consider? Give me a little more time. Then, I'll retrieve the remaining energy we need."

"That won't be necessary." Vilevelious persisted. "The dawn of a new moon is upon us, and I got a huge wager on the line."

"A wager?"

"Yes! I made a huge bet with my acquaintances the previous week. If we overtake Mathias before the next moon, we'll be at the very top."

The Meister then recalls the emperor meeting with Mr. Rare on the rooftop of a building, shaking hands.

"I see."

"And yes! With your last monster ensuring the mirror's destruction, nothing can get in our way. So the odds are in our favor."

Meanwhile, back with Alistor and the company down below...

"I can't believe this. Bamboo actually got arrested."

The party is seen hanging by a café watching TV. Video footage shows Bamboo being cuffed and surrendering to authorities.

"Dude...This isn't good for him. We have to get him out somehow."

"I know. But it won't be easy." Katty nodded. "Wanted for fraud, forgery, and even tax evasion. The tables against him."

The news shows Bamboo being accused of helping the enemy. The disappointment was seen in Alistor's eyes.

"This entire time. The free ski trip, theater tickets, concert passes, cruise passes, driver's ed, and Bon Festival. All one big lie."

His head lay flat on the table.

"Hey! Nobody's perfect." Maigashi shrugged. "So what if he pulled some shady business. He's not such a bad guy."

"Indeed! If everything was perfect, there's no point existing." Auroa added. "He even helped us in our fight against Rondo. Don't you remember when we were in a tight jam?"

They recall their battle with Rondo. Flames and ingredients were flying everywhere.

"I don't know." Alistor nods. "Right now, my feelings are mixed."

The TV shows Bamboo detained behind a holding cell. The scene transitions to him during an interrogation with the guards.

"Admit it! You planned to conspire with the enemy the whole time. We got the evidence against you."

The table was being slammed.

"Look here!" Bamboo snapped. "This is all just one big misunderstanding. It was a job! They needed a new chef, and the money was good. I could care less who the employer is. My cooking goes everywhere."

"Yeah, but of all places, it had to be Aggerona? That dreaded Vilevelious?" Pointed the guard.

Viper's Labyrinth

"Hey! It was a one-shot gig." Bamboo shrugged. "He tried my food and didn't like it. So I was quickly fired."

The questioning continued to commence in the room. But, again, the entire department's eyes focused on their suspect.

"If that's true, it makes you in the wrong place at the wrong time. But it still doesn't change the fact for your other charges."

A big quake suddenly shakes the room.

"What was that?"

The sound of explosions commenced outside as the shaking continued.

"We're under attack!!!"

The labyrinth eclipses the city as the light fades to darkness.

A battalion of Whoopers and Musker grunts is seen raiding the entire city. Alistor and the company head outside to witness the destruction.

"They're everywhere! Dude, they're going all out."

"Judgment day already?" Maigashi sighed.

The team begins to clash with a pack of oncoming Aggerona soldiers. The Meister is seen swooping by.

"There's too many of them," Katty shouted. "We need to find the way into the heart of their base. A gate or an entry into the labyrinth."

Tannen's lens begins to react.

"Already done! Follow me."

The party begins following Tannen as he leads the way through the chaos. Finally, Maigashi and Auroa send a group of Whoopers back with wind and lightning.

"Another wave approaching!" Alistor pointed.

"We got this," Katty assured.

Axe kicks away a couple oncoming soldiers while Katty cuts through the rest with his speed. Finally, Tannen makes a detour through an ally.

Max Mathesius

"We're almost there!"

The party continues another block down. Again, a group of Muskers was seen lined and ready to fire at them.

"Tannen! They're gonna..."

"We're here! I got this."

Tannen pulls out his scythe as the Muskers fire away. He deflects the oncoming shot with his weapon, sending it back at them. The area was quickly familiar to them.

"You're kidding me. This place?" Alistor dropped.

It was none other than the Grand Arcade standing before them.

"The lens points to here," Tannen assured. "Reeking with negative energy."

They suddenly spot the emperor from a nearby television screen. He is seen high above, making his way to the kingdom walls.

"Hey? Isn't the capital building on the other side?" Axe wondered.

"Yeah, miles away!" Maigashi informed. "Looks like soldiers are lined and ready."

The scene transitions to the emperor overseeing the defense down below.

"Humph! Such pitiful worms."

Weapons are seen aimed toward him. Thousands of arrows and shells fired away as he stood motionless.

"Now it's time to demonstrate some real power."

A great earthquake commenced collapsing the entire ground below. Large branches are summoned, walling Vilevelious.

"Was that your best?" Vilevelious laughed.

The roots fall over, crashing through the kingdom walls and ending the battle. As soldiers are scattered across the city, smoke and debris are left from the ruins.

"And now for the finishing touch."

Viper's Labyrinth

The emperor begins clasping his hands together, forcing all the roots to merge. A great tree formed within moments. Leaves and flowers were sprouting away as they overshadowed the castle. The Meister immediately appears behind him.

"Over already? Well, that was quick." The general snickered.

"Sigh...Such a lovely attack. Good for showcasing but too much strain on energy."

The emperor was showing signs of fatigue.

"Nya! I came to warn you. Those pecks are snooping by the arcade. They're closing into our labyrinth, and our forces require reinforcement."

"What? Then deal with them." The emperor ordered. "I need to rest for a bit. Don't let any of them through that door."

"As you wish."

The Meister vanished before his very eyes. Back down below, Alistor was shaking up from the emperor's display of power on screen.

"Come on! Stop being a scaredy-cat." Maigashi pestered.

"That's one huge tree!" Alistor jumped. "Did you see how he just leveled the entire area down? This is...this is too much."

He begins to step back.

"Hey! There's no backing down now." Katty grabbed. "We came this far, so you better get a hold of yourself."

Alistor took a moment to clear his mind.

"We wasted enough time. Let's head inside." Maigashi kicked the door right open.

Inside, machines were seen lined in complete working order.

"Just the same as last time."

"Right there! Beyond that basement door is the entrance to the labyrinth." Tannen points.

The party approaches the door. Again, chilling air is felt.

"We got some company!" Auroa pointed.

Max Mathesius

A tremendous yellow top hat drops down the center revealing the Meister before them. The team readies for battle as a keen look was in Katty's eye.

"Alistor, are you ready for this?"

"What?" He nervously stumbled.

The party soon spots Aggerona soldiers approaching the building.

"You guys, hold off the guards outside. Leave the Meister to the both of us." Katty insisted.

"Fine then." Maigashi shrugged.

Tannen, Auroa, Axe, and Maigashi head out the doors while Katty and Alistor face the general. He snickers at the two of them.

"Ha! If you think your moves will work on me, they won't. But, thanks to Barrel Man, I memorized all of your techniques." Snapped the general.

Some degree of doubt crossed Alistor's mind.

"Remember our training together." Katty reminded. "We can do this."

Meanwhile, outside the arcade, the four begin fending off the approaching Whoopers and Muskers with projectiles. Axe suddenly steps aside.

"Dudes! I'm gonna go and bust Bamboo out."

"You sure?" Maigashi asked.

Axe quickly kicks an attacking Whooper from behind.

"Leave it to me!"

With one thumb up, he leaves the battle as they clear his path. Back inside, the Meister begins emitting a yellow aura.

"Here goes!"

Katty starts off with a barrage of ninja stars. The Meister responds with a magnetic force stopping the attacks in midair.

"Kids game!" Snickered the general.

The Meister sends it back at the two as they take cover behind a couple machines.

Viper's Labyrinth

"Great start." Alistor sarcastically said.

"Not if you can do any better?" Katty responded.

"Well, now it's my turn."

Alistor begins rushing at the general with his Star Breaker.

"HA! That same move! You haven't learned your lesson from last time."

The Meister begins launching doors directly at him from his cape. A door comes crashing his way, but Alistor quickly sidestepped.

"NYA?"

More doors continued to slam down, but he avoided the fire, using every arcade machine to his advantage. The doors impact various devices as he appears behind the Meister with a fully powered Star Breaker.

"Now it's over, Meister!"

His attack pierces through the Meister from the back.

"YES! A direct hit!"

No sound of pain or reaction came from the general. But, from the look in his eyes, they knew something wasn't right. The Meister's body fades in seconds, leaving a blank yellow cape.

"Over there!" Katty pointed.

"Fools! Do you think it's that easy to hit me? You fell right into my optical illusion."

The yellow cape begins wrapping across Alistor, binding him as he gets sent flying back. Katty pulls out his katana to start rushing him. The Meister sends more oncoming doors in his path.

"Nya! You'll never land a hit on me."

With a few quick swipes, Katty destroys the incoming doors. Then, he makes a huge dash in the air, ready to stab the general.

"Not so fast!" The general snapped.

Katty phases right through the general as multiple copies begin appearing. But, unfortunately, Meister continues to belittle them.

"Some teamwork? It won't be enough to beat me!"

Axe continues to stroll casually downtown through the chaos. He makes his way back to his hotel. Opening the doors to his room.

"Blade! Lance! Bow! Dudes, we need to break Bamboo out!"

Axe confronts his crew as they come crawling out of their hiding place.

"But it's too dangerous out there." Lance cried.

"Yeah! We're doomed. This concert is never going to happen." Bow moaned.

His three bandmates continue to cower.

"It won't ever happen if we sit and do nothing." Axe pointed. "Alistor and his team are fighting for our sake. Bamboo needs our help, and if we don't try, Vilevelious will win."

Axe quickly bolts out of the room; his crew hesitates for a moment but quickly has a change of heart.

"Dudes! You guys came!"

"We got your back!" Bow nodded.

The band is seen strolling through the flames and destruction. Soldiers in the background clashed against the Whoopers and Muskers.

"How far is the station?" Blade asked.

"Just around the next corner."

"For the concert!" Lance yelled.

"STEEL SPECTERS FOREVER!!!"

Returning back to Katty and Alistor's battle. The two are seen blasted away from Meister's lightning attack.

"NYA, HAHA! That was my signature, Thunder Beam!"

Multiple clones of the Mustache Meister float across the room. Laughing away at the both of them.

"Damn, there's seven of him. Which one is the real one?" Alistor asked.

Viper's Labyrinth

"Give me some time."

The Meister prepares for another attack. Seven beams are sent directly toward them as Alistor runs for cover.

"Don't move!" Katty yelled.

The beams passed through them, destroying an arcade machine on the far right side.

"How did you know?" Alistor surprisingly asked.

"If you had dodged, that beam would have likely hit you. So you see, there may be seven of the Meister, but only one of his attacks is real."

"Nya! So you finally see through my illusions? That was fast."

The two quickly huddle up for a plan.

"I think I know how we can beat him," Katty assured.

"You do?"

"If we combine our attacks, we can take out those copies and end him. Follow my lead."

Alistor readies his Star Breaker once more as Katty pulls out his katana. The Meister unleashes his defensive doors, but he swiftly cuts through them. Alistor charges in with the Star Breaker as the Meister readies his Thunder beam.

"Ninja Dispersion!"

At the same time, the two jumped into the air. Katty dispersed Alistor's Star Breaker with one blow, scattering as it surprised the general.

"What!"

"A direct hit this time!" Alistor snapped.

The clones quickly dissipate, leaving nothing but smoke in the air. In moments, victory was still from reach as they saw the Meister emerge unharmed from a top hat.

"You got to be kidding me? How many tricks does this guy have up his sleeve?" Katty furiously asked.

"Nya! I won't fall that easily. You can never touch me! Your attacks are useless."

"Damn…No matter how hard we hit. The Meister's one step ahead of us." Alistor admits.

Max Mathesius

"There must be a way, there has to be one, and I know it."

Meanwhile, back with Axe and the crew, they arrive at the police station seeking Bamboo.

"His cell is just right there. Beyond that wall." Axe pointed.

The crew gives him a boost up the window.

"Yo! Bamboo, we're gonna bust you out."

Relief was in Bamboo's eyes as the crew began breaking the wall down. Back to the battle, the Mustache Meister continues toying with them.

"Gya!!!"

Alistor gets punched by the Meister through a door. Katty jumps in but slams into the wall as the general summons a ladder.

"You cannot win! As long I have my mustache, I am invincible. You'll never get through that door. Nya ha, haha. Give up!"

The two got up, standing vigilantly. Determination still burned through Katty's eyes.

"You deranged fool! How far will your ego drive? Never in my life have I seen someone this vain. You're even worse than those school girls." Katty shouted.

The Meister emits a magnetic force once again. Pushing Katty away as he struggled to get close.

"Nya! It's you who are deranged if you possibly think your attacks can work on me."

The general sends Katty right back, but Alistor quickly catches him. The Meister readies for his Thunder Beam once more.

"We tried Katty…We tried…" Alistor whispered. "Our training wasn't enough."

"I am the Mustache Meister! A proud general of the Aggerona Empire."

An idea caught Katty's mind.

"There's still one thing we haven't tried."

"Like what?" Alistor asked. "We used everything."

The two take their final stand against the general as he unleashes his attack. Katty readies his katana at the approaching beam.

Viper's Labyrinth

"Here goes!"

The beam clasped against his katana as he felt an electrical surge through his body.

"Are you crazy? We can't block that." Alistor reminded.

"I know! But no one said we can't deflect it."

An enlightened look was now in Alistor's eyes as he went to support him. The two clasped their blade against the general's beam.

"Nya! Stalling for the inevitable? You can't block it! No one can!"

The Meister continues to emit his magnetic force pushing the two back. Alistor was beginning to break a sweat.

"I don't think I can hold on any longer."

"Don't worry! I won't let it end this way." Katty assured. "We've been through a lot in the past. We've come back from worse. Beyond that door, Vilevelious waits, so we can't lose now."

With determination, Katty applies the last of his strength against the beam. Pressing the palm of his hands against his blade as his hands began to bleed.

"It ends now! Flashfire!"

Katty unleashed his attack at the general's beam, sending the blast back at him.

"WHAT!"

The Meister attempts to absorb the thunder, but a force impacts him.

"Impossible....To be defeated by my own weapons."

It was none other than one of his doors.

"I had a feeling you would try and absorb that." Katty snapped.

"But how?"

He begins explaining to the general.

"Right after I pulled my final attack, we used one of your doors below and sent it back at you. None of our attacks worked this whole time, but yours do. In fact, you left yourself wide open."

The Meister's body begins to break apart in midair.

"NYA! THE POWER!!! It's LEAVING MEEEE!!!"

The general fade into nothing in one flash of light, leaving only a yellow gem behind. Alistor goes to collect the final stone.

"And that's a wrap."

Katty suddenly drops to the floor as the others arrive on the scene.

"We heard a loud explosion. Is everything alright?" Maigashi asked.

He presents the final gem to the rest. Katty was wrapping his hands up as the rest helped him back up.

"I used up a lot of power in this fight, sadly. I still have some fight left, but not very much."

"It's ok." Alistor smiled. "You take it easy. We'll handle the emperor from here."

A determined look was now in his eyes. The fear of the emperor's power no longer crossed his mind. The party now faced the door before them. Opening up the basement, they find a portal directly below.

Chapter 20

Destiny Foretold:

Till we meet again

The party begins to approach the dark portal.

"Well, it's now or never," Maigashi smirked.

"What about Axe?" Alistor asked.

"It seems he's still busy." Tannen shrugged. "We'll have to go without him."

As they go through the dimensional door, Axe and his crew bash the walls with blunt objects. Barely making any cracks or dents.

"Dude! This is not working."

"This is going to take ages. We need something bigger." Lance sweats.

Then suddenly, Axe spots a box of barrels from the far corner.

"I got it!"

"Whoah! Are you nuts! Those are explosives." Blade jumped. "We can't handle that sort of stuff."

"We won't know till we try. It's our only chance."

The crew begins placing the barrels by the walls of Bamboo's cell.

"Dude, you might want to step back. We're gonna use Barrel Man's explosives to bust you out."

"Wait, what?" Bamboo hesitated.

He takes a few steps back as the crew lit the explosives. The walls blew open within moments taking out a good portion of the station.

"Success!"

"Good work! You guys are a lifesaver." Bamboo cried.

The celebration was quickly cut short as things shakeup. The labyrinth continued to expand on the horizon. Finally, a group of Whoopers approaches the crew.

"Look like we'll have to bust some skulls. Alistor and the rest will need your help, maybe. They're probably at the Emperor right now."

Bamboo pulls out his frying pan.

"Leave it to me. I have a score to settle anyway. My cooking is not third-rate."

Axe and his crew begin to engage the Whoopers.

"Bamboo, we'll cover you. Then, head down to the arcade to reach the Emperor. We'll catch up later."

Bamboo dashed off from the scene. Meanwhile, high above, the party finds themselves inside the labyrinth's heart. A great set of stairs appear before them.

"So… You've made it this far."

"Vilevelious!"

The Emperor appears before them atop the stairs as they draw their weapons. He is seen applauding them.

"A lovely view, isn't it? But, unfortunately, in minutes, the labyrinth will engulf your world with complete darkness."

"You're out of monsters and the only one left." Alistor pointed. "Let's end this here and now."

The Emperor was barely amused.

Viper's Labyrinth

"Monsters! It won't matter because once the darkness spreads. I'll just open a gate restoring all my followers endlessly. Better yet! The soul of a dark warrior rests within this very room. Once awakened, who knows what else this labyrinth is capable of."

"Not going to let that happen."

He stood firm with confidence with the party by his side.

"I see you acquired a nice team, but five-on-one is not my style." The Emperor hissed. "I have one last monster I would like to try."

"You're bluffing! You have no monsters left." Alistor pointed.

"You're all standing on it."

"Say what?"

A massive monster formed beneath their feet within the very second, scattering them apart. Taking the form of a humanoid golem. Walls quickly encased across its entire body.

"I present my greatest monster. The labyrinth itself, Mazetress!!!"

The party didn't hesitate to stand down.

"That's one huge ugly thing," Maigashi commented.

"Very big indeed." Auroa agreed.

"What comes up must go down," Tannen added as he made the first move.

The monster slowly moves in, but he easily maneuvers around, slashing an arm off before it can strike. Then, a large piece comes crashing down.

"Too easy."

"Wait for a second, look!" Maigashi pointed.

In a split second, the monster reformed its arm. It sends a wave of stalagmites crashing down on them. Auroa deflects it with his wind.

"We may need to combine all our attacks. Find the weak spot." Katty thought.

The five of them unleash their best attacks at the monster. Breaking it piece by piece as it came crashing down. The labyrinth quickly reformed itself.

"What? This isn't getting us anywhere." Alistor realized.

"Ha! Fools! My labyrinth monster is indestructible. As long I stand, it won't go down." The Emperor laughed away.

"He established a link with the labyrinth. So one of us must take him out while we keep this thing busy." Auroa said.

Vilevelious begins to take his leave as all eyes are focused on Alistor.

"Ok, I know. Fine, I'll do this alone." He insisted.

Alistor heads up the stairs while the rest hold off the monster. He follows the Emperor to the highest point in the room.

"And here we are once again. Let's see if you are the same helpless runt who needs his friends. Ha! First, move yours!"

"I'm not the same as before."

He didn't hesitate to charge right in at full power. Enraged by the Emperor provoking as he aimed at the face. The Star Breaker impacts his face, creating a burst of smoke.

"Is that all?"

Vilevelious stood unfazed by the strike as he found his blade blocked by the tip of his jacket. He gets swatted back.

"What? No fair!"

"A small, simple turn to the side, really. My jacket has state-of-the-art protection and is in high demand for fashion."

Vilevelious counters back with a wave of lasers, but Alistor swiftly avoids them. He makes a dash toward him once more. The Emperor sends some branches but quickly cuts them away with his breaker.

"Foolish boy!"

The Emperor steps to the side again but feels a cut through his fingertip. Blood dripped from one of his fingers.

"You cut me?"

An irritated look was now on Vilevelious.

"Your torso may be fully covered, but not your arms. So I can hack at it all I want."

The Emperor begins to step back.

Viper's Labyrinth

"Why you....... Curses! I used too much power in that one attack. I still haven't regained enough energy."

The Emperor recalls the moment he destroyed the kingdom walls. Then, bringing the whole castle down as a great tree formed.

"What's the matter, too scared?" Alistor pestered back.

"No! In fact, I have something else in store."

Dark energy begins pulling into him.

"What are you doing?"

The Emperor begins to transform before his very eyes. Doubling in size as a monstrous snake demon overshadows him.

"Time to end this game!"

Meanwhile, Alistor's friends continue to clash with Mazetress as it continuously reforms. But, on the other hand, the monster is seen creating walls before them.

"Now die!!!"

Vilevelious begins slamming his tail down as the room starts getting wrecked. Alistor takes cover behind the throne.

"Damn... I'm almost out of strength. Only enough for one last shot."

Vilevelious destroys what remains of the chair as Alistor emerges from the smoke with a Star Breaker at his heart.

"This is for everyone!!!"

The attack impacts the Emperor, barely stunning him for a brief second.

"Nice try, boy. But it's not enough."

He slaps him off as he wraps his body tightly with his tail. The Emperor tosses Alistor aside as he struggles to get back up.

"Damn it...."

The five general spirits can be seen cheering from a stand high above.

"Stick it through him!" Mushogun blabbered.

Max Mathesius

Silly party hats are seen worn over their heads.

"We look stupid in these." The Admiral nodded.

"Come on! Live a little for a change." Shellshock teased. "It's not like we get a chance to party so often, ya know."

The Meister was not amused.

"Nya! Quit copying my style."

"Oh, stop being so grumpy. Ya put up a good fight but lost to your own door."

Scrap-Ram and Mushogun were seen messing with some party poppers. Popcorn was seen flying all around them.

"Nya! I lost stupidly. If I ever come back, I'll get them for this. One day you'll see. One day!" The Meister raged.

Some popcorn lands over the Mustache Meister's head as Mushogun and Scrap Ram mess around.

"Enough with the popcorn!"

The Meister begins fighting with the other two generals on the stand while Shellshock cheers the Emperor on.

"Sigh…At least we'll see how this ends." The Admiral shrugged.

The Emperor continues to take his time with Alistor.

"As expected. You don't possess the power to defeat me. Within moments your world will be consumed by the labyrinth. Just give it up."

Alistor drops to the floor while the others hold off against Mazetress on the other side. The Emperor continues to overshadow him.

"It's true…I don't have the power to overcome you." He quietly admits.

"Glad to hear, but sadly we'll have to cut our talk short. You shall spend the rest of eternity under these shrubs."

The monstrous Vilevelious calls forth branches from the ground. Snaking its way to his body as it encased him within seconds. The five essences slipped out of his pocket. His blade drops to the floor.

Viper's Labyrinth

"My follower's gems. I'll be sure to restore them once I'm done. Too bad you never utilized their powers; oh well, now it's too late."

The Emperor charges for his final laser but gets called out.

"HEY, YOU!!!!!"

Vilevelious turns his attention to the person he least expects.

"Bamboo?"

Fixed atop a high standpoint, he overshadows the Emperor.

"I'm done! You can take my restaurant, wreck my car, bomb my noodle stand, and even fire me. But not take my pride."

He pulls out a plate of Grass Jelly.

"EAT THIS!"

He tosses the Jelly straight into the Emperor's mouth, causing him to gag within contact. He then coughs and wheezes in disgust as he reverts to his original form. Alistor frees one of his arms and immediately grabs a purple gem.

"Mushogun's Essence. How does this work?"

He begins looking back at his battles and immediately triggers something. Mushogun's aura begins shrouding the room. Then, a ball of sludge drops down, destroying the roots that bind him.

"Dessert is served." Bamboo nodded before leaving the scene.

Vilevelious attempts to regain his posture. Continuously vomiting as power begins to slowly leave him. Finally, the Emperor tries to fire back with a wave of stalagmites raining down.

"This one better work."

Alistor makes his way to the next gem. The red one triggers Shellshock's soul as Comet Shots blast away the stalagmites.

"You will pay!!!" The Emperor lashed.

Vilevelious desperately fires his energy, but a wall of junk nullifies the entire blast. Nevertheless, the green gem was now in his possession.

"Now it's time for some offense."

Max Mathesius

He retrieves the final two gems. Admiral Bombshell and Mustache Meister's energy quickly levels the playing field.

"NO!"

As Alistor moves to the high ground, water floods the room. The Meister's essence followed with a vortex of lightning electrocuting Vilevelious.

"The Meister's Thunder Beam."

The Emperor was now seen smoking up. Refusing to fall as all five gems suddenly merged, forming a tremendous white sphere.

"What's this?"

The Shrine Maiden's voice could be heard as it sent the chills down Vilevelious. Alistor stood clueless with her spirit appearing before them.

"Is this possible? Yoko? No!" The Emperor refused to believe. "Even in death, you are still a pain under my thorn."

Bamboo enters the scene to explain things.

"Even if the Meister ensured the destruction of the mirror, her prophecy still came. The Shrine Maiden gave her life to seal you but knew you would one day return. If the mirror would fail, then the five gems she previously encased within your generals would be the secret to ending you."

The Emperor continues to choke from the aftertaste.

"Curse her!"

The spirit of all five generals' souls appeared behind, standing motionless. The White Gem begins to violently resonate as the weakened Emperor attempts to fire a blast once more. Alistor quickly avoids the attack.

"Now, let go. Put an end to this and bury this wicked past." Yoko commanded.

The white gem breaks open with one slash unleashing a great light impacting Vilevelious head-on as sparks and explosions commence.

"This… can't be happening."

Vilevelious was down to the last minutes of his dying breath as Alistor approached with his blade.

"Now tell me. I want answers." He demanded.

Viper's Labyrinth

The Emperor merely jested.

"Tell me!"

"What difference does it make?"

"Argh! Tell me now! Your connection with Mr. Rare and my past. Where I came from and my parents. You know something."

The Emperor grasped tight onto the rib portion of his jacket as blood poured out.

"My business with Rare is none of your concern. But tell you what….for a bastard child. Your parents. COUGH! Brother…My brother. Brother... Avenge ME!!!!!"

Vilevelious suddenly collapses to the ground unleashing an incredible explosion. Alistor wasn't sure how to feel as Bamboo helped him right up.

"This place is going down. We must get out."

Back at the other battle, the monster Mazetress fades away moments after the Emperor's defeat.

"Well, it's about time." Maigashi panted.

"Vilevelious lost his link with the labyrinth. This whole place is going down. We got to get out." Katty jumped.

The party runs for the exit, quickly catching up with Bamboo carrying Alistor.

"Just over that ledge."

A pile of rubble suddenly falls over the doorway; Tannen quickly slashes it away with one swipe from his Scythe. As the six jumps through the portal, the labyrinth crumbles from above the city.

"They actually did it!" Axe smiled.

Within moments, the team found themselves back under the Arcade Basement. Cooped up and cramped while struggling to get through the stairs. Then finally, the doors open with Axe and his bandmates to greet them

"Yo, dudes!"

A while later….

"Do you really have to go?" Alistor asked.

Max Mathesius

Bamboo was seen waiting by a bus stop, making a call. His bag is packed and ready as the sun slowly sets. Finally, the party goes to say goodbye.

"Sorry, but I can't stick around. I have too much heat on my shoulders. On the run with the law." He nodded.

"Yeah, it sucks," Maigashi admits.

"Wanted for fraud, counterfeiting, tax evasion, and even conspiring with Vilevelious. Man, the list goes on." Katty slapped.

Bamboo takes one final look back at the party. Then, he lightly pats Alistor on the shoulder with a cheerful smile.

"Don't worry; we'll cross again one day. Till we meet again...."

Waving goodbye, he boards the bus as it sets off into the light. He took his seat with a crowd of wacky figures along for the ride.

"Hey! I know you."

"Oh, you're that Opera guy plastered all over the billboards. What brings you here?" Bamboo asked.

"Not anymore...My fame was cut short thanks to circumstances. I am Marvo, by the way."

"Tell me about it. I'm on the run."

Three circus creeps popped up from behind.

"Me too! I'm Mi, and this is Re and Do. So we are Do Re and Mi."

"Nice to meet you all."

Within moments, Bamboo quickly got acquainted as the bus vanished into the setting sun. In the city, Alistor was seen recuperating by the shores near the docking bay. Gazing at the horizon as the waters pushed back and forth.

"Something on your mind?" Auroa asked.

He approached his side as a breeze quietly passed by.

"Dunno...I don't know what to feel about this."

"About what?"

Viper's Labyrinth

"Vilevelious has only been defeated by using someone else's powers. I didn't have the strength to overcome him. Now that he mentions another brother…this could be bad."

The Emperor's final words flashed back into his mind.

"Is that really it?" Auroa kindly shrugged.

"Are you kidding? This is bad. I barely survived against him, and now that we know of another brother, who knows how strong he could be."

"When the time comes, you'll know. You have much to learn, but maybe we can train you."

"You mean it!" Alistor jumped as he grabbed hold of him by the collar.

He quickly brushed him off.

"One thing at a time first."

"So, what's the first thing?" He asked.

Auroa lets off a brief sigh.

"Well, let's see. The first thing we must do."

"Yes, what?"

He waited with anticipation.

"Of course!" Auroa snapped. "We must be at Axe's concert. Come on! These backstage passes won't last. The others are waiting."

Alistor immediately stumbles as Auroa rushes to join the rest at the city stadium. And moments later, they were seen seated within the heart of the concert. Axe makes his way to the front stage.

"Hey, Dudes! YOU READY TO ROCK!!!"

Flames and explosions set off on stage as a song begins to play. A roaring cheer commenced in the background. A group of spirits can be seen watching from above the stadium from a distance. Finally, the five generals joined, along with several previously defeated monsters.

"Hey! Those are my explosive barrels." Barrel Man pointed.

"I'm hungry…You guys stop hogging the food." Potty Mouth whined.

Mushogun and Scrap Ram were seen snacking away.

"Well, at least we get to see the credits roll." Shellshock shrugged.

"Eh! Quit your yapping." The Meister snapped.

Viper's Labyrinth

Max Mathesius

Viper's Labyrinth

Max Mathesius

www.ingramcontent.com/pod-product-compliance
Lightning Source LLC
Chambersburg PA
CBHW071057250626
47159CB00002B/494